ANGEL

by Petra Laurent

This is a work of fiction. Names, characters, places, and incidents are either the product of the author's imagination or are used fictitiously, and any resemblance to actual persons, living or dead; events; or locales is entirely coincidental.

Dorrance Publishing Co
585 Alpha Drive
Pittsburgh, PA 15238
Visit our website at *www.dorrancebookstore.com*

ISBN: 979-8-88812-169-6
eISBN: 979-8-88812-669-1

For George, Ian and Nina
each of them, first love

and

In loving memory of George Themistocles Petropoulos
my hero, champion and forever angel

"I've tried to forget you
But the light of your eyes shines
You shine like an angel
A spirit that won't let me go."

JON SECADA

PROLOGUE

Of all days for his car to break down.

Jamie Nelson groaned, checked the time again and gave the ignition one last try. Nothing. He leaned back into the seat, shaking his head at the unlit dashboard. With a resigned sigh, he got out, reached through the back seat window and grabbed his gym bag. He was late—and that was not the way he had intended to begin his senior year.

"This is just great," he mumbled to himself, kicking at the dirt as he began walking the remaining three blocks to Lakeview High School. "I'm gonna catch so much grief for this." Feeling his phone vibrate, he fished it out of his pocket.

His spirits lifted. Charlotte had texted him.

He couldn't wait to tell his friends he had a date with Charlotte Sanders for Friday after the pep rally. Jamie grinned at the thought. He'd drop it into the conversation, casually, as if Charlotte wasn't the hottest girl in school. Their mouths would drop open.

But first he had to get there. Throwing his bag over one shoulder, Jamie began to jog, while texting Charlotte back.

"Get out of the way!"

The warning came too late. Caught completely off guard, Jamie jerked to his right, barely able to avoid colliding with a girl on a speeding bicycle. She cut the street corner, tires skidding.

"Hey! Slow down!" he yelled to the girl's back. She was pedaling away as if the world were on fire. Her wheels screeched to a stop and she looked over her shoulder. Jamie's eyes narrowed. He had never seen her before, and unless he was wrong, she was hiding a smile.

"Are you okay?" she asked, her tone too measured, too polite.

He had been right. She was definitely holding back laughter. "Yeah, sure. Perfect. What makes you ask?" Jamie removed his right foot from the mud puddle it had landed in. Shaking it, he glared at her.

The girl sucked in her breath. "Hey, I'm sorry about that. I wasn't paying attention. My bad. I just need to get there before *he does*." She turned to look ahead of her and Jamie followed her eyes in time to see a boy turn the next corner on a bike of his own, hands in the air, claiming victory. "You only think you're winning!" the girl called out. "I'll catch you!" Leaning forward, she gripped the handlebars tightly, then glanced back at Jamie.

He was hopping on one foot, stomping his muddy shoe on the ground in yet another unsuccessful effort to shake the mud off. Laughter bubbled out of her. Looking up, Jamie snapped his eyebrows together. She clamped her hand over her mouth.

"Uh, even the way you ride that thing, I wouldn't bet on you catching up."

Her response was to whip her right pedal up to a ready position, without looking away. Despite his morning mishaps, Jamie was unexpectedly amused. Resuming his jog, he caught up to her. She watched him, her eyes still dancing with laughter. Shaking his head, Jamie could not help a small smile.

"Sorry to slow you down," he said, as he passed her, still stomping his foot.

She laughed again and pedaled around him. "No worries. I'll catch him. But you might want to reconsider the texting and running thing!" she called over her shoulder.

Jamie Nelson, star athlete of Lakeview High, slowed to a walk. He was suddenly out of breath.

She was the most beautiful girl he had ever seen.

CHAPTER ONE

"What is your name, please?"

Sarah looked into the stern eyes of her new English teacher, Jeanne Dixon. "Sarah Giannopoulos."

"Sarah Gia-what?" It was one of her new classmates making fun of her name already. The joke hit home. Muffled laughter could be heard around the room.

"That will be quite enough, Todd. I'll be sure to let you know when your comments are welcome." The austere woman peered over her glasses at Sarah. "You are late, Miss Giannopoulos."

"I'm sorry, Mrs. Dixon. There was...traffic."

The teacher nodded sharply. "I understand this is your first day, but know this: Habitual tardiness is unacceptable in my classroom. And it's *Ms.* Dixon. Take the empty seat by the window, please."

Sarah turned and made her way to the empty desk. *'Ms.' Dixon*, she thought to herself. *Shocker.* She kept her head high, avoiding all eye contact. She could still hear the snickering around her. She pretended she didn't.

"Summer is over, boys and girls, and there is no one more sorry than I. Time to get to work. We will begin our unit with Browning, page 35. His work is a fine example of subtle analysis in English poetry..."

Sarah turned the pages mechanically, lost in her thoughts. She had dreaded this day for weeks. How had this even happened? The last two months since the move to North Carolina, she had asked herself that question a thousand times. How could her life turn upside down so quickly? They'd all worked so hard in New York. Together, the three of them had made the restaurant a success. It had not been easy. The years after her mother's death had been long and hard for all of them. But together, her dad, brother and she had stuck it out—and they had made it. That is, until the fire.

She ran her finger over the scar on her left hand—the last one. It too, was almost gone. Gone, like the life she had left behind, the only life she had ever known. She had tried to fight the move, tried to convince her father to stay, even though deep down she always knew he had no choice. Necessity had forced Andreas Giannopoulos to skimp on a good fire insurance policy. After the fire, he had practically nothing to rebuild with.

Then the bank had called in his loans.

Who knows what would have happened if Uncle George had not insisted his brother move to Kernersville and manage a pizzeria he had invested in? He'd helped them buy a small home and Aunt Patty had even furnished it for them. So, here she was: a senior at a new school, in a room full of strangers.

She could feel the curious looks she was getting. She could hear the whispers around her, even over Ms. Dixon's monotone voice. They were taking in everything about her: her face, her clothes, her northern accent, and her foreign last name. Sarah flipped another page. It wasn't as if her cousin, Toni, had not warned her about the kids at Lakeview before she had left for college last week. Kernersville was a small town, she had explained, her eyes sympathetic. Cliques had been the same for years and years and went beyond school to long-time family friendships. New faces were considered by many to be nothing more than unwanted outsiders.

You weren't kidding, Toni.

Sarah sat up straighter in her chair, locking her eyes on Ms. Dixon. She would focus on the bright side.

First period was almost over. Only seven more to go.

CHAPTER TWO

"Jamie! Over here, man!" Walt called across the crowded lunchroom, his mouth full of potato chips.

Jamie walked over to the senior football players' table and sat down, glad to have finally made it to lunch. "What's up?'

"Summer's over, so nothing good," his friend Gaston answered between greedy bites of an oversized burrito. "Where've you been?"

"Yeah, Coach K's already been by here looking for you," Walt informed him.

"My car broke down halfway here this morning. I had to run to make Ms. Dixon on time. Then, my phone died. I just now called home to let them know."

"Man, that blows," his best friend Robby said. "And so will practice this afternoon. Coach is still ticked off after that scrimmage." Jamie couldn't help but smile at the dread in his voice. "Don't laugh, I'm serious. I heard him yelling in his office this morning. Said something about running extra, heat be damned." Robby gave Jamie a thump on his back. "And maybe something about how Nelson better step up as quarterback and get his team in line."

"He said that? You heard those exact words?" Gaston asked, nervously.

"Yep. That burrito might be a big mistake."

Jamie laughed, leaned back in his chair and popped a barbecue chip in his mouth. He said nothing for a moment; when he spoke, it was as if he were thinking out loud. "Guess I'll be too worn out to stop by Charlotte's house tonight."

"Charlotte's house? Charlotte Sanders?" Walt was the first to bite, dropping his sandwich in his plate.

"Yeah, ha-ha. No way, man," Gaston piped in. "Charlotte Sanders has been dating Dirk Bowens, local town hero and NC State quarterback, since the day she was born."

Jamie brought his chair back to the floor. "Thanks for the update. But here's a new one: seems Bowen's been out of the picture for most of the summer. We've been out twice this week. And she's coming with me to Grant's, after the pep rally."

Robby grinned, while Walt and Gaston gaped. Walt spread out his arms, his expression one of sheer awe. "Whoa! Why didn't you tell us? Jackpot, pal!"

"Dude, you are one lucky dude," Gaston said, giving Jamie a fist pump.

Jamie shrugged, then smiled. They were right about him being lucky. The son of James and Daisy Nelson, he'd never lacked for anything. His dad was a doctor and his mom a lawyer, though she had not practiced since his older brother, Ben, was born. Ben was a sophomore at Wake Forest this year; his little sister, Hillary, was a sophomore at Lakeview.

And he was finally a senior: quarterback, team captain of the basketball team, guitar player in a band with his buddies—and best of all, dating Charlotte Sanders. Everyone at Lakeview wanted to date Charlotte Sanders. Everyone.

"Did y'all get a load of the new babe?" Gaston's words interrupted Jamie's thoughts. "She's Greek, from New York. She's in my second period pre-calc class."

"Greek? Well, that's different. Easy on the eyes?" Robby asked.

"Definitely. But, not too friendly. I tried to get her attention. I think she avoided me on purpose."

"Smart girl," Walt commented dryly.

"How do you know she's Greek?" Jamie asked.

"Her last name's Giannopoulos. That's not French, buddy."

Jamie thought of the carefree girl he had almost collided with earlier that morning. The same girl he had watched walk stiffly across the room in Ms. Dixon's Lit class. She had spoken to no one.

"Come on, man." Robby was waving his hand in front of Jamie's face. "Snap out of it, the bell rang."

"What's her name?"

"Who?"

"The new girl. Giannopoulos."

"I think Gaston said it was Sarah. Move it, James, we're late." Robby started for the door.

Sarah. Jamie let the name sink in. "I'm right behind you, bud."

CHAPTER THREE

"I'm never going back there. Never."

"Come on, Nick. It's not that bad."

"Not for you, maybe, but for me it is, Sarah. The guys in my class are total losers. Toni warned me, and she was right. I'm not going back. I mean it."

"Then what are you going to do all day?"

"Get a job."

Nick Giannopoulos stood facing his sister, shoulders squared and fire flying from his eyes. It was a look Sarah was accustomed to, and often shared with her younger brother; a look they had inherited from their mother.

Maria Giannopoulos, as beautiful as she had been smart, had possessed a remarkable zest for life. She had always stood up for what she had believed in, no matter what the costs were. How many times had Sarah watched her face their father with her hands on her hips and that same fire coming from her eyes? Andreas Giannopoulos would argue as best he could, but in the end he'd almost always give in, for no other reason, Sarah suspected, than to simply hold her close. How he'd loved her spirit...

Mom, I miss you so much.

"I'm wasting daylight talking to you. You're not even listening, " Nick accused.

Sarah sighed. "I'm listening, Niko. I hear you. But you're being too dramatic. This was our first day. First days are the worst days. You've just got to hang in there and give it time."

"Time for what? What's gonna change?"

"They'll change. You'll change. Things will change."

Nick put his head down. "I miss home, Sarah."

Sarah knew him well enough to know he was fighting tears, just as she knew he would never cry in front of her. Sometimes it was hard for her to remember just how young Nick was. He had been through so much for a boy his age. At thirteen, he was already a man. Sarah felt a warm rush of love for her little brother. She wanted to hug him, but knew he was too proud for that—and would only push her away.

"This is home, Niko," she said softly. "And I need you to be strong for Dad and me. School will get better, if you give it a fair chance. Those kids in your class will come around. I'll bet you'll be friends with them before you know it. Just be yourself." Sarah took his hand in hers and placed them on his heart. "We're keeping where we came from right here. No matter where we go, we're still the same. You, me and Dad."

For a moment Nick said nothing. Then he nodded, pulling his hand away. "I'll give it one more day."

"I had more like a month in mind."

"Ugh. That sounds terrible."

"It's reasonable, Niko. Deal?"

"I guess."

Sarah gave him a playful shove. "You think school was bad. Wait until we get home and I tell Dad you got beat by a girl again!" Jumping on her bike, she began pedaling. Seconds later, Nick sped by her. Triumphantly, he held his fist over his head.

Sarah smiled. Maybe she'd take her own advice and give Lakeview a chance. Maybe, just maybe, it really would get better. She pedaled faster.

She'd changed her mind about letting him win.

CHAPTER FOUR

"Jamie! Jamie-e!" Daisy Nelson stood at the top of the stands, waving to get her son's attention.

Jamie jogged up from the football field, jumping the stairs two by two. His mother watched him, smiling. The pride she felt for her handsome, athletic son radiated from her face.

"What's up, Mom? I'm in the middle of practice."

"I can see that. I just thought you may want your car keys. It's fixed." Daisy Nelson started to hold his keys out, only to pull them back, as if she had changed her mind. "Of course, if you're too busy to take them, I could always let Hillary take a spin around town. She really needs the practice, and..."

"Okay, Mom. Sorry I snapped at you," Jamie interrupted. "Coach K has gone crazy today. He's decided we're in terrible shape. I think I'm having a heat stroke."

"You're forgiven this time. And you look fine, just keep drinking water." She dropped the keys in his hand and reached out to ruffle his hair. "Hillary and I are going to the mall and your father is working late tonight. I guess we should all be home around eight or so. If you get hungry, there are leftovers in the fridge."

"I think we're gonna grab a pizza after practice. If we're still alive."

"Well, that ought to help you boys get into shape."

"Wow, Mom, that's funny."

Daisy laughed. "Just be careful driving, my grumpy boy." Her voice took on a more serious tone. "They're calling for thunderstorms tonight."

"Mom, I think I can handle it. I'm going to college in less than a year, remember?"

His mother's tone remained unchanged. "I remember. Speaking of college, if Ben calls, tell him to call back after nine. Your father needs to talk to him."

"Yes, Mother. I need to get back on the field. Thanks for bringing me the keys."

"What, no kiss for your sweet mama?" she called after him.

"I'm saving it for when you tuck me in tonight," Jamie called back to her, as he jogged down the stands.

Daisy lingered to watch as he joined his teammates, reveling in that familiar sense of contentment she always felt around her son. She loved all her children but Jamie was the easiest to love. From the beginning, he stood out. Unlike her other two, he'd been born with a full head of dark hair, like James's side of the family. She had taken him in her arms and he had immediately began to suck his thumb. They had all laughed at how relaxed he looked. Daisy remembered the way his eyes had quickly drifted shut, as if he fully expected the world to comfort and protect him.

Over the years, she'd made sure it had. Her baby boy had grown into a purposed young man, ready to take on every challenge, yet comfortable and confident in the process. Well over six feet, his lean frame and handsome face turned heads when he entered a room. His hazel eyes sparkled with wit and kindness. His smile always looked mischievous. He was easy-going, loyal and sure-footed—with a wonderful sense of humor to boot.

He was her pride and joy.

You'll be a catch for some lucky girl, Jamie Nelson. Just like your father, you are. I just hope you find one as worthy as she is lucky.

CHAPTER FIVE

Steve's Pizzeria was packed. Robby was the first to spot a table, sit down, and lay his head on the cool surface. Jamie, Walt and Gaston followed, slowly.

"Man, that was ridiculous. I've pulled muscles I didn't know I had," Walt said, grabbing a menu. "I want a large for myself—and a gallon of tea."

"Me, too. I'm starving," Jamie agreed. "Hillary says this place is awesome."

"Where's a waitress? I need a drink," Gaston groaned.

"I'm right here. And don't worry, the drink machine should be fixed in the next hour or so."

Jamie looked up from the menu, recognizing the cheery, not-so-Southern voice. Sarah Giannopoulos smiled as she flipped the page on her order pad. She was dressed in a red and white pinstriped shirt, jeans, red apron and a red baseball hat that said "Steve's" in big white letters. She gave Gaston a sunny smile and a wink to let him know she was kidding about the drink machine. Then, her eyes met Jamie's—and her smile widened.

"Nice to *run into you* again." She paused, giving a little laugh at her pun on words. "Don't worry, you're safe this time. I promise not to race with anyone when I bring over your pizza."

Embarrassed, Jamie looked back down at the menu. He could feel the surprised stares he was getting from the guys. He knew they were wondering how he knew this girl. He had just finished impressing them with his stories about Charlotte and himself. He wasn't sure how to respond, an unfamiliar feeling for him.

He didn't really know her, anyway. She had recognized him from this morning but she didn't even know his name. She was being polite, just doing her job. And with his friends sitting there, he should play it cool.

"I'd like a small, extra cheese and pepperoni, please. And a large tea." He handed her the menu and with a quick, impersonal smile, looked away.

Sarah felt her cheeks redden. He had pretended he had never seen her before! She felt like a complete fool. She turned to Robby, intent on regaining her composure. "And for you?" Her voice was indifferent, her eyes on the order pad.

"I'll have the same," Robby said slowly, realizing something had just happened between Jamie and Sarah. Something Jamie was definitely playing down. He smiled up at her. "Hey, aren't you new at Lakeview?"

"Yes, I am," Sarah replied stiffly, as she wrote down his order.

"Well, hey there, then. I'm Rob Gates."

Sarah looked up. She returned his smile with a brief one of her own, before turning to Walt. "And for you?"

"Just make it the same for all of us." He handed her his menu without looking at her. "Except make one a large. And we're in a hurry, babe, make it fast."

Walt's tone was unmistakably condescending. Her previous embarrassment forgotten, Sarah felt her temper flare. *Babe? These guys have some nerve.*

"No problem," she responded coolly, collecting the menus and tucking them under her arm. "We are a New York pizzeria. And New Yorkers are fast."

"Really..." Walt replied, leaning back in his chair. Crossing his arms across his chest, he gave her a cocky grin. "Well, honey, one thing's for sure, us Southern boys sure do like fast girls."

Sarah met his eyes but said nothing. Then she turned and walked away.

"What the hell, Robby?" Walt said, as soon as she was out of hearing range. "Well, hey, hi," he imitated. "You're such a geek, man. Even you can do better than some exchange student waitress."

"Whatever, Walt, she's hot." Gaston leaned back in his chair, smiling. "I dig chicks in aprons. And I also happen to like foreign languages."

Walt burst out in laughter. "Gaston, you *dig* any girl that has a pulse."

"True." Gaston agreed, with a shrug of his shoulders. "So, what's up, Rob?"

"I was just being nice," Robby said, uncomfortably. "Besides, Nelson's the one who knows her, not me."

"What? No, man, I don't know her." Jamie kept his tone casual. "She must have thought I was someone else."

"Walt, dude," Gaston said. "Now I know why they never let you on the welcoming committee."

"Yeah, man, that was cold. I think I'd rather be a geek," Robby muttered.

Jamie tuned them all out, suddenly not feeling too good about himself. What was the matter with him? Why had he pretended not to recognize Sarah? Why had he sat there and let Walt insult her for no reason? She had been so nice and he had dissed her. Something he couldn't define had caught him off guard, just as it had when he had seen her that morning. She was beautiful, this Sarah Giannopoulos. And now, she hated him.

"Here you go, boys." She was back with their drinks. Jamie couldn't help but notice the way she stressed the word *boys.* He glanced up at her, surprised to find her smiling. He felt a welcome wave of relief. *Maybe she's going to let me off the hook. Maybe she missed Walt's crude remark or decided he had only been kidding. Maybe I could even be extra-nice to her the next time I see her and make up for pretending not to recognize her—without the guys around.*

"This is for you," she said, a little too sweetly, Jamie noticed, as she handed Robby his drink. "And for you..." Gaston took his and gave her a smile. She smiled back. "For you." Jamie reached to take his glass from her, but purposefully ignoring him, she slammed it down hard on the space of table in front of him. Some of it spilled on his lap.

Or maybe not, Jamie corrected himself.

"Easy!" Walt said, irritably. "You spilled it all over him! Grab us some napki..."

Sarah didn't let him finish his sentence. Instead, she leaned over and dumped a Steve's super large sweet tea over his head.

"*Bless*," she said, with an exaggerated Southern accent. "We New York gals may be fast, but we can be ever-so clumsy!" Narrowing her eyes, she leaned closer as she glared at Walt, who watched her stunned, his mouth gaping and his face dripping. "Since you hicks didn't ask the new girl's name, let me tell it to you *any-ol-way*: It's Sarah Giannopoulos." She lowered her voice, as if she were about to tell them a secret. "In case your tiny little pea brains don't recognize it's Greek, let me inform you that it is. To put this in terms *y'all* might understand: I'm Greek. *And* a New Yorker. That combination means I pack a temper and there's no way I'm going to let a bunch of idiots like you insult me." She picked up the empty glass, keeping her eyes on Walt.

"As for your tea," she added, with a satisfied smile, "don't you worry *honey-bunch*. It will be my pleasure to bring you another. And *fast*."

CHAPTER SIX

Jamie was finding it next to impossible to concentrate on Browning. He was too absorbed in watching Sarah. From where he was sitting, all he could see was her back—but that was the way he'd planned it. He wanted to watch her without her, or anyone, knowing. He wanted to think about her undisturbed.

He couldn't help but smile to himself as he remembered the night before. The look of total disbelief on Walt's face was nothing compared to the look of total triumph in hers. Her eyes were full of fire, daring him to provoke her further.

The fire had died out, or at least lessened in intensity when a large man, who Jamie surmised was her boss, demanded she explain herself at once. Sarah had crossed her arms across her chest and stood her ground as he fussed over Walt, apologizing over and over again. He had turned furious eyes to Sarah and ordered her to the kitchen. And she had gone. But not before her own eyes met and held his with total defiance.

She had affected him in an odd way, this new girl from New York. From the very first moment he'd laid eyes on her, he'd felt as if he were on unfamiliar ground. It wasn't her looks alone; he'd seen plenty of beautiful girls before her. It was something else, something he couldn't put his finger on. Whatever it was, it was new, and it had kept him thinking about her the rest of last night and most of the morning.

He had to find a way to talk to her, to apologize for his behavior at Steve's. Maybe she was going to Grant's party on Friday night and he could talk to her then. Except he was taking Charlotte. Even if Sarah did show up, it would be hard to get a chance to talk to her alone.

Jamie turned the page, though he hadn't read any of it. Sarah had already managed to make herself an outsider after one day at Lakeview by antagonizing his friends. They didn't like her. Maybe he should just stop thinking about talking to her. Showing any further interest in her would make him look like a loser to the guys. Why would he want to do that? For a girl he knew virtually nothing about?

And yet, there she was, for some unknown reason, tempting him to.

Sarah Giannopoulos, self-proclaimed Greek New Yorker who had no tolerance for idiots, sitting three desks in front of him, studying her Browning.

Jamie mechanically turned another page. He was being ridiculous. He would force himself to concentrate on Charlotte. And Browning.

Suddenly, they both interested him about the same.

CHAPTER SEVEN

"Aunt Patty packs a mean sandwich," Sarah said to herself as she savored the last bite of her lunch. Between the pizza mistakes she snacked on daily and her aunt's amazing cooking skills, she knew she would reach "the point of no return", as Nick called it, in no time. "I'll have to remember to diet—tomorrow. There are worse things than having to get new jeans." Smiling, she popped a bite of brownie in her mouth, leaned back, closed her eyes and relaxed in the warm September sun. She hated to admit it, even to herself, but the weather was really wonderful in Kernersville.

Nothing like New York this time of year.

"Nice outfit, Amelia. They must be running a sale at the consignment shop this week."

Sarah opened her eyes and turned in the direction of the voice to see a group of girls standing over the student they had called 'Amelia'.

"Leave her alone, Jocelyn," one of them coaxed, sarcastically. "She can't help that she's a loser."

Sarah stiffened at the cruel words. But this Amelia person wasn't saying a word. Instead she was keeping her eyes focused ahead. Sarah looked too, expecting to see someone there. All she saw was a tree.

"Charlotte, you are just too nice. But I'm not. I'm wondering if Amelia is too stupid to know when someone's just not interested." She leaned over and flicked a piece of Amelia's hair. "Like Justin. *My* boyfriend. He would never be interested in you, so stop trying. You're pathetic."

"What are you so worried about then?" Sarah heard herself saying, immediately wishing she hadn't. *What am I doing, getting involved in somebody else's drama?* The group of girls turned towards her. Jocelyn stared at her in surprise. Sarah popped another brownie piece into her mouth and met her eyes. *Too late, Jason Statham, too late...*

"Why don't you try minding your own business?"

"Exactly what I was trying to do." Sarah lazily stretched her legs in front of her and smiled as she chewed. "But your insult hurling sort of made that impossible."

"Hey, aren't you that girl from the Bronx who dumped tea on Walt for no reason last week?" one of the girls in the group asked.

Sarah laughed. "I'm from Long Island. And yes, I did. But for a very good reason."

"Which was..."

"He's a jerk with an oversized ego. Kind of reminds me of...you."

"What did you call us?" Jocelyn's voice was shrill, her eyes wide. She moved to stand directly in front of Sarah.

The last thing Sarah wanted to do was repeat what she had said, especially since she couldn't even begin to believe she had actually said it. *No turning back now, Miss Congeniality.* She stood, her face inches away from Jocelyn's, and opened her mouth to speak. But she didn't get the chance.

"She should have called you something worse," Amelia said, making her way through the group that had gathered around Sarah. "For the record, your boyfriend came onto me, Jocelyn. He must be bored. Can't say I blame him—but I can do better."

"Wha..." Jocelyn looked from Amelia to Sarah in disbelief, but recovered quickly, and flipped her hair in a nonchalant manner. "I can't believe you actually have a voice, Amelia. Just remember what I said about Justin. Because I mean it. Stay in your pitiful little loser world and keep away from him." She turned to glare at Sarah, her eyes narrowing. "Same goes for you, Bronx girl." With another flip of her hair, she turned away, motioning for the rest of the group to follow.

Still angry and suddenly embarrassed, Sarah fought the urge to call out to Jocelyn. *Shut up, big mouth, what's the point*? She turned to gather

her belongings, instead. "Bronx girl", they had called her. She had thought they hadn't noticed her since school had started, too absorbed in their perfect world to think about including her. That, she had expected. But "Bronx girl"? They had noticed her, all right. They already looked down on her. They had already decided she wasn't good enough to be included. And now she had given them reason to hate her.

"Sarah?"

Amelia was still standing there. "Hi."

Sarah straightened and smiled. "Hi."

"I've seen you in third period French. I'm in there, too." She was looking at the tree again, nervously. "I...uh...thanks for what you said. I can't believe you said it. I've been taking their crap since the third grade. I don't know why. It's not like I want to be friends with them or anything, but I guess I just always tell myself they aren't worth the aggravation...or something." She turned sad, blue eyes to Sarah. Sarah smiled again, this time supportively.

"But you," Amelia continued, "you come here not knowing anyone—and you stand up to them. Just like that, without even having to. You did what I should have done a long time ago." Her voice lowered to a guilty whisper. "You didn't exactly make friends just now. Sadly, those girls are the 'it' girls at Lakeview."

Sarah digested that piece of information. "Yeah, I kind of figured that."

"If they don't like you, nobody—well, that's anybody who's anybody—will," Amelia added, softly.

Sarah sighed, braved a smile, and shrugged her shoulders. "Hey, don't worry about it. They'd made up their minds about me before today." *Surely she can see that. The way I talk, my clothes, my name... everything about me is different than these girls.* She fought the tears threatening to fill her eyes. *But it's only for a year. After that, I'm out of here.* Sarah forced another smile. "Besides, you're somebody. I've never been a big fan of the 'it' girls anyway."

"Yeah, I know what you mean." Amelia smiled. "In all my life, I'll never forget Jocelyn stomping away, her lame groupies practically running to keep up."

Both girls laughed at that. "So tell me," Sarah asked her new friend, as the two of them headed back to their classes, "did you really come on to Justin, whoever he is?"

"Nah. I wouldn't go for someone else's boyfriend. Even if the girl is Jocelyn Jones. It's not like Justin is Lakeview's hottest guy or anything."

"So, who is?"

"What, hottest guy at Lakeview?" Amelia smiled. "That would be Jamie Nelson."

CHAPTER EIGHT

Jamie was exhausted. The September sun was showing no mercy and neither was Coach K. Practice was miserable. Finally the whistle sounded, signaling a break and prompting countless groans of relief from the exhausted players.

"Water," Jamie said, gasping for breath.

"I'm in too much pain to drink," Walt complained, holding his side.

"Exactly what you should have said last weekend, dude," Robby joked.

"Robby, you're such a pansy."

"Whatever. Drink up and start running or we'll all have to run extra." Robby put a cup of water in Walt's hand. "Do you need help getting it to your mouth?"

Jamie grinned, still doubled over.

"Hi, boys!"

Squinting up at the sun, Jamie straightened and smiled. "Hey, you."

"Practice looks tough today." Charlotte smiled back, and reaching over, brushed the hair back from his eyes.

"I'm thinking the heat has gotten to Coach. He's a madman today." Jamie did his best to ignore Robby and Gaston sending him thumbs up signs behind Charlotte's back. "Are y'all practicing?"

"Yeah, we are. It's tragic today but we're almost done. We need to get our moves down before the game Friday night," Charlotte answered with a nod towards the far end of the field. Jamie followed her gaze to find the rest of the cheerleading squad, one prettier than the other. He'd gone out with almost all of them. All of them, but Charlotte.

Handing her a cup of water, he noticed she didn't show a single sign of heat distress. Her hair was perfect; her make-up was perfect. *The last thing she needs to worry about is getting any kind of moves down. She is so hot.* As if she could read his thoughts, Charlotte smiled and brought the cup to her lips, keeping her eyes on his.

"I had a great time the other night at Jocelyn's party. I only wish your band had played. You guys are good."

"Thanks. I think we'll play some at Grant's Saturday. You still up for it?"

Charlotte delicately wiped the corners of her mouth with her index finger. Then, she reached over and did the same to Jamie's. "Of course. What time are you picking me up?"

"How about eight?"

Charlotte smiled and handed him the empty cup. "Don't be late," she said and walked away, pausing to give a little wave to Robby, Gaston and Walt. Jamie smiled at their dumbfounded expressions, as they all watched her go.

Just then, the whistle sounded again. His friends took off and Jamie backed up to the cooler for one more drink.

Where he was sidetracked again, this time by the unexpected.

Sarah was there, getting herself a drink of water. He watched her fill two cups and offer one to Amelia Patten. He couldn't help but stare. She was drenched in sweat, standing a few feet away from the rest of the cross country team. Just a few seconds ago, he had been impressed with Charlotte's lack of perspiration despite the intense heat. But never in his life had he seen a girl look as good as Sarah did, greedily drinking water. She wiped her forehead with the back of her hand and burst into laughter at something Amelia was saying. Jamie felt nervous, a feeling strange to him. He felt his stomach tighten. He wanted to say something, but after what had happened at Steve's, his mind was drawing a blank.

At that moment, as if sensing she was being watched, Sarah turned. Their eyes locked for one brief moment before hers narrowed and the laughter left them. She looked away. Instinctively, Jamie did the same and moved closer to the cooler, aware of how close he was to her.

Reaching out to fill his cup, he could almost touch her. *Say something. Even if it's wrong. Now. Just do it.*

"Come on, Amelia," he heard her say, instead. "Let's run some more laps."

"What? You gotta be kidding!" Amelia complained. "You just said you were done, finished, exhausted and hotter than..."

"I just caught my second wind," Sarah interrupted, moving away from Jamie and towards the track.

"Geez, let me finish my water, at least."

"Don't worry, if you pass out, I'll take you home."

Amelia watched her start around the track. With a groan, she threw her empty cup away, noticing Jamie as she did so. "More like the closest Urgent Care. I see dehydration and probable collapse in my immediate future," she said, wearily.

Jamie smiled and watched Amelia run to catch up with Sarah, as he greedily gulped down water. He had wanted to talk to her, but she had definitely not shared that desire. He watched as she and Amelia turned the corner. She was definitely a runner. Her long, lean legs moved in an almost effortless, smooth rhythm. She looked as if she were at total ease with the fast pace she was keeping, as if nothing could slow her down. Jamie got the feeling not much could. She was confident, that much was clear. The girl was no pushover. Remembering Walt, drenched and dazed, Jamie smiled again as he crumpled up his empty cup and tossed it into the trash.

Next time, I won't pass up the chance to talk to her, he told himself as he started jogging towards the center of the football field. *The hell with what everyone thinks. I don't care.*

CHAPTER NINE

"Jamie Nelson is definitely staring at you."

Amelia and Sarah were cramming for their French quiz while eating lunch outside on one of the school picnic tables. Sarah swallowed her bite of turkey and avocado sandwich and raised an eyebrow. "Who?"

"Jamie Nelson. Two tables over on your left. But look casually. He's watching you," Amelia replied, while pretending to be reading the label on her water bottle.

"You mean the guy in the light blue shirt?"

"That's the one."

"Yeah, well, he's not staring at me." Sarah took the bottle from her and took a sip.

"Oh, he most definitely is. And he stared at you at practice yesterday, too. I watched him watch," Amelia insisted, with a knowing smile.

"You had all the symptoms of a heat stroke at practice, Amelia. Let's study." Sarah put what was left of her lunch away and pulled her notes out of her book.

Amelia smiled bigger. "First, I want to ask you something."

"This better be a French question."

"Why are you avoiding the subject of Jamie Nelson?"

"Because he's not even remotely looking in this direction."

"Yes he was, and...wait for it...yup, there he goes again!"

Sarah looked up from her notes. "What makes you so sure he's not looking at you?"

"I have 20/20 vision." Amelia smiled again and dropped her head in her hands, a dreamy look in her eyes. "He's into you. The *it-chicks* are about to get rocked."

Sarah rolled her eyes, picked up her notes and blocked Amelia's face with them.

"Fine. Ignore me. Keep studying French. It still won't change the undeniable fact that I'm right."

"Whatever, Amelia. Where was your 20/20 vision at practice yesterday when he was practically panting over Charlotte and her perfectly-poofed-up pony tail?"

Amelia's eyes grew wide. She reached over the table and smacked Sarah's notes away. "You've been watching him, too!"

Sarah shrugged her shoulders. "I notice everybody. I'm new, remember?"

"Honestly, I just didn't see this one coming," Amelia said, smugly. "But you're right, we should study."

"And also, you really think I would be into that arrogant jock?"

"Yep."

"Well, let's do you a favor and chalk that up to you just not knowing me well enough yet. Maybe him, too. For your information, I tried to be nice to him—before I knew how big his head was—when I first came here. And guess what he did? He blew me off. In a big way. Did I fail to share that with you?"

"No, I think I know this story. In retaliation, you soaked Walt with a Coke."

Sarah tried not to smile but failed. "It was tea. That's all you people seem to drink around here. And Amelia, you're really beginning to annoy me."

Amelia laughed and reached for her book. "I won't lie, you're a little scary when you're mad. Like when you yelled at the little guy at the Quickie Mart yesterday for running out of cotton candy."

"He was 6'4" and a jerk. Can we please just study now?"

"Mais, oui!"

Sarah flipped her notes over. "Amelia?"

"Yeah?"

"Not that I care, but was he for real looking at me?"

"For real, for real."

Sarah eyed her friend thoughtfully. "Amelia, why are *you* not looking at me?"

Amelia kept her head down, trying to hide her smile. "Because I'm going to laugh and you're gonna get mad. I don't want to risk it."

"Why would I get mad? And why would you laugh?"

Amelia looked up at Sarah's confused expression and burst out laughing. "Because, girl, you've fallen for Jamie Nelson, just like every other female at Lakeview before you."

Sarah couldn't believe her ears. "I have not! He is the last guy at this school I would fall for!" She tried to keep her voice low. Her temper was threatening to erupt and she didn't want it to. She knew Amelia meant well and she didn't want to make too much of this. But she was wrong and she had to be set straight. "Amelia. Listen to me. Guys like him don't waste their time staring at girls like me. I'm an outsider, a waitress, the complete opposite of the *it-chicks*, as you call them. And he can have any one of them; you said so yourself. All he has to do is snap his fingers. They'll come running."

Amelia tried to interrupt but Sarah continued. "But if—and believe me I know better—but if this *boy prodigy* of Lakeview was even remotely interested in me, I would never, ever get involved with him. I know what guys like Jamie Nelson want from girls like me. I learned it the hard way." Her eyes turned sad for a brief moment. "I won't forget it anytime soon."

"In New York? Anything you want to talk about?" Amelia's tone was concerned.

"Nah. It's in the past. I'm more worried about failing this French quiz right now." Sensing she had worried her friend, Sarah smiled.

Amelia smiled back. "Okay, we study now. But I just have one more thing to say."

"Can I stop you?"

"No. What is it you called him, Sarah? *Boy wonder*?"

Sarah sighed and reached for her French notes again. "I think I said *boy prodigy.*"

"Well, I think it may interest you to know, *boy prodigy* is heading this way."

CHAPTER TEN

"Hey, Amelia. What's up?"

"Not much, just studying for a quiz," Amelia said, trying to keep her tone casual. She tried to remember the last time Jamie Nelson had spoken to her. She couldn't. She smiled up at him. "That calculus test was inhuman, wasn't it?"

Jamie nodded, smiling back. "Yeah, it really was."

As he spoke, he glanced at Sarah. Amelia didn't have to look at her friend to know she was keeping her attention on her book and ignoring Jamie completely. "So, are you ready for the game tomorrow?"

"I hope so. I think the team is looking in better shape." He leaned back on his heels, digging his hands into the pockets of his jeans. Amelia nodded, agreeably. She couldn't come up with anything else to say to him.

The silence began to be awkward.

"Y'all coming to the game?" Jamie finally asked. He looked from Amelia to Sarah, who flipped a page, as if she had not heard a word.

Amelia had had enough. "Yeah, of course. Can't wait! Jamie, do you know Sarah? She's new this year."

"I don't think we've met. But we have run into each other," Jamie said, grinning.

Looking up, Sarah met his grin with a sarcastic smile. *That's cute. Oh, we've met,* she felt like saying. *Only when your friends were around it was more convenient to pretend you'd never seen me before. Surprise, surprise, none of them seem to be around now.* "Really? Can't say that I remember that," she said instead, before returning her attention to her book. She couldn't believe the nerve of him! What was he doing? Was this some kind of plan to get back at her for the other night at Steve's? If so, how? Why was he being so...nice? *Just keep ignoring him. He'll talk to Amelia and then he'll go away. He probably just wants to talk about calculus anyway. Take a chill pill, Sarah.*

But she knew, even as the thoughts were forming in her head, she couldn't ignore him. She could feel his eyes on her. Her peripheral vision told her he had squatted down to the level of the table. Sarah slowly lifted her eyes to his, without lifting her head.

"What are you studying for?" he asked, his tone annoyingly cheerful.

"French."

"I take Spanish."

"I guess that means if we were both in Europe, there would be no chance we could communicate." *Sorry, hot shot, you so walked into that one.*

"Ouch." Jamie grinned back at her. "We could use sign language."

"Or not." Sarah was pleased to see his eyes cloud over. He said nothing for a moment but just looked at her. She smiled cheerfully at him.

"You're a good runner," he finally said, breaking the silence.

What the heck is this? Sarah reached for her notes and looked back down at them. "Thanks. So, I really have to study." *There. He'll leave now for sure.* For some reason, she couldn't get her thoughts in order. *He's being so nice. But why? It's so weird.*

"Hey, I'm sorry about the other night at Steve's. We were complete assholes. I...it won't happen again."

Sarah lifted her head in surprise. She couldn't believe it! He had ignored her sarcasm and actually apologized to her. *Could Amelia be right about him?* As soon as the thought crossed her mind, she dismissed it. She had thought they would be friends when she had met him on her bike that first day of school. He had seemed like a genuinely nice guy and she had felt a strange sort of connection with him. But that was before she found out he was Jamie Nelson, star of Lakeview High. And before he pretended he'd never laid eyes on her when he'd found out she was a waitress at the local pizzeria.

"So, what do you say, am I forgiven?" Jamie was still watching her. Amelia looked at her, hopefully.

Sarah stood. Surprised, Jamie did, too. And found himself so close to her that for a moment, he forgot his own question. He thought about speaking but realized he was having trouble catching his breath. She literally took it away. She was taller than he had thought, able to stare him squarely in the eyes just by barely lifting her chin. Her eyes...they were incredible. He was lost in the depth of them. In that moment, he was sure he had never seen anything like them before. There was an intensity in her eyes, an energy that seemed to communicate without words. Somewhere, in the back of his mind, as if it were a dream at the edge of his consciousness, he realized she was talking. He blinked and willed himself to listen.

"No big deal, don't worry about it," Sarah said, shrugging her shoulders. "I gotta go." She reached over to gather her books and in doing so put some distance between them. Without another word, she turned and walked away.

Amelia suppressed a sigh as she watched her friend leave. One glance at Jamie confirmed he was watching, too. "She really is nice, Jamie," she said softly, as if to make up for Sarah's indifference.

Jamie nodded. "Yeah, she seems great. I'll see ya, Amelia."

"Yeah, see you at the game. Good luck."

All Jamie could do, as he made his way to his next class, was think about her. His apology had not had the outcome he had thought it would. Instead, Sarah had made it painfully clear she had no interest in talking to him, apology or no.

And yet...there was that look. The look of fire he had just seen in her eyes.

CHAPTER ELEVEN

Grant's party was definitely a success. Of course, that came as no surprise to anyone for two reasons: Grant had a party practically every weekend on his parents' farm; and he was dating Gertie Walker, a cheerleader and Charlotte's best friend. Grant's parties were the place to be on a Saturday night, for anyone who wanted to be seen with the *in* crowd. Which in high school was, of course, everybody.

Grant smiled as Sarah walked by and she smiled back, ignoring the stuck-up expression on Gertie's face. *Her personality is as phony as her hair extensions.* She couldn't help but smile at the way she, Charlotte and Jocelyn tossed their hair in perfect unison. They were giggling, excitedly. *Planning brunch at the country club, no doubt.*

Sarah laughed out loud at the thought, and turned to look for Amelia and Derek. Derek was Amelia's new boyfriend. He was sweet and easy to talk to, and Sarah liked him. Tonight was their third date in two weeks, and she knew Amelia was excited. Sarah scanned the dark room for what had to be the tenth time since she had gotten there, hoping to spot her friend in the crowd. But there was still no sign of Amelia. *They're probably in a dark, quiet corner getting to know each other better. They're so cute.*

She began to make her way toward the cooler for a drink. *The question becomes, however, why did I ever tell Amelia I would come tonight? I should have never let her talk me into it. Now, here I am, lost in this gigantic kitchen, awkwardly searching for a drink and my only friend. I should be helping Dad. They're probably so busy right now and I'm not there to keep them calm.* She smiled at the thought of her father and Niko running around Steve's, yelling at each other to get out of the way.

"Sarah! You made it!"

It was Michael Capitano, the other reason she had agreed to come. He ran cross-country with her and had invited her to meet him tonight. Between Amelia's coaxing and her inability to come up with an excuse not to, she had agreed. So, here she was.

"Hi, Michael. Sorry I'm late."

"No problem," Michael replied with a smile. "You're just in time to hear the BBDs." He pointed to the back of the room, where a band was setting up.

"Woah...a band at a house party? Are they local?"

"Nah. They're just some seniors from school. They practice in a garage. But they're not bad. Folks are starting to hire them out this year."

Sarah smiled at his deep Southern drawl, still getting used to words like "folks". She was actually starting to enjoy herself — until she got a look at the band members. Sarah stifled a groan. Walt, Robby, Gaston, a guy she didn't know and...Jamie. They were all there. *Seriously? He's in a band, too? Is there anything Boy Wonder doesn't do?*

She allowed her gaze to linger on Jamie, since the room was dark and he was too occupied to notice. He was hard at work, wiring up a speaker. Sarah watched as he pulled the wires apart. She had to admit Amelia was right about one thing: He looked good. He was dressed in jeans that were worn and a plain grey t-shirt. It should have looked sloppy, but on him, it looked clean-cut. She liked the way he kept his hair short—it brought out his deep-set eyes. They were definitely his best feature. When he was absorbed in thought, or working on something like he was now, his eyes were hard to look away from. And when he smiled...

"Sarah! You still with us?" Michael laughed, waving his hand across her face.

"Yeah, I'm sorry. I was just thinking about Steve's. I...I'm worried it's busy and I'm not there to help. My dad says the restaurant business gets in your blood and stays there, but I didn't think it would happen to me—and so soon."

"If you want to go, I'll take you."

Sarah smiled and shook her head. "That's so nice, but it's okay. I know you want to stay. And I do, too. Thanks for inviting me."

Michael smiled back. "Okay, then. You want something to drink? A beer?"

"Actually, a bottle of water sounds great."

Sarah watched him make his way through the crowd, stopping to talk to almost everyone he walked by. Michael was a great guy. She was glad she was getting to know him. Even as the thought formed in her mind, she found herself watching Jamie again. He was still working on the wires, tiny specks of sweat forming over his scrunched up brows. *Okay, the boy is hot. So what? Michael is, too. Minus the arrogant, self-obsessed factor, or every girl at Lakeview throwing herself at him.*

At that moment, Jamie looked up and straight at her, as if he had somehow heard her thoughts. Their eyes met and held for a moment before he flashed her that perfect grin of his. It was as if he had expected to find her staring at him. Annoyed with herself for giving him the satisfaction of catching her doing just that, Sarah turned away.

Where is Michael anyway? How long does it take to find a drink in this monster of a house? She hated standing there alone. She looked around the room again, hoping to spot Michael, or better yet, Amelia and Derek.

"Hi, Sarah. Come to hear me and the guys?"

She knew the voice belonged to *him*. Sarah turned and smiled her very best fake smile. "Don't you mean the guys and you? Oh, wait, what am I thinking, Jamie, you seem like the type of guy who always puts himself first."

Jamie smiled broadly. "Ouch. Again. You're just not going to forget that unfortunate incident at Steve's anytime soon, are you?"

"What incident?" she asked innocently. *Yeah, that's right, you spoiled, arrogant, ego-maniac. I've already forgotten all about you and your stupid friends.*

Jamie crossed his arms over his chest and leaned back on his heels, as if studying her but said nothing.

Go ahead, All-Star, hit me with your nastiest comeback. Sarah felt her heart kick up its rhythm as she waited for him to respond. *I can play this game, Jamie Nelson, as well as you. In fact, I can...*

"Your eyes are incredible."

Sarah felt her cheeks redden and thanked the powers above for the darkness in the room. She couldn't believe what she was sure she had heard him say. *Or maybe... I'm not so good at this game. Maybe I suck at it.*

"I...have to go," she managed, in what she hoped was her normal voice.

"Why? Michael's a patient guy."

He's been watching me! What is going on right now? Amelia, where are you? "Ha-ha, yeah, but I..."

"Jamieee!"

Charlotte was making her way over to the two of them. Sarah was so relieved, she smiled as if she'd just seen her best friend. *Yay! Charlotte! You're evil, but who cares, I love you right now! You go, girl!*

Charlotte scowled at her, before fixing her gaze on Jamie and transforming into a smiling vision of sweetness. Sarah watched the change in amazement. Charlotte slipped her arm through Jamie's and gave him an Oscar-worthy flirtatious pout. "Hey, you. I've been looking for you." Her voice was pure seductress, as if Sarah was not standing there.

Jamie smiled, eating it all up. "We're setting up to play. Charlotte, have you met Sarah?"

"Hi!" Her friendly tone effectively masked her indifference, but Sarah knew better. Sure enough, Charlotte did not wait for a reply before turning her body to speak more privately to Jamie. "Everyone's waiting for you to sing. Me, especially." She flashed him a sexy smile. "You're the best guitar player I've ever seen."

Seriously? What a fake! Even Jamie has to see right through her.

Except he didn't. He was smiling back at her as if it were only the two of them in the room. Sarah looked away from the pair in disgust. *I can't believe I almost fell for that ridiculous line. He's with Charlotte. The world makes sense again. Who knows why he even said what he said? Maybe he says that to all the girls he meets. Hey there, I'm Jamie the magnificent. Your eyes are incredible.*

"It was nice to meet you, Sally," Charlotte was saying, in the plastic voice that was uniquely her own. She laughed and gave Jamie a playful shove towards the stage.

"It's Sarah. Nice meeting you, too," she replied to their backs, scrunching her nose as she smiled with exaggerated cheerfulness.

"See ya around," Jamie called to her. "Hope you like the band."

Sarah pretended not to hear him, as she busied herself scanning the crowd for Michael. She was convinced now, beyond a reasonable doubt that Jamie Nelson had to be the most conceited guy she'd ever met.

Definitely not the sharpest tool in the shed, either.

"Sorry I took so long." Sarah heard Michael's voice in her ear about the same time she registered the smell of alcohol on his breath. She turned and took a step backwards, to put a little more space between them. No wonder he had been gone so long. Gone was the shy polite boy she had been talking to earlier. His voice was too loud and his eyes were glassy.

At least he had remembered her bottle of water. Sarah took a grateful swig. The lights lowered and the stage lit up. The crowd let out a rowdy cheer and Sarah felt Michael's arm around her shoulder. He whistled right into her ear. At that moment, she decided she had had enough for one night. She was about to tell Michael she was leaving when she noticed Jamie watching her, as he secured his guitar strap over his shoulder. He looked irritatingly amused. Without thinking, she looked up at Michael, and smiled a smile Charlotte would surely have been proud of. Returning her gaze to the stage, she saw Jamie was focused on the crowd, not her.

Michael's arm tightened around her, in response to her obvious encouragement. Sarah cringed. *Smooth, genius. Drunk boy thinks you like him. Now what?*

"Hey, y'all! Having fun?"

"Amelia! Hi!" Sarah moved out of Michael's arm and hugged her friend with grateful enthusiasm. "Where have you two been?" she asked, smiling warmly at Derek.

At that moment, the band started playing and loud music filled Grant's crowded den, ending any conversation. To Sarah's surprise, they were good. So good, she became aware she was holding her water bottle to her lips but not actually drinking any of it. Her body was swaying to the beat. She hoped no one had seen. Especially *him.*

"So, what do you think?" Michael bellowed, leaning in close to her.

Besides that I'm now deaf in one ear? I think you're a putz.

"They're pretty good, right?" Michael persisted, spitting on her cheek.

You can't make this up. One beer and he's a spewing megaphone. Ew.

"They're okay I guess." She shrugged indifferently and pretended not to see Amelia frown at her. Michael put his arm around her shoulder again.

Sarah wiped her cheek with her sleeve and downed her bottle of water. This night was getting complicated. She should have just worked at Steve's.

CHAPTER TWELVE

Jamie was beginning to tire. He tried to remember just how many laps he had run but couldn't. It didn't matter anyway. He had left the house irritated that morning, gotten in his car and ended up at the track. His house had been chaos for the last several hours, with Ben home from college and Hillary's friends spending the night after the game the night before. Usually he would have enjoyed all the noise and activity. But not today. His mind felt clouded and he needed to clear it. Running felt good. He knew it would have.

He had not played well the night before. He had thrown two interceptions, the second one resulting in a touchdown for the other team. They had managed to win anyway because of Walt, who got an interception and scored in the last two minutes of the fourth quarter. He thought of the exhilaration on his friend's face and felt some of his tension ebb. Then, he remembered that same face completely dumb founded after Sarah Giannopoulos poured a Steve's super-sized sweet tea all over it.

Sarah. She was the reason for this mood he was in. There was something about her that kept her on his mind. He didn't understand it—and he didn't like it. She blew him off like he was nothing more than a pest. No girl had ever done that before. Still, he knew she was nice from the way she had befriended Amelia. And Michael Capitano.

Jamie ran faster. Michael must have been the guy she was racing on her bike that first day of school. They must have gone out over the summer.

She had left Grant's party soon after the band had started playing. He'd noticed her go, even though he had pretended not to. He had hoped to talk to her again and was bummed he wouldn't get the chance. If only Charlotte had not come up to them when she had, they could have talked longer. He had thought Sarah was beginning to warm up to him a little—and maybe forget how stupid he had acted at Steve's.

Jamie slowed to a walk, too tired to run any longer. What did it matter anyway? She was Michael's girlfriend. She had made that more than obvious at the party. And besides, she didn't like him. So why should he even care what she thought? He had Charlotte—and Charlotte was the hottest girl at school.

Jamie scooped his sweatshirt from the ground where he had thrown it and pulled out his car keys. He had Charlotte, all right. She had been all over him at Grant's.

Except, to his complete and utter amazement, he didn't want her.

He leaned against the giant oak tree that he had grown up playing around and watched the sun climb up past its branches, dying leaves dancing around him as they fell. The bright light spread welcome warmth into the early morning. Jamie breathed it in.

And he knew then. He wanted Sarah. Like he had never before wanted anything in his life.

Somehow, someway, he was going to get her.

CHAPTER THIRTEEN

"Sarah! Table twelve's complaining their pizzas are all wrong! That makes three tables tonight! What's the matter with you? We're running a business here, in case you forgot. A business with a lot of bills to pay! *Your* bills!"

No one would ever describe Andreas Giannopoulos as a soft-spoken man. The fact was, there was not a patient bone in his body. He yelled, as he was doing now, at every opportunity. Whether he was genuinely upset or not, the man yelled. It was simply his way.

"Maybe you shouldn't give me so many tables, then," Sarah muttered in response, as she edged around him. "There are other waitresses at this *business*. Spread the joy."

"I heard that!"

Sarah ignored her father and made her way to the bar. "I need two Miller Lites, Mac," she told the bartender with a sigh. "And better make it quick before the boss blows another gasket."

Mac laughed at her frustrated expression. Everyone at Steve's knew Sarah was her father's lifeline. She was the joy of his life, along with Nick. His two children were well-rounded, smart and full of personality. If there was a smile on Andreas's face, the staff knew it was one of them who put it there. "You got it, gorgeous."

Sarah smiled, rechecking her orders while she waited. She knew better than to make any more mistakes tonight.

"Sarah, take four on seven," Andreas's voice boomed from behind her, causing her to jump. She smiled at Mac again, adjusting the Miller Lites on her tray. "Is it me, or does he seem to know few words besides 'Sarah'?"

"He pays me, so I'm not answering that," Mac answered, with a knowing wink. Sarah laughed and made her way around the crowded dining room to deliver the beers. *Is it busy tonight, or what? Why is it that people come out on the same night, at the exact same time? Oh well, the tips will be worth it. And Dad, for all his yelling, will be a happy camper at night's end.* She dropped off the beers, grabbed a basket of breadsticks and headed towards table seven.

"Hi," she began, in a polite, cheery tone. "I'm sorry you've had to wai..." Her voice trailed in mid-sentence when she saw who sitting there. Jamie, Walt, Gaston and Robby—all staring up at her.

Oh boy. Classic déjà vu. Or more like a recurring nightmare.

From the looks on their faces, they weren't any happier to see her than she was to see them. "Your waitress will be right with you," she recovered as best she could. Dropping the breadsticks on the table, she quickly turned away and headed for the waitress station.

"Lucy!" she whispered fiercely. "Switch tables seven and sixteen with me." Lucy stopped smacking her gum and glanced worriedly towards Andreas.

"C'mon, Luce, he won't notice. If he does, I'll take the heat. I really can't stand those guys. But they are good tippers! Please, please, please..."

Lucy resumed smacking and looked over Sarah's shoulder at the foursome of boys. "Hey, that's the kid you threw tea at, right?"

Sarah nodded, clasped her hands together, as if in prayer, and closed her eyes tightly in response.

"Okay, okay, don't get your panties all in a wad, I'll do it," Lucy conceded. "But after they leave, you have to tell me which one it is you've got the crush on."

Sarah kissed her on the cheek, giddy with relief. "Thank you. I love you. But don't be silly. I just told you, I hate them. All four of them."

"Yeah, right, honey. I hate a whole lot of people, too. But there's only one or two I can't talk to."

"Clearly, you missed your calling as a therapist, Luce. But for now, do you think you could just get to the table before I get into more trouble?" She gave Lucy a gentle push in the right direction, picked up another basket of breadsticks and headed for table sixteen.

Which one I've got a crush on... Ha! Must be Walt...

⁂ ⁂ ⁂ ⁂ ⁂ ⁂

Sarah took extra care not to make any more mistakes that evening. She kept as busy as possible waiting on her tables, bussing everyone's tables, taking cash and hostessing. Even Andreas gave her a nod of approval. Most of all, she made a point to ignore table seven completely, along with Lucy's lifted eyebrows and knowing smirks.

Finally, a glance at her watch told her it was almost closing time. And a glance towards table seven confirmed they were still there. Sarah groaned. She was running out of things to do. *What are they doing? Discussing world peace? Impossible, they're too dumb.* She turned and headed for the kitchen. *Maybe Mac needs more glasses for the bar.*

"Sarah, take cash for me. Mac needs more glasses from the kitchen," her father instructed, as he moved past her.

Sarah let out a deep breath. She just knew it was them. She knew it without a doubt, without turning around to look. And there was no getting out of it now. Straightening her shoulders, she moved behind the register.

"Dude, I got this one. I'll meet you outside." *Oh, yeah. No mistaking that voice. It's him.*

Sarah didn't look up, although she knew Jamie was standing directly in front of her. He placed his check on the counter. "How was everything?" Sarah asked, pleasantly, as she punched the numbers into the register.

"Great. Really good, thanks."

Ding.

"I'm glad. That will be $42.80, please."

"Here you go, Sarah."

Her heart skipped a beat at the way he said her name. She ignored it. Glancing at him, she took the cash out of his hand. "Out of $60.00 then."

"I have to say it's a little disappointing that you don't look at your customers. Just check 'em out and send 'em on their way."

There he went, antagonizing her again. Suddenly, Sarah felt completely at ease, her previous nervousness forgotten. *Two can play this game, you arrogant quarterback jerk.*

"That makes $17.20 your change, then." She handed him the change and looked up at him with a smile so sarcastic that even he could not mistake it for the least bit genuine.

He didn't. Jamie's eyes flashed with amusement. "Thank you, Sarah," he responded with an easy grin. His hand brushed hers as he took the change and for a second, Sarah felt her knees get shaky. He handed her back a ten dollar bill.

"For our waitress. She was great, too."

"I'll be sure to tell her." Behind the counter, her knees wobbled again.

Big deal, shaky knees. You're tired, Sarah, it's been a long night. And you need more iron. That's all. It means nothing!

"Thank you."

"You're welcome." Her voice could not have been icky-sticky sweeter.

"Goodnight, then."

Sarah leaned over the counter, casually resting her chin in her palms. "Have a good one," she said, still smiling.

Her smile was goofy and he knew she was faking it, but Jamie felt his insides draw up at the picture she made, just the same. He didn't move. He made no effort to leave. Instead, to Sarah's surprise, he stood and watched her, his expression changing from amused to thoughtful. "Wait. Aren't you forgetting something?"

Sarah straightened. "No, I don't think so. I gave you your change and a receipt."

"Yes, you did. But you haven't invited me back."

Sarah smiled and shrugged her shoulders innocently, pleased with the opportunity he had just given her. "Like I said, I don't think I've forgotten anything."

Jamie laughed. "Oh, okay, I see how it is. I guess I had that one coming."

"Yeah, you really did." Sarah couldn't help but laugh at the pitiful expression on his face, as phoney as all the smiling she had been doing. "But, hey, I need to get back to my customers. Have a good night."

"I was your customer. I heard your boss give you our table."

Oh, boy. Sarah felt her cheeks redden and her confidence quickly fade. Her expression sobered. "And you're surprised I didn't want to wait on you?" she managed to ask, in what she hoped was a normal tone.

"No. Not really. You didn't feel comfortable waiting on us, Sarah and I get that. That's one of the reasons we came tonight. The way we acted the last time we were here was wrong and I'm really sorry. It won't happen again."

Just like that. He had apologized so smoothly that suddenly she felt as if she were the bad guy. She looked away. "Yeah, well, don't worry about it."

"I mean it, Sarah. I won't let anyone treat you that way again."

Sarah looked at him, confused. She tried not to blink. Had he really just said that? "Um, thanks, but really it's no big deal. I've already forgotten about it."

"So, I'm forgiven and you don't think I'm a big jerk anymore?"

Sarah found her first real smile since the conversation had begun. He looked like a little boy standing there, all innocent and hopeful.

"Yes, you're forgiven, but let's not get crazy."

Jamie laughed. "That's a start. Hey, listen, I was wondering if..."

"Sarah!" Andreas yelled in his customary booming voice—which always seemed to come through a megaphone—but didn't.

"My dad, as well as my boss," she explained to Jamie, with a resigned shrug of her shoulders. Andreas wiped his hands on his apron, as he walked up and addressed his daughter. "Michael is on the phone. Tell him not to call you here. This is a business and we are busy!"

"Yes, sir."

Andreas's eyes narrowed at her militant response, but relaxed again when he noticed Jamie watching them. "How was your dinner, young man?"

"Excellent, sir."

"Good, good." Andreas gave him a good-natured slap on the back, his large, forceful hand causing Jamie to almost lose his balance. "Come back soon, son, and be careful out there." Looking over Jamie's shoulder, his eyes narrowed again. "Lucy! Don't carry the glasses without a tray! How many times do I have to tell you people the same thing..." Both waitress and boss disappeared into the kitchen, leaving Sarah and Jamie alone once more. This time the silence was awkward.

When Jamie finally spoke, his voice was distant. "I'll let you get that call. See you around."

He left before Sarah could reply. She watched the door swing shut behind him and somehow felt disappointed. The reason for that made no sense to her. He had been about to ask her something. But, what? Surely he wasn't going to ask her out? He was dating Charlotte Sanders. Still, it had sounded like he was going to invite her to something—until Michael's call had ruined the moment.

Sarah shook her head as if she could force her thoughts to clear. Jamie had been so sweet tonight. But that had to be all there was to it. He was just being nice. Like a friend. And that was all she wanted, anyway, for the two of them to be friends. Wasn't it? She thought of the way she had responded to the touch of his hand on hers.

"Lucy!" She grabbed the arm of the now exasperated waitress, as Lucy attempted to fly by her. She was careful not to cause her to spill the drinks on her tray.

"What now? Girl, I can't talk. Your dad's about to blow a gasket again."

"Give me that, you've got to do me a favor." Sarah took the tray and handed her the phone. "Tell this person I've already gone. Pleaaasseee?"

"Yeah, sure, kid," Lucy replied, smirking at her as she had all night. "In a million years, I couldn't guess why. Nothing to do with *Mr. Table Seven*, right?"

CHAPTER FOURTEEN

"Sarah, I'm seriously feeling nauseous..." Amelia was bending over and stretching her legs, her head upside down. Watching her from the grassy spot where she was sitting, her legs stretched out in front of her, Sarah could not help but laugh.

"Maybe that's because the blood is draining to your head. Chill, Amelia. It's a cross-country meet, not a college interview."

Amelia straightened. "Chill? Did you say to chill? Of course, you did. Probably because you can run three and a half miles like it's nothing. Me, on the other hand, they will have to wait for after everyone else has come in. Maybe, they will even leave."

"Don't worry about me leaving. You drove, remember?" Sarah joked.

"Don't wait, just take the car and go. Come back for me in a few hours."

"Hey, now," Sarah said, her voice softening. "Come on, Amelia. We're both going to do fine. You just need to relax. Take some deep breaths."

Amelia nodded and dropped to the grass, crossing her legs and closing her eyes. She began to take some of the deepest breaths Sarah had ever seen a person take. Sarah cupped both hands over her mouth to stifle the laughter bubbling out of her and hoped Amelia didn't hear. But she did. Opening one eye, she glared at her friend. "I can see my misery is funny to you." She sat up. "Forget about taking the car. You are so going to wait for me."

Sarah burst into laughter. "I'm sorry! I can't help it, you should see yourself right now."

"Hey, what's going on?"

"Niko!" Sarah hopped up to hug her little brother. "You came! I can't believe Dad let you skip prep time! How did you get him to?"

"Skills, big sis. I'll teach you someday." Nick gave Amelia a wink. "Plus, I told him it was my best chance to see hot girls running around in shorts."

Amelia smiled. "Aw, thanks, Nick. It makes me feel better to know everyone isn't here to judge my athletic ability."

"Wait," Sarah interrupted. "Are you saying you'd rather people judge your legs than your running? That actually makes you less nervous?"

Amelia shrugged, stretching her legs out in front of her. "And this surprises you, why? I have decent legs, right, Nick?"

"Yes. Yes, you do," Nick agreed, grinning.

Amelia smiled up at Sarah. "See? Your brother even thinks so."

"Only because he is young and easily impressed."

Amelia winked at Nick. "Sounds like someone is jealous of our relationship, Nicky."

"No doubt about it." Nick shook his head at his sister. "It's eating her alive."

Sarah laughed. "There is something seriously wrong with you two. Amelia, we better get to the track."

The smile left Amelia's face and she let out a deep sigh. Sarah shook her head and gave her bag to her brother. "Hold this for me, *playa.* "

"Where should I watch from?"

Amelia turned to point to the stands. "Everyone watches from the home stands."

"Everyone being five people, little bro." Sarah gave Nick a quick hug. "Thanks for coming."

"Yeah, thanks, Nick, you really are..." Amelia stopped in mid-sentence. "Whoa...there's one person I've never seen at a cross-country meet before! Yo, Sarah, baby, check out who came to watch!"

Sarah looked towards the stands and saw Jamie, sitting next to a man in uniform. She quickly looked away.

"Who are we looking at?" Nick asked, not recognizing anyone he knew.

"No one." Sarah kept her tone nonchalant.

"Apparently, *someone* is a fan of your sister," Amelia told him, smiling. "You know, Sarah, suddenly I'm feeling too amused to be nervous."

"Whatever, Amelia. He is not here because of me." Sarah busied herself looking for her hair tie in the gym bag Nick was holding.

"Uh-huh. You're probably right. I mean, I'm sure Jamie Nelson is here because he has nothing else to do. Or because cross-country is so darn exciting to watch."

"Jamie Nelson?" Nick chimed in. "I've heard about him. He's the quarterback, right?" He didn't wait for an answer. "He's Livvy Ryan's cousin or something. She's a girl in my grade." He motioned towards a girl stretching with the younger team members. "That's her. Her dad's the sheriff. He picks her up in his patrol car every day." He turned to look at Sarah. "All the girls in my grade are in love with Jamie Nelson. And he likes you? Cool!"

"No, not cool. And definitely not true. Obviously, he's here to watch his cousin." Sarah pointed her index finger at Amelia, her eyes on her brother. "She is crazy. Never listen to anything she says, Niko, especially about Jamie Nelson." Turning her brother around, she zipped the bag shut and gave him a push towards the stands. "Now, go watch."

"Okay, alright, I'm going! Can I sit with Jamie and the sheriff?"

"No. And don't talk to him. Not a word, or I promise I will hurt you."

"I'm so scared right now." Nick smiled at Amelia. "Good luck. And don't worry, I'll always listen to you."

"Thanks, Nick. See you in a couple of hours when I finish." Grabbing her bag from the ground, Amelia fell into step with Sarah and the two of them headed for the track. "I hope you know I can't run to the best of my ability now. I'm too insulted," she complained.

"What? Not you, the girl whose legs are the envy of every eighth grade boy." Sarah laughed at her own joke and looked up at her friend, only to find her waving a cute little half wave. Thinking she was waving to Nick, Sarah turned and followed her gaze.

Instead of Nick, her eyes met Jamie's. He held up his hand in greeting. Sarah forced a quick smile and looked away. Her breath caught in her chest.

"I cannot believe you did that. I hate you, Amelia Patten. I mean it. What the..."

"Sarah! Amelia! Let's go!" Coach Adam impatiently motioned the pair to the starting line.

Like I can run with him watching me.

"Oh, God, Sarah, they look fast." Amelia shook out her hands, nervously shifting her weight from foot to foot.

Sarah glanced at the girl standing next to her. Amelia was right. She looked to be in great shape. So did the girl beside her. *Okay, Sarah, focus. Forget him. You can beat these girls. Don't think about Jamie Nelson. He's just another rich, spoiled jock with an overinflated ego. He's probably meeting Charlotte here and has some time to kill. Maybe the sheriff made him come. He couldn't care less if you're running in this race or not.* She took a deep breath and let it out, jogging in place and stretching her arms. *You've got to run well. Focus. You owe it to this stupid school. To the team.*

"Runners, take your marks!"

To yourself. Sarah dropped her arms, placing one foot in front of the other.

To Mama. She waited for the sound of the gun.

And if by some miracle you win, he'll see you do it.

The gun went off with a loud bang and Sarah pushed herself to get to the front of the pack. Only one girl was ahead of her. She heard Niko calling her name in encouragement and then nothing. All she could hear was the sound of her breathing and the steady rhythm of her feet hitting the ground. For the next two miles, she allowed no one to pass her, keeping directly behind the girl in the lead. In the last mile, she focused on closing that lead, until the gap between her and the leader was small. They were about to reenter the track, for the final lap.

"Go, Sarah, you got this!"

That's Coach Adam! He thinks I can take her! C'mon, c'mon, her brain urged her legs. *Move, move faster! No, don't pass her yet, be patient, not in the turn!* Sarah cut the turn hard and after coming out of it, gave it all she had. Somehow, she caught her competitor and managed to run past her. *Got ya! Keep pushing, keep going...* She could barely feel her legs and had no idea where the other girl was. She knew she was pushing too, and could pass her at any second. Suddenly the finish line came into focus and Sarah closed her eyes and crossed it, still running as fast as she could. Voices pushed into her consciousness and she slowed to a stop, doubling over and gasping for air. She wanted to ask if she had won, but she couldn't catch her breath, couldn't even look up. She could hear Nick yelling and knew she had done well. She had given it all she had. It felt good.

"Number 17—Sarah Giannopoulos, of Lakeview—first place!"

Sarah looked up in amazement. She simply could not believe she had heard correctly. One look up at the stands at Niko's beaming face confirmed it. Sarah smiled, happily. *If only Dad had seen it...this would truly be perfect.*

"Great run, Sarah!" Coach Adam stepped by her, stopping to give her a pat on the shoulder. That's a new personal best for you. Way to kick it on that last lap. I had you coming in third. You just beat two of the top five runners in the state."

"Rea-ally? Thanks, Coach! I heard you call out to me when I was coming back on the track. It really helped!"

Coach Adam smiled, looking up from his clipboard. "Wish I could take credit but that wasn't me. Great job, kiddo. Get you some water, now."

Sarah turned to look towards the end of the track—and blinked in shocked surprise. Jamie was standing at the track entrance. Slowly, it dawned on Sarah it was he who had urged her on. He was standing alone, his hands in his pockets, watching the runners come in, one by one. When he turned to look at her, she didn't look away. His eyes settled on hers for a long moment. Then he grinned and gave her a thumbs-up sign. Sarah smiled back, a bubbly, happy smile she felt all the way to her toes. Jamie *had* come to watch her. More than that, he had helped her win.

In front of anyone who cared to watch.

She looked away, almost embarrassed with the realization. Still, the happiness that was blossoming inside her felt so welcome, so good. She straightened and let her eyes wander back to him. He was still watching her, his expression now intent, his eyes still smiling. Their gazes locked and suddenly, more than anything, she wanted to go to him. At that moment, she didn't feel inhibited by her previous misgivings. She couldn't deny the attraction she felt for him, the same feeling she'd had since she'd met him on her bike that first day of school. Her pride had kept her from admitting it, but she knew now it was real. As he stood there, only a few feet away, looking at her the way he was, she felt powerless to do anything else but give into it.

Two runners crossed in front of him and onto the track. Sarah came out of her trance-like state and realized one was Amelia. She was running neck and neck with another girl. "Go, Amelia, Go!" she yelled excitedly, as she watched her friend.

Seconds later, Amelia crossed the finish line ahead of the other runner. Sarah jumped for joy and rushed to hug her friend. Then, she turned to look for Jamie.

He was gone.

CHAPTER FIFTEEN

"Heading out, son?" Doctor James Nelson knew better than to ask his teenage children detailed questions on a Saturday morning. It was a time to keep conversation minimal. He folded over the newspaper he was reading.

"Just going for a run," Jamie answered, irritably. He was trying to untangle the cord of his earphones without much success.

James Nelson took a sip of coffee and eyed his son with amusement. Sensing he was being watched, Jamie looked up from the task. "What?"

His father leaned back in his chair and crossed his arms over his chest. "Well, frankly, Jamie, I'm surprised to see you. I don't think you have been up this early on a Saturday morning since you were seven."

"Yeah, I've got some stuff on my mind and I feel like running." He finally managed to untangle the cord and felt his mood improve. He smiled at his father. "How 'bout it, Dad? Wanna tag along?"

"My running days are behind me, son," the older man replied with a sigh. "Back in the day, I would have left you in the dust, though."

Jamie grinned. "Dad. I was kidding. Stick to the golf course."

"You know, the truth is," Doctor Nelson added casually as he picked up his newspaper again, "you may just be a little worried I could keep up. Maybe even show you up." He took another sip of coffee and ignored Jamie's burst of laughter. "I do admire your confidence, buddy. But someday you might crawl out of that bed on a morning just like this one and find me waiting in the driveway."

"In that case, I'd better start training now." Jamie bit off a piece of toast, smiling at his dad as he chewed. "Thanks for the heads up though."

"Sure thing, son." Doctor Nelson opened the paper to hide his smile. "Have a good run. And Jamie, whatever it is you are worried about—try not to be. The greatest gift life has to offer at your age is that it usually works everything out for you."

"Thanks, Dad. I'll try to remember it's that easy," Jamie replied, laughing.

"Now, your mother on the other hand, running in here hysterical about you not coming home last night when she discovers your bed empty—any minute now—is definitely something to be concerned about." He looked over the paper at Jamie with a knowing smile. "Lucky for you, the years have definitely worked to my advantage when it comes to handling your mother. You go enjoy your run. I'll enjoy the peace while it lasts."

"Right. Poor Mom. You're going to mess with her and pretend you haven't seen me since yesterday, aren't you, Dad?" Jamie said, more than asked.

"Why in the world would I do a thing like that?" He held the paper in front of his face. "Now go, Jamie. Oh, and close the door quietly behind you."

Jamie laughed again. "Whatever you say, doc. Have fun." Swinging open the kitchen door, he let himself out, taking care not to make too much noise.

The air was both crisp and damp as Jamie began to jog. He smiled as he recalled the conversation with his father. Too bad he had not had the time for another of their many father-son debates. It was their favorite thing to do, argue over whatever issue they deemed worthy of debating, until one clearly proved the other wrong. James Nelson was a superb debater. He had taught Jamie the art—one of the reasons Jamie was considering law school, eventually.

He knew he was lucky to have such a great dad and better yet, such a good relationship with him. He wanted to make his dad proud. Law school would make him happy, he knew. Maybe, even a football scholarship to college. There was nothing Dr. James Nelson would appreciate more than a reduced college tuition.

And Sarah. Without a doubt, Jamie knew his dad would like Sarah.

Where had she been all day Friday? He had been—almost—finally sure of what to say to her. Only after first period English, he had not seen her all day.

Something had happened at the cross-country meet Thursday afternoon. He was pretty sure she had felt it, too. He thought of her doubled over, trying to catch her breath, smiling at him from across the track.

The memory had the same devastating effect on his senses as when it happened. She was the most intriguing girl he had ever met. She had put her all into that run. It had surprised him how badly he found himself wanting her to win. He was barely aware of the fact that he had left the stands and gone to the edge of the track to cheer her on. He had shouted, urged her on, unable to take his eyes off her. He had known she would win from the determined look on her face when she started the race. It was a look he knew he wouldn't forget.

Jamie turned a corner and ran faster.

Her smile...it had not been the usual sarcastic or polite. It had been a smile that would make anyone stop and stare. And it had been meant for him.

That smile had made his world shift in a weird and crazy way. And for the first time in his life he had not known what to do or say. It was a lot to sort out and he had left, not wanting to push; not wanting to ruin it; thinking he would talk to her at school the next day. Only she was nowhere to be found. And she had not come to the game last night. His guess was, she probably had to work.

Charlotte had been there, though. He sat through dinner at *John Paul's* with the team and his friends afterwards and she had been all over him. After dinner, he told them all he had a headache and went home. Charlotte had texted him on the hour until the wee hours of the morning, but he had not responded.

Jamie turned and started to head home. Hopefully, his dad had had his fun by now. He thought about what his father had told him and decided he was right. It was time to stop worrying about things and just let them happen.

But there was nothing wrong with helping them along a little. He would go home, call Walt and make sure he was still having a party tonight.

He felt a rush of adrenalin, more powerful than the ones he felt after throwing a great pass or even scoring a touchdown.

With a little luck, tonight, Sarah would be there.

CHAPTER SIXTEEN

Sarah was at Steve's, unsuccessfully trying to solve a calculus problem, when Nick called her to the phone.

"It's Amelia," he shouted, poking his head out from behind the kitchen door. He was covered in flour.

"Thanks, Niko," she answered with a laugh. "Looking good, bro..." He made a face and let the door swing shut. Sarah was still laughing as she walked over to the register and picked up the receiver. "Hello?"

"Hi! You never answer your cell phone. Why do you even have one? And what's so funny?"

"Hey, bestie! I'm fine, how are you?"

"Yeah, fine, whatever. You'd better be going to Walt's party. You promised me you'd go," Amelia said, in the tone Sarah had come to recognize as one she used when she was on a mission.

Sarah sighed. "No, I did not! What I said was I would *think* about going. Big difference. How's skiing? Is there snow up there?"

"No. But it's cold. It's pretty fun, actually. We went on a four-mile hike through the mountains today. So, that was cool. The downside is, my parents are driving me nuts, and my little cousin and I have to share a bed. He kicks me all night long. But my older cousins are awesome. You'd like them!"

"I'm sure I would." Sarah was fond of Amelia's family. They were close and did lots of fun things together, just as her own family had done before her mother's death. And after that, the fire. There had not been time—or money—for trips since then. Still, somehow they had gotten along just fine. Sarah knew it was because of her father's resolve to keep them a close, loving family, no matter what. And they were.

"So, what are you wearing?" Amelia asked, interrupting her thoughts.

"Sweats and a..."

"To the party, you geek. You have got to go. Oh my God, your dad's not making you work, is he?"

The panic in her voice kept Sarah from lying, though she considered it.

"No, but for once, I wish he would. Amelia, I don't want to go by myself. I can't stand Walt Patterson. And I'm guessing he's not exactly crazy about me, either."

"But his best friend is."

Sarah let out a sigh. "I sincerely doubt that's the case."

"Ugh, Sarah, what's it going to take for you to just admit he likes you and you like him? Why do you make things so hard? Anyway, go for *me*. Derek is going to be there. We just finished talking! He called to say he misses me!" Amelia giggled into the phone.

"He did? Called, not texted?"

"Yes! And Hudson is going. You like her, right? She's great. And she said she's only going if you go. So you have to go! Both of you have to keep an eye on Derek and tell me if there is any interaction with that scheming Lexi Taylor."

"His ex? She seems nice."

"Yeah, well, trust me, she is not what she seems. I just know she is going to hit on him now that he and I are going out." Amelia's voice became quiet. "I wish I was there."

Sarah heard the worry in her friend's voice and felt badly for her. "C'mon Amelia, you know that's not going to happen. The boy really likes you. He even called you instead of texting, and that's huge. I mean you just left last night. Which means he's thinking about you and not Lexi—or anyone else."

"Yeah, I guess. I wish I were confident, like you are. I'm so darned insecure when it comes to guys. I mean, look how cool you are about the whole Jamie thing." Her voice became more animated. "Sarah! You have *got* to go! He likes you! You never know what could happen if you don't go! And Hudson really wants you to."

Sarah sighed. "But I'm working on calculus and it looks like it might get busy here. They might need me."

"Sarah Giannopoulos, it's four o'clock in the afternoon. How can you tell it's going to be busy?"

"I don't know, I just can. It's a restaurant thing."

"That's ridiculous and you know it," Amelia said, exasperated.

"What do you know about the restaurant business? It just so happens that lunch was slow and when that happens, dinner gets busy."

"I might not know the restaurant business, but what I do know is you are scared to go to that party."

"Okay, now *that's* ridiculous!"

"Prove me wrong, then. Go to the party."

"I'll think about it." Sarah's voice was firm.

Both girls fell silent. Amelia finally spoke, her tone resigned. "Okay. Well, look good if you go. And if anything happens with Jamie, call me immediately. I don't care what time it is, I'll be awake."

"Don't wait up, dear, nothing is going to happen."

"And make sure Derek is behaving himself," Amelia continued, as if she had not heard her.

"I will. I will make a sign that says: 'Property of Amelia' and hang it around his neck. If I go, that is."

"Good idea. Thanks, best friend. I'm so glad I called."

Sarah giggled at Amelia's defeated tone. "Aw, me too! Seriously, Amelia, have fun and I hope your little cousin takes it easy on you tonight. Call me when you hit the city limits Monday and don't forget to keep your eyes open for hot skiers."

"No one is as hot as Derek," Amelia said, her voice deliberately dreamy.

"Whipped in less than a month. That might be a record. Bye-bye."

"Bye, Sarah."

"Oh, wait! One more thing!" Sarah's tone became serious.

"What?"

"*If* go, I'm wearing my sweats."

For a few seconds, there was silence. Then, with a click, the line went dead.

Sarah laughed out loud, hung up the phone and picked up her calculator. Amelia was the best friend she had ever had. Funny she had found her in this temporary place, in her last year of high school. She had dreaded the move so much and now here she was, with a real best friend. A best friend who wanted her to go to this party so badly, she had called her from her family mountain trip to tell her so. Although she had used Derek and even Hudson as excuses for wanting her to go, Sarah knew it was largely because she knew Jamie would be there. Amelia had her back. And she really liked Jamie.

The thought of him made Sarah forget the numbers she had just punched into the calculator. With a sigh, she cleared it and started over. She stared at the numbers, and chewed on the eraser of her pencil, unable to concentrate. She had avoided Jamie like the plague at school on Friday for reasons she could not explain, even to herself. It wasn't as if she didn't want to see him. Far from it. She could no longer deny there was something between them after what happened at the meet. But it was just too much to process. The feeling was all too familiar, the script writing itself the same way as before, except this time, the feelings were even stronger. She had just barely survived Jake. She could not let herself head down that same destructive road. Her heart needed a break, not to be broken again.

Sarah groaned and buried her head in her hands. "Why? Why do I have to go and find the popular, rich, know-it-all, always-gets-it-all, adored-by-all superstar jock like Jamie Nelson to like? Again? Really?" she mumbled to herself.

She knew it could never work between them. Not in a million years. They were complete opposites. All she would do is end up hurt.

Again.

Even so, she could not let the past dictate her future. Her mother never would have. *Never run scared, love, you'll only regret it,* she'd say. *Be smart but be bold.*

"Sarah? Are you okay?" Nick stood over her, his eyes concerned.

Sarah lifted her head. "Yeah. I was just thinking."

"Well, that explains it. I know that's not easy for you," he teased, grinning.

"Ha ha, good one, Niko. Do me a favor and tell Dad I went home to get ready."

"Ready for what?"

"Walt Patterson is having a party tonight." Sarah clicked off her calculator and smiled at her little brother. "And I've just decided to go."

CHAPTER SEVENTEEN

"Great party, Walt!" Robby came up behind his friend and gave him a bear hug.

"Get off me, man." Walt shrugged him off and spun around. "What the hell was that?"

Robby raised his cup to his lips, grinning. "Just happy to see you, I guess."

"Yeah right. What's up, Rob? You drunk or switching sides?"

Robby ignored him and smiled over Walt's shoulder. Walt turned to look and saw Sherri Bray standing with a group of friends, smiling at Robby. When she saw Walt turn, she looked away. Walt took a swig of beer and laughed. "Well, that's a relief. She's looking good, bro. What is she a sophomore? Isn't she Mary Elizabeth's friend?"

"Yeah, but she's a junior. She plays field hockey with Mary Elizabeth. She's good, too. I went to their game this week and hung around to talk to her afterwards. And here she is tonight." Robby grinned again and clinked his cup to Walt's.

"Well, good luck talking to her with Mary Elizabeth here, buddy," Walt said, amused.

"What about Mary Elizabeth?" Gaston walked up behind the twosome. "When did she start looking like that? I was just noticing, she is looking good..."

That wiped the smile off Robby's face. "Don't even think about it, Gaston. My sister is off limits to you. For life. As in, forever."

"Chill, man, I'm only saying she's pretty," Gaston replied in his usual good-natured manner as he took a sip of drink. Then his face turned thoughtful. "Wait, I think I'm offended. What, I'm not good enough for your sister, Rob?"

"No. No, you're not." Robby had to smile at Gaston's wounded expression. "Hey, no worries, man, I'll find you somebody..."

"Save it for someone who needs your help. Me, I'm going to talk to Mary Elizabeth's friend, the field hockey player. She's hot and unlike you, Mary Elizabeth is my friend, and will say nice things about me to Sherri."

"Sherri? Since when do you talk to Sherri Bray?" Robby asked, his eyebrows coming together, his tone anything but friendly.

Gaston shrugged in response and started towards Sherri and Mary Elizabeth. Robby stepped in front of him, blocking his way. "Not gonna happen, buddy."

"Who's gonna stop me?" Gaston challenged, his tone equally unfriendly.

Robby started to reply but was interrupted by Walt's loud laughter. He looked from Robby to Gaston and laughed again. "Rob, he's playing you, man."

Robby looked at both, confused. Gaston smiled, then burst out in loud laughter and gave Walt a fist pump. Robby shook his head. "Good one. Very nice."

Gaston held his cup up. "Here's to me not being good enough for your sister!" The three laughed and drank together, Robby's good mood back in full swing.

"It's gonna be a good night," he said, glancing at Sherri again.

"Not likely. Sidney's in a foul mood. Not even coming," Walt complained.

Gaston eyed him with amusement. "I don't know how you hang with her, man. She's way too high maintenance. I say you forget about Sidney tonight. Turn off your phone and let's have a good time with girls who appreciate all we have to offer."

Walt smiled into his cup. Reaching into his pocket, he pulled out his phone and pushed the off button. "You're right, buddy. The night is young and full of possibilities. The BBDs are playing and there are girls here I've never seen before. What else could we..." Walt's voice trailed, as he stared intently at something behind Gaston, his expression one of surprise. Gaston and Robby turned to see what had caught his attention.

"Wow." It was Robby who spoke first.

"What's up?" Jamie walked up from behind the group, pushing Gaston's baseball hat down over his eyes.

"Cut it out, Nelson. I'm busy here!"

Jamie laughed. "You don't look busy."

"Jamie, shut up and get a load of this." Robby pulled him in, so he could see for himself what they were all looking at. "There," Robby indicated, with a nod of his head.

Jamie looked across the darkened room. "What? What is it?"

"Not what. Who. Now I know where the expression *Greek Goddess* came from."

Robby kept talking but Jamie was no longer listening. He finally saw who they were all gaping at. He blinked to see more clearly.

Sarah was standing towards the far end of the room, laughing. She was dressed in a black sweater dress that hung off one shoulder and enhanced her slender figure by just barely clinging to the curves of her body. The dress was short, her legs long and lean beneath it. Her dark hair fell freely around her shoulders, contrary to the reserved ponytail she usually wore it in. Tonight, it was like the wind had whipped through it just a little, giving it a wild, untamed look. She looked like a goddess, Robby was right. She took his breath away, just like she always did; each time, it seemed more than the time before. This time, more than ever.

"So, the waitress has left the pizzeria," Walt commented dryly.

"Whatever, man. She looks so hot. Even you have to admit it, Walt," Robby said, still staring at Sarah.

"She looks cheap and I can't believe she has the nerve to come here," Walt replied, irritably.

"Chill, man. Just don't offer her tea," Robby said, sending Gaston into another fit of laughter. Walt glared at them, swiped Gaston's hat off his head and sent it sailing.

"Hey, lay off the hat!" Gaston picked his hat up off the floor and brushed it off. "Dude, you need to lighten up."

"Is she alone?" Robby asked.

"Who cares? I say we ignore her so she leaves," Walt mumbled, gulping down his drink.

"She's with Hudson," Jamie observed, quietly.

Walt rolled his eyes. "C'mon, Gaston. I need another drink. By the time we get back maybe we'll get lucky and she'll be gone."

"Give her a break, Walt," Robby said. "She's dressing up the place. You may not like her, but the girl's a knock-out."

"Says you. I say she's bad news. She's got no class and she's weird." Walt leaned close enough to Robby to point him in the direction of Sherri and her friends. "Sherri, on the other hand, is hot. If I were you, I'd make my way over there before someone else does."

"Yeah, that's right," Gaston warned, adjusting his hat and giving Robby a pointed look. "You should be worried." He turned and followed Walt to the kitchen.

Jamie tore his eyes away from Sarah and looked at his friend, eyebrows raised.

"Sherri Bray? What grade is she in? When did this happen?"

"Yes, eleventh, and tonight, I hope." Robby looked over Jamie's shoulder in time to catch Sherri glance his way. "I'm gonna go talk to her."

"You'd better, before Gaston gets back and snakes your girl," Jamie said, smiling. "We still playing?"

"Yeah, in about thirty minutes. We were waiting for you. Hey, man, what do you think of Sher..." He stopped short, noticing Jamie wasn't listening to a word. Instead, he was watching Sarah again. Robby studied his best friend for a moment. "Interesting girl," he said casually, watching for Jamie's reaction.

"Who, Sarah? Yeah, I guess." Jamie took a sip of his drink and waited for Robby to say what he knew was coming. They had been best friends since pre-school. Robby knew him better than anyone.

For a moment, the silenced became awkward. Then Robby let out a breath and shook his head. "I'm just gonna say it. I don't know, man. She's new and really hot. But Walt has a point, dude. She's...well, she's different than you...than us."

"Yeah." Jamie didn't hide the irritation in his voice. He wasn't surprised by Robby's criticism of Sarah, or that it bothered him. What surprised him was how much.

"Look, man, I don't want to see you lose all you got over some pretty face, that's all. That girl's not your type."

"Lose what, Robby? My friends?"

"Naw, man, that's not what I mean. You know what I'm talking about." Robby looked away, uncomfortable.

"Yeah, I think I do."

"What about Charlotte? She's the hottest girl in the county and she wants you."

Jamie nodded, his eyes distant. "You should go talk to Sherri. She keeps looking over at you."

Robby watched him, thoughtfully. "Yeah, I will." He paused. "You know I'm just looking out for you, right?"

Jamie looked away, his expression guarded. But the genuine concern in Robby's voice reached him and he smiled. "I know. Go get the girl, Rob, she's definitely into you. Remember, we play in a few minutes."

Robby watched his friend walk over to center of the room, where Walt, Hughey and Gaston were setting up the band. He wondered if he should have said anything. Then he saw Sherri smile at him again—and decided to think about it later.

CHAPTER EIGHTEEN

Sarah pretended not to notice Jamie making his way through the crowded den. The band was setting up. *He's going to play tonight*, she thought to herself. Her knees felt annoyingly weak. She wanted to talk to him, but didn't have the nerve.

"Hudson, are you sure I look okay? I think I overdressed..."

"Sarah, you look hot! Go talk to him," Hudson urged. "He's definitely into you; he's been checking you out."

"Who?" Sarah asked, surprised.

"Oops. Sorry." Hudson made a remorseful face. "Amelia kind of told me you have a crush on Jamie Nelson. Only because I swore I wouldn't tell anyone though, and I won't, so don't worry. I'm a steel trap."

"Oh, God. Keep your voice down!" Sarah whispered, panicked. "Hudson, I don't know what Amelia told you, but I do not have a crush on him! He just did something nice for me at the meet last week and I wanted to talk to him and say...thanks."

"You want to say 'thanks'? Really?" Hudson smiled mischievously.

Sarah couldn't believe it. At this rate the whole school would know by Monday. It would be all over social media: *Sarah Giannopoulos is the newest loser girl to have a thing for Jamie Nelson, king of studs, because he came to a cross-country meet she happened to run in.* Sarah closed her eyes at the horrible thought. That was it. Amelia was a dead girl. She opened her eyes and fixed them on Hudson.

"Okay, Hudson, listen to me." Sarah chose her words carefully. "Jamie Nelson is nice and he is extremely hot, no doubt about it. But he's just not my type. He's used to having every girl he wants."

Hudson nodded, cheerfully. "And then some."

Sarah's eyes became angry. "My point exactly. He uses them and tosses them aside when he's through. Why would I want to get mixed up with him? Believe me, I've been down that road before. And I have promised myself to never, ever go there again."

Hudson saw the expression in Sarah's eyes—and believed her. She would have to remember to ask Amelia about this ex-boyfriend. For now, it was clear that changing the subject would be the best idea. She liked Sarah and didn't want to upset her. And Sarah definitely looked upset. "I'm sorry, Sarah, I didn't mean to be nosey. Forget about it. C'mon, let's get a drink."

"You mean, like a beer?"

"Um, no. Or maybe? I'm sorry, Sarah, Amelia told me you don't drink alcohol. I can't say anything right tonight." Hudson shifted her weight uncomfortably. "I mean...um...we can just grab a soda."

Sarah smiled. "I'm Greek, Hudson. There is no drinking age in Greece and alcohol has never been taboo in my family. My dad would rather Nick and I drink a glass of beer or wine with a meal than soda. He says it's better for us and that soda is poison."

Hudson's mouth made a small, surprised "O". "Well, there's something I don't hear at my house. Or anywhere. Ever."

"It's no big deal. I don't drink at parties because I don't want to. I'll wait until I'm legal. Honestly, it doesn't taste that good to me. But I'm cool if you do, I get it."

Are you sure? It's not like I'm a big drinker or anything but...I don't know, I mean, everyone does here."

Sarah nodded. "Sure. No worries, I promise I don't care. As long as you're good with me sticking to poison-soda, I'm good to drive us home."

Hudson smiled. "Could you be any cooler? I think I'll stick to poison-soda tonight, too. Sounds far more dangerous and thrilling now. Let's go."

Sarah tried not to stare as she followed Hudson towards Walt's kitchen.

His house is ginormous. Three families could live here, she thought to herself. *Of course, Walt Patterson needs a house this big, so his ego can fit in it.* She suppressed a sigh as she made her way through the crowd and thought of the conversation she had just had with Hudson.

She didn't belong in this place, with these people. She had made a mistake in coming.

CHAPTER NINETEEN

It was about an hour later. Sarah was still out of sorts. Jamie's band had played and was taking a break. She had been unable to keep from watching him throughout the BBDs' performance, and only hoped Hudson had not noticed. There was an honest and real feel to his singing. Though it pained her to admit it—even to herself—he was good at that, too.

He had caught her once. Their eyes locked for what had seemed to her an eternity. Unnerved, she had been the one to look away—only to find her traitor eyes wandering back in his direction.

What is it about him? she thought to herself, as she sipped on her water bottle. She thought of the way he had been on the sideline of the track, urging her on; the way he had apologized at Steve's; the way his deep-set eyes slit when he smiled at her—like he had the first time she had seen him, that day she almost ran him over on her bike.

Sarah took another sip and sighed. No, it definitely was not good looks that had her thinking about Jamie Nelson far more than she knew she should be. It was his way.

"Sarah!" Hudson's voice was urgent. "Derek's here."

"Oh, yay!" Sarah replied, happily. "A friendly face at Walter *Gatsby's* manor! Where is he?" She looked over Hudson's shoulder.

"Upstairs in a bedroom."

"Let's go find...what?" Hudson's serious tone suddenly registered with Sarah. She cocked her head and lifted her eyebrows in question.

Hudson sighed. "I was looking for an empty bathroom and the door was cracked so I walked in. There he was, making out with his ex-girlfriend, Lexi Taylor."

"Unbelievable." Sarah looked past Hudson to the stairs. "Amelia leaves for one weekend—one little weekend—and he hooks up with his ex?"

"The sleaze didn't waste any time," Hudson replied, her voice sad.

"Which one?" Sarah snorted in disgust.

"Oh, God, Sarah, are we gonna tell her? I mean we have to tell her. She needs to know! But she'll be so devastated, so maybe we shouldn't. What a jerk..." Hudson's voice dropped to little more than a whisper. "She told me she thinks she loves him."

Sarah's heart sank. Amelia had confided the same thing to her. *What an asshole.* She felt her breath quicken and knew she was too angry to stay there a minute longer without doing something she would later regret. *Leave, now. Leave this stupid mansion and go home,* she told herself, even as she looked to the stairs once more. "Which bedroom?" she asked, instead, spitting out the words.

Hudson's eyes widened. "First one on the right, at the top of the stairs. Why?"

"Did he see you?"

"No. At least, I don't think he did. He was too busy sucking the lips off her face to notice much of anything. Sarah...what are you going to do?"

"Not let Derek Quigg make a fool out of my best friend."

Turning, Sarah started for the stairs. And ran smack into Jamie, spilling his drink all over both of them.

"Um...yeah...I was just thinking it was a little too warm in here for me, so that feels much better," he joked, wiping the front of his t-shirt. "However, I am running out of shirts, since every time I see you, there seems to be a drink prob..." Jamie paused mid-sentence, registering the furious look in her eyes.

Sarah looked down at her wet dress and wiped the liquid away. "Sorry. I have to go."

Jamie didn't get a chance to respond. She was gone, taking the stairs two by two. There was no mistaking the angry look he had seen.

She was worked up about something. It was the same look he had seen her give Walt and the rest of them that night at Steve's. Walt... The thought occurred to him that Walt may have said or done something to Sarah in retaliation for the Steve's incident. He saw Hudson move towards the stairs and touched her arm. "Hudson, what's wrong with Sarah? Did Walt say something to her?"

Hudson looked at him, confused. "What?"

Jamie could feel the tension building inside of him. Sarah was clearly upset. Walt had to be responsible. "Sarah is obviously angry. Do you know why?"

Finally, Hudson understood what he was asking. "Oh, no, no. It's Derek. He's with Lexi upstairs. Derek goes out with Amelia." She shook her head. "You probably don't even know what I'm talking about." Hudson was talking faster than usual and as a result, running out of breath.

"Yeah, I heard about that."

"Well," Hudson continued, "Amelia is on a family ski trip—and Derek's hooking up with his old girlfriend, and I saw him, and that's it, really, except that Sarah just went up there."

Hudson took a breath. Jamie's eyes narrowed.

"I'm gonna go up," she said.

"I'll come with you."

The two hurried up the stairs and towards the bedroom, where Sarah had just flung open the door. Flicking on the lights, she took a step inside the room.

"So, you think you're a player, Derek?"

Derek jumped off the bed, fumbling with his jeans. "Sarah! Hold on, I can explain this. And keep your voice down, will you?"

"Nope. Actually, I don't think I will." Sarah planted her feet and faced him. "Did you just say *'explain'*? Derek, you're pathetic and I'm not just talking about what you're putting away there." Sarah heard chuckles behind her and realized they had an audience. She didn't care. Not one little bit.

"I...we were talking, that's all!" Derek looked past her, his eyes desperate for escape.

"You've got lipstick all over your face, Derek. And I recognize the shade as Lexi's favorite: slut red."

That earned a gasp from Lexi, who was busy buttoning her shirt. She glared at Sarah.

Sarah refused to look at her. Not yet. Her eyes were fastened on Derek. "You told Amelia you love her, you lying snake."

"Sarah, calm down!" He was pleading with her now. He looked over her shoulder again. The room was suddenly crowded.

"You told her you love her, you pathetic dirtbag!"

Derek stared at her. He couldn't believe what was happening. Everyone he knew, it seemed, was witnessing what he was sure was the worst moment of his life. It was true, he had told Amelia he loved her. And he had meant it, but at the same time, it had scared the living daylights out of him. When Lexi had come on to him earlier, he had not let himself think about it. Now, it would cost him Amelia for sure. His mind raced. Unable to come up with a better option, he decided to at least save some face.

"So, sue me. I lied." He returned Sarah's furious glare with a defiant one of his own. "What's it to you, Sarah?"

Sarah ignored the question, turning to look at Lexi still sitting on the edge of the bed. "And you. I've heard you're a great actress; now I can see it. You pretend to be everyone's friend and you're obviously smart enough to pull it off. You don't even know how to be better, do you?" Lexi opened her mouth, closed it and looked away.

Sarah turned to look at Derek. When she spoke, her voice was quiet. "You just lost the very best thing that should have never happened to a loser like you."

Derek shrugged with indifference, but his eyes told another story. Sarah turned away from both of them, feeling spent—and suddenly, so sad for Amelia.

She was stunned to see all the people standing behind her. The room was full. One girl was already on her phone, texting. Sarah's heart sank. It would not be long before Amelia heard. She hated that but there was no stopping it. She noticed Jamie watching her and realized he had been right behind her the entire time. Again. Seeing the sympathy in his eyes, she felt tears threaten to spill from her own.

"You go, girl," Hudson said quietly, giving her arm a squeeze.

"All right, all right!" Walt's voice boomed across the still mostly-quiet room. "Show's over. The party's downstairs people, let's get back to it." The crowd came to life, chatter filling the room, as they filed out the door. Walt made his way to Sarah, a fierce scowl on his face.

"Okay sweetheart, listen up. This is *my* house and *my* party. I don't know about you Greeks, but this is the South. We know Jesus and we like peace. People came here to have a good time, not witness another one of your scenes. You should go."

Sarah met his angry eyes and defiantly lifted her chin. "My *name* is Sarah. And since you mention Jesus, here's a fun fact: His teachings were originally written in Greek. They called it The New Testament. It became the number one selling Book of all time, translated into every language. I bet you even own a leather copy with your initials on it. Double or nothing, you've never read a word of it. The point is, you're too elitist to know Jesus."

"Elitist?" Walt's nostrils flared.

Sarah shrugged. "New word? Google it later. Also, there is nothing I want more than to leave your house."

"So, why are you still standing here?" Walt replied, his voice hard as stone. He moved to the side, motioning with his arm for her to move past him.

"Walt, chill, dude..." Jamie started, only to have Sarah stop him.

"No, he's right. I made a huge mistake in coming here tonight. I'm leaving."

"I'm coming with you, Sarah." Hudson gave Walt an icy look.

The two girls started for the door, but Sarah paused. Turning back, she smiled demurely and crossed both hands over her chest.

"Why, I almost forgot. Where *are* my manners?" Her tone was sarcastic, mimicking a Southern accent. She batted her eyelashes at Walt. "Thank you, Walter, for a most lovely evening. Your home is as charming as you're not—you dirtbag."

CHAPTER TWENTY

"You sure do have a lot of nerve, Sarah Giannopoulos," Hudson said between fits of laughter, as the two friends made their way down Walt's stairs. "That was hysterical!"

"I don't have a lot of nerve, Hudson," Sarah sighed. "Just a terrible temper I have never been able to control, coupled with a mouth that just runs independently of my brain. Right now, my heart's beating way too fast, my stomach is in knots and I just want to go home and pretend this whole entire night never happened." She grabbed Hudson's hand as they made their way through the crowded house. "Thanks for coming with me."

"Are you kidding? I've got your back, you've got Amelia's—that's how it works. Except we are not going home. We're going to Three Spoons for something incredibly chocolaty." She smiled at Sarah. "We've got a lot to talk about."

Sarah smiled back. "Sounds good to me."

"Sarah! Wait!"

Sarah felt her body stiffen and at the same time, her knees turn to jelly. There was no mistaking Jamie's voice, louder than it sounded when he was singing into the microphone. He was calling to her, from what sounded like the top of the stairs. But why? Was he going to team up with Walt and insult her some more? Her heart pounded even harder. She grabbed Hudson's hand again, this time in a death grip. Keeping her eyes straight ahead, she pulled her surprised friend towards the front door.

But Hudson was not being cooperative. She tried to pull Sarah back. "Sarah! Jamie's calling to you!" she whispered, loudly.

"Pretend you didn't hear him," Sarah urged, pulling her forward. They were almost at the door.

"Sarah, wait!"

Sarah stopped dead in her tracks and caught her breath. From the sound of his voice, he was right behind her. Reluctantly, she turned around, only to find herself the center of attention for the second time that night. Except this time, everyone was crowding behind Jamie—and all the way up the stairs. Unable to do otherwise, she lifted her eyes to his and squared her shoulders. She would take whatever Jamie Nelson had to say in front of practically everyone in the senior class with her head held high. Then, she would walk out the door, go home and cry for the rest of the weekend.

It wasn't a great plan, but things had gotten way out of control at this nightmare of a party—and there was no changing that now.

"Good thing for Lakeview, you run cross-country," Jamie said, breathing hard. "I didn't think I'd catch up to you."

Sarah was not sure how to respond, so she said nothing. An almost eerie hush had fallen over the room. She felt the silence go through her.

"So, probably not the best time to ask but I was wondering if you want to go out sometime." Jamie shoved his hands in the pockets of his jeans. "With me."

Sarah stared at him blankly. The entire room was watching her, wide-eyed. She wondered if her own eyes were just as huge. Her mind raced, trying to make sense of what Jamie had just said. Her knees felt as if they would buckle any minute.

Did he really just ask me out? Like on a date?

His expression added to her confusion. He looked sincere, hopeful and very sure of himself, all at once. She, on the other hand, was at a complete loss of what to say or do. She wasn't even sure she had heard him right. The whole scene was absurd.

Pull yourself together, Sarah. Chill. You can fall apart later. But not here.

"Sometime?" She heard herself ask, her voice sounding like it belonged to someone else.

"Yeah. Like, Friday? After the game?"

Sarah tried to take that in. She couldn't. Her mind simply could not register or catch up. He was standing there watching and waiting, confusing her beyond belief.

Jamie Nelson is asking me to go out with him and everyone in this house is as shocked as I am. We're all just standing here like zombies. And we should be. This is crazy. He's so hot; he could have anyone here. Why me? It makes zero sense.

She could feel all eyes on her, waiting for her response. It was completely surreal and she wanted to say yes, but somehow, even in the midst of her confusion, her logic managed to prevail. Her thoughts cleared and her legs steadied.

She was worlds apart from everyone in that room. Except, possibly for Hudson.

The reason this is beyond weird is because it doesn't fit.

Sarah smiled, sure now of what she needed to say. "I have to work on Friday. I waitress at Steve's, the pizza joint you guys sometimes come to. With my dad and brother. It's not ours, of course. It belongs to my uncle. He helped my dad out, by giving him a job last summer. He can't afford to hire much help, so we're pretty much it."

There. She had said it. She had shown them all she knew she didn't belong in their mansions, at their parties or in their it-kid cliques. Most of all, she had shown she knew who she was. She had said the words out loud. Strangely, it felt good.

"Thanks, anyway, though. It was nice of you to ask," she added, almost shyly. She turned and started for the door. Hudson followed, her mouth stuck in a stunned "O" shape. Sarah pulled the door open, letting Hudson walk through first. She followed her friend onto the porch, breathing in the crisp night air with relief.

Thank you, God. I promise to never again go to Walt's horrible house.

"How about Saturday?" Jamie's voice came from directly behind her, the question as natural as if he had been walking with them outside.

Sarah turned around slowly, her eyes locking on his. Hudson gasped, jumped and whirled around. She peeked out over Sarah's shoulder and smiled at Jamie.

Jamie smiled back before returning his gaze to Sarah. "Or even Sunday. Isn't Steve's closed on Sundays?" He sounded both determined and confident.

Sarah nodded, overwhelmed with surprise. He had to have understood what she had just told him. She knew he had. Now, he was telling her he didn't care. He was telling her in front of all of his friends he was aware of the differences between them.

And that it didn't make a difference to him.

Maybe I'm dreaming all this. Because this isn't real life stuff. It's more like a teenage series on Netflix. Or teenage Pretty Woman, minus the whole prostitution thing.

"Saturday's good...I think," she said out loud, her eyes still on his.

Jamie grinned. "Great. We'll talk at school and I'll get your number without..." Purposefully, he leaned back against the door frame, causing the crowd of curious onlookers to stumble backwards into one another. "Without them."

She couldn't help but smile. "Sounds good. Goodnight, Jamie."

"Goodnight, Sarah. Bye, Hudson."

Sarah turned and walked off the porch into the dark night, pulling Hudson along with her. She heard the door close behind them and exhaled deeply.

Her mind was still spinning. It was almost too much to take in. It was real; it had happened but she just could not believe it. And from the looks of her, neither could Hudson. She just kept staring at Sarah and shaking her head, her eyes huge.

Sarah pulled out her phone. She had to tell Amelia.

I'm going on a date with Jamie Nelson on Saturday. Is this crazy or what?

The thought of Amelia jolted Sarah back to the night's confrontation with Derek. Sighing, she put her phone back in her coat pocket. She wasn't ready to make that call.

Because when she did, she would break her best friend's heart.

CHAPTER TWENTY-ONE

"C'mon, Amelia. You have to start getting over this."

Sarah stood just inside the door of Amelia's room. It was Friday afternoon and the two friends were spending it as they had every other afternoon since Sunday, when Sarah had explained what went down with Derek: Amelia either crying or not saying much of anything, and Sarah doing her best to cheer her up.

"I just still can't believe it. I can't believe it was all a game to him. I can't believe he did that to me." Lying on her bed, Amelia buried her head in her pillow. "And, I *really* cannot believe what a fake Lexi Taylor is. She pretends to be my friend, but she has a black soul."

Sarah sighed. "She's that competitive high school girl who thinks boys and the homecoming crown are the pinnacle of success and will do whatever it takes to get them. She's insecure and spends every day trying to paint herself as happy and confident, when she is just the opposite. What gets me is that Derek couldn't see through that. I couldn't believe it when I saw him with her and I still don't understand it." Sarah plopped down next to her on the bed and picked up a stuffed dog that looked like it had survived a major world war. "But he did it, Amelia; it is what it is. You've got to get over him. He's not worth it." Sarah looked at the dog more closely, wrinkling her nose. "How long has this pitiful creature been lying on your bed? And what on earth did you do to the poor thing? He doesn't even have a nose."

Peeking from underneath her pillow, Amelia smiled through her tears. "That's Flatso. He was in my crib before he made it to my bed. His nose was a choking hazard, so my parents pulled it off."

They looked at each other and began giggling. Amelia sat up and took the dog from Sarah. Her expression sobered. She hugged it for a moment, and closed her eyes, a lone tear rolling down her cheek. "He didn't care about me. All he wanted was for me to sleep with him," she said, quietly. "The worst part is, I almost did."

Sarah didn't say anything. She leaned over and laid her head on Amelia's shoulder.

"He told me he loved me. No guy has ever said that to me before. I should have known better, I should have never believed him. But I did, Sarah. I really did."

"Well, why wouldn't you? You had no reason not to," Sarah replied, gently.

Amelia laid her head on top of Sarah's. "I was thinking about sleeping with him," she admitted again, miserably. "That's still what bothers me the most."

"But you didn't."

"No, but I feel like an idiot for considering it. For not seeing through him."

Sarah sat silently for a moment, then got up and walked to the window. The leaves on the trees were changing colors. They were bright and beautiful.

"My mother once told me that you're never a fool for believing in something—or someone. It's when you see the bad, the red flags, and you continue to cling to your belief, knowing that it's anything but what it should be—then yes, you're fooling yourself and probably being made a fool of." Sarah turned and smiled sadly at her friend. "Believe me, I should know. I don't want to talk about it but I definitely learned to love myself the hard way." She shrugged her shoulders and sighed.

"You, on the other hand, had no reason to think Derek would cheat on you with Lexi. Now that you know, you'll move on—and be just fine without him. Or her. And you'll find a great guy, Amelia, because you are anything but a fool."

Amelia rocked herself gently on the bed as she listened. Finally, she nodded, wiped her tears, looked up at Sarah and smiled.

"What's this?" Sarah threw her hands up in the air, victoriously. "A major breakthrough! Flatso, that's two smiles in one day! Our girl is back!"

"Yeah, well don't get too excited. I don't know how long it will last." Sniffling, Amelia walked over to her friend and hugged her. "Let's go to Three Spoons for hot fudge sundaes. I'm tired of crying over Derek the Putz."

"Yay you! And yes to chocolate therapy! But let's go now." Sarah hugged her happily. "I have to work tonight and Andreas is grumpier than usual. Ugh, I hope it's busy so he lightens up by tomorrow." They grabbed their coats and headed out the door.

"Sarah?" Amelia asked in a quiet voice. "I'm sorry we've been constantly talking about Derek and me this week. I am so happy about your date tomorrow night. Hudson said the night at Walt's was incredible. I've known Jamie Nelson since kindergarten and I have never seen him act like that—for anyone. He must like you a whole lot."

"I don't know about that. I mean, to be honest, I am still in shock over the entire thing. Tomorrow night will be interesting, that's for sure."

They drove the rest of the way to Three Spoons in silence. Sarah was thinking about her mother's advice—the same advice she had just given Amelia. She knew Jamie's friends didn't like her. He was part of the 'in-crowd', part of a different world. That world was all he had ever known. It meant everything to him and she knew she would never fit in it. She didn't even want to. So, what was she doing, going out with him tomorrow night? It was stupid and she knew she was heading for trouble. Again. Unwelcome memories of the past filled her mind. Stubbornly, she fought them away.

It's only a date, Sarah, she told herself for what she was sure had to be the thousandth time that week. *One little date. And afterwards, you will get over this crazy infatuation you have for this boy and he will get over...whatever it is he's got going on in his head. And that will be that. Whatever. No big deal.*

So why were her knees shaking again?

And Amelia thinks she's the idiot. I'm developing a nervous condition over a singing quarterback. And we've never even gone out. It's like my brain stopped functioning. I can't wait to get this date over with. He'll brag all night, I know he will. I'll hate it.

"Sarah?"

"Yeah?"

Amelia put the car in park, sat back in the seat and smiled at her friend. "Thanks for the advice you gave me back at the house."

Sarah smiled back. "I hope it helps."

"It did. It does. Your mom sounds like she was a special person."

"She was, Amelia. She really, really was."

CHAPTER TWENTY-TWO

"Every single person here is staring at me," Sarah groaned, as she self-consciously edged her way between Amelia and Hudson in the stands. "It's the halftime show and no one is watching the cheerleaders, even though they are clearly gifted athletes, judging by that routine. Instead, they're watching me making a complete spectacle of myself."

"Sarah, chill. Be nice about the cheerleaders, they amuse me. And did you really just say 'spectacle'? Hudson, did you hear that?"

Hudson laughed. "I heard it."

"Well, that's what I am because you forced me to come here." Sarah sat down and crossed her arms over her chest.

"It's a football game, Sarah! The only one you have come to this year! I mean, Steve's is out of power. As in, closed. As in, woo-hoo, you don't have to work! Were you really just going to sit at home and do homework on a Friday night?"

"Yes."

"No. It's your only opportunity to see a game, hence you are."

Sarah looked at Hudson. "Did she just say 'hence'? Who says 'hence' unless they are reading from the British Lit book in English class?"

Hudson laughed again. "I have a word! Both of you are whack-a-doodle."

Amelia smiled, closed her eyes and tilted her face up towards the sky. She took in a deep breath. "Good one, Huddie. Y'all, feel that wonderful breeze. How good does that feel? I love Indian summer nights."

"Yeah, we don't get these in New York. Crazy weather, huh? Hard to imagine, a little over an hour ago, the lightning was so bad it threw out the power at the restaurant." Sarah pulled her phone out and checked it. "I hope they get it back on soon."

"Relax and enjoy being a normal teenager." Amelia grabbed her phone and threw it back into her purse.

Sarah looked around for a minute and then straight ahead. "They are *staring*. And whispering. I hate this." She looked at Hudson. "Where is that hat you had earlier? Did you bring it in?"

Amelia and Hudson looked at each other and burst into laughter.

"Oh, that's nice. Go ahead and entertain yourselves." She looked down at the field and sighed. Charlotte and the cheerleaders were posing for a selfie. "*They* know why I'm here. This is beyond humiliating."

Amelia grunted. "Oh my gosh, Sarah! This is so un-you! We are at a football game, the only one you've ever come to because you work every Friday. After Walt's, I'd say everyone is aware of that. And believe it or not, football is the most popular sport for high school students—which, correct me if I'm wrong—we are."

"Okay, you are wrong. Basketball is definitely the most popular and far-superior sport for high school students—and people of all ages."

Amelia rolled her eyes. "So, you have a date with Jamie tomorrow," she continued, ignoring her. "Big deal, you've said all week. Now you can't even go to a football game because he's playing in it?"

"Well, he *is* the quarterback. Not to mention, totally hot. I'd be seriously nervous," Hudson said, chewing on a piece of gum and grinning.

"Don't speak, Hudson," Amelia said, laughing at the horrified expression on Sarah's face. "Unless you want to tell her how dramatic she is being."

"Sarah, stop being dramatic, hence paranoid."

Sarah could not help but laugh. Maybe she was being paranoid. She sighed and reached into her purse again, this time pulling out a box of Chocolate Raisinets. Popping a couple into her mouth, she decided to take the advice of her friends and relax. It really was a nice night. And it was nice to have it off.

"Yum, can I have one? Those look great!" Amelia asked, holding her hand out.

"Sure. They *are* good. A little rough around the edges, but good." She laughed. "Kind of like you guys."

"That's really funny, Sarah." Amelia and Hudson both made a face as they each took a handful of the candy. For the next few minutes, conversation was limited, as the three friends happily munched on chocolate.

"Of course," Amelia said casually, as she picked up the last morsel, "he is both the quarterback *and* team captain."

Sarah's eyes widened. She stopped chewing.

"Yeah, it's definitely all about him," Hudson chimed in. "And the date *is* tomorrow night."

"Yeah, now that I think of it, it is sort of...well, a coincidence this is the first game you came to," Amelia continued, thoughtfully.

Sarah looked from one to the other. With a resigned look on her face, she dropped what was left of the Raisinets back into the empty box. "Fine. Perfect. Enjoy yourselves at my expense. Just don't expect me to watch any of this stupid game." She turned the box over and began to study the writing on the back.

"Oh, look! There's Jamie!" Amelia pointed him out, as the players ran onto the field. "You may want to stop reading your candy box. Just sayin'."

"Really? Stop pointing! What is wrong with you?" Sarah grabbed Amelia's arm and pulled it down. She glared at her friend, not that Amelia even noticed. Her attention was on the field.

"Oh, the boy is looking *good*. And, he happens to be looking up at that pretty face you're making right now. Girl, look up and smile."

"I do not believe you can be this immature." Reluctantly, Sarah looked towards the field. Her friends were right about Jamie looking good. Her heart began to beat faster and she was once again thrust into that confused state of being with which she was beginning to feel well acquainted with. A smile formed on her lips as she watched him. Maybe it was wishful thinking, but she thought she saw him smile back.

"Sarah," she heard Amelia saying, "Jamie Nelson is crazy about you."

"Yeah, right. He smiled at me. It's truly amazing," she replied, sarcastically.

Seconds later, Jamie threw a perfect pass down the field to Robby, who carried it in for the touchdown. The trio cheered and Sarah could not help but think about what Amelia had said.

Much as she hated to admit it, for whatever *whack-a-doodle* reason, she hoped her friend was right.

❦CHAPTER TWENTY-THREE

In the end, it was a horrible game. The weather had suddenly turned again and rain poured relentlessly. The Lakeview Hawks lost 21-7. Jamie had played well, but not his best, according to Amelia and Hudson. The stands had slowly cleared out as the game progressed, and what few loyal fans remained, began moving out in the final minutes. Sarah, Amelia and Hudson stayed until the end.

"Let's go before I have to see Derek," Amelia urged.

"Darn...and there are tons of people here I want to shoot the breeze with," Sarah replied, sarcastically. "If Charlotte and her posse disliked me before, it's pretty much a given they despise me now."

"Yeah, well, not a big loss," Amelia answered. "At least you don't have to deal with Lexi still trying to be your best friend. The girl has as much class as she has a conscience."

"Classic sociopath move. Like I said, she is as fake as her homecoming crown. She's worse than Charlotte; she's a pretender. Feel sorry for her, her whole life is a lie."

Hudson stepped right in the middle of a huge puddle. She lifted her dripping left foot up in frustration. "Dang this rain!"

Sarah laughed. "Let's make a run for it!"

"Sarah!"

Still laughing, Sarah turned and saw Jamie calling to her from the bottom of the stands. Strangely, she wasn't nervous. She waved to him.

"Give me a minute to talk to him," she told her friends. "I'll catch up."

"We'll get the car and come back for you," Amelia promised, as Hudson and she broke into a run towards the parking lot.

Sarah began making her way down the stands as Jamie started up towards her. They met halfway.

"Hi." He was muddy and soaked from head to toe.

"Hey." Sarah smiled. "You look like you enjoyed the rain. And the mud."

"Yeah, nothing better than getting our faces shoved in the dirt. That was terrible."

"Nah, it just wasn't our night," she said, lifting her hand over her eyes to see him better through the driving rain. "You played well, Jamie."

"Thanks, but we stunk it up out there. We'll pay for it in practice next week."

"Maybe the rain will hold up and you won't have to."

Jamie laughed. "That's optimism. Heck of a first game for you to come to. Sorry we didn't make it worth your while."

Sarah shrugged. *He noticed it was the first game I've come to.* "Well, since you brought it up, winning would have been a tiny bit more impressive."

"Ouch. Thanks for making me feel better about the whole 'getting our asses kicked' thing." He shook his head but he was still laughing.

Sarah laughed too, completely at ease. Jamie grinned from ear to ear, watching her. In that split second, he wondered if she had any idea how gorgeous she was. Somehow, he doubted it. What was most attractive about Sarah was that she seemed unaware of her looks. Even standing there, drenched from head to toe, she seemed comfortable. He couldn't ever remember a girl who was so real—or that had him so completely rattled. He had to remind himself to keep from staring at her. He couldn't believe he was taking her out on a date. *I can't wait for tomorrow night.*

Sarah pulled a strand of wet hair out of her eyes and Jamie snapped out of his thoughts. Reaching into his athletic bag, he pulled out his baseball hat. Leaning closer, he put it on her head. "This should help," he told her, looking into her eyes.

Sarah felt her cheeks warm and prayed the rain would hide the now familiar unease she felt when he got close. Instinctively, she let her playfulness take over.

"So, the quarterback is a gentleman."

The boyish grin that was uniquely his instantly covered his face. "I try."

Sarah laughed. "Thank you, Jamie. I'll be sure to get it back to you."

"Don't worry about it. Consider it a *thank you* for sitting through that game."

They stood there together, Jamie Nelson, star athlete of Lakeview High and Sarah Giannopoulos, star of nothing. Yet, as they laughed together in the pouring rain over nothing really funny at all, all they saw in each other's eyes were stars.

CHAPTER TWENTY-FOUR

It was seven-thirty in the evening. Sarah put on her earrings, stepped back and appraised herself in the mirror. She had spent every last penny of her tip money on her outfit, but she was pleased. Her dress was casual but pretty and her new boots made the outfit both chic and playful at the same time. She hoped Jamie would like it. She put on her jean jacket, pulled her long hair out from under the collar and smiled. She was ready.

Walking over to the window, she looked outside. Not seeing Jamie's car, she crossed over to her bed and sat on the side. Her eyes rested on her mother's smiling face, in the only picture she kept on her nightstand. Sarah picked it up.

"I hope you won't think I'm being naive, Mama, but I think I'm kind of falling for Jamie. I've only recently admitted it to myself and I'm not ready to tell anyone but you, yet. I was not expecting to feel this way—in this place, and in this last year before college. There's just something about him... He's different...well, I mean, I'm not stupid, I know he's different than us in lots of ways, but I think he understands who I am and where I come from. I mean, you saw him at Walt's...he asked me out in front of all of them." Sarah paused, looking into her mother's warm brown eyes. "So, I'm going to take a chance, Mama. I have no idea what will come of it. My life is changing so fast and college is just around the corner. But don't worry I'm not going to rush into anything. I'm not going to put my heart on the line again. You always said to do one thing at a time and do it right. My focus is school and Daddy and Niko. I won't forget that. But he's worth this...friendship. A lot of those kids at school aren't, but he is. He really seems genuine, Mama. I hope I've learned how to tell the difference after Jake..."

Sarah closed her eyes. "Do you hate hearing his name as much as I hate saying it? I try to block him out, because I'm scared if I don't, I'll never let my guard down again," she whispered. "And I don't want these walls anymore, Mama. I want to be brave. I want to go for it, like you taught me to. Like you always did."

Opening her eyes, she smiled. "Not that I plan on caring about Jamie or anyone else like that again. Not now, anyway. Lesson learned, don't worry. But Jamie is...well, he does put on a certain act for the benefit of others, but around me—when he looks at me—it's amazing, Mama. Like last night at the game. You had to have seen it. He makes me feel like it's only he and I, like no one else is even around. You know that after Jake..." her voice cracked for a moment as she fought the unwelcome memory, "I promised myself I'd wait until I was much older before I cared about someone that much again. And that they would have to prove themselves to me first. But Jamie broke through all that. He changed it, somehow, and I'm so glad he did. I don't want to be scared anymore. I don't know if tonight is a beginning or just a date. What I do know is that I want to give whatever it is a chance. Because the thought of him makes me happy and nervous and excited all at the same time." Sarah paused again, bringing the worn picture frame to her lips.

"Watch over me tonight, Mama. I know you always do."

Carefully, she placed the picture back on her nightstand and once again walked to the window, glancing outside. She checked her watch. Seven-forty.

Jamie was late.

⁂ ⁂ ⁂ ⁂ ⁂ ⁂

"Jamie, dude, have another one. Daisy's not in town tonight," Walt coaxed, popping the top off a can of beer.

"Dude, I need to get going." Jamie was beginning to feel light-headed. He didn't really want another beer. He just wanted to watch the second half of the UNC-Clemson football game—and he wanted Clemson to win. His mom had graduated from there and had taken him to every game she could in Death Valley. It was an awesome place. He was in the minority, but Jamie loved the Tigers.

"Game's not over, they're gonna come back," Robby said, taking the beer from Walt.

"What's up, Jamie?" Walt sat back in the oversized chair he was sitting in and gave his buddy a questioning look. "Where do you have to go?"

"Yeah, dude, what's better than this?" Gaston chimed in.

Without looking away from the TV, Jamie knew all eyes were on him. He casually reached over towards Walt. "Yeah, I told Daisy I'd do some raking, but I guess it can wait. Hand me a beer, man."

Walt got him one, and the four friends turned their attention back to the game. They had met at Robby's house to watch it since he had a movie room with a huge screen. His parents were in the mountains with Jamie's for the weekend, and when Walt and Gaston had walked in with the beer, watching the game had turned into an afternoon party. Jamie checked his watch. Four-thirty. He would need to leave as soon as the game was over. He didn't want to be late for his date with Sarah.

"Dude, what time is it?"

Jamie looked up to find Walt smiling at him. "Shut up, Walt."

Walt laughed and took another sip of his beer. Then, he sat up in the chair and leaned forward. "Let me guess. Your pizza chic doesn't like drinking?"

Jamie shrugged. "Her name is Sarah. And I don't know if she does or not. You got a problem, Walt?"

Walt laughed again. "Nah. It's all good. Just seems like you don't want to hang with us."

"Yeah, Jamie. What's up with you today?" Gaston asked, his words slurred.

"I just want to watch the game. Walt is the one with the problem."

"He iss?" Gaston asked, confused. The way he asked made Robby laugh and the tension in the room eased.

Walt leaned back in his chair again, still eyeing Jamie, as he took another sip. He crushed his beer can and reached for another. "So, you're really going out with the waitress tonight?"

Jamie drained his beer. "Yep."

"Sarah? She's hot," Gaston stated, matter-of-factly. "She can wait on me anytime."

"Walt, not so much," Robby said, drawing laughter from Gaston and Jamie.

"Whatever. That girl needs anger management." Walt popped open the can and took a long swig.

"Why, because she doesn't like you?" Jamie challenged.

"Because she's trouble and she's gonna bring you down." Walt shrugged. "I'm just trying to look out for you, man."

Robby saw Jamie's jaw tighten. He knew what that meant. Reaching into the cooler, he tossed another beer to him. "If you girls are done yakking, the game is on."

Jamie caught the can and popped it open. He knew Robby was trying to keep him from blowing up at Walt, who was obviously intent on being a real pain in the ass. What he didn't understand was why. He saw Robby exchange a look with Walt before turning back to the TV. The unspoken communication made Jamie feel like an outsider.

It was a feeling he did not recognize. Or like.

The four friends had hung out every Saturday afternoon since Jamie could remember. They played video games, basketball, baseball and football until dinner, when one mom would finally take them all in for the night. What he did not remember was ever feeling awkward with his best friends. Until today. Frustrated, he took another sip of beer. Walt was right, Sarah was different. But he liked her. He wanted to get to know her better. So what? It had nothing to do with his friends and he wouldn't let it change things with them. They had been friends all their lives. Walt didn't like Sarah, that much was clear. But he would come around, Jamie was sure of it.

He watched the Clemson quarterback run the ball in for a touchdown and jumped off the couch at the same time Robby did.

"That's what I'm talking about! Williamson is money!" Jamie yelled, excitedly.

"That was pretty sweet," Walt agreed.

"Did the doorbell ring? Did someone order pizza?" Gaston asked, getting up and walking to the front door.

Walt, Robby and Jamie burst into laughter, all of them glad for the welcome distraction from the conversation before. "Nah, we didn't. But, still, you'd better check. If he's not at the front door, check the back, Gaston," Walt called after him.

"I'm on it like a tick on a dog," Gaston called back, sending the trio into another fit of laughter.

They ended up ordering pizza, mostly to enjoy the entertainment factor in watching Gaston place the order. But they never heard the doorbell ring when it finally came. The game went into overtime, but they didn't see that happen either. Alcohol, combined with a long week of school and football caught up with them—and all four fell asleep in the den.

⁕ ⁕ ⁕ ⁕ ⁕ ⁕

The first thing Jamie thought of when he woke up on Robby's couch was how dark it was. His head hurt and his neck was sore from the way he had fallen asleep on it. Sitting up, he rubbed his eyes and tried to clear his throbbing head. They had been watching the game and Gaston and Walt had brought beer. They must have drunk too much. They must have fallen asleep. And now it was dark.

Dark! Sarah...the date...

He pulled his phone out of his pocket and checked the time. Almost ten o'clock. The throbbing in his head intensified. Jamie sat back and closed his eyes.

He couldn't believe it. He had slept through his date with Sarah.

❋ ❋ ❋ ❋ ❋ ❋

Sarah remained dressed until nine. After that, she hung her still-new outfit back in the closet, turned off her phone and crawled into her bed. She reached over to turn out the light and her eyes inadvertently rested on her mother's picture. She took it in her arms, hugged it tightly and since no one was home to see, soaked her pillow in tears.

CHAPTER TWENTY-FIVE

It was 8:20 a.m. Time was running out. Jamie had stood in the same spot for almost an hour waiting for Sarah. He couldn't wait much longer. School would be starting soon. Where was she?

He kicked at the ground in frustration. His thoughts were racing in a million different directions, always ending with Sarah. How could he have been stupid enough to miss their date? The whole thing was a disaster.

Jamie checked his phone again. 8:22. He kicked at the dirt once more, harder this time. The last two days had been miserable. Gaston's parents had come by to check on them at Robby's house and discovered the beer. They were all in a heap of trouble.

He had shaken his parents' trust. And he had blown it with Sarah. He thought of the way she had looked at him after the football game, her beautiful brown eyes full of playfulness. And he had stood her up.

Approaching voices interrupted his thoughts and he looked up to see Sarah and Nick, riding their bikes towards him. Taking a deep breath, he stepped on to the road to meet them.

It was Nick who reached him first and stopped, grinning. Sarah stopped too, but her body language told him that if not for Nick, she would have blown right by.

"Hey, Jamie!" Nick greeted him enthusiastically, obviously unaware of the situation, much to Jamie's surprise.

"What's up, Nick?" Jamie gave him a fist pump and smiled. "I was just waiting to talk to Sarah."

"Yeah?" Nick glanced from Sarah back to Jamie, finally sensing the tension between them. "Okay. I'll just head on to school, then. See you guys later."

Sarah nodded and Jamie smiled again, waiting until Nick was out of earshot. He braved a look at Sarah, but she still had not looked at him. She was watching Nick ride away, her expression unreadable.

"I'm sorry, Sarah," he said, his voice quiet.

She shifted her eyes to him. They were hard and indifferent. Jamie laid his hand on the handlebar between hers. "I...I'm...well...I know *sorry* sounds lame, but I was watching the football game with the guys and we...um...had some beer and I guess we were all so tired we just fell asleep and the next thing I knew it was ten o'clock. I mean, I could lie and give you a reason that makes me look a whole lot better than this, but the simple truth is I just messed up and lost track of time. I called you three times yesterday, even at your house. I texted, left messages on your phone, and also with your dad. Did he tell you?" His voice trailed, as he paused, feeling like the complete idiot he knew he sounded like, and waited for her to say something. She didn't.

"I was really looking forward to Saturday night with you. All I can say is, I'm sorry." He wanted to keep explaining, but thought better of it. She remained still, her expression blank and unchanging, as if she had not heard a word he had said.

"Sarah." He hoped his voice didn't sound as desperate as he felt. "Please, say something." Her silence was not what he had expected and it overwhelmed him. For the first time in his life, Jamie found himself at a complete loss. He had no idea what to say or do.

In the distance, the school bell rang.

Sarah looked past him in the direction of the sound. Then, her eyes returned to his. Jamie watched as they became angry, lit with fire. He braced himself. He had seen that furious look before. She was about to let him have it.

"I'm late," was all she said, turning the wheel sharply, so that his hand fell.

She rode off before he could respond.

CHAPTER TWENTY-SIX

"Sarah, you're moping again. If you're tired, we can call it a day and go home." Amelia waited for a response, but didn't get one. "Hellooo! Can you hear me?"

Sarah looked up, her expression apologetic. The two friends were spending Saturday afternoon at the mall. "I'm sorry. I really am having fun." She smiled as big as she could and held up her shopping bags. "I mean, look at all my stash!"

"Yeah, whatever, you are not. You're buying scarves."

"I happen to love scarves."

"And you're grumpy—yelling at strangers and judging people for the way they chew a cookie."

"I am not grumpy; that guy jumped in front of us and I was hungry. And that lady shouldn't let her annoying kid spit out his cookie wherever he feels like, which happened to be on my shoe."

"It was an accident! Sarah, he was just a little kid! This is definitely not you having fu...ooooh, look at that dress!" Amelia stopped suddenly, causing Sarah to run into her, to point at a dress in the shop window.

So very Amelia, Sarah thought to herself in amusement. "It's kinda bright. So many colors..." she said, relieved that Amelia had changed the subject.

"I know! Awesome, right? Come on, I want to try it on!" Sarah followed her animated friend inside and to the dressing room. Once there, she collapsed into a chair, playfully shielding her eyes as Amelia tried on the dress. They both giggled.

She had lied, of course. The truth was she was having a miserable time and had exhausted herself trying to prove otherwise. But Amelia had gone to great lengths all day to try and cheer her up. Sarah knew that; the last thing she wanted was to let her down. Sensing Amelia watching her, she looked up and grinned, as if she didn't have a care in the world. "You are so right about that dress. It's great on you. I wonder if it's on sa…"

"Nah. Actually, I hate it. The colors are ridiculous." Amelia pulled the dress over her head. "So, I talked to Jamie."

Sarah blinked in surprise, her mouth gaping open. "What?"

"He called to explain what happened and asked me to ask you to answer your phone tonight so he can try and explain it to you. He said he's tried all week and you won't listen to him."

Sarah started to speak, but Amelia quickly continued, her voice gentle. "He said Gaston and Walt got some beer and took it to Robby's house where they were watching the game. Robby's parents were out of town. The game was close, they were worn out from practice, one beer led to another and before they knew it, they were all passed out and didn't wake up until Gaston's parents came and busted them. He said he's embarrassed and feels really badly about the whole thing." She paused to check Sarah's reaction to what she was saying. She couldn't read it.

"I believe him. I think he knows he screwed up and just wants another chance." Amelia hung the dress back on the hanger and sat down on a chair opposite from Sarah. "Sarah, you know I love you. But you are way too stubborn. You like him and he likes you. Maybe it leads somewhere, maybe not. Girl, there's only one way to know. And that's not by pretending you don't care." She leaned over and laid her hands on Sarah's knees. "Don't be mad at me, okay? It's just that you don't get to do some things again. Believe me, there aren't too many guys out there like Jamie Nelson."

Sarah looked at her and sighed. "I don't know… Maybe you're right about me being stubborn, but I really don't want to talk to him. Don't you think it's weird that he texted you instead of trying to talk to me all week at school? Texting you is safe, but he doesn't want his friends to see...that he even talks to me."

"Actually he called, not texted. And he sounded genuinely sad. Sarah, the boy asked you out in front of the entire school. He says *you* won't talk to him."

"I did! And I told you what he said: that he's *so* sorry because he 'lost track of time' and that he had really wanted to spend Saturday night with me. What did *that* mean anyway? Does he think the desperate pizza waitress would have put out for him?"

"No, I don't think he meant it like that."

Sarah shook her head. "I'm telling you, Amelia, something is weird about this whole Jamie thing. I mean he asks me out, then gets drunk and passes out. Why would I even want to be with a guy who does that?" She stood up and picked up her bags. "Anyway, let's not talk about this anymore." She unlatched the door. "I'll wait for you outside, okay? Razzle-dazzle looks good on you. You should get the dress."

Escaping the dressing room, Sarah walked through the store without looking around, trying to ignore the lump in her throat. What if Amelia was right? What if it were just a misunderstanding, bad luck even? He had gotten drunk. He had gotten drunk and forgotten all about their date. *How could he have let himself do that if the date had meant anything to him? How could he do that if he's such a good guy? Wake up, Sarah...maybe he's not such a good guy. Maybe he's...like Jake.*

Absorbed as she was with her thoughts, Sarah failed to notice Charlotte, Jocelyn, Gertie, Lexi and Sydney standing together a few feet away. When she finally noticed them approaching, she quickly turned to the nearest display, only to find herself admiring a sock collection. *If I don't move, they won't notice me,* she thought to herself.

"Well, hello there, Sarah," Charlotte cooed, in her annoying Southern-belle tone.

So much for wishful thinking.

"Hey," Sarah replied with a polite smile, before returning her attention to the socks.

"My, my, such concentration. But I guess socks can do that to a girl."

Sarah fought to hold her tongue and ignore the sarcasm.

"Seriously, Sarah, I'm actually glad we ran into you. I know we never exactly got off on the right foot, but I want you to know I hate what Jamie and the guys did to you. Believe me, I told him it was a cruel and childish thing to do. And Sidney told Walt the same thing. It was just a completely tasteless prank. We all think so, and I just wanted to tell you so in person. None of us approve of that sort of thing."

Prank? Sarah's mind raced in confusion. *As in joke? What is she talking about? Whatever this is, I know Charlotte's intentions are as fake as the rest of her. Careful, Sarah, stay cool. Don't react and don't talk. Or you'll play right into her games. Ignore her and she'll go away.*

She chose a pair of fuzzy pink socks and turned them over to look for the price before casually looking up. "Sure, whatever."

"So, you're still in the dark." Charlotte sighed. "That makes me even sadder. Sarah, the boys played a sick joke on you. Their whole group—Jamie, too, I hate to say it, but as I always say, the truth is the truth—well, anyway, they think it's funny to make these silly bets with each other to see who they can get to go out with them. They pick some—how can I say this and not hurt your feelings—some *out-of-the-loop* girl, this time, you, to agree on a supposed date that's never going to happen. Then, they ghost her. It's not funny at all but they think it is. They bet things like basketball tickets, like they can't get those anyway. Like I said, completely tasteless. Just immature and mean."

"Yeah, it was mean for him to get your hopes up," Jocelyn chimed in. Even you didn't deserve that."

"That's right, Jocey. I mean it, Jamie is going to have to be on his best behavior to get me to forgive him this time," Charlotte said, with empathy Sarah was certain she didn't feel. "I made him promise to apologize to you. I thought he would have by now."

"Really," Sarah replied, as indifferently as she possibly could.

"Oh, yes. Like I said, we all agree." Charlotte smiled, sweetly. "Of course, I'll have to forgive him eventually. We can't ever seem to stay mad at each other for long."

"Yeah, try for like, five minutes," Sidney said, laughing.

Sarah felt numb. She tried not to stare at them, but the room seemed to spin around her as their words sank in. It had all been a joke. The whole, entire thing had been a joke...on her. The *'out-of-the-loop'* girl. Suddenly, it all made sense. She fought to keep her expression chill, but the faces of the girls seemed to be swimming in front of her. In her mind, she played back the night Jamie had asked her out. She remembered the way he had called to her from the top of the stairs. She had thought it nothing less than amazing that he had done that in front of everyone.

In front of everyone. At Walt's house. So they could all see firsthand.

Sarah swallowed the bile that was suddenly rising up her throat. *I almost bought the whole thing! How could anyone lose track of time and not show up for a date? It was a pathetic excuse. Followed up by the damage control call to Amelia. He scores with the joke and now everyone forgets about it. Who does that?* She could feel her temper begin to flare. *Finally, the insanity at Walt's party makes sense. He intentionally set me up in front of everybody because it was the perfect opportunity for their little joke. He played me like a pro. All for basketball tickets—and a laugh.*

"Charlotte? Charlotte, sweetie, is that you?" Sarah turned to see Daisy Nelson and her daughter Hillary make their way towards them. She watched the striking woman walk straight to Charlotte and hug her warmly. Sarah stood statue-like as they exchanged pleasantries, the pink fuzzy socks still in her hand. All of them were comfortable with one another, as if they had known each other for a lifetime.

Sarah realized they probably had.

"Hi, Sarah," Hillary said, the first to acknowledge her standing there. Daisy Nelson pasted on a smile, but Sarah did not miss the condescending look in her eyes. Her disapproval was evident and she made no attempt to hide it. Charlotte saw it, too. Smirking, she slipped her arm through the older woman's.

"Have you met Sarah Giannopoulos, Mrs. Nelson? She's a waitress at Steve's Pizza. You may have seen her there."

"Why, no, I don't believe I have."

Sarah tried not to react to the indifferent tone of the woman's voice and instead, pasted on a smile of her own. She let the pink socks drop to the table below.

"Actually, Mom, Sarah is in Jamie's grade at Lakeview. She moved here recently from New York," Hillary said cheerily, with a sharp look towards Charlotte.

The kindness in Hillary's tone diffused some of Sarah's anger, leaving her feeling even more exposed. "I have to go," was all she managed to say before turning away. Holding her back rim-rod straight, she walked out of the store, through the mall and out to the parking lot. Only then did she allow the first tear to roll down her cheek. She wiped it away, closed her eyes and gulped in the cold November air.

Never again, Jamie Nelson, she told herself, angrily, swiping at the tears that refused to stop streaming down her face. *Never again will I give you, Charlotte or your horrible 'prankster' friends another chance to get to me.*

She started to walk home, not bothering to wait for Amelia. She would call her later and explain, but for now she needed to walk, breathe and be alone. All she wanted was to get home and forget this day had ever happened.

⁕ ⁕ ⁕ ⁕ ⁕ ⁕

Back at the mall, Charlotte had watched Sarah until she disappeared from sight. Then, with a satisfied smile, she had winked at Lexi before turning to the rest of her friends. They were still chatting with Hillary and her mother.

"Mrs. Nelson," she had said warmly, "we were just about to go to Starbucks. Won't you and Hillary join us?"

CHAPTER TWENTY-SEVEN

It had been an unending night for Sarah. At long last, she politely wished Steve's last customers a great night and locked the door behind them. Leaning against it, she sighed heavily.

"It was a good night, eh?" Andreas grinned and patted his daughter on the head as he walked past her.

"You read my mind so well, Μπαμπα," Sarah replied sarcastically, pulling to her feet and moving to lean against the counter. "I was just trying to decide if my feet have ever hurt more and thinking what *a great night* it was."

Andreas closed the register drawer and laughed. "You are not getting out of cleaning up," he said, as he moved behind her, pausing to twirl her ponytail. "You and Lucy show Angie what needs to be done. Niko," his voice turned into the commando mode that always made Sarah wish she could have seen him in his army days, "I'll see you in the kitchen."

Sarah stifled a smile at Niko's grim expression, as he grudgingly stomped after his father. She grabbed the cleaning solution and a towel and started wiping down the counter. "Ah, life at Steve's," she said on a sigh. "Ain't it grand?"

Lucy smiled. She tossed Angie, the new waitress, a towel. "It sure is, sugar."

Sarah fluttered her eyelashes at both of them. "Did you catch my 'ain't', Luce? I'm a Southerner now!"

"Sure you are, honey," Lucy replied, smacking her gum. "But don't knock your bread and butter. We made good money tonight."

"Is it always that busy?" Angie asked. "The night flew by. I like your restaurant, Sarah. I had a lot of fun tonight."

"So did all the males you waited on, " Lucy replied, smiling. "Honey, the way you look, tips will be good for you whether it's busy in here or not."

Angie looked up from cleaning a cheese shaker. "Aw, thanks." She smiled at Lucy. "I'll settle with looking half as good as you two."

"Yeah, I wish. I haven't seen my knees in three years." Lucy shrugged and smiled. "But, sugar, that's sure sweet of you to say."

Sarah locked the register and laughed. "Oh, come on, Luce, you know you're the reason all those thirty-something single guys come in here. More importantly, you know I count on you to teach me the art of making men worship me the way they do you."

Lucy grinned and blew a big pink bubble with her gum. "Sure, I could do that. I'll start with that Jamie kid. Although, I've noticed you seem to be doing surprisingly well with the whole 'I can't see you' strategy you've got going."

Sarah rolled her eyes. "I take back all nice things I say about you. Angie will teach me."

Lucy giggled and blew Sarah a kiss. "No worries, precious. I will speak of the kid no more—unless you tell me different."

Sarah couldn't help but smile. She knew there was no stopping what came out of Lucy's mouth. Ever. "Deal. For now, I'll get the mop. Angie, would you mind finishing the counters? Nick's already gotten most of the tables clean. We need to mop so we can stack the chairs," she explained to the new girl.

"I refuse to move a muscle without music. Good music, Sarah." Lucy stuck out her bottom lip. "Please?"

"Anything to avoid further comments about my non-existent love life," Sarah muttered, turning off the easy listening CD they all detested and tuning into what she knew was Lucy's favorite station. She grinned when she recognized the song "I Can't Get No Satisfaction" by the Rolling Stones.

"Satisfied?" she teased and disappeared into the kitchen in search of a mop. She returned, seconds later, to find Lucy and Angie using saltshakers as microphones and singing along to the music. Sarah laughed at the picture they made. Seeing her, Lucy picked up a ketchup bottle and threw it at her. Sarah caught it, shook her head and put it on a table. "No, no, you two have it covered," she yelled above Mick Jagger's voice.

"C'mon, you scared?" Angie called back and began swaying her hips to the beat. Sarah's mouth dropped open in a big, surprised smile. "What have you done to her in one night?" she called to Lucy.

"She learns fast, kid. Unlike you, who needs lessons. Well, here's one now. Take it, if you dare," Lucy challenged. She rolled her shoulders provocatively and swung her hips like a hula dancer.

Sarah smiled, and raised both eyebrows mischievously. "I didn't want to show you older ladies up, but if you insist..." Pulling off her apron, Sarah hopped on a stool and then onto the counter, mop still in hand. She loosened her hair and tied her shirt in a knot above her waist. Using the mop for both microphone and balance, she began belting out the words and swaying to the music, dropping low on the mop, as if it were a pole in a night club.

Lucy and Angie whistled and whooped in delight. "You go, girl!"

Sarah laughed and continued dancing with her mop on the counter, forgetting that only minutes ago, she had been too exhausted to move. Lucy and Angie danced and sang around her. When it was time for the chorus, the trio huddled up and sang in unison, laughing heartily at the imperfect harmony they made.

⁂ ⁂ ⁂ ⁂ ⁂ ⁂

Jamie, Walt, Gaston and Robby were walking home from Sydney's house where they had been hanging out, when Gaston happened to glance across the street into the dimly lit dining room of Steve's Pizzeria.

"Dudes," he laughed. "Get a load of this!"

The others turned to look—and saw Sarah dancing on the counter with a mop. Two attractive women danced around her, singing into pretend microphones.

"That's hot. They're so hot," Robby said, stopping to take in the scene.

Walt shook his head. "How appropriate. Sarah and her friends are practicing for their future careers in pole dancing."

"Shut up, Walt," Jamie said, his eyes locked on Sarah. "They're just having some fun."

"Sarah's got moves," Robby said, impressed.

"Yeah. I wonder what song that is," Gaston said, and let out a slow whistle. "Day-um those girls are gettin' it."

Walt smiled smugly at Jamie. "I rest my case. Strippers in the making."

Jamie didn't respond. He was too busy watching Sarah. Her body flowed in such fluid rhythm, he felt as if he could actually hear the music. Her long hair was loose, as it rarely was, and it tousled wildly about her as she provocatively swayed her hips and rolled her head. She was having so much fun, she failed to notice Andreas march into the dining room. The other two women did. But Sarah continued to dance and sing—and Andreas stood with both hands on his hips, watching her.

"Oh, boy," Robby said, laughing. "That can't be good."

Jamie nodded in amused agreement. "Wait for it...and there it is. She sees him."

Sarah froze, the mop over her head, upon seeing her father. Glancing towards Lucy and Angie, she found them giggling while busily wiping away at what had previously been their microphones. Turning back to her father, she smiled meekly and shrugged. Then her smile became determined. Throwing down the mop, Sarah jumped down from the counter and took Andreas's big hands in hers.

The huge man protested for only a moment before a broad smile replaced his previously tired features. Andreas danced with his daughter, twirling her around and around before finally dipping her. Bowing deeply before her, he brought her hand to his lips. Sarah laughed in delight and flung herself into his arms. Lucy held her hand to her heart and smiled while Angie clapped and whistled through her fingers.

"That's it. Enough already. I'm gonna barf." Walt began walking away and Robby and Gaston followed, laughing. But Jamie lingered for a moment, appreciating the tender moment between Sarah and her father.

Later, after parting with his friends to walk the remainder of the way to his house alone, his thoughts turned once again to the girl who seemed to occupy his mind more and more frequently. He thought of the way she had looked dancing on the counter and found himself grinning from ear to ear. He doubted he would think of much else for a while. She was just...so free. So sure of herself—and hot as hell.

Hands down, the most intriguing girl he'd ever met. And he had blown it with her.

Jamie stopped walking and looked up into the myriads of stars that lit the night sky. "You're a tough one, Sarah," he said, quietly to himself. "But I've never been a quitter. Like you, I give as good as I get. And I'm not ready to give up on you."

CHAPTER TWENTY-EIGHT

"Amelia. It's me. Listen, I need your help. It's Nick." Sarah kept her voice low, as she nervously looked around her, shivering from nerves, not cold.

"Whoa. Slow down! Where are you?"

"Outside the Quickie Mart on Main Street."

"What are you doing there?"

"Following my brother. And freaking out." Sarah put her phone down and peered around the corner of the building, trying to see more clearly through the night. "Listen, Amelia, it's a long story, but Nick has been acting strangely all day. About an hour ago, he just left Steve's in the middle of setting up. On a Friday. Without saying one word to anybody, not even me."

"You're right. Very weird."

"So I followed him and get this: He went to the alley across the street, behind that sketchy bar, Troll's."

"What? Are you sure? "

"Yeah. And he wasn't alone. He's with three thugs that look around our age."

"Thugs? Oh my gosh, why? Sarah, I can barely hear you. What's that beeping?"

Sarah's breath caught at the panic she heard in Amelia's voice. It mirrored her own. "My phone is running out of battery. Amelia, what do I do? I can't breathe..."

"Stay right there," Amelia replied with instant resolve. "Do not, I repeat, do not go into or behind that bar until I get there. Then, we'll decide what to do together."

"Okay, I won't...but hurry!" Sarah whispered urgently and hung up.

Amelia threw on her jacket and quietly slipped out the door, hoping her parents wouldn't hear her. Checking the time on her phone, she relaxed a little. She still had a couple of hours before dinner. She hopped on her bike and started riding towards Main Street as fast as she could.

✻ ✻ ✻ ✻ ✻ ✻

Daisy Nelson was in exceptionally high spirits. All three of her children were home, the football team had a bye and the five of them had just enjoyed dinner at *Della Ventura's*, their favorite restaurant. She had reveled in their togetherness all evening, unable to keep from admiring her brood. *Just look at them. I love devoting my life to their happiness,* she thought to herself. *Who wouldn't? They are amazing.*

Her gaze lingered on her eldest son, Ben. He had grown into a strikingly handsome young man, a mirror image of his father in his youth. He was at the top of his class at Duke University, and dating a darling young girl from a prominent South Carolina family.

Hillary was hanging on to his every word. It touched Daisy to see the adoration for both her brothers in her eyes. Hillary was blossoming into a lovely young woman with a sharp mind and a strong will. Both were traits Daisy deemed essential for any young girl in such a fast-paced, competitive world.

And just today, she had run into sweet Charlotte Sanders. She had been thrilled to hear Jamie was seeing her again, after fretting over his infatuation with the Greek girl from New York, who waitressed at Steve's. Daisy frowned at the thought of her youngest son, who of her three had always been the one to make the wiser choices, dating, perhaps even marrying a girl like that. She had worried about it since she had heard from Libby, Charlotte's mother, that Jamie had asked Sarah out in front of the whole class. She had quickly confided her concern on the matter to James, who simply shared none of it. He liked Sarah. His opinion was that she was terrific, always smiling and joking with him when he went to Steve's for take-out. Daisy had walked away, letting James see she did not approve of a girl with Sarah's background for Jamie. The last thing she heard as she left the room was James's stern warning for her not to meddle.

As if she needed a warning. Daisy had learned long ago not to openly meddle in her children's lives. She knew the cost, so instead, she watched and waited to see how things would play out. Still, she began to pick up the Steve's take-out herself and made sure she addressed Sarah with remote, cool politeness. Admittedly, the girl was unusually beautiful and Daisy could understand Jamie being attracted to her good looks. But there was a lot more to a successful relationship or marriage than good looks, and there was no doubt in Daisy Nelson's mind that her son had a lot to learn when it came to women.

But for this night, things were good. Jamie was seeing Charlotte again. Daisy said a silent prayer of thanks, watching her three children laugh together, as they walked ahead. She looked up at James, who seemed to know—like he always did—what she was thinking. Smiling down at her, he linked her arm through his, took her hand and brought her fingers to his lips. Daisy moved closer to him, feeling blessed and content.

"Ice cream, anyone?" she said out loud.

CHAPTER TWENTY-NINE

Sarah had never felt so cold. She was shivering so intensely, she could feel her body twitch. *Amelia...where are you?* she asked herself, nervously. But it was Niko who appeared instead, along with the three boys he had gone in with. Sarah felt her stomach knot at the sight of their ratty clothes and menacing looks. From what she could tell, they were old enough to be in high school, probably close to her own age. Her eyes narrowed when the biggest one shoved Niko ahead of him. She knew her brother's body language well. Niko was not there of his own free will. The big guy shoved him again and all four began walking away from the bar.

Sarah's fists closed tightly. Her shivering ceased and her adrenalin took over. Moving quietly and deliberately, she fell in behind the foursome, carefully keeping a safe distance and staying close to the shadows of the buildings.

Amelia turned the corner on her bike just in time to see Sarah disappear into the darkness. "Where are you going, Sarah?" she said to no one at all. "What are you thinking? I told you to wait..." She glanced nervously around her, trying to decide what to do.

It was then she saw the entire Nelson family crossing the street and walking towards her. Instinctively, she smiled politely and looked away, hoping they would do the same. But Jamie stepped away from his family to speak to her.

"Where is she going?" he asked, his voice low.

"Who? Sarah? Oh, yeah, I...didn't see her," Amelia stammered.

"C'mon, Amelia, you saw her. Where is she going?"

Amelia let her breath out in a rush. "I think she's in trouble, Jamie."

"What does that mean?" Jamie asked, his voice even, but at the same time, impatient.

"I don't know but I'm freaking out. She told me Niko slipped out of Steve's earlier today with some 'thugs'. So she followed him here, to Troll's and called me but her cell phone started dying on her while we were talking. She was scared. I tried to get here fast enough, but they must have come out before I got here. I saw her round the corner by herself, which means she is still following them. I was trying to figure out what to do when you walked up," she finished, completely breathless.

"How many guys?" Jamie's voice took on a more urgent tone.

Amelia shuddered and shook her head, her eyes big with worry.

"Okay, Amelia, calm down. I'll go check on her." He pulled his cell phone out. "Give me your number. I will call if you need to get help." Amelia glanced at the spot she had last seen Sarah as she punched in the numbers. Jamie flicked his phone off and put it back in his pocket. "If you don't hear from me in an hour, call the police."

Amelia grabbed his arm. "What? Jamie, I'm scared. Should we get your dad or your brother?"

"No. It would take too long and I need to go now. I'm guessing they're heading down to Doogie's Point. If you have to make the call, send them there."

"Doogie's Point? Isn't that where drug deals go down? Oh God," Amelia whispered, bringing her hands to her face and closing her eyes in disbelief. "No, Jamie, I think you're wrong. Niko wouldn't go there. There's no way."

"Unless he didn't know what he was getting into. Stay here and stay to yourself. Just keep your phone on and wait for me to call."

Amelia nodded, her eyes fearful. "Be careful," she whispered, as she watched Jamie walk back to his family. He spoke to his parents briefly, then walked briskly in the same direction she had seen Sarah disappear just a few moments earlier. It had gotten darker. She watched him until she couldn't see him anymore.

⁕ ⁕ ⁕ ⁕ ⁕ ⁕

Daisy Nelson had followed the exchange between Amelia Patten and her son with great interest. She didn't think Amelia was a girl Jamie socialized with much. It had not been a casual exchange, that much she could tell. And unless her eyes had deceived her, she had seen Sarah Giannopoulos a few minutes earlier. One look at Jamie told her he had, too. He had more than noticed her. Her guess was he had asked Amelia where she had gone. Had he followed her? Why would he do that?

"Something is up with Jamie," Ben commented to his parents, as they walked towards Spill the Beans, the family's favorite ice cream parlor.

Daisy sighed. "Not something, Ben. Someone. The Greek waitress."

"C'mon, Daisy. Her name is Sarah," James said, pulling his wife closer. "She's a very pretty girl," he added, winking at Ben.

"Yeah, Mom, quit being such a snob," Hillary agreed.

That earned her an irate look from her mother. "I am not a snob, Hillary," she corrected, firmly. "She's just not the type of girl I see Jamie with, that's all."

"Let Jamie decide that, honey. You don't even know her," James coaxed.

"Hmph. I know enough."

Ben watched the exchange between his parents with interest. Then, he stretched his arms out and yawned. "Y'all, I'm beat. I think I'm going to have to skip ice cream, head home and watch the game."

"What? You're passing up Spill the Beans pistachio ice cream?" his father questioned with a laugh.

"Hillary will eat my share, Dad," Ben replied, with a playful jab to his younger sister's shoulder. Leaning over, he gave his mom a kiss on the cheek and grinned. "Watch them, they should both be dieting."

"So much for the Nelson family reunion," Daisy complained.

"Nonsense. I love it when a plan comes together. I save money and I get my two girls alone," James said, pulling Hillary to his other side. "Now, I know my little Hillary won't turn down double-dark chocolate with her super-hip parents. Am I right?"

"Of course you are, Daddy," Hillary said, laughing. Pulling herself closer to her father's ear, she whispered softly, "You know Ben is going wherever Jamie went, right?"

James gave his daughter a small nod and a knowing smile.

"What are you whispering about, Hillary?" Daisy asked, sighing.

"The toppings I am about to order."

Daisy had to smile at her daughter's cheery expression. "You heard what Ben said, sweetie. Listen to your brother. The prom's not far away."

"It's plenty enough far away for me and my toffee crunch," Hillary said. "And Daddy's getting toppings, too. He wants M&Ms. And he's paying, so that's that."

The trio laughed, and James opened the ice cream parlor door for his girls.

CHAPTER THIRTY

"Lucy! Looceee!"

Lucy nearly jumped out of her skin at the booming sound of Andreas's angry voice.

"Take it easy, boss!" she said, clutching her hand against her chest as he stormed towards her. "You nearly gave me a heart attack!"

"Missy, the way you go through boyfriends, whether you have a heart or not is debatable." If Andreas noticed the offended look Lucy gave him, he showed no sign of it. "Where is everybody? Are we running a business here, or a playground?"

"I don't know," Lucy replied with distinct emphasis on each word.

"Do you know what time it is?" Andreas thumped his thumb on his watch so hard, Lucy was sure it would never work again.

"Almost opening time?"

"That's right!" Andreas threw his hands up in the air and then ran them through his graying hair. "Που ειναι τα παιδια μου?" he yelled.

"Mr. Giannopoulos, you know I don't know what that means. Please stop yelling at me! If you're upset because Sarah and Nick are not here, I saw them leave about an hour ago," Lucy said, lifting her chin and staring at her boss with as much defiance as she dared.

"Together?" He bellowed the word so hard, Lucy wondered if the windows shook.

"No. First Nick. Then Sarah."

"Did they look sick?"

Lucy fought the sudden urge to smile. He was a softie at heart. "Not that I saw," she said evenly.

"You saw? What do you mean, you saw? Evidently, you saw nothing!"

With that, he stormed to the window and looked outside, mumbling things in the language Lucy had come to recognize as Greek—and at times, desperately wished she could understand. Others, she thanked her lucky stars she didn't. She watched Andreas become quiet and knew he was making a decision.

"You and Liliane handle the cash. The two of you do the best you can. Apologize to our customers and don't take any take-out orders until I get back," he instructed, as he walked to her and handed her the keys.

Lucy nodded. Andreas exhaled deeply and pulled off his apron.

"Lucy, you know I yell at you because you're like one of the family. I thank God for you every Sunday in church. Thank you for taking care of things here. I'll be back as soon as I can."

"I know. No worries." She dropped the keys in her pocket. "Good luck, Mr. G," she called out to him as he went out the door. His response was a string of Greek.

"I hope they're okay," Lucy mumbled to herself, as she made her way to the kitchen to let Liliane, Angie and the cook know they were in for a long night—alone.

CHAPTER THIRTY-ONE

Jamie carefully made his way through the woods leading to Doogie's Point. It was dark and he saw nothing out of the ordinary. Still, he walked cautiously, his senses keen to every sound. He hoped his gut feeling would pay off and he would find them. His first thought when Amelia had explained what Sarah was up to, was that Nick had somehow gotten involved with the school's gang of drug users. A kid like Nick would be the perfect choice to sell their drugs. He was young and he was new to Kernersville. He didn't know a whole lot about who was bad news in town.

Jamie knew enough about the gang to know they were dangerous. Ben had warned him years ago to stay away from them—and he had. Still, he had heard enough sad stories to know the effects they had on more than a few kids. He had watched a few of his friends throw their future away because of their drugs. He had been in middle school when his uncle Teddy had come down on the gang hard, after a fifteen-year-old girl had overdosed and died. But Jamie knew the gang had not gone away. Now they were more careful. Now they used younger kids like Nick to do the selling for them—and get caught for them.

A slight rustling sound caught his attention and he noticed a form crouched in the bushes just ahead of him. He squinted, trying to see through the moonlight. He recognized Sarah's jacket even though he could not see her face. She was watching something—or someone. Silently, Jamie moved away from her, keeping her in his line of vision. Peering through the bushes, his fears were confirmed.

Nick and three high school-aged boys dressed in black stood in the ravine that overlooked the city. They were silent, just standing in darkness, framed only by the faraway city lights. Jamie knew they were waiting. Just then, from the other side of the ravine, headlights flickered on and off three times. One of the boys held up his phone and flashed back. Jamie swallowed. It was time for the exchange.

"No!" Nick's quivering voice pierced through the cold darkness. "I've changed my mind, like I said before. I'm going home. You can keep your fifty bucks."

"Kid, like *I* said before, shut it," one of them hissed, pointing his flashlight in the direction of the headlights, as he handed it to Nick. "It's too late to back out."

"So go," the second one ordered. Opening his jacket, he pulled out a small package and held it out to Nick. "We'll be right here waiting on you. Easy as pie."

"No."

The first boy stepped closer to Nick. Taking the package from his friend, he thrust it into Nick's empty hand. "Go. Now. If there's trouble, run but don't drop the package. And remember: if you get caught, you never saw us. Or your pretty sister is dead."

Nick swallowed back the bile rising in his throat and looked down at the brown package in his hand. He couldn't believe this was happening. He had no idea what was in the package, but there was little doubt now that whatever it was, it was against the law. Drugs? For what seemed like the hundredth time that night, he thought about running. But there were three of them, and they scared him to death. They had said they would hurt Sarah. After what Jake had done to her, he had vowed to let no one hurt her again. He would do it, just this one time and then stay away from them. He ignored the sweat trickling down the side of his face and willed his feet to move.

"Who is *that* supposed to scare? Him or me?"

All four heads looked up in surprise. Sarah stood just in front of the trees, her hands in her pockets. She looked casual and relaxed, as if she were joining a group of friends.

Jamie bit back a curse and hung his head. His mind raced with options. Sarah had not given him time to come up with a plan. He checked his watch and groaned inwardly. Only twenty minutes had passed since he'd left. If he tried to text Amelia, they might see the light coming from his phone. Help was not coming anytime soon.

"Sarah!" Nick yelled, only to have his mouth covered by one of the gang members.

"Get your filthy hands off him," Sarah warned with quiet fury.

"How about you just come down here and make me, princess."

Sarah glared at him. "Because unlike you, I'm not an idiot. I've called the police and they'll be here any minute. If there is any brain left at all in your obviously fried skulls, you'll leave him alone and get out of here while you still can."

"Honey, you just scare me silly," the bigger one who held Nick leered. "My friend Ryan is coming up to help you down here. Since you want to join the party, we're all going for a little ride together. That's after your brother takes care of business." The others nodded in agreement and the one he had called Ryan started to make his way up the hill towards Sarah.

"Listen, Ryan, if you have any sense at all, you'll ditch your loser friends and run. I've called the police, I swear it," Sarah urged, calmly. Ryan turned blood-shot eyes to her, and hesitated.

"Shut up, bitch! Ryan, hurry up," the big one growled, angrily.

Sarah began to search the ground for a stick to use as a weapon. She spotted one near where she stood, picked it up and braced herself. "You guys are the biggest losers in school. I'm new and even I know that. But this stupid? I never knew this level of stupid existed," she called down to them, gripping the stick tightly. "Don't worry, Niko, the cops are on their way. You be sure to tell them you had no idea anything illegal was going on and that they forced you to come with them!"

"I said shut up!" the apparent leader yelled back. Ryan stood still, unsure of what to do. He watched as Sarah raised the stick behind her like a batter about to swing. "Ryan, get moving. She didn't call any cops, not with her brother here. Shut her up."

Encouraged, Ryan smiled up at Sarah. With a quick bound, he landed four feet in front of her. "Settle down, sweet thing. Pretty girls like you shouldn't play with sticks. Now you're coming with us, one way or another. We'll show you a good time with real men, not those girly boys you're used to," he said, slurring his words, his glazed eyes sweeping over all of her.

"When I see a real man, I'll let you know," Sarah replied coolly, adrenalin and anger replacing what should have been fear.

Ryan's response was to lunge at her awkwardly. Sarah swung the stick with all her strength and hit him hard in his side. Cursing, he grabbed his side in pain. Sarah used the opportunity to ram the stick into his stomach and push him off balance. Ryan rolled halfway down the hill, with a muffled cry.

There was a burst of cursing from the gang and Sarah looked to Nick, relieved to find him unharmed, still held by the leader. "Now, that, princess, was a mistake. You've made me mad and you're gonna pay for it," he said. His voice sent a shiver down Sarah's spine. "Kenny, go help him. Now!"

For the first time since she had confronted the gang, Sarah felt panic seize her chest and constrict her breathing. She tried to will herself out of it as she watched Kenny help Ryan up. The two began closing in on her. *Maybe I should try to run for help. But I'd never make it... They know these woods, and I can't even remember which way we came from...and I can't leave Niko...*

She stood her ground and braced for their attack, wishing she really had called the police, wishing for a miracle. She decided to swing at Kenny first, since Ryan was at least a little hurt and clearly stoned. Just as she raised the stick, she heard a thudding noise. Sarah watched in confusion as Kenny dropped to his knees and grabbed his head. She saw blood dripping between his fingers at the same time she registered he'd been hit by a large rock lying on the ground next to him. Muffled sound became a familiar voice calling her name, telling her to run. Terror seized her as a form shot out of the darkness and lunged at Ryan.

It was Jamie.

CHAPTER THIRTY-TWO

Andreas turned his truck onto Main Street for the third time, searching for any sign of his children. Again, he found none. His anger was beginning to be replaced by a gnawing fear deep in his stomach. His eyes narrowed as he recognized Jamie's family on a park bench eating ice cream. He noticed Jamie was not with them. Slowing to a stop next to them, Andreas rolled down his window.

"Dr. Nelson, have you seen my daughter tonight?"

"A man of pleasantries he's not," Daisy mumbled to herself, as she smiled politely at Andreas. James got up and walked to the other man's truck. "No, Mr. Giannopoulos, I'm sorry to say I haven't seen Sarah. Everything all right?"

"I don't think so. Dr. Nelson, where is your son?"

"Jamie? Well, until a few minutes ago, he was here, but he left to meet his friends." James frowned at the concern in Andreas's eyes. "Can I help?"

"Something is wrong. Both my children disappeared right before opening time. They told no one where they were going and no one has seen them since."

Daisy's eyebrows came together as she listened. Anxiously, she got up and came to stand beside her husband. "I saw Sarah walking that way," she motioned as she spoke, "about a half an hour ago. Jamie may have followed her."

"And Niko? My son? Was he with her?" Andreas shifted the truck into reverse and was moving even as he spoke.

"No...I didn't see anyone else. But Jamie spoke to Amelia Patten before he left and I noticed she hasn't budged since..."

Without another word, Andreas pulled away. The Nelsons watched as the truck pulled up near Amelia. She was still standing by her bike, her back to them.

"Amelia!" Andreas boomed, causing her to jump in the air, startled. One look at her stricken expression told him she knew something. She was visibly upset. Andreas's stomach knotted, but he forced control into his voice. "Where is Sarah, Amelia?"

Amelia bit her lip, her eyes filling with tears. "I don't know," she rasped. "Mr. Giannopoulos, I don't know. But I think she's in trouble. Maybe Nick, too."

Andreas put the truck in park and hopped out. Taking her by the shoulders, he started to say something. But when he felt her shaking and she looked up, tears flowing down her stricken face, he only hugged her tight. "Come on, settle down now. Get in the truck and tell me where to find them. I'll take care of it, I promise." He kissed the top of her head, before letting her go, swallowing the bile that was rising in his throat. Amelia nodded, wiped her tears with her sleeve and bolted for the passenger seat. Throwing her bike in the truck bed, Andreas jumped in the truck and hit the gas.

Across the street, James Nelson watched the exchange with worried eyes. "Daisy, Hillary, time to go. Hillary, give me your keys, I'm driving."

Daisy grabbed her sweater from the park bench. "James, what's going on? Where do you think they are? Do you think Jamie is with them?"

"I don't know. But we're going to follow that truck and find out."

❦CHAPTER THIRTY-THREE

"Sarah! Sarah! What's happening? Sarah!"

Sarah registered the panic in Nick's screams as she tried to make sense of the incredible scene playing out in front of her. Jamie and Ryan were fighting—and Kenny was rolling on the ground, holding his head. Where had Jamie come from? Somehow, he had managed to hit Kenny in the head with a rock and then jump Ryan. How had he known to come? Had he followed her? She shook her head, as if to make sense of any of it. Narrowing her eyes to see more clearly, she searched the ravine for her brother. She saw he was struggling to get away from the leader.

Rage filled her and Sarah started down the hill towards them. "Let him go! Now!"

"Come and get him, sweet thing. So, that's the police you were talking about. Designer jock boy. He is definitely scaring me." Nick felt the larger boy's grip loosen on his shoulder, twisted and lunged into him. Surprised, the gang leader lost his balance, but only for a moment. Straightening, he punched Nick hard in the stomach, sending the smaller boy face-first into the dirt. Nick struggled to get up, but the leader kicked him hard. Nick collapsed and was still.

"Niko!" Sarah screamed, throwing herself on the leader, so angry she could barely see him even as she attacked him. He grabbed at her hands, but she raked at his face as hard as she could. She heard him howl in pain and felt the victory all the way in her toes. But not for long. The much larger boy quickly overpowered her, grabbing both her wrists and pushing them painfully behind her. Yanking her close to him, he stared at her, his eyes cold as steel, his face bleeding where her nails had left their mark, his breath heavy with alcohol—and something else she didn't recognize. Sarah tried not to react to his stench or his stare. Boldly, she fixed her eyes on his.

"Don't worry, wildcat. I've got what you need. As soon as Ryan is done with pretty boy up there, I'm gonna give it to you." He pulled her even closer so his mouth was almost on hers, licking the blood off the corner of his lip. His bloodshot eyes locked on hers. "And little brother's gonna watch." The evil in his whispered threat sent shivers down Sarah's spine but she did not look away, determined not to show him fear.

"Let her go."

Sarah looked over his shoulder, trying to recognize the boy standing behind them. She couldn't. He looked older and somehow familiar, but at the same time she had no idea who he was. One of the gang members trying to stop this from going too far? No, even in the darkness, he looked too clean-cut to be one of them. She watched as the stranger silently took off his jacket and threw it to the ground.

The gang leader jerked her face back around to his. Leaning into her ear, he whispered, "I'll be back in a minute, wildcat." Then, he abruptly let her go.

Moving slowly, he began to walk towards the stranger. Sarah ran to Niko. Wrapping her arms around his waist, she helped him to his feet. Her eyes searched for the best way to run, now that she had him. But the darkness was enveloping, she had no idea where she was and Niko was limp against her. "It's all right, Niko," she whispered into his ear. "It's going to be okay. Be ready to run." She looked up the hill to Jamie. She knew she couldn't leave him. Her heart sank when she saw Ryan land a punch square on his face. Jamie staggered but stayed on his feet. Ryan swung at him again, but Jamie ducked and head-butted him in the stomach. Ryan went down, but he pulled Jamie with him.

Nick whimpered and Sarah turned towards a strange clicking sound. The clouds gave way to a sliver of moonlight and in it she saw the shiny blade of a knife in the gang leader's hand. He hissed and began to move closer to the stranger who had come to Sarah and Nick's defense. The stranger remained silent, his eyes locked on the knife. Who was he? Sarah wanted to cover her eyes and cry.

I'll be back in a minute, wildcat. The leader's menacing threat played back in her mind and Sarah felt her resolve strengthen. Taking advantage of the moonlight, she searched the area for a weapon. For whatever reason, this stranger was helping them—and she was not about to leave him or Jamie. From the corner of her eye she noticed Nick pushing a rock closer to them with his foot and knew he was thinking the same.

Suddenly, a large figure, one she would recognize anywhere, stepped out of the darkness and into the moonlight. Sarah and Nick watched in amazement as their father walked between the two boys and stopped in front of the gang leader.

"Put that knife down before you hurt somebody," he warned him, his voice both quiet and firm.

"Get the hell out of here, old man. This ain't none of your business." The gang leader began to slice the knife through the air, his glazed eyes now wild.

Without hesitation, Andreas moved in on the boy, moving so quickly he caught him off guard. Andreas had told Sarah and Nick many stories about Desert Storm, stories they only half-believed. But, as they watched their father paralyze the boy by hitting him between the eyes, then expertly catch the knife mid-air, they became believers. Leaning over the gang leader's crumpled form on the ground, Andreas grabbed his stringy hair and forced him to look up, even as his eyes rolled back in his head. "You deserve everything that is about to happen to you. When they do let you go, remember me. Come near my daughter or son again and I will kill you. Do you understand?"

"Yeah..." the gang leader groaned, his features contorted with pain.

Andreas let the boy's head fall into the dirt. As if on cue, sirens sounded in the distance, coming closer. Ryan froze and Jamie took the opportunity to tackle him and hold him down. The stranger took off running up the hill and together they subdued Ryan easily. Breathing heavily, Jamie searched the ravine for Sarah. She was there. She was all right. He felt his body shudder in relief, even as he smiled at his brother. "Thanks, Ben."

Ben nodded and smiled back. "Anytime, little brother. I got you."

From the ravine, Sarah watched the exchange between Jamie and the stranger in a daze. She felt a wave of relief that both seemed fine. Then she and Nick were enveloped in her father's strong arms. "Παιδια μου," he whispered, kissing them each, over and over. "Thank God." Tears ran down his cheeks unchecked, as he hugged them fiercely to him.

"I'm so sorry, Dad," Nick said between sobs. "It was all my fault. I almost got Sarah really hurt..."

"Shh, Niko," Andreas soothed his young son. "There's time for that later." Squatting down, he put one hand on Nick's shoulder, the other under his trembling chin. "Look at me, son. Stay right next to me now. Say nothing to the police without me. Answer their questions, but don't add anything. Understand?"

Nick shuddered and nodded.

"Jamie? Ben?" Sarah jerked at the terrified sound of a woman's voice. She looked up and saw Dr. and Mrs. Nelson running towards Jamie and the other boy.

Ben? Who is Ben?

Suddenly, realization dawned. The stranger standing next to Jamie was his older brother, Ben. Sarah closed her eyes and shuddered. Terrible things could have happened to the Nelson family because of her tonight. But, amazingly, all was well. Relieved and exhausted, she buried her face in her father's shirt. His arms tightened around her.

James reached his boys first and began to check them over. "Are you both okay?" he asked, his expert eyes examining them from head to toe. He frowned when he saw a cut above Jamie's eye but was relieved to see it was the reason for the blood on his son's face.

"Oh, James, why is he bleeding so much?" Daisy Nelson asked from behind him, her breathing ragged from running, her voice calmer now that she could see both her boys seemed to be well-enough.

"He's fine, nothing's broken." James fished a handkerchief from his pocket and gently forced Jamie's head back so he could apply pressure to the cut.

"Yeah, he's still the looker in the family, Mom, no worries," Ben said, grinning at his younger brother. He pulled a leaf from his hair, then ruffled it.

Jamie held out his fist and Ben brought his own down over it, a gesture they had used since they were boys. "I've never been more glad to see you," he said, more to the air than his brother, as James continued to hold his head back. "How did you know?"

"Gut feeling," Ben replied, still grinning. "But brother, I was a little worried until *The Rock* showed up. Who is that man? He's a giant!"

Jamie smiled, then grimaced from the pain it caused. "That's Sarah's dad."

CHAPTER THIRTY-FOUR

After that, everything had been a blur. Police sirens and blue lights filled the ravine with light and sound; the police handcuffed the drug gang and took them away, and Amelia held Sarah's hand until they both managed to stop shaking. Sarah and Nick and then Jamie and Ben answered questions the police asked. Finally, Andreas announced he was taking the kids home.

"C'mon Jamie, we need to get that eye stitched up," James told his son, patting him gently on the shoulder.

The two families began to silently walk together, Amelia staying close to Sarah and Nick. The Nelsons had left Hillary's car a little further down the field that led to the ravine so they reached Andreas's truck first. The group stood together for an awkwardly silent moment before Andreas opened the door and motioned for the kids to get in.

Jamie glanced at Sarah for what seemed like the hundredth time since their ordeal had ended. She was holding Nick's hand like she would never let it go again. Again, he felt relief wash through him. As if sensing his gaze on her, she met his eyes. He tried to smile, but winced instead at the pain the movement caused. He tightened the handkerchief his father had given him to the wound above his eye. Sarah caught the movement, her expression concerned.

"Jamie, I am so sorry. Are you...is that going to be okay?" In the soft light spilling from the truck, she saw his eye had begun to swell. Gently, she reached out with her free hand to touch the spot. His jaw muscle jerked at her touch. "How did you get here?" she asked, her voice barely more than a whisper.

"Amelia told me you might be in over your head," he explained, disappointed when she moved her fingers away.

"What you kids did tonight was completely, utterly foolish," Daisy Nelson spoke sharply, moving to stand by Jamie. Pulling his hand back, she examined his cut, frowned and had him resume the pressure on it before turning to Sarah. "Unbelievably foolish," she repeated, with contained anger.

"I am so sorry," Sarah managed, dropping her eyes to the ground.

"He's fine, we all are," Ben said, aware that Sarah was fighting tears. She braved a look at him and tried to smile. Ben winked at her. "This town needs a little excitement. And sir, I have to tell you," Ben grinned at Andreas, "I don't know how you did what you did back there. I've never seen anything like it."

Andreas smiled sadly. "Lessons of war, son, something I hope you'll never have the misfortune to see." He held out his hand and shook Ben's firmly before doing the same with Jamie. "Thank you both for what you did tonight. I will never forget it."

Nick pulled his hand from Sarah's and stepped close to Jamie and Ben. His head hung low and he did not look up. "I'm s-sorry," he choked, his voice small and shaky.

"It's ok, Nick."

But Nick shook his head, tears rolling down his cheeks. "I thought... I wanted to make some money, just this once. I didn't think it through, I was so stupid."

"Niko, time for that later," Andreas came to stand behind him.

"When I saw those headlights flicker, I got so scared. I couldn't move, like I was stuck. It was weird, I had seen them before. I don't know where or..."

"That's enough, son. Like I said, there's time for that later." Andreas took Nick by his shoulders, turned him around and hugged him. Nick buried his head into his father's chest.

"James, we need to get Jamie to the ER," Daisy said, through what sounded to Sarah like gritted teeth. She swallowed miserably, tears welling up in her eyes. Andreas reached out his arm and pulled her close.

"C'mon, angel, get in the truck. Niko, Amelia, you too," he ordered. "The Nelson boy needs to get to the doctor." Letting them go, he stepped around Daisy and shook James Nelson's hand before making his way to the driver's side. Nick and Amelia followed. But Sarah could not move. Not yet.

"It was a very brave thing you did for your brother, Sarah," James said, ignoring Daisy's glare. "It's over now. That gang is going away this time. And our town's better off for it."

Sarah tried to smile, her lips trembling. A lone tear made its way down her face. Taking a step closer to Jamie, she reached up and kissed him softly on the cheek.

"You saved our lives tonight," she said, her voice little more than a whisper. "Thank you can never be enough. But, thank you."

Jamie could not find the words to answer her. He was lost as he looked into her tear-filled eyes. His heart began to thunder in his chest, as he fought an unexpected urge to reach for her and pull her into his arms. He wanted to tell her it was okay, that he was just glad she was unhurt. But all he could do was stand there.

"I'm sorry," Sarah said more loudly, turning her eyes to the ground. She stepped inside the truck, closing the door softly behind her.

Jamie tried to think of what to say to make her stay a little longer. He couldn't come up with anything. Frustrated, he watched the truck as it pulled away, hoping she'd turn around. She didn't.

" Let's get a move on," James said, intentionally breaking the silence. He wondered about the look he had just seen on Jamie's face. The family walked to their car, James falling into step beside his youngest son. Hillary was excitedly asking Ben questions about the fight. Daisy led the way, not saying a word.

"I thought you were more responsible than this," James quietly admonished him. "Thank God Ben sensed you were in trouble."

Jamie nodded. "I know, Dad. And I'm sorry. Around here, we know about those guys. But Sarah's brother doesn't. He's a good kid. I knew she was too late to stop him."

"Still, you should have gotten help before you followed her. I was right there. I don't have to tell you, this could have ended very differently."

"I know. I should have, but I thought I could get to her and warn her in time. You should have seen her, Dad, jumping out from behind the trees, ordering them to leave her brother alone."

"Jamie, you endangered your well-being—and hers—by not thinking things through. You know better, son. God knows you've seen the law at work all of your life." James lowered his voice. "On the other hand, I can't wait to tell Uncle Wyatt and Teddy. Because I'm damned proud of you. And I wish I could have seen her do that."

Jamie suppressed a smile, knowing it would hurt. "Thanks, Dad."

"Don't tell your mother I said that."

Jamie laughed, then winced. "I won't."

"How's your eye?"

"Since we're being honest, it hurts like hell."

James chuckled. "It's a hero's price, son," he said. "A hero's price."

CHAPTER THIRTY-FIVE

In her room, Sarah stared at the ceiling.

She couldn't sleep. The night's drama kept playing over and over in her mind. Something was nagging at her consciousness, but she had no idea what. She turned to look at the clock. 2:30 a.m. Groaning, she closed her eyes and pulled the covers up over her head.

One drug dealer, two drug dealers, three...

A faint purring noise pierced the quiet. Sarah sat up, listening. The front door opened and closed.

You gotta be kidding me, Niko, what now?

Flinging the covers off, Sarah moved quickly and quietly to Nick's room. Cracking open his door, she let out the breath she had been holding. Nick was sound asleep in his bed. Relief coursed through her. But only for a second.

Who had opened the door downstairs?

Oh, God, the drug dealers...

On tiptoes, Sarah ran to her father's room and looked inside. He wasn't there. Confused, she stared at his made up bed.

Lights suddenly flashed through the bedroom window. Instinctively, Sarah dropped to all fours, then crawled towards it. She reached it just in time to see her father back out of the driveway and onto the street, his headlights off.

From across the street, lights flickered again, blinding her. She shielded her eyes and tried to see what they were.

A dark car. The same car Niko had seen at Doogie's? She watched it reverse, trying to make sense of what she was seeing. She couldn't.

Her father turned his headlights on. Slowly, he began to follow the car.

The memory struck fast and sudden. Sarah ran back to her room, as quietly as she could. Throwing on jeans and a sweatshirt over her night shirt, she hurried down the stairs to the kitchen, careful to avoid the squeaky step. She didn't want to wake up Niko. Finding her keys, she let herself out the back door, locking it behind her.

She grabbed her bike and walked to peer around the corner. The cars were no longer in sight. Running, Sarah got to the street in time to see her father's taillights dissolve into darkness. She climbed on the bike and pedaled as fast as she could toward them. Her teeth chattered in the cold night air. And yet, she was sweating.

She knew now why she couldn't sleep. She had been digging deep for memories she had worked to suppress—to remember what Niko had not.

In the chaos earlier that night, she had missed her father's odd reaction to Niko's accounting to both the police and Jamie. But now she knew exactly why he had kept him from saying too much.

Because she knew exactly where Niko had see the pattern of flashing lights before.

It had been the Christmas before the fire. Niko and she had gotten their first iPhones and they were huddled by their bedroom window using the moonlight to see through the darkness. They had been warned by their father he would confiscate the phones if they used them late at night. So, they were taking turns listening for his footsteps in the hall as they watched YouTube videos.

Suddenly, bright light had flooded the room.

At first, they thought Andreas had busted them and had his flashlight pointed at them from the front yard. They had turned off the phones and hit the floor. Niko had been the braver of the two, daring to peer over the window at the steady pattern of flashing light.

It's not Dad, Sarah. It's a car or something. Wow, that's weird. I think it's in the Davises' yard. Like in the middle of the yard.

She had looked up then. They had looked at each other. They had stayed low, watching the lights flick on and off.

Flash, flash, off. Flash, flash, off. Flash, fla...

Their father's footsteps on the stairs had sent them scrambling to their beds. The door had opened, ever so softly. Then closed again.

They had not dared to move, had lied silently in the darkness, watching the lights continue to light the bedroom walls.

Flash, flash, off.

The front door had opened and closed. Quietly, Sarah had gotten up to look outside the window. She had seen her father get in his truck and roll down the driveway, facing the lights. He had flicked on his headlights. Across from him, a dark sedan.

Flash, flash, off. Flash, flash off. First one, then the other. She had watched the sedan turn onto the street and drive away.

And her father follow.

Sarah, what's going on? Where did the lights go? Where's Dad? Did he leave?

Shhhh, Niko, go to sleep. It's just cars. Dad probably had to go to the restaurant.

In the middle of the night?

Shhhh. Go to sleep. He probably remembered to do something like check the alarm or ovens. He'll be back any minute.

Are you sure? I'm scared.

I'm sure. I'm going to sleep and so should you. Night, Niko.

But she had not slept. She had stayed awake for what seemed like hours until she heard her father return home. Only then, too exhausted to think about where he had been anymore did her eyes flutter shut.

The next morning, she had asked her father if he had left the house in the night. He had said yes, because he was worried he had left the cooler door open at the restaurant. The Davis boys were having a party again and had kept him up late. He was sorry to have scared them. All perfectly normal. She had been so relieved.

After that, Andreas installed a home alarm system. And cameras.

So you are never again afraid if I have to leave at night. I'll always be here in the morning.

Niko and she had loved how safe the alarm made them feel. How safe *he* made them feel. They never saw—or thought of—lights in the night again.

Until that spring, anyway. Until the fire.

Up ahead, Sarah could make out both the sedan and Andreas's truck stopped at a red light. Snapping out of her thoughts, she hopped on the curb and rode the sidewalk, staying low, shielding herself behind the trees. She slowed to a stop and waited. The light turned green and both vehicles turned right.

From a safe distance, Sarah followed.

CHAPTER THIRTY-SIX

Minutes later, both vehicles turned onto a dirt road. Sarah waited until she could barely see red taillights bopping up and down in the darkness. She hid her bike behind the brush by the street and followed on foot, glad for the moonlight peeking out from behind the clouds. She avoided stepping on anything that would make noise.

Twice in one night. It's official. My family is completely whacked.

The darkness thickened and Sarah realized the red lights were no longer glowing in the distance. She crept closer to the bushes, careful to stay low. She rounded a corner and saw soft yellow lights ahead.

A cabin? Yes...there's Dad's truck parked behind the sedan.

Sarah pulled her hood up and ran to the side of the cabin. She could hear voices inside. She closed her eyes and let out her breath. Her heart pounded in her head.

Carefully, she inched over to the window, dropped to the ground and looked inside. Her father was sitting at a table with two other men. The men had their backs to her. She had no idea who they were; they looked comfortable and calm.

But her father's face sent a chill down her spine. He was angry. No, he was furious. He had a look she had never seen before as he spoke to the men. His eyes were ice cold. The color had gone out of his face.

And in his hand, he had a gun.

Oh my God, Dad, what are you doing here? You have a gun? Who are these men? Do they have guns, too?

Her father was talking. Sarah tried to listen but Andreas was keeping his voice low. She looked around her, trying to think, to help—to do anything but hide by the window. Staying low, she fished her phone out of her pocket and ran back to the sedan. She turned off the flash and snapped a picture of the license plate. Then, after making sure the phone was on silent, she made her way back to the window.

Inside, the voices had gotten louder.

Now what, Dad? Gunfire at any minute? What do I do, Dad, what do I do?

Sarah braved another look through the bottom corner of the window.

And locked eyes with her father.

She froze, unable to move. Andreas let his gaze wander as if he had not seen her, rolled his eyes and yelled, "No!" before slamming his fist on the table. Sarah ducked out of sight. She heard chairs scraping. Keeping low to the ground, she ran. She didn't stop until she got to the street. Hopping on her bike, she raced home, trying to focus on nothing else but getting there. Fear rushed at her but she refused it.

Not now. Please, God, get me home to Niko. Please don't let them catch me.

By the time she got to the house, she couldn't feel her legs. Paralyzing fear had set in two streets back. Her cheeks were soaking in tears and she was shaking all over. Dropping her bike to the ground, she ran up the steps to the back door. But as she turned the key in the lock, she paused. She hated being afraid.

Mama would get answers. She wouldn't freak out and hide.

Wiping her eyes with her sleeve, Sarah willed her breathing to slow. Then she turned, walked to the front porch and sat on the swing.

She waited for her father to come home.

CHAPTER THIRTY-SEVEN

Andreas pulled into the driveway minutes later. He saw Sarah sitting on the front porch swing and for the second time that night, their eyes locked. His resigned, hers angry. Andreas turned off his engine, plunging them both into darkness. He crossed himself, closed his eyes and exhaled.

Help me, Maria. Help me not lose her tonight.

He let himself out of the car and slowly walked up the steps to her. He could feel her eyes still on him. But he couldn't bring himself to look at her. He stopped and stood in front of her.

"Are you okay?"

"Yes."

"Can we talk about this in the morning?"

"No." She scooted over to make room for him.

Andreas sighed and sat down next to her. He reached for her hand but Sarah pulled away.

"I want you to know I was planning on telling you all this one day."

"Well, that worked out well." Her voice was barely more than a whisper.

Andreas turned to look at her. "I don't have to get into all this with you, Sarah. None of this was supposed to happen tonight, but you and Niko are safe. If that's enough for you right now, we can leave it for another time. I think it would be best if we do."

Sarah looked up at him, her eyes blazing with anger. "Niko could have been hurt tonight, Dad. Or worse. And Jamie and Ben. And me. I remembered the lights, I know what happened was because of you, not Niko."

Andreas looked away from her. For a moment he said nothing. Then, he slapped both hands on his legs, nodded and stood.

"Let's go inside, then. I'll put on some coffee. We're both going to need it."

CHAPTER THIRTY-EIGHT

"So, Sarah," Michael Capitano was saying loudly, trying to hear himself over the music, "how does it feel to have outrun Shannon Moore?"

Sarah smiled. "Pretty good!" she replied, her voice bright with enthusiasm. She had beaten the "unbeatable" Shannon in the final cross-country meet earlier that afternoon. Shannon Moore was a senior at Riverside, Lakeview's biggest rival. Sarah grinned. She still could not believe she had won. Running was turning out to be a passion for her and she was so glad she had joined the team. It was going to be a great asset on her college applications. Better yet, it was fun and she had made new friends because of it—friends like Michael Capitano.

They were at Hughey Weinstein's house along with what seemed to Sarah like the rest of Lakeview High. Hughey's house was so big that it would be impossible, at least in Sarah's mind, to fill it with people or things. But tonight it was full, inside and out. Sarah had been surprised to see people were even swimming in the pool. Amelia and Hudson had quickly informed her it was heated.

Hughey was an only child and his parents adored everything he did. He was funny and laid back and Sarah liked him. Judging from the mob of people at his party, so did everyone else at Lakeview.

Aware that Michael was saying something to her, she shifted her gaze and pretended to listen—a skill she had perfected over the years in the restaurant business. She nodded politely at whatever he was saying, but the noise and her thoughts kept her from really paying attention. She had come to Hughey's party for a reason. Hughey was cool, but she knew Jamie and Charlotte would be there together. During the three weeks since Doogie's and the supposed date, she had been through more emotions than she cared to admit. She had even begun to forgive Jamie—after all, he did risk his life to help Niko and her. She cringed at the memory of that awful night and what could have been.

She had ended up sitting at the kitchen table with her father through what had been left of the darkness. She had listened in disbelief as he quietly told her things that had thrown her world off its axis. She had just sat there, staring at him numbly. When he finally finished, pain, fear and loss had overwhelmed her and she had crumbled into him, sobbing. Andreas had held her, his own face covered in tears.

Afterwards, he had sworn her to secrecy. They had watched the sun rise together. Then, they had each gone to their rooms. When Nick woke up, they had all gone downstairs for breakfast, as if none of it had happened.

But it had happened. Even now, she could not take it all in.

And then there was Daisy Nelson's judgment of her. That had gotten to her. What she had seen in the woman's eyes made her want to crawl into a hole.

Oh, Mrs. Nelson, if you only knew...

Sarah concentrated on reining in her thoughts. She and her father had made a pact: They would never discuss that part of his past again. They would put it behind them where it belonged. She had promised to bury it, if for no other reason to protect Niko—and her dad. And she intended to. She was her mother's daughter and she would hold her family together, no matter what. Her father was a good man. The best man she knew. It was time to move on, to focus on the present.

That means putting all the Jamie drama behind, too.

Sarah sighed. She had tried to thank Jamie at school that next Monday but never got the chance. It seemed Jamie went nowhere without his friends. And Charlotte seemed to always be in the mix. So, she had stopped trying. Sarah knew herself well enough to know that no matter how much what Jamie did for them at Doogie's meant to her, no matter how her life forever changed that night, she would not forget the joke. Nor the fact that she was, and now more than ever always would be, an outsider.

But, at the same time, Jamie had helped her. Maybe even saved them. Having had time to think about it, she had realized the in-crowd's stupid high school joke had affected her long enough. Outsider or not, Sarah knew she was built strong. She would not cower. She would be no one's victim.

Tonight, she would show anyone who was interested, that she no longer was.

"Earth to Sarah!" Michael was waving his hand in front of her face. Uh oh. She had forgotten to pretend to listen.

Sarah laughed, embarrassed. "I'm sorry, Michael. It's been a great day but I think I'm a little out of it. What were you saying?" She moved closer, determined to pay attention.

"It's Jamie, isn't it?"

Sarah felt her cheeks redden. "What? No, of course not."

"I don't mean to get in your business or anything, but I know he stood you up, Sarah, and I know it must have hurt you." Michael smiled sympathetically, as he watched for her reaction.

The simple truth of his words, along with the genuine concern for her in his eyes, were soothing to Sarah. Still, her cheeks reddened for the second time. He knew about the joke. Of course he did. Everyone knew.

"Yeah, well, no worries. They picked the wrong girl. I don't do drama and I won't be a victim." She shrugged. "That said, it was pretty pathetic that I fell for it."

"Don't beat yourself up. All I have to say is Nelson's not worth it. Everyone has always thought he's so cool, but if you ask me, he's an idiot. He's too caught up in his status which is why he blew his chance with an amazing girl like you."

"Thank you, that's really sweet of you to say."

This time, it was Michael's cheeks that reddened. "I mean, if I had a chance with...someone like you, I'd consider myself the luckiest guy in North Carolina."

"Aww, Michael." Sarah smiled, touched. "That means a lot to me. You're a great friend." It wasn't what he wanted to hear, she knew. But she said it anyway. Though she had tried, she felt no attraction for Michael. He felt like a friend. And she sure did need one now. She reached up and hugged him, laying her head on his shoulder.

Her father had told her time after time she was cursed for falling for the wrong guys. Sarah sighed. There was no doubt about it—the curse was holding strong.

❋ ❋ ❋ ❋ ❋ ❋

From the other end of the room, Jamie watched Sarah and Michael embrace and was filled with the overwhelming urge to break Michael Capitano's jaw. And Sarah... How could she be with that loser? How could she pretend there was nothing between them? He knew there was. And he knew that she knew it too. The feeling was too strong to be all in his head. Yet, there she was, acting as if she could care less if he were dead or alive. It wasn't as if he hadn't apologized every way humanly possible for not showing up for their date. He had called her every day that first week, sent her notes, tried to trap her in the hallways at school, even tried to get Amelia to plead his case. He knew he was in the wrong, but she was taking it too far. Had the girl never made a mistake? His friends had watched him practically humiliate himself over her. So in the end, he had decided to give up on the whole thing.

And then came Doogie's. He was sure she had been afraid for him that night. She had looked at him with real concern...and something else. He had really thought things would be different after that. But he had thought wrong. Sarah had been as distant as ever.

She wouldn't give him the time of day, no matter how hard he tried. And there she was, standing in a dark corner with Michael Capitano.

"Enough, Sarah Giannopoulos," he muttered to himself. "I'm done. No more playing the fool for you, trying to live up to your perfect expectations."

He walked over to his friends and put his arm around Charlotte. "Did you save a dance for me?" he asked her, with an easy grin.

Robby and Gaston exchanged surprised looks. Walt smiled broadly.

"You know I did." Charlotte smiled, wrapping her arm around his waist.

"Hey, Hughey! Play a slow one, will you?" Jamie said loudly, hoping his voice carried across the room. *Take that, Sarah.*

Hughey cranked up the music and pulled Hudson in for a dance. Couples started slow dancing and Jamie pulled Charlotte close. She buried her head into his neck, her fingers doing a slow dance of their own in his hair. As they moved to the music, Jamie glanced to where Sarah had been standing, and found her watching him. Their eyes locked briefly before she looked away. A slow ache began to build in his stomach and he loosened his hold on Charlotte. It was there, in Sarah's eyes. That same hard, unreadable expression he had seen on the day he had tried to explain missing their date to her.

What was he doing, dancing with Charlotte because of his stupid pride? He knew what he wanted, what he had wanted for weeks now. And it wasn't Charlotte. Everything felt upside down. Unable to stop himself, he looked again towards Sarah.

She was gone.

CHAPTER THIRTY-NINE

The rest of the night had been a blur for Jamie. He had looked for Sarah everywhere and just when he had come to the conclusion she had left, he found her in the living room with a small group of people. She was talking to Amelia, Michael, Hudson and a couple of other guys. Whatever the conversation was, the girls were in stitches. He watched Sarah laugh and realized once again she didn't care if he was there or not. She was enjoying herself and if he had any sense in his head, he should leave it alone. Jamie smiled. How many times had his mom complained that he had no sense at all?

Just do it. Go big or go home.

Putting his hands in his jeans pockets, he casually strode over to the group—and tried not to notice the awkward silence that greeted him. Or how quickly Sarah's laughter faded. He smiled, rocking back on his heels. "Hey, how's it going?"

"Hey, Jamie," Amelia spoke first, smiling, as she glanced sideways at Sarah. Jamie knew from past experience Sarah would not look his way. He turned towards her and tried hard not to notice there was not even a hint of a smile left on her face. "Can I talk to you for a minute?"

"Nope." Sarah's voice was hard—and her eyes angry.

Determined not to give up, Jamie turned to the others. "Would you guys give us a minute?" he asked again, more to Amelia than anyone else. Amelia nodded, taking Hudson's arm and nudging her forward. "Of course, no problem."

"Actually, Nelson, it *is* a problem." Michael put his arm around Sarah possessively, his voice anything but friendly. "Sarah is with me and she doesn't seem to want to talk to you. How about you save it for another time?"

"How about you get out of my face?" Jamie replied, taking his hands out of his pockets and moving closer to Michael.

"How about you make me?" Michael let his arm drop from around Sarah's shoulder.

"Okay, stop it," Sarah interrupted, stepping in between the two boys. "It's all right, Michael," she said with what she hoped looked like a convincing smile. The last thing she wanted was to cause another fight and Jamie be involved in it. "I'll just talk to him for a minute. It's no big deal."

But Michael wasn't moving. His nostrils flared as he stared Jamie down. Amelia gently touched his arm. "C'mon, Michael. Let's get something to drink."

Michael hesitated, but with one last glance at Sarah, he followed Amelia and the others. At the door, he turned. Sarah smiled reassuringly and waited until he was gone. Wearily, she turned her eyes to Jamie, bracing to hear what he had to say.

"Can we go outside?" Jamie struggled to reign in his angry feelings towards Michael. He was not sure what he was even mad at him about. He just was.

"Sure. Whatever you say." Jamie knew she was angry, too. And not at Michael. He motioned towards a door he knew led out to a balcony and followed her outside. The late November air was crisp. Sarah wrapped her sweater closely around her.

"Well, what's the matter, Jamie?" she asked with false cheeriness. Are they out of slow songs or are you just taking a breather?"

I danced with Charlotte to get you back for being here with Michael, he wanted to say. Instead, he took a deep breath and let it out slowly. *What am I even doing here?*

"Okay, hotshot, your minute's up. This truly has been fascinating, but how about I do us both a favor and just go back inside now." She started past him, but he grabbed her arm. Sarah yanked it free and turned to face him, her eyes spitting fire.

"Not yet, *Angel*." Sarah stiffened at the sarcastic use of the nickname she knew he had heard her father use. "Of course, you're going to make this hard because it's what you do. But tonight, the air needs clearing, so I'm going to clear it. I'm going to talk — and you're going to listen."

Sarah lifted her chin. "I guess somewhere between the crack on my personality and the rest of that ultimatum, I'm supposed to feel... intimidated?" She stressed the last word as if testing it out to see if it fit.

Jamie's eyes narrowed. All he wanted to do at that moment was shake the smugness out of her. It seemed all he did was try. And all she did was mock him. He leaned in closer, his face inches from hers. "I'll settle for you just feeling. I know why you do it, why you make it so hard, Sarah. It's your defense against what you can't control. It's how you protect yourself."

"What are you talking about?" Her voice trembled with anger. "How many beers has it been tonight, Jamie? Is that how you keep control? By losing it? Like you almost just lost it with Michael? Like you *lose track of time*?"

Jamie shrugged. "Exhibit A. There you go again."

"And just what, in your once-too-many concussed mind, is it that you think I can't control?"

"The way you feel about me."

Sarah's eyes filled with fire. "Jamie Nelson, you are the most arrogant..."

"Call me what you like," he interrupted angrily, grabbing her shoulders and pulling her even closer to him. "But your eyes, Sarah, tell me everything you won't."

As if to punish her, to shut her up, he kissed her.

Sarah barely heard those last words, as he whispered them harshly, completely caught up in the surprise of what was happening, and unable to react in time to stop him from covering her mouth with his. He kissed her, angrily, crushingly, and she fought him, her anger matching his. Furious, Sarah held her lips together and waited, thinking how hard she would slap him at the first opportune moment. But then, she felt his lips soften, and amazingly, her own respond. She couldn't think. She couldn't move. The warmth that overtook her was impossible to resist—and she didn't want it to end. Vaguely, she became aware of his arms dropping to her waist and her own arms circling around his neck, holding him to her, as if they had a will of their own.

Somehow, for whatever reason, it felt right. She had never before felt anything like what she felt in that moment, standing on that balcony in Jamie's arms. She wanted to stay there. Maybe forever. It was nothing like Jake... Like a lightning bolt, the memory jolted her back to reality. Jake, Charlotte, Walt, Jamie, the joke...

And this kiss...this kiss could even be part of it...

Sarah broke the kiss and pushed away from his arms. Shaken, she walked to the edge of the balcony, hugged her sweater tightly around her and tried to steady her breathing. She needed to think, to collect her thoughts and make sense of what had just happened, but the beating of her heart echoed too loudly in her head.

"Sarah..." Jamie was behind her, his breath warm in her hair. Sarah closed her eyes, thankful her back was to him. Even the way he said her name was unlike anyone else ever had. It sent chills down her spine.

"Why can't you just leave me alone, Jamie? You've had your fun. When is it enough for you?" She struggled for composure, but her traitorous voice trembled.

Jamie gripped her shoulders, gently turning her around to face him. He searched her face but she wouldn't look at him. "Sarah, what are you talking about? I know I screwed things up that damned Saturday but I've apologized for it again and again. That's not me playing games with you." His voice softened. "Call me crazy, but something happened between us a minute ago that was...I don't even know what to call it, except pretty epic. And it's been happening between us for a long time now. So, if you're waiting for me to say I'm sorry I kissed you, I won't. Because that would be the biggest lie I've ever told."

Sarah looked at him, as if in a spell. Their eyes locked for a long moment. Jamie let her go and stepped back. "I'm going to kiss you again if you look at me like that. God knows I want to, but we need to clear this up." He reached for her hand and intertwined his fingers with hers. "Talk to me, Sarah."

"Thank you for what you did at Doogie's". With her free hand, she reached up and touched the scar still healing above his eye. "I'll never forget it."

"You've already thanked me. Say you forgive me, Sarah."

Sarah couldn't stop the sigh that escaped her lips. She wanted to forgive him, that much she knew. But she was confused, her mind clouded with things she could not make sense of. Even worse, she wanted him to kiss her again. She pulled her hand from his and looked away. "For what?" she asked, softly. "The joke?"

"For screwing up our da...what joke?" Jamie sounded both confused and irritated. "Why can't you just let it go, Sarah? Why do you have to make things so hard? What joke are you talking about? And what does it have to do with us?"

Sarah eyes blazed with renewed anger. "Oh, like you don't know. Feel free to cut the act anytime now. *I* make things hard? Really? Well, here's me making things easy for you, James Nelson the third, or fourth—or whatever number you are: I know all about your little joke. That's right. The one where you and your buddies make bets to see if you can get the new girl to think you actually want to go out with her, then stand her up. *That* joke, Jamie. The one you think makes you really cool."

Jamie's hands dropped to his sides. The fire in her eyes and the weight of what she was saying threw him for a loop. "What? Sarah..."

"No. Don't say anything. You're smooth, Jamie. Really smooth. I mean, I don't know how you can be these two different people. The first time I met you, you were so nice. At Doogie's, you risked your life for

Nick and me. But when your boys are around, watch out. It's not like I didn't see it; I saw it. I'm no rookie when it comes to guys like you. I'm pretty sure now there's one of you at every high school. Still, you had me going. Like that meet you came to. That was beyond smooth. You caught me off balance and I admit, I couldn't figure you out. But, now I can, Jamie. I know why you asked me out in front of everyone. It worked like a charm and you had your fun. But guess what? I'm still standing. So maybe, just maybe, the joke's on you. You and those losers you call your *friends*." Breathing hard, Sarah lifted her chin and waited for the onslaught she knew was coming.

Jamie said nothing. He started to and then stopped. He simply could not make sense of what she was saying. *What joke?*

Sarah took his silence as proof of his surprise the gig was up. She felt vindicated, strong even. Arching an eyebrow, she smiled. "So, Jamie, I have only one question for you: Why the kiss tonight? Are your buddies hiding behind the curtains, looking out the window?" She strained to look past him. "When's the game over? You've won, you know." Bringing her eyes back to his, she stared at him coldly. "I bought it. I believed you. I was ready Saturday night and I waited for hours. Go tell your buddies that. Tell them I spent every last dime I had on a new outfit. Tell them to pay up, if they haven't already. When you asked me out at Walt's that night, I bought it, hook, line and sinker. Must have been quite the scene when I left. I bet you didn't stop laughing fo..."

"Enough, Sarah." Jamie's voice was hard, his eyes narrowing into slits. "Who told you this?"

Sarah batted her eyelashes. "Why, who else? Charlotte, your plastic cheerleader, bobblehead girlfriend. Wait, was she not supposed to? Too early? Was tonight *Part Two*? Whatever, I don't even care anymore. And I'm done talking about this. I'm going inside."

She started past him, exhausted, and yet, somehow relieved. She had gotten to say her piece and now it was over. Things made sense again. But Jamie grabbed her arm and stopped her. Exasperated, Sarah looked up at him. The tension in his face surprised her. His demeanor had changed from surprised to angry. He was practically glaring at her.

"Charlotte lied."

Sarah stared up at him and blinked. It was the last thing she had expected him to say.

"She lied to you, Sarah. There was never any joke. It's the truth, I swear it."

His arm dropped and Sarah stood there, trying to process what he had just said. His eyes were hard and unreadable, though his expression softened a bit. She looked away and tried to think. Could it really be the truth? Would Charlotte make up a story like that? Even worse, could she have fallen for it that easily? No, no. Charlotte had to have known she would find out. The whole thing was too outrageous to be a lie.

"I would never do that to a girl, Sarah." Jamie's voice broke through her thoughts. "I would never do that to you. Think about it. I know you haven't known me long, I know I can be a jerk sometimes. But I'm the guy who's been tripping all over himself trying to get a chance with you. Why would I do all that? Yeah, I came to the meet. I wanted to see you run because I think about you all the damn time. I followed you to Doogie's because I was worried and I still feel my stomach knot when I remember the way you tried to take those guys on with a stick. And I asked you out in front of everyone because I couldn't stop myself from doing it. *That* is the truth, Sarah."

Sarah closed her eyes. Her heart started kickboxing in her chest. She didn't want to believe him. She knew she shouldn't. And yet, she did.

"I know what I feel. And I know you feel it too. I saw it in your eyes that night at Doogie's. And again tonight. There's no way in hell either one of us faked that kiss." Jamie's voice softened and he lifted her chin. "Look at me, Sarah, and you'll know I'm telling you the truth. There was no joke. But there *is* a you and me. So, let's go back. Let's start over, this time without the bullshit. Because we started the minute you side-swiped me on your bike." His fingers gently stroked her chin and side of her face. "And then told me to watch where I was going even though you were totally in the wrong."

Sarah couldn't help but smile at both the memory and his words. Still, she shook her head and sighed, freeing her face from his touch. "We can't do that, Jamie. You have a way with words, with…everything, and you make things sound so simple, but the truth is, you and me, it would never work. I mean, look how much has happened already and we haven't even been on a first date!" She sat down in a patio chair. "We're just so different, you and I…" Her voice was almost a whisper.

"I don't think we're that different." Jamie pulled a chair close to hers and straddled it, facing her. He watched her guarded expression for a moment. Sarah looked at him, half-smiled and shrugged. She looked vulnerable and cute and he wanted to hug her. "How, Sarah? How are we so different?" he asked her, instead.

She raised an eyebrow. "How? Well, in every way that matters. You're this boy who grew up in a world that belonged to him, that had unending gifts waiting for him. And, as a result, you're so very gifted. And so very adored. That matters to you. As it should. I don't blame you for that. It's what you know, it's who you are."

Jamie opened his mouth to speak but Sarah quickly continued. "And me, I'm the daughter of two dreamers whose dream somehow kept getting away. As a result, I have to work for things, even little things. And they don't usually come with praise or adoration, Jamie. Life's hard when you're poor. My family survived one crisis after another but we did it. We survived, we're here. I love my family. But I'm a girl whose childhood wasn't easy—and you're right, I have built walls. I don't fit in your world. You've been raised to stay in the box, Jamie. My side of town is way outside your box. It is what it is."

Jamie watched her for a moment. Then he stood and pushed the chair back. Squatting down, he took both her hands in his. Looking into her brown eyes, he was amazed, like always, at how they had a life of their own. Gently, he brushed a stray strand of her hair back in place with his fingers. "So, you've got walls. And I live on Easy Street. Boxes are made of paper, they're easy to take apart. Walls are harder, I hear you. But they're a choice, too. People are different, Sarah. It's cool to be different. I like you. You're safe with me. Give me a chance to show you."

You're safe with me. The words echoed through Sarah's mind, reminding her of the past. It was all too much. She had been down this all too familiar road before. The memory of it was so fresh, it hurt. If Jamie only knew about her...Sarah sighed and shook free of his touch. There was no choice to be made. It was time to grow up, to think with her head instead of her heart. She stood and walked over to the railing, trying to ignore how much she already missed his hands holding hers.

"I believe you about the joke, Jamie. I want you to know that. But...I can't."

"Look at me and say that." His voice was quiet.

Sarah took a breath, resolved. She turned around and looked at him, ignoring the ache in her chest, determined to save herself this time. "I'm sorry, Jamie. I can't."

"You can, Sarah. What you mean is you won't."

"Hey, what are you crazy kids doing out here?" Hughey's loud voice boomed good-naturedly from behind them as he pushed the patio door open and stepped outside. His expression quickly sobered as he registered the tension in the air. He looked from Jamie to Sarah, awkwardly. "Uh, Jamie, they're waiting for you to play inside, man, but if you're busy, it's cool."

"No, it's fine. I have to go," Sarah said, walking past Jamie without looking at him.

"Hey, sorry if I interrupted," Hughey said, still looking from one to the other.

"No worries," Sarah said, stopping to give him a quick hug before she walked into the house. "You throw a great party, Hughey. See ya at school."

Jamie heard them exchange goodbyes but didn't say a word. He didn't try to stop her. His feet were glued where he stood, as if he were frozen. Again. He had pretty much just opened his heart to her. And she had turned him down. He couldn't believe it. Why was she so scared? What joke had she been talking about? Would Charlotte even do something like that? Was it made up? None of it made any sense.

Tonight had been the moment he had been waiting for. When it had just been the two of them, it had felt right, just as he had somehow known it would, from the first time he met her. And she had felt it, too. That much he was sure of. He thought of the fire in her eyes when she had been angry with him, and the way her body melted against his when he had kissed her. She had fit in his arms like a puzzle piece snapped into place to finish a picture. She couldn't react that way and not be into him. Something was holding her back. And it was more than some made-up joke.

"Uh, Jamie," Hughey stammered uncomfortably, still standing in the doorway, "you ready to play, man? It's getting late, but there's still time. The guys are waiting for ya. What do you want me to tell them?"

His words snapped Jamie out of his stupor.

There's still time.

Hughey was right! Sarah wasn't gone yet. There was still time.

He grinned at Hughey, as he rushed by him. "I'm ready. Let's go."

CHAPTER FORTY

Hughey had to walk fast to keep up with Jamie. They ran into Robby as Jamie maneuvered his way through the crowded room. "Wrong way, buddy," Jamie said, grabbing his friend by the shirt and pulling him along. Robby looked back at Hughey, who shrugged his shoulders and threw his hands up in the air. His expression said: *Don't look at me. I got no idea.*

They reached the spot where the band had set up and still Jamie spoke to no one. Strapping his guitar over his shoulder, he used his free hand to adjust the microphone in front of him. He looked over his shoulder and grinned at Gaston, already on the drums. Gaston grinned back. "Where you been, dog?"

"Sorry. Okay, listen." He spoke loudly so Robby and Walt could hear him as they strapped their guitars on. "Just follow my lead on this one. Remember that Rick Springfield song from his album *Hard To Hold* that Hillary was into during her '80s song phase? It's called 'Don't Walk Away.' We had just gotten the band together. Remember how we played it for her birthday?"

"Yep," Gaston replied.

"No," Walt chimed in. "Come on, man. Let's do what we're good at."

"Lighten up, Walt. You liked it as much as Hillary. Follow my lead. It will come back to you."

"I said no. That was ages ago. Why play a song we haven't practiced?"

"This crowd will like it, trust me. Let's go. I'll lead you in."

"I got you, man, let's play." Gaston hit the drums, in warm-up, and the room exploded in cheers.

Robby leaned close to Jamie. "You sure you know what you're doing?"

"Yeah, I think so. You got my back, buddy?"

Robby nodded. "Always."

Jamie smiled, grabbed the microphone and clicked it on. "Hey everybody, thanks for waiting on us. We're going to try something a little different tonight. Because different is good, right?" The room exploded in cheers again. Jamie waited a moment for them to die down.

His fingers began to play the familiar tune Hillary had loved years ago. His only hope was she was still in that room. The words, words he had not until that moment known he even remembered, filled his consciousness and poured out, one by one. His voice was steady, strong and resolved to be heard. By her.

I know just what you're doing, you don't want to put the hurt on someone.
You keep trying to convince yourself, you're better off if you just turn and run.
But I'm gonna hold on tight, I've got a feeling
You'll only happen once to me,
And no one, not even you, is ever gonna make you wrong for me.
Don't walk away,
Or are you looking for a price to pay,
Is that your master plan?
Don't walk away.
I'll do anything to make you stay.
I've got to make a stand.
Don't walk away.
I'm not afraid.
Don't walk away.

Jamie played his guitar, lost in the moment, oblivious to the hush of the room and his captivated audience. Robby held a hand up and Walt and Gaston paused, letting all the music come from him. Jamie didn't notice. He played on, his soul strumming through his fingers into the room—and into the message he was trying to get to Sarah.

You used to be the one
Who used to be so strong.
What happened to your rationale?
Your heart is on the line,
It happens all the time...
Don't walk away.
I'm not afraid.
Don't walk away.

He finished to a thunder of applause. Turning to Robby and Walt, the three strummed their guitars in unison, and Gaston unleashed a vicious drum finale. Robby held out his fist and Jamie met it with his own. Walt nodded, smiling. Jamie smiled back. Gaston finished and bowed his head, sticks high in the air. The room went wild. The sound was deafening. They loved it.

Looking into the crowd, Jamie searched for her. And she was there, standing next to Michael, clapping. Unavoidably, their eyes locked. Jamie felt the breath catch in his chest in an incredible rush of feeling for her. He blinked, trying to steady his breathing, and see her more clearly. It was then he saw her eyes were filled with tears. He smiled over the chaos of noise, wanting to comfort her, to make her understand everything would be all right.

She smiled back at him. Jamie drank it in, hoping it meant what he hoped it did. He cocked an eyebrow in question, knowing she would understand. Sarah stopped clapping, rested her chin into her still clasped hands and nodded slowly.

Jamie felt a wave of relief and excitement wash over him. It was finally going to happen. She was giving him another chance. His smile became huge and he laughed out loud. "Thank you," he said into the mike, and the crowd roared anew.

But his eyes stayed on Sarah. And she knew the words were meant for her.

CHAPTER FORTY-ONE

"You okay?" Jamie's voice was tender. Sarah smiled. She loved the tone of his voice when they were alone. They were in his car, driving to Robby's house for a party.

It had been three weeks since the night at Hughey's—and they had been going out ever since. Jamie picked Nick and her up every morning for school, walked her to what classes he could and spent his free period with her, since they had the same one. Lunch, they ate separately. Sarah told him this was a good thing because they needed their space and time to spend with their friends. After school, they would wait for one another to finish practice—Sarah was practicing for track and Jamie had started basketball season. After that, Sarah would rush to work at Steve's. Jamie would often come by after her shift was over and they would do homework together. On weekends, they would go to dinner after the games, or maybe to a movie.

Initially, Sarah had been concerned about her father's reaction to Jamie. After all, his own memories of Jake couldn't be too far behind. She had been pleasantly surprised on the night of their first dinner date. Andreas had been civil. After eyeing Jamie silently for several minutes, he had even smiled.

"Your eye healed up well," Andreas had told him.

"Yes, sir," Jamie had replied, respectfully.

"Have her back here before midnight." The smile was gone.

"Yes, sir."

It had been Sarah's turn to smile. She knew her father was trying. And she knew Jamie had not forgotten her father's swift actions at Doogie's. He had nodded in agreement when Sarah told him he would need to pick her up and drop her back at Steve's, not her house. Sarah had almost gotten the feeling he had been glad there were other people around. She giggled a bit at the memory. When they had lived in New York, she used to get upset over her father's many rules. Now, she understood him better. He had good reason to worry. She still complained about his over-protectiveness and gruff manner. But she knew he only wanted safety and happiness for Nick and her. After all, the two of them were all he had left in the world. She loved them both so much.

Andreas had sensed her need for his approval of Jamie. And he did like him, Sarah thought. For one thing—and it was a big one—he had come to the aid of Niko and herself with little concern for his own safety. Still, her dad always started mumbling on the nights Jamie would come to study with her after her shift was over.

"That boy is here *again,*" he would scowl. "Why does he have to come here so much? Maybe to get away from his overbearing mother? I don't know how the doctor deals with that woman. Does she even feed her boy? He's bone thin."

"Μπαμπα...if you can't say something nice..." Sarah would pause, "... you must be talking about Daisy Nelson." And the two of them would laugh. That was when he was in a good mood. When he wasn't, Jamie would walk in the door and Andreas would pull her in the kitchen. "Have you finished your homework? I don't like *that boy* coming here on weeknights," he would tell her at a near yell.

"We're studying together. If you want, we can go back to the house where it's more...quiet." Andreas would either growl and walk away or half-smile. Sarah knew he loved her wit. He had told her many times how much it reminded him of her mother.

But always, no matter what his mood, he would make sure Jamie heard him tell Sarah, "I'm not sure about *that boy*. I'm watching him." Then he would narrow his eyes at Jamie, yell at somebody about something, and disappear into the kitchen.

Nick was another story altogether. He made no secret of his admiration for Sarah's new boyfriend. He gave anything Jamie said his complete attention. Sarah appreciated the way Jamie would patiently listen to her little brother's stories. She loved the serious expression he wore when he was focused on something, whether it was listening to Nick, playing sports or studying. Sometimes, he would sense her watching him, look up, grin and wink at her before turning his attention to whatever he was doing. Every time he did it, she felt a tingle all the way to her toes. There was no doubt in her mind: Jamie Nelson could win anybody over. Even Andreas Giannopoulos.

"You okay, Sarah?" Jamie repeated, pulling her from her thoughts. Taking her hand, he pulled her towards him. "Where are you, baby?" he asked, with a hint of a smile.

Sarah shrugged. "I was just thinking. I guess I'm a little nervous tonight," she admitted.

Jamie parked the car, unbuckled his seatbelt and turned to her. "Sarah, if you don't feel comfortable, we don't have to go in. It's no big deal. We can just go see a movie or something."

"Ha, ha, I think we've seen them all. No, I want you to hang out with your friends. I like Robby, I really do." Sarah smiled and tried to sound convincing. "I mean of all your friends, he's the most…the most…likable."

Jamie laughed. "Okay, listen. I know you don't have a very high opinion of my friends but they will grow on you. Trust me, they're cool. And they like you."

"Ha. Ha. Ha." Sarah smiled at him, amused.

Jamie smiled too. "Well, they do." He pulled her closer to him. "But you should know it's only because you're seriously hot. It's true they have limited appreciation for other qualities."

Sarah giggled. "But you do. You like me for my mind."

"Yes, ma'am, I sure do." Jamie cupped her face in his hands and brought her lips to his, brushing them softly, as though he was kissing her for the first time. Sarah melted into him, wrapping her arms around his neck, encouraging him to deepen the kiss, which he did with an urgency that thrilled her. She felt excitement take over every part of her body, the intensity of it so great, she almost could not breathe.

Jamie felt it, too. Reluctantly, he parted his mouth from hers, pulling her into his chest. He held her, waiting for his ragged breathing to return to normal. It amazed him, the effect Sarah had on him.

For some reason, Andreas flashed through his mind. He thought about the intimidating man's watchful eye where his daughter was concerned. Surprisingly, he didn't find it annoying, but perfectly natural.

Because what mattered to Andreas was now the same thing that mattered to him: Sarah's happiness.

CHAPTER FORTY-TWO

Robby's living room was full of people. It was so cramped, Sarah and Jamie could barely move through the crowd. Jamie held her hand and led the way. "I don't see the guys anywhere," he said loudly to her, above the noise. Sarah nodded in response. She didn't see Amelia or Hudson, either.

Jamie slid open a porch door and led them outside, where thankfully there was room to move. It was a cold December night, but the fresh air was a welcome respite for both of them. Sarah leaned over the railing and looked down. Jamie put his arm around her. "Don't jump, baby, I'd have to come after you."

Sarah laughed and snuggled close to him.

"Cold?" he muttered into her hair, kissing the top of her head.

She looked up at him. "Not now." She kissed him quickly, then turned with her back against his chest. Jamie's arms came around her. "I wanted to show you the lake. I have always loved the way it looks from here at night. The land around the house is like a hundred acres. Robby and I have explored every bit of it. Some of my best memories are on this lake." He nuzzled her cheek, chuckling. "Robby broke his finger swinging on that tire swing in the seventh grade, right before basketball tryouts. We were devastated. We cried like little girls. It was the end of the world, we were sure of it."

"Aw, did he not get to try out?"

"Nope. But his parents took him to the NBA finals and I got to go."

Sarah laughed. "Classic rich kid probs. Of course they did."

"Be nice. The finals were awesome that year."

"I'm sure they were. I can see you now. Bet you took a private plane."

Jamie was silent. Sarah turned around in his arms and looked at him, her eyes wide. "Oh my gosh, Jamie Nelson, you seriously took a private plane?"

Jamie tightened his arms around her and pulled her face close to his. "Company plane. Not my company." He grinned at her. "Bet you wanna kiss me right now."

Sarah smiled. "Really? What makes you think so?"

"'Cause you're imagining what a cute kid I was with my face plastered on the window, all excited to be going to the big game."

She rolled her eyes. "On your sexy, private plane."

"Hey, it had a window and my face was plastered on it."

Sarah laughed and kissed him playfully on the cheek before turning back around in his arms. "I bet that was pretty awesome. And I bet you had tons of fun growing up here. I love land like this, endless with lakes, hills and mountains. It's so beautiful. Six months ago, I was dreading leaving New York. Now, I'm so glad I did."

Jamie nuzzled her hair. "'Cause of me, right?"

Sarah smiled. "'Cause of the open land, the mountains and the lakes, weren't you listening?" she teased.

"I was. What about the hills? You said hills, too."

"Hills are the best because they're fun to run over."

Jamie nibbled at her ear. "Hmm. So, it's all topography for you? What about me?"

Sarah laughed, feeling the tingling in her toes again, as he pressed small, soft kisses on her cheek. "Well, the mountains and land and hills are pretty impressive. They turn the land into a tapestry of color and texture. And you're just a guy in high school who plays football and basketball and flies around on private planes, so..."

"Company plane. You forgot the lakes, they're way better than hills, by the way." Jamie kissed her throat. "Because the water feels amazing on your skin."

"You think so?" Sarah was beginning to have a hard time concentrating.

"Definitely. Also, I play soccer."

Sarah rolled her eyes. "Yes, of course you do. I bet you're a defender. Your head is so big, I bet no one heads the ball like you do."

Jamie chuckled. "Forward. MVP last two seasons, but let's get back to why you like it here."

Sarah laughed. "Now that would be impressive if I didn't suspect you got a personal trainer when you were two." She heard Jamie chuckle again. He rested his head on hers and hugged her tight.

"So I'm really not even a little bit of the reason you like it here?" he asked, his voice purposefully adorable.

Sarah smiled. "Well, since you do play the guitar *and* have been known to sing a heck of a good song to the girl of your dreams, at the risk of making that big head of yours even bigger, yeah, I guess I like it here because of you, too."

"Thanks, baby. Don't worry, my head doesn't feel any bigger."

"That's good news." Sarah giggled, happily. For a moment, they were silent, watching the moonlight reflect on the gentle ripples of the lake below.

Jamie nuzzled her hair. "The girl of my dreams, huh?"

Sarah heard the smile in his voice. She felt her cheeks redden, embarrassed by her own teasing, annoyed with herself for having said such a stupid thing.

"I was joking...I didn't mean me..."

"Sarah," Jamie interrupted, his voice barely a whisper against her ear, "sometimes, when you look at me I forget where I am and what I'm doing. I pray you're not a dream, that's how perfect you are to me."

Sarah felt her heart skip a beat. She turned around in his arms, and as they kissed, on that corner of Robby's deck, it felt to her as if they were the only two people in the world.

Of course, they weren't. Charlotte was there, too. And she was watching them.

CHAPTER FORTY-THREE

There was definitely more than the topography Sarah had come to love about living in a small southern town in North Carolina. Time Out was one. The place was a dive but never in her life had she tasted better fried chicken biscuits. She was looking forward to repeating the experience as she pushed her menu aside and smiled across the booth at Hudson. Next to her, Amelia sighed contentedly.

"What are you getting?" Amelia asked, perusing the menu.

Sarah laughed. "The same thing I always get. For that matter, the same thing you always get, so why you obsess over the menu every time we come here is one of life's great mysteries."

Hudson didn't look up. "How you two eat like you do is one of life's great mysteries. I mean, it's two in the afternoon. Y'all are ordering a meal. And y'all look like you do. I really hate you both, I don't even know why I hang out with y'all."

"Stop fishing for compliments," Sarah said, smiling. "You're the pretty one and you know it."

"Pshh," Hudson replied, closing her menu. "Pleasantly plump is what I am, my own mother can't deny it. All because I was born with a bad metabolism. So not fair."

"Actually, it's because you won't join the track team, babe. Spend half the day running, and eat anything you want," Amelia said, still reading the menu.

"That's funny, Amelia. You know these chubby legs don't run. Whatever, but one day, maybe even today, some hot guy will walk through these doors, take one look at how much there is to love and fall desperately and completely in love with me."

Amelia peered over the menu at her, trying not to smile. "Today? Do you think it could really be today? Because if you do, I have make-up you can use. At the very least, some lip gloss?"

Hudson made a face, snatched the menu from her and sat on it.

Sarah busted out laughing at their antics. "Rough crowd," she teased, reaching across the table to give Hudson a hug. "Huddy, you're gorgeous. The hot guy is a sure thing, with or without lip gloss."

"Oh yeah, no doubt. You are gorgeous—but I'm still going to have to tell your *hot guy* what a baby you are," Amelia said, getting up from her seat next to Sarah and squeezing in on the opposite side with Hudson. "Here comes a hot guy, but he's already Sarah's," she explained, as she pushed Hudson over and reclaimed her menu.

Jamie walked up, pulled off his baseball hat and slid in the booth next to Sarah. "How did I know you'd be here? Eating again?" he asked her, grinning.

"Nah, Hudson was hungry," Sarah said matter-of-factly. Another menu came flying from across the table. Sarah caught it, laughing.

"That's it!" Hudson said, pushing Amelia. "Let me out."

"No way. In case you have already forgotten, we are waiting for your hot guy to make his entrance. And don't worry, love. When he gets here, I promise to let you out so you can wow him with your sexy walk." Amelia couldn't stop the laughter from bubbling out of her. Neither could Sarah. Hudson shook her head and looked at Jamie.

"They're hostile because they're so skinny," she whispered loudly, as if they couldn't hear her. "All that running makes them just plain hangry."

Jamie let out a whistle and smiled. "Rough crowd today."

Sarah linked her arm through his. "That's what I said. We're so in sync, baby." She noticed Robby, Walt and Gaston sitting at the counter. "What are y'all up to?"

"Just hanging out. We had Charlie Wood come out and watch us rehearse today. He helped us with a song Gaston wrote. Mr. Wood thinks it has a shot at being recorded. He says he's going to get Gaston in touch an agent and see what happens."

"What? Jamie, that's awesome!" Amelia said, clearly impressed.

"Wow," Hudson echoed. "That's really cool, Jamie."

Sarah dropped her head into the palm of her hand and eyed him sideways. "Imagine, girls," she cooed in her best Southern accent, "I'll be *datin'* a real *stahr*."

Jamie laughed. "You're such a nerd," he said, knocking her hand out from under her head. For a moment, he looked at her. Sarah smiled and batted her eyes. Grinning, he leaned over and whispered in her ear, "Bet you wanna kiss me right now."

Sarah laughed. Turning, she whispered in his, "And yet, I'll control myself."

"I don't think you can."

She straightened. "Self-aware, aren't ya?"

"Whatever, I roll big style and you're into it." He winked at her.

"Did you say *Big Style*?" Sarah tried not to smile.

Jamie grinned. "Yep."

Laughter bubbled out of her. Jamie pulled her close, taking her hand in his. He smiled at Hudson and Amelia. "Sorry about that, ladies, I can't seem to keep her off of me." He winced as her elbow connected with his rib. "But thanks. For real though, I don't know if we want to do that. Honestly, we're not good enough and besides, we're all going to college in the fall. I mean the band has always been just for fun, that's all."

"What would it hurt to let an agent hear it?" Sarah asked him, her expression becoming thoughtful. "I think you should, *Big Style*."

"Yeah, so you could have a reason to dump me because your dad would never let you date a rock and roll dude."

"Rock and roll dude? Dude, I thought you were talking about being a recording artist," she corrected.

Jamie laughed and yanked on her hand, causing her to lean into him. "I think I'll stick to law and let you draft my arguments," he told her, his face inches from hers.

"Up to you, but that's gonna cost ya. I would charge by the minute." Sarah patted him on the chest. "Better be a rock and roll dude on the side, so you can afford me."

"I'll do it for free, Jamie," Hudson offered, with a smile. "And you won't have to deal with a hangry person."

Jamie laughed. "Thanks, Hudson. That's a deal. And no worries, the pay will be more than generous." He winked at her. "Seven years from now. You and me."

"What about *hot guy*?" Amelia asked.

Hudson shrugged. "He's late. I have struck my deal and there's no turning back now."

The foursome was still laughing when Jamie stood, pulling Sarah's arm. "Come with me a minute. I need to talk to you about something."

"You two stay put," Amelia said quickly, getting up and pulling Hudson with her. "We're going to the bathroom. Huddie needs make-up before the love of her life walks through that door." Hudson rolled her eyes and followed, mumbling.

"I'll order the usual for you," Sarah called after them, laughing. She waited for Jamie to sit back down. "So what do you need to tell me that you couldn't say in front of them?" she asked him. "Careful, you know I'm a good girl..."

"I know, I know, that's why I have *those* conversations with you only in my mind." Jamie laughed as he watched her eyes go wide. "No, seriously, I was looking for you to tell you we just got tickets for tonight to the Hornets-Lakers game in Charlotte. Gaston's dad got them and we're taking off in a few minutes. So, we can't go to dinner tonight but I'll come by Steve's when we get back, around eleven or so."

"I'm not working tonight, *Jamie*."

Jamie did not miss the way she stressed his name. "Uh-oh. You're mad." Sarah said nothing, and he continued, more carefully, "I know you're not working, but I thought you might hang out there and wait for me so we can see each other."

"Well, I can't." Sarah crossed her arms over her chest and glared at him.

"Okay." Jamie tried not to smile, but failed.

"What are you smiling about?" Sarah asked him, her eyes, it seemed to him, changing color. "Did I say something funny?"

Jamie tried to look serious, but failed again. He reached for her hand. She pulled it away. "Okay, Sarah, no, nothing is funny, except you look like my sister when she's seriously ticked at me and…it's obvious you are seriously ticked at me." He brought his face closer to hers and lowered his voice. "Is this our first fight, baby? C'mon, don't be mad. I'll only be late, we'll still see each other."

"No need to rush back, we're seeing each other right now."

"C'mon, Sarah, lighten up. It's not a big deal, I'll just be a few hours late. These tickets are hard to get."

"Oh, I know they are." Her eyes had taken on that unreadable expression that was uniquely hers. "For most people."

Jamie's brows came together. "You know how much I love basketball. It's the Lakers. I'll come by Steve's when I get back, or to your house, if you want."

"I don't want. Not tonight." Sarah unfolded her arms, pulled her phone out of her purse and began to scroll through it. "Have fun," she added, without looking up.

For a moment, Jamie watched her. "Really, Sarah? What, you're dismissing me? Seriously? You're mad because I have the chance to go to an NBA game with my friends? I can't believe you're acting like this. I would never get mad at you for that." His voice was loud enough for Walt to look over at them.

Sarah put down her phone and faced him. "Really? Seriously?" she mimicked. "You can't believe it?" Purposefully, she kept her voice low. "Maybe that's because you don't have to beg to get the night off like I do, Jamie. You're ditching me because something better came up and you want me to be your booty call when you're done?" She picked her phone up again. "Well, prepare to be disappointed. I won't be. And yes, I'm mad." She looked past him and waved at Walt, who quickly looked away.

"So, let me make sure I have this straight. You are telling me I can't hang out with my friends." Jamie's voice was angry.

Sarah didn't look up. "No, that's what you heard, not what I said. I said don't ditch me whenever something better comes up and expect me to be available."

"I'm not doing that, Sarah. This isn't something better, it's a pro-basketball game," he practically growled.

Sarah shook her head and looked at him again. "Okay, this is getting us straight to nowhere. I've got the night off, Jamie, and I'm not going to stay home or be at Steve's waiting for you. I'm going to enjoy it."

"What the hell does that mean?" His nostrils were flaring.

Sarah's eyes flashed defiantly at his angry ones. "It means I'm going out."

"And that's it?"

Sarah shrugged. She could see how angry he was but she didn't care. Strangely, she felt calm. "I want you to hang out with your friends, Jamie. And I don't want you to miss seeing the Lakers play. But I am not going to be the little girlfriend who's hanging around when you decide you have time for her. I don't want to be that girl. You changed the plans, that's your choice. Now I'm changing mine. I'm going out with the girls and then I'm calling it a night. I'm sorry you're mad, but it's how I feel."

He surprised her by getting up and walking away without responding. Just like that, Sarah was angry again. She felt her eyes fill with tears.

"What the..." Amelia began, as she and Hudson slid back into the booth. She stopped short when Sarah held one hand up, the other wiping away a tear. "I cannot believe I'm crying right now. I never cry. What is wrong with me?"

"It's okay, sweetie," Amelia said, noticing the angry expression on Jamie's face, at the counter with his friends. "You're not crying, you're trying not to. Let's go."

Sarah nodded, keeping her head down. Hudson leaned closer. "Whatever it is, Sarah, you'll fix it when you go out tonight. Wait 'til he sees you in that red dress."

Sarah shook her head. "We're not going out tonight. He's changed his plans. He's going to Charlotte to watch the Lakers play the Hornets with his buddies." She looked up, her misty eyes flashing with anger. "That's the second dress I blew all my paycheck on for nothing. I guess I should be grateful he let me know beforehand this time."

Amelia and Hudson exchanged worried glances. "Let's go," Amelia said again, grabbing her coat. "We'll get sundaes at Three Spoons."

Sarah nodded, careful to avoid looking in Jamie's direction, as she busied herself getting her coat on. She followed Amelia and Hudson outside. The cold December air hit her like a welcome friend and she gulped it in.

"Sarah. Wait up," Jamie's voice came from behind them.

Amelia smiled supportively at Sarah and linked her arm through Hudson's. "We'll just walk ahead and wait for you," she said gently. "See ya, Jamie."

"Yeah, thanks, see y'all," he replied.

Sarah shoved her hands in her coat pockets for warmth and exhaled. She turned and looked at Jamie, expecting more angry words, but he was staring at something past her shoulder. Surprised, she turned to follow his eyes. She saw nothing there.

"I got rid of my ticket," he said, his voice strange.

Sarah sighed. "Jamie, that's not what I..."

"I know it's not about the ticket now, Sarah," he interrupted, locking his eyes on hers. "I just wanted you to know I got rid of it."

"What do..."

"I mean what does it matter," he continued, as if she hadn't spoken. "No fun with the ticket, no fun without it."

"Well, I think you should just go to the..."

"The point is, this is all new to me, Sarah."

Sarah blinked. She opened her mouth to speak, but thought better of it and closed it again, waiting to see if he would continue. He didn't. Instead, he watched her in silence. Sarah felt a shiver go through her—and she didn't think it was the cold. "What are we talking about here, Jamie?" she finally asked, her voice quiet.

He shrugged. "Honestly, I don't even know," he said, just as quietly. Sarah watched him take his hands out of his jean pockets, cross his arms across his chest and lean back on his heels, all the while watching her. "That's just it," he said. "I don't know. I've had this same fight before. I love basketball. I like hanging out with my friends. But I broke our date, so you had a right to get mad. I should have realized you would."

"Jamie, it isn't one or the other; me or your..."

"No, no, I know that. That's not what I'm saying, Sarah. What I'm saying is I got kicked in the gut in there. Yeah, that's it...it feels like a football hit me in the gut when I wasn't expecting it. Except there's no ball."

Sarah shook her head. "I don't understand." She wanted to say more but her mind was trying to catch up. Jamie wasn't acting like Jamie at all.

Jamie nodded. "Yeah. Like I said, me neither. I guess I just wanted you to know. Have fun tonight with...whatever you do. I'll see you around."

With that, he pivoted on his heels and walked back inside. Sarah stood and watched him for a moment, then turned and began to walk towards her friends. She wanted to run. For the second time that hour, she felt tears stinging at the corners of her eyes.

What just happened? Did he just break up with me?

She practically ran into Amelia and Hudson as she rounded the street corner.

"What was that all about?" they both asked in unison.

Sarah blinked back tears. "I have no idea."

Amelia linked her arm through Sarah's and the trio started walking. "What do you mean?" she asked her friend gently. "Is he going to the game or not?"

"Not. But his gut hurts because a loose football hit it. Except there was no ball." Sarah knew the words made little sense. "He didn't let me get a word in. He said...he said he'd see me around."

Amelia and Hudson were silent. Sarah tried to clear her head as they walked. She felt her body shiver again and hugged her coat more tightly against her.

Jamie had not expected me to be angry. He said he'd been through all that before. Does he think I'm possessive? I want him to be with his friends, he knows that.

"I shouldn't have said anything," she mumbled out loud. "I should have just let him go and talked to him about it when he got back. He loves basketball." She shook her head, even as she finished the sentence. "But it's like the third time he's broken a date for whatever reason. It's not easy for me to get off work, he knows that. It just makes me mad."

"That's because it should," Hudson said.

"Yeah, you did the right thing," Amelia agreed.

Sarah sighed. "He's mad, too. He didn't expect that from me."

"And he will get over it, " Amelia said, stubbornly. "I'll bet he wouldn't like it if you did that to him."

Sarah thought that over for a minute. "You know, honestly, I don't think he'd mind. He just kind of goes with the flow." She sighed again. "Unlike me. Maybe I'm wound up too tight, like Niko always tells me."

"Well, yeah, but you don't want to be a pushover," Amelia insisted. "No way, Sarah, you totally did the right thing. You were honest. That's never wrong."

Sarah couldn't argue with that. They walked in silence the rest of the way. "Do you guys think he just broke up with me?" she asked, as they walked into Three Spoons.

"Over this? No way," Amelia told her as she led the way to a booth by the window. "But I think you need to think the conversation over." She slid into the booth first. "To tell you the truth, I don't get what you guys talked about—at all."

"That makes two of us." Sarah sighed and slid into the opposite side.

"Well, ladies, chocolate fixes everything. Let's order some and figure this out." Hudson smiled and slid in next to Sarah. "Like the Three Musketeers we are."

Sarah smiled back, glad for her friends. "Thanks, you guys. Maybe we should let it sit for a little while. Let's talk about you, Huddie."

"From confusion to boredom..." Hudson lamented, dropping her face into her hands. "Didn't we just go through this?"

Sarah and Amelia laughed. "Aw c'mon. It's almost Christmas. The most magical time of year. You still talking to Hughey? Or is it just Reed now?" Sarah asked, glad for a moment to not think about Jamie and what had just happened between them.

"Just Reed. Here and there. He says he's bad at communicating."

"He communicated pretty well at Robby's over Thanksgiving break," Amelia pointed out, smiling.

Hudson groaned. "I know, right? He's so hot and he knows I like him. We talked forever that night. I told him Hughey and I are just friends. And then, nothing."

"Maybe he's overwhelmed by the hotness of that kiss you laid on him," Sarah said.

Hudson dropped her head back into her hands. "Yeah, that's the even worst part. A kiss like that, and then, nothing."

"Like she said," Amelia motioned towards Sarah, "it's almost that magical time of year...bet he asks you to prom."

Hudson perked up. "Do you think so? Should I do anything to encourage him? I've never texted him first. Should I?"

Sarah's mind wandered back to Jamie at the thought of the prom. What had happened earlier? Amelia was right. If she had pretended not to be upset, she would be a fake and a pushover. Maybe that's what Jamie was used to, but she had to stand her ground. He needed to understand how she was before they got too involved. Maybe he had realized it today. Maybe that's what he had meant when he said he had been kicked in the gut. Maybe he had realized she wasn't going to be as low maintenance as he wanted.

Well, he'll just have to get over it. I refuse to be the little girlfriend that caters to his whims and is waiting around when he has nothing better to do.

She tried to focus on what Amelia and Hudson were saying but she kept seeing Jamie's face and remembering his distant expression. For some reason, she felt lonely. She had no idea why. Sarah took a deep breath and forced her mind to go blank. She wasn't getting anywhere with her problems. Maybe she could help Hudson with hers.

⁂ ⁂ ⁂ ⁂ ⁂ ⁂

Jamie walked along Main Street, barely noticing the crowd of people around him. He nodded absentmindedly as Santa went by in his sleigh, heartily wishing everyone a Merry Christmas. He was buried deep in his thoughts, the main one being why he didn't care his best friends were well on their way to watch his favorite basketball team play without him. Instead, all he saw in every cheerfully decorated window was Sarah.

He wasn't sure how he felt about that. He'd been through his share of girlfriends, never sticking with one too long, starting with the first grade. Three had fought over him that year, and he had agreed to be the boyfriend of all three. He smiled a little at the memory. He still remembered them running to him after recess so they could hold his hand on the walk back to class. The one left out would pout all the way. Since then, he had come to the conclusion girls were going to be difficult, but well worth the effort.

And he was proven right. Not that he minded, he actually liked the challenge. Of all the girls he had gone out with, Charlotte had been the hardest to win. She had always had an older boyfriend and he had wanted to date her since middle school.

But that was all before Sarah. What had she done to him? She was all he thought about. Sometimes he would lose focus around her. That had never happened before. His friends thought he was nuts to be into her, especially when he could have Charlotte. That had never happened before, either. Everyone had always followed his every lead. But now? Not so much. And to top it all off, Sarah didn't think twice about putting him in his place. It didn't seem to matter to her at all that he was the most popular guy at school. That had definitely never happened before.

"Hey, man, watch your step! Hell, you've ruined it."

Jamie snapped out of his thoughts and looked down. He had stepped on a large piece of paper with charcoal artwork he quickly recognized as the ice skating rink across the street. He stepped back and picked the paper up, trying to dust off his shoe print. "I'm sorry, sir. But hey, it's coming off." He handed the sheet to the irate man, then glanced over at the real thing. "That's pretty good."

"It was." The artist, a man who looked to be in his late twenties, snatched his work and blew on it. Glaring briefly at Jamie, he laid the paper under his chair and resumed sketching. Jamie glanced down and saw he was drawing Three Spoons, festive and filled with happy diners. Impressed, he looked to the shoppe to compare the likeness when his eye caught a familiar form inside. He squinted to see better in the evening light.

There was Sarah, her head thrown back in laughter at something Amelia and Hudson were saying. Jamie dug his hands in his pockets and smiled. She was doing the talking now, waving her hands as she talked, sending the other two into a fit of laughter.

That's my girl...

And that's when it hit him. Just like that, he understood. The smile faded and his pulse quickened with the realization he had just made. He stood unmoving, watching her.

"Dude, are you gonna stare at those girls all night?" the artist asked, without looking up. He had the most monotone voice Jamie had ever heard.

Jamie stared down at him. The artist looked up. "Seriously, kid, you're weirding me out."

Jamie shook his head as if to clear it. "Sorry, man, it's all good. That's my girlfriend." He motioned to a box of blank white paper by the chair. "Hey, can I borrow one of those? And a pencil?"

The artist rolled his eyes. "If you're gonna write on it, you're not borrowing it, just to be clear." He reached down, grabbed a piece of paper and a pencil and shoved them towards him.

Jamie tried not to smile. "I'll just borrow the pencil then, thanks." The artist rolled his eyes again, waved him off and resumed his work.

Jamie crossed the street and walked towards the soda shoppe window where Sarah was sitting. Amelia spotted him first. She motioned to Sarah, who was still laughing when she turned and saw him. Jamie stopped in front of her and grinned. Sarah held her hand up and waved, her eyes curious. She noticed his cheeks and nose were red from the cold. What was he doing out there? She became aware Hudson was asking the same question out loud.

As if he understood, Jamie held up his finger in a "just a minute" gesture. Then, bending over, he began to write something on a large piece of white paper. Still grinning, he held it against the window, his face peering over it.

"I figured it out," Amelia read out loud, as if the others couldn't read.

Sarah brought her face closer to the window. *God, he looks adorable. Like the hot guy in a Hallmark Christmas movie.* "What?" she mouthed to him, a little dazed.

Jamie held up his finger again. Taking the paper, he put it backwards on his knee and began to write. It took longer this time. Sarah looked at her friends. "Anybody have any idea what's happening?"

"Not a clue," Hudson replied, "but he just put that sheet back up in front of your face. Read out loud, please."

Hudson didn't wait. Peering over Sarah's head, she read: *"The punch in my gut. Were you even listening?"*

Sarah shook her head. "I...well, yeah but...what?" she mouthed, holding up her hands in confusion.

Jamie nodded, still grinning. He turned and crossed the street.

"He's leaving?" Hudson gasped. "Sarah, go after him!"

"Take it easy, no he's not," Amelia corrected. "He's talking to the guy who's been drawing over there." All three watched Jamie speak to the artist. "Does Jamie know him? He's hot," Amelia observed.

"Yeah, in a scruffy kind of way, he is," Hudson agreed. "But he looks seriously ticked off. I'm not getting a friend vibe from him. Look, he's giving Jamie paper."

"Jamie's coming back," Amelia said, excitedly. "Sarah, what is going on?"

"I told you, I have absolutely no idea," Sarah replied, her eyes fixed on Jamie walking towards her. He reached the window and smiled at her, his expression smug, like he knew a big secret. Sarah's eyes narrowed. He wrote something else down, then held the paper in front of his chest. *"It's all new to me."*

Sarah felt a thousand butterflies fluttering around in her stomach. Her heart began to hammer in her chest. She thought she might be beginning to understand. At least she hoped she did. Her eyes met his for a long moment.

Jamie's expression went from playful to serious. Then he put the paper on his knee again, flipped it over and wrote.

Amelia and Hudson both read aloud when he held it up in front of him: *"I just wanted you to know."*

Know what? Sarah's eyes silently asked him the question. His smile broadened and she knew he understood. He held up his index finger, then turned and jogged across the street.

"Hot, scruffy guy's giving him more paper," Amelia observed.

"He didn't even look up this time," Hudson added.

Sarah heard them both, but their voices sounded like they were coming from far away. She watched Jamie cross the street. As soon as he had, he leaned down and wrote as he walked towards her. But as he was about to reach the window, he stopped. Sarah looked from his face to the paper he was holding and back to his face again. He just stood there, watching her, as if he were thinking something over. Then, he crumpled the paper and let it drop to the ground.

Sarah followed it all the way down with her eyes. Her first instinct was to go outside and get it. She wanted to know what it said more than anything. She knew without a doubt that it was something important, though she could not begin to explain how she knew. She lifted her eyes back to his and found him watching her. Her brows came together in question. He leaned back on his heels, stuck his hands in his pockets in the stance that was uniquely his and smiled up at her. Sarah had to smile back at the picture he made, standing there grinning like a satisfied little boy. She didn't know what was on that piece of paper or what was even going on, but at least, she didn't think he was breaking up with her. Still, for whatever reason, her heart was pounding so loudly, she thought he might be able to hear it through the glass.

Amelia and Hudson looked from Jamie to Sarah and then to each other in confusion. Across the street, the artist put down his pencil and watched, as well.

Jamie's smile slowly faded and his eyes became serious. Keeping them on Sarah, he walked the few remaining steps to the window. He leaned in, his face almost touching the glass. Unconsciously, Sarah did the same.

"I love you." He spoke the words loudly enough for Sarah to hear, despite the barrier of glass—and the thundering of her heart.

Amelia clamped her hand over her mouth and stared wide-eyed at Hudson. From across the street, the artist leaned back on two legs of his chair, folded his arms across his chest and smiled. Passers-by stopped to look. Only Sarah didn't move. She couldn't. She felt as if she were suspended in time, her eyes glued to Jamie's.

Jamie watched her a moment longer. Then, he smiled, shrugged his shoulders and put his hands back in his pockets. "I just wanted you to know," he mouthed silently. Stepping back, he turned and walked away.

Sarah finally blinked, staring at the empty spot where he had just been standing.

"Unbelievable," Amelia muttered. Hudson nodded, speechless.

Sarah looked from one stunned girl to the other. "Huddie, let me out, please!" she urged, flinging herself out of the booth, as Hudson jumped out of her way. Running outside, she stepped into the crowd of people who had gathered to watch, oblivious they were even there. Crossing the street, she paused by the artist, who raised his brush, grinned and pointed down the street. Sarah smiled back and started running along the sidewalk in the direction Jamie had gone. It took only a moment before she spotted him walking in the crowd, a few short feet ahead. She slowed to a walk and was ready to call out to him when, as if sensing her there, he turned. Seeing her, he smiled. Sarah smiled back and started towards him. She closed the space between them just as Jamie's arms opened for her. Sarah jumped into them—and Main Street erupted with cheers.

⁂ ⁂ ⁂ ⁂ ⁂ ⁂

The next morning, Jamie discovered an envelope under the windshield wiper of his car. Neatly folded inside, he found the piece of paper he had crumpled up the night before. Surprised, he unfolded it. The words *"I love you"* he had written were still there. But next to them, in Sarah's writing, was one more: *"too".*

CHAPTER FORTY-FOUR

"There's something I have to tell you."

It was two weeks later and Sarah met Jamie in her front yard. Giving him a kiss, she slipped her arm through his and walked him up the steps to the front porch.

"Lemonade? For me? Thanks, baby." Jamie smiled as Sarah poured him a glass, dropped his duffel bag and pulled out a fresh shirt.

"How was practice?" She scrunched her nose. "Smells like it was a good one."

Jamie laughed, peeling off his sweaty shirt and using it to wipe his forehead. Sarah raised an eyebrow as he changed. "You look good, Big Style," she said, playfully. "But I can't help but think you saved changing for when you got here."

Jamie chuckled and pulled her close. "Glad you approve, baby. Now come here and kiss me proper."

Sarah did, loving the way he held her. He smelled wonderful, even after a work out. After a moment, she pulled back, handing him the glass. "Sit down, I have to tell you something."

Jamie sat on the porch swing, gulped down the lemonade and stretched his arm for her to slide in next to him. She didn't. Taking his empty glass, she sat on the edge facing him. He smiled at her. It felt like forever since he had last seen her—and it had only been the night before.

"God, you're beautiful."

"Jamie. I have to tell you something. And you're not going to like it."

"I doubt that, baby. Your eyes are doing that thing they do. That's worth whatever you're going to say. Do I have to bus tables at Steve's tonight?"

Sarah smiled. "You're an idiot."

"But you love me anyway."

"Whatever. I have to tell you something, Big Style. Please shut up and listen."

Jamie reached for her empty hand. "Okay. But first tell me you love me before your eyes go back to normal."

Sarah sighed and rolled her eyes. "I love you."

"I love you too, baby, but you kinda ruined it with the eye roll."

Sarah laughed and pulling her hand away from his, put his glass on the table next to them. "Okay, be serious. I have to tell you something."

"Yes ma'am, tell me something." He reached for her hand.

She pulled it back again. "Stay on your side so I can talk to you."

"Sit on my lap. I listen better."

"No. Pay attention. I'm serious."

Jamie's raised an eyebrow and nodded. "Okay baby, I'm listening."

Sarah sighed again and met his eyes. "It's about my dad."

Jamie sat up. "Oh, hell, what did I do?"

Sarah shook her head. "No, it's nothing you did. It's something he did."

"That's a relief." He sobered at the uneasiness he saw in her eyes.

Sarah looked down, wringing her hands together in her lap.

Jamie reached over and covered them with his. "What's going on? Tell me, baby. It's okay, whatever it is."

Sarah shook her head. "I'm not sure you'll think so after I tell you."

"Try me."

Sarah looked at him and exhaled. "I am. I mean I will. Give me a minute, this is hard."

Jamie smiled. "Don't tell me your dad's in the Greek mafia."

Yanking her hands back, Sarah jumped off the swing, her eyes wide. "What? Jamie, how..." She stopped, mid-sentence and looked away.

From the swing, Jamie watched her. "Well, I was obviously kidding."

Sarah closed her eyes and let out another breath. Then she sat back down, facing him again. "So, the thing is...he was. He participated in unlawful activities for a powerful family in New York." Her body began to shake. "Italian, not Greek."

"Holy shit."

"Yeah." She moved closer to him and lowered her voice. "What I am telling you today could destroy my family. Especially Niko. But not telling you makes me feel dishonest. So, I've decided to tell you what I can. Not all of it. Some of it. The part that matters, the part you need to know. But I need to ask you first: Can you hear this, Jamie? No matter what happens with us, can you hear this and promise to never repeat a word of what I tell you to anyone?"

"Yes." His answer came quick. "Unless it's to save you."

Sarah's brows snapped together. "What does that mean?"

"It means you come first. I promise to always do whatever it takes, if it saves you."

"Jamie, my family means everything to me."

"I know. I understand."

Sarah looked down at her lap, her hands wrung together. She let out a breath and looked up at him. "God, I don't want to tell you."

"I see that, baby. Tell me anyway."

Sarah nodded. "When my mom got in the accident, the medical bills were huge. My dad couldn't cover them. Business was slow and he was shaken to his core; he couldn't be everywhere he needed to be. There was Niko and me to take care of; the restaurant; and my mom, in the hospital in a medically induced coma."

Jamie reached out and stroked her cheek. "God, Sarah, I'm sorry."

Sarah sighed. "So, I could go on about the how and the why but my dad made a terrible choice. He made it because he was too upset to think clearly. But he made it and that's what matters."

She took another deep breath, then let it out in a shudder. Jamie stayed silent.

"Before he met my mom, my dad was a rebel. He wore his parents out. My grandfather was a priest. Did you know that?"

Jamie shook his head.

"Well, he was. And my dad, his only son. He was such a trouble maker that my grandfather apologized for him to the entire congregation. Granddad tried everything, sent him everywhere he knew to get him to follow the rules. He couldn't."

Jamie looked surprised. "He sure follows them now."

"Granddad gave him a choice: jail or the army. My grandfather didn't play. Dad chose the army. And came back a changed man. He met my mom and the changes stuck."

"She was a rule follower?"

Sarah smiled a little. "No. Anything but, actually. But she was so confident. So strong. She was a force for good. My dad was crazy about her. And he loved her too much to ever disappoint her. So, he didn't."

A tear rolled down Sarah's cheek. Gently, Jamie wiped it away.

"Until the accident. With her in the coma, he got desperate. We were so young. We couldn't help him. Most of our family lived in Greece. He was alone with all of it. Or at least, that's what he told himself."

"What did he do?"

Sarah met his eyes. "In his wilder days, before my mom, before the army, he made some *deliveries* for a powerful family in New York. Italians—enough said. He loved the easy money and they kept him in the dark about what he was delivering which made him feel like he could opt out anytime he chose. When my grandfather heard rumblings about my dad's side job from a parishioner, he had him followed to a *delivery*, confronted him with proof and gave him the choice: jail or the army. My dad left the next day. A few months later, he shipped out to Afghanistan."

"Damn."

"Yeah. My grandfather never gave up. He saved him. Well, my mother and he did. My dad met my mom the week he got home. He was older, wiser and ready. I doubt it was an accident. My grandfather probably arranged for them to meet. They threw a church dance in honor of my dad; the whole town was so proud of him. My mom was there. She was beautiful—and a little wild herself."

Jamie smiled. "I bet she was."

Sarah smiled back. "He fell in love with her the moment he saw her, standing by the punch bowl."

"But she wanted nothing to do with him."

Sarah blinked. "How did you know that?"

Jamie winked at her. "Wild guess, baby. Keep going."

"Well, he was persistent and in time, she fell for him, too. They got married, opened the restaurant in New York and had us. We weren't rich but we were happy." She smiled at the memory. Then, her eyes clouded over. "And then, the accident."

"Can you tell me about that?" Gently, Jamie rubbed her fingers with his own.

Sarah's eyes filled with tears. "She picked us up from school. She was taking us for ice cream and we were singing together in the car when someone hit us head on. Our car was old, no air bags worked. We were in the back seat and Niko flew forward. Miraculously, the windshield wiper held him in the car." She paused, turning her gaze to a red bird perched in a tree by the porch. "I think it was my mom's hand. They say it couldn't have been because the steering wheel crushed her chest and she couldn't have moved. But I know I saw it. And I know my mom."

She turned sad eyes back to Jamie. "Anyway, Niko broke his jaw, but other than that, we were fine. My mom ruptured the major artery to her heart and had serious head trauma. After successfully getting her through a long operation to repair the damage, they induced a coma, hoping her age would pull her through. But six months later, the doctors told us we had to let her go. The machines were the only thing keeping her alive."

Jamie felt his chest ache at the sorrow in her voice. He waited, still rubbing her fingers with his own.

"During the six months, we barely saw our dad. My aunt Patty came to take care of us for the first few weeks, but after that, it was friends and neighbors who pitched in for dinners and carpool to school. Every night we went to bed alone. But every morning, my dad was there, in the kitchen, cooking us pancakes and packing our lunches. We didn't question him; we thought he was out late working at the restaurant and spending time at the hospital. And he was."

Sarah exhaled deeply, pulled her hands away and stood. "Except between the time the restaurant closed and the part of each night he spent with my mom, he started making *deliveries* again."

Jamie sat back in the swing. "Aw, man."

Sarah looked down at him, her eyes filled with grief and loss.

"It must have been so hard for him, Sarah, to lose your mom like that. And to worry about you and Nick with no help. I kinda get it."

Sarah shook her head. "Well, that makes one of us. I don't." She sighed. "But I forgive him. I love my dad so much. He would give his life for us and it wouldn't be a sacrifice. He needed help and the bills kept coming. I just wish he had more courage."

"Baby, he fought in Afghanistan. He has courage. It sounds like his heart was shattered to pieces and maybe he got a little angry about it."

Sarah shrugged. "Sense, then. I wish he had had more sense."

"You're here, so I guess he didn't get caught. Did your grandfather save him again?"

"No, my grandparents had moved back to Greece. Both have since passed away. I'm just glad they missed all this. Dad made *deliveries* until the fire. After our house burned, he told them he was done, that he was taking us away to live here."

"And they let him go?"

Sarah sighed. "He thought so. They told him so over drinks at some seedy bar. They wished him well while Niko and I ate dinner at a hotel alone. And that was that. We moved here, Dad started working at Steve's and he was no longer *'the delivery man'*."

Jamie sat up. "Well, babe, I won't pretend I know much about what you call "powerful Italian families" but from my limited movie knowledge, if they let you out, you're out. It sounds like your dad got lucky."

Sarah laughed sarcastically. "Yeah. He thought so too. Until Doogie's."

"Shit." Jamie's voice was quiet.

Sarah sat down again, facing him. "That wasn't some random kids trying to score a drug deal. The family found them and tried to lure Niko into their group so they could have my dad where they want him. Apparently, the North and South Carolina coasts are perfect for *deliveries*. And my dad seasoned enough to be a perfect choice to make them."

"What's the family's name?"

"You don't need to know that. The less you know the better. You are getting the bare bones. It's enough, trust me." Sarah let out a deep breath and hung her head.

"All right. And then? What happened after Doogie's?"

"My dad confronted the family. He met with them and told them he is staying out. Then, he told me all about it. And armed our house with security cameras." She motioned with her eyes towards the camera above the swing. "We are just hoping it all goes away. But nothing is for sure. We watch Nick all the time. He's getting older and I guess eventually, my dad will tell him, too. Nick's been through a lot, we don't think he can take any more right now. And my dad seems to trust these guys will keep their word."

"Why does he think that?"

Sarah shook her head. "That's the million dollar question."

Jamie leaned back, crossing his arms across his chest. For a moment, he said nothing. Then, his eyes met hers. "Maybe your dad has something on them. Something they can't get to."

"If he does, he's not sharing that with me. Dad says it's in the past, that we need to leave it there." Sarah sighed. "I just hope he's right."

"Come here, baby, " Jamie said, pulling her close. Emotionally spent, Sarah slid close to him and leaned her head against his chest.

"I'm sorry, Jamie. I really am."

Jamie kissed the top of her head. "You have nothing to be sorry for. I'm just glad you told me. I can watch over you and Nick. It's going to be okay."

"I don't know about that. You and Ben have already been in harm's way because of my dad. I couldn't bear it if something bad happens to you because of me."

"It won't."

Sarah looked up at him. "You need to be careful, too, now because of me. Your mother is right to not like me. Can you imagine if she knew all this?"

Jamie smiled. "To be honest, I'd rather not."

Sarah laughed, amazed that she could after what she had just told him. She shook her head, staring into his strong eyes. "How can you be so wonderful, Jamie? You really don't care? You still want to be with me after what I've just told you?"

Jamie sat up and turned to gently take her face in his hands. "Your dad's past is not something you can run away from. None of it is in your control and none of it is your fault. Of course I want to be with you. I love you, Sarah. More now."

Sarah leaned her head against his. "Your mom has it right, you deserve so much better than me," she whispered.

"My mom doesn't know you well. After she does, she'll love you too."

Sarah smiled. "Before or after she finds out I'm a mob princess?"

Jamie laughed, pulling her into a hug. "We never speak of this again, Sarah," he said softly into her ear. "Your dad's right. You need to leave it in the past, where it belongs. But if you become worried, you come to me and we handle it together. Okay?"

"Okay. Thank you, Jamie."

"You're welcome, baby."

She pulled out of his arms and kissed him. "And you'll never tell anyone, you swore, don't forget," she said, looking into his eyes. "No matter what."

"I won't forget my promise. You have my word."

"My dad's a good man, Jamie. Life kicked the legs out from under him and he buckled. Afterwards, he had to find his way back up. He did the best he could."

Jamie nodded, saying nothing.

"He worshipped my mom. She was everything to him. Losing her brought him to the cliff's edge. And there was no one to hold him back. Do you understand?"

Jamie kissed her forehead. "Yeah, baby, I think I do."

Sarah sighed again, laid her head against his chest and closed her eyes. She wasn't sure she had done the right thing in telling him what she had. But she couldn't live a lie. She loved and trusted Jamie, that much she did know. For the first time in months, she felt lighter—and less alone. Still, she could not stop from shaking.

Gently, with his arms wrapped tightly around her, Jamie swung the swing until her shaking stopped.

CHAPTER FORTY-FIVE

Sarah found herself humming as she strolled through the nearly empty mall. It was almost Valentine's Day and the mall was filled with hearts and balloons, stuffed animals and chocolate. *This holiday was made for me,* she thought to herself.

It had been the best week. Her dad had called a family meeting and announced to Niko and her that he had paid off his New York loans in full. Not only that, but he had made his brother an offer to buy Steve's and her uncle had agreed to it. Sarah smiled as she walked. It was all working out. North Carolina was really starting to feel like home. Even Niko was happier. He was making friends at both school and church. Maybe it really was a new beginning for all of them.

She wondered what to get Jamie for Valentine's Day. Maybe she would get him basketball tickets to a Clemson game. Jamie loved the Tigers. They could go together and make a romantic date of it. She wanted to make it special, the way he always did for her. She looked down at the bracelet Jamie had given her for Christmas. It was a simple gold weave, but it was perfect. She had been speechless when he had brought it over to her aunt's house on Christmas Day. Aunt Patty had *oohed* and *ahhed* over both—the gift and Jamie. That was a good thing, since Andreas's frown could have melted the snow that had fallen outside.

The holidays had been hectic but happy. Steve's had been almost too busy to handle and Andreas had been a bear the whole month. But Sarah knew, underneath it all he was the happiest he had been in a long time.

Jamie had taken her to his house for dinner for the first time the week of Christmas. That had not gone so well. Sarah had tried to keep an open mind and it was surprisingly easy to do with Jamie's dad, brother and sister. Daisy Nelson, however, was another story. She didn't like Sarah and she didn't pretend to. Jamie had apologized for his mother when he had taken her home, explaining it was because of the night at Doogie's and that she would get over it. He had insisted there was nothing else and that in time, his mom would love her. Sarah had not argued about it but, in her heart, she knew there would be no winning Daisy Nelson over.

She wanted someone better for Jamie. Someone like Charlotte Sanders.

You think Doogie's was bad, Daisy. If only you knew the rest of it...

Sarah sighed. Daisy must not have been too excited to hear about the prom. Still, she could not help but smile at the memory. Jamie had asked her last week and it had been perfect. She had gone to Tuesday's track practice, and was on time, which was unusual for her. Coach Adam had yelled for her to start running without warming up because she was late. Sarah had shrugged her shoulders and done as he said, figuring he was just in a bad mood.

But when she had started around the track, she had discovered her name written out across the lanes in colorful chalk. As she reached the first corner, the word *PROM* was written across the lanes, with a big question mark after it. Her heart beat with happy excitement as she had come across the next message, only to burst into laughter. It read: *Keep Running*. She had reached the finish line, to find Jamie's name written across the lanes. Coach Adam and the team had clapped excitedly and many of the girls had followed her to the gym, where she had enthusiastically accepted by throwing herself into Jamie's arms.

"Hey, you!" Sarah snapped out of her thoughts at the sound of Amelia's voice. "What are you smiling about?" Amelia walked towards her, arms outstretched.

"Hi! Nothing, really. It's just so happy in here," Sarah said, as she hugged her friend.

"Yeah, yeah, Valentine's Day, blah, blah." Amelia rolled her eyes and grabbed Sarah's arm. "Whatever. Help me find a sweater for Michael's party tonight and let's go to Three Spoons."

Sarah laughed. "Okay. But, for the record, I love Valentine's Day! It's fun and romantic and..."

"Pshh. For you and Jamie, maybe." Amelia squeezed Sarah's arm and giggled. "Oh my gosh, I still can't get over how the boy asked you to prom! I've never seen an *ask* like it; it's just the coolest, sweetest thing ever."

Sarah smiled at her friend. "You're the coolest, sweetest thing ever, Amelia Patten."

"Aw thanks, boo. I try. Speaking of not cool, did I tell you about Lexi?"

"No, what did the *queen of fake* do now?"

Amelia laughed. "You're gonna love this. Laura said when we were all so happy and excited for you, you know, when you were running on the track and reading Jamie's messages, Lexi was so jealous, she said: 'Whatever, it's going to rain tomorrow and wash it away.'"

"Really? She said that? That surprises me. I mean, not that she is awful and would think that, but that she would say it. She's usually too smart to show her true colors."

"I know, right? Watch her. She really has it out for you," Amelia warned. "She's kind of obsessed with the whole 'I love everybody and would never say a bad thing about anyone, especially sweet Sarah, *but*...'"

Sarah laughed. "My turn: pshhh. She can do her worst. She has a black soul and I feel sorry for her. Nothing is real in her life. She just reinvented herself on social media and got people to buy it. I really think people like Lexi, who live a lie, end up going crazy. It's just sad."

"Seriously, it is sad. But you're right, people buy it."

"Yeah, for now they do. She's having her day in the sun. But think of the big picture. I mean, look at her. She's pretty and smart and has a lot going for her. Instead of being happy, she competes and lies relentlessly. My mother used to say you can never compete with a liar, but that karma is nothing to mess with. Lexi Taylor should be worried about some serious karma in her future."

Amelia nodded in agreement. "Girl, I believe it. What you do to others is going to get done to you. What comes around goes around."

"Right. Maybe she's not as smart as we give her credit for."

Amelia smiled. "Or maybe she's had bad parenting."

Sarah linked arms with Amelia as they walked. "That's impressively insightful. So, in other news, I sent in my Clemson application. Cross your fingers."

Amelia squealed with joy and crossed her fingers on both hands. "Roommates!"

"Maybe," Sarah said, laughing at her antics. "You know my grades could have been better in New York. I mean, I'm glad it's done and I'm glad you talked me into it, but I'm nervous. It's a reach for me. Are you nervous?"

"Oh, yeah." Amelia crossed her fingers again and hugged her tight. "You wait and see, you'll get in. You speak Greek and you have track and work experience."

Sarah hugged her back. "Yeah, Greek, the language of commerce two thousand years ago. Oh, well, we've sent them in. Now we wait." She spotted a sweater in a store window and turned Amelia around. "Hey, what about that sweater?"

"That sweater has potential. Like you." Amelia grinned, as she followed Sarah into the store. "So…I have to tell you something and this is a good place since there's lots of people around." She turned and faced her. "Promise you won't get mad."

Sarah frowned. "What is it?"

"Promise you won't get mad first," Amelia insisted.

"There is definitely something wrong with you, but I promise."

Amelia scrunched her eyes shut. "I have communicated with *The Nameless One*. He texted me yesterday and asked to take me to Michael's party." She opened one eye. "And I said *yes*."

Sarah's mouth dropped open. "What? Amelia! Did you forget what he did to you? How he and *the queen of fake*…"

"Don't say it, I haven't forgotten," Amelia interrupted. "Of course I haven't forgotten. My fingers just went crazy and said yes before I could stop them." She smiled. "It's just a party, right? I mean, you'll be there."

Sarah studied her friend. She'd known Amelia wasn't over Derek. She had not been the same since they broke up. But to go out with him again after what he had done...it was nothing less than a terrible idea. "Text him back, Amelia. Tell him you forgot you were riding with Jamie and me."

"It will be fine, Sarah. I can handle it. I just want to find out why he did it, you know? It'll be closure for me."

"Closure," Sarah repeated. "Closure is going out on a date?"

Amelia shrugged, shifting her weight, uncomfortably. "But you'll be there. And Huddie, too. It's not a date. It will be fine."

Sarah sighed. "Yeah, yeah, I'll be there. I'm taking him pizza from Steve's."

Amelia hugged her. "See? We'll have great friends and great pizza. And karma on our side. How can it not be a good night? It's fine. No worries."

"No worries," Sarah repeated, shaking her head. "It's fine, everything's fine."

Amelia laughed. "Actually, you took this better than I thought. Now, stop being my echo." She picked up the sweater in her size. "Let's try this on and go get yogurt."

Sarah followed Amelia to the dressing room. Suddenly, she had a very bad feeling about Michael Capitano's party.

CHAPTER FORTY-SIX

"Jamie! Over here!" Sarah motioned him over to where she was filling glasses with ice. Steve's was beginning to get busy.

He grinned and made his way through the narrow waitress station. Stopping a few feet away, he held his hand to his heart. "God, you're beautiful. That's...an amazing dress." He took a few more steps and pulled her into a hug. "Did you know red's my favorite color?" he whispered in her ear.

Sarah laughed. "Your favorite color is green. God, you're smooth. But I like it."

"It's how I roll." Jamie winked at her.

"How you roll? How exactly do you roll?"

"We've been through this. Big style, baby. 'Cause I've got you."

Sarah laughed again. His arms tightened around her. "Did I tell you how beautiful you look tonight?" His voice was barely a whisper in her ear.

"Yes, but suddenly I'm becoming a fan of repetition. I should tell you, flattery will get you everywhere with me."

Jamie smiled. "Everywhere?"

Sarah smiled back and pulled away. "Not *exactly* everywhere."

"You're a tease."

Sarah looked over his shoulder for her father; not seeing him anywhere, she reached up and brushed her lips—just barely—against Jamie's. "Maybe, a little. I can't help it. It's how I roll," she whispered. She kept her eyes on his and ran her index finger down his neck and the front of his shirt. "I like your shirt, Big Style. You look hot." Jamie swallowed and moved closer. As he reached for her, Sarah abruptly shoved two glasses in his hands. She laughed at his wounded expression. "Help me finish filling these before my dad changes his mind about letting me get out of here."

Jamie chuckled and picked up the scooper. "You're a cold woman, Sarah Giannopoulos, to tease the way you do." He pointed the scooper at her. "But I'll do what you ask because of that dress."

Sarah patted his shoulder. "Good boy," she joked. "I'll be right back."

"Where are you going?"

"To the kitchen. Michael's pizzas should be ready by now. You and I are taking them to the party for him."

Jamie stopped scooping ice. "And when were these arrangements made?" he muttered, but she had already walked away and didn't hear him. Irritably, he began shoving ice in the glasses again, his good mood soured. Michael Capitano. Why was he always hanging around Sarah? And why did it get to him the way it did? *Because he's a dirtbag and he's crazy about your girlfriend.* Jamie put the last glass down with a hard thud.

"Wow, you're fast." Sarah was back with the pizzas. Jamie had to smile at the picture she made. Just the sight of her lightened his mood. He leaned over and took the boxes from her. "I used to be. But my girlfriend's a tease and my moves are taking a hit."

Sarah laughed. "Maybe your moves need work."

"Maybe you need to let me practice more," he challenged.

Sarah laughed again, and shoved him towards the door. She paused to give her brother a kiss on the cheek, not at all surprised when he rolled his eyes in response. It was Jamie's turn to laugh.

"Niko, tell μπαμπα we've gone. When he yells about it, just walk away."

"Genius plan. That never works," Nick replied, waving to Jamie and following Lucy into the kitchen.

"Lucy's in love with our new cook, Mario," Sarah said as they stepped outside. "He's Italian and he's hot."

"That's worrisome."

"Lucy can handle him."

"That's not what I'm worried about."

Sarah eyed him, playfully. "We could always double date. Bet he could give you some tips from his hot Italian playbook."

Jamie grinned at her. The February air was cold as they walked to his car and he wanted to wrap his arms around her. But he couldn't. They were already full, carrying pizzas for Michael Capitano.

CHAPTER FORTY-SEVEN

Jamie's mood soured again as the night wore on. In fact, it went from bad to worse. It seemed to him, Sarah was helping Michael with way too many party tasks. They were acting like a couple throwing a party together. To top it all off, Amelia had shown up with Derek. When Sarah wasn't with Michael, she was off somewhere with her. It was obvious to Jamie, Sarah was not into spending time with him. To make matters even worse, for the first time he could remember, his friends and he had very little to talk about. All that seemed to interest them was scoring with girls. The subject bored him. He already had a girl he wanted to be with, even though he had no chance of scoring.

But she was having too good of a time without him to notice.

Gaston had brought a few beers and after having a couple, Jamie managed to get in the swing of things with the guys. He even began to enjoy himself a little, accepting that it was just going to be one of those nights.

⁂ ⁂ ⁂ ⁂ ⁂ ⁂

Charlotte Sanders was really good at pretending. Right now she was pretending to be engrossed in Walt's stories from a concert he had recently been to. But what she was really doing was keeping on eye on Jamie. And noticing that for the first time in a long time, Sarah wasn't attached to him like a fixture to the wall. What Jamie saw in Sarah Giannopoulos, she could not understand. The girl was pretty enough but she was dull—and not one of them. Charlotte had been certain the two of them would be over by now, but for some reason

Jamie kept her around. One thing she did know: There was no way she was going to let Sarah Giannopoulos win. Tonight, something was wrong. Charlotte knew an opportunity when she saw one. And she was ready for this one.

"Walt," she interrupted, softly, laying her hand on his arm. "Please promise you'll finish telling me all about it when I come back. I see the line to the bathroom has finally gotten better." She smiled up at him, batting her eyelashes just once, knowing full well the picture she made.

Walt smiled back. "Well, sure. I'll just grab another beer. You want one?"

"No, I'm good. But Jamie looks like he needs another," she suggested casually over her shoulder, as she walked away.

Walt drained the rest of his beer and watched her leave the room. He couldn't believe his good luck. Michael's party had started out being the drag he had known it would be. But then, out of nowhere, Charlotte had suddenly become interested in everything he had to say. Now that Jamie was out of the picture, and Sydney was being a pain in the ass as usual, maybe he should think about asking Charlotte to the prom. He smiled to himself. It sure would annoy Sarah to be with Charlotte all evening. The thought made him frown and he wondered why he cared at all what Sarah Giannopoulos thought about anything.

Charlotte let herself into the bathroom, locking the door behind her. Carefully, she reapplied her lip gloss and fluffed her hair. Examining herself in the mirror, she smiled at her reflection. Then, she fished her phone from her purse and started texting.

Everything was going according to plan.

CHAPTER FORTY-EIGHT

"Michael? Hi! I'm Ali Brockman. I don't know if you remember me..."

Michael looked up from the trash bag he was tying up to the pretty girl in front of him. He smiled. "Hi, Ali. Sure, I remember you. You're in my pre-calc class." Ali nodded, cheerfully. "How do you like Lakeview so far? I guess your dad got transferred or something for you to move after the school year started."

"Yeah, something like that. And I like it a lot so far."

"That's great. Can I get you a drink?"

Ali followed him to the kitchen where he poured her a Coke. She smiled at him shyly and took the cup. Michael guessed she was uncomfortable with the unfamiliarity of her new surroundings, not having met a lot of people yet. He smiled back, warmly. She seemed nice. He would have to introduce her to Sarah.

"I really like your house, Michael," Ali said. "Everyone here is really nice, especially your girlfriend. She was my mentor this week at school. She's been so sweet to me."

"My girlfriend?"

"Yeah, Sarah. I assumed you two were dating..." Ali's bubbly voice trailed as she glanced past Michael to where Sarah was busy refilling a bowl with chips. Michael followed her eyes and Ali watched his expression change from friendly to thoughtful. "I'm sorry...I guess I shouldn't have presumed anything. It's just that she talks about you so much and I always see the two of you together."

"No problem. But no, she's not my girlfriend, we're just friends. Hey, I'll see you in a minute, I need to run this outside."

Ali took the hint. There was no mistaking she had struck a nerve and he didn't want to talk about it. She smiled, embarrassed. "Sure, see you later, Michael."

Michael heaved the heavy bag over his shoulder and started for the back door, thinking over in his mind what Ali had suggested. He glanced at Sarah from the corner of his eye and realized it was true. She was spending all her time helping him tonight, instead of hanging out with Jamie. Had they broken up? Wouldn't she have told him? What did it mean that Ali said Sarah talked about him a lot? Was he missing something? Or was it wishful thinking?

He stepped outside into the cold night air. One thing was for sure. If he ever got a chance with Sarah, he would take it, no questions asked. Maybe Ali was on to something... Michael dismissed the thought, even as it formed in his head. He knew better. Ali was new and had made a mistake, that's all. Sarah had made it crystal clear she thought of him as a friend. Michael threw the trash bag into the can and slammed the lid shut. He sighed, turned and walked back into the house.

❋ ❋ ❋ ❋ ❋ ❋

Sarah fumed as she picked up empty cups and plates from Michael's den. What was Jamie's problem tonight? Why was he ignoring her like this? She had not really expected him to pitch in and help Michael out but she had thought he would at least hang out with her some. *Really? Why would you think that? How cool would that look to his oh-so-cool friends?* Frustrated, she looked across the room at Jamie. He was laughing at something Robby and Gaston were saying, the cheerleaders all around him, hanging on to every word.

That does it. I'm getting a ride home with Derek and Amelia, who came together and are actually hanging out together. Guess I was wrong about them, too. She glanced towards Jamie again and saw him chugging a beer with Gaston, obviously racing. Charlotte and her friends were cheering them on. Feeling her temper flare, Sarah turned and made her way through the crowd to the kitchen. Throwing the cups and plates she had collected in the trash, she grabbed her phone. She would ask Derek to take her home. She couldn't wait to get out of there. Opening the door, she stepped outside.

Michael came into the kitchen in time to see Sarah slam his trashcan drawer so hard it rattled, then storm off to the back patio. There was no doubt something was wrong. Concerned, he followed her outside.

CHAPTER FORTY-NINE

"Ali, meet Jamie Nelson. Jamie, this is Ali Brockman. She's new in town and just started school here last week," Robby said to his best friend.

Jamie shook Ali's hand. "Nice to meet you, Ali."

"I like your name, Ali. Is that short for Alice?" Gaston asked. The group laughed, the beer responsible for making things seem funnier than they actually were. Gaston put his hand on Robby's shoulder. "Man, where have you been? I just beat Nelson in a chugging contest."

"Looking for Mary Elizabeth. My little sister being old enough to come to parties is a definite buzz-buster. But Ali says she just saw her, so I guess she's okay."

Gaston nodded, his eyes serious. "Yeah. I don't know, man, I'd be worried. The way Mary Elizabeth looks tonight worries me too. I'd better go look for her."

Robby grabbed his t-shirt, pulling him back. "Thanks, but we've been over this. I'm sure she'll turn up."

Gaston looked at Ali, his expression wounded. "Alice. Don't you think it's rude that I'm like his brother but he doesn't think I'm good enough for his sister?"

The group laughed again. "You guys are hilarious," Ali said, taking a mini bottle from her purse and mixing it in her drink. She took a sip and smiled. "This is a great party. Michael and Sarah know how to do it up right."

The laughter dissolved and was quickly replaced with awkward silence. All eyes zeroed in on Jamie, waiting to see his reaction and whether or not he had picked up on what Ali had implied. He had. His eyes were stone cold as he watched Ali, as if he was absorbing what she had just said.

Ali seemed to be the only one who hadn't noticed the change. She rattled on cheerily, "They are both super nice. They have to be worn out with all these people here. I wasn't surprised to see them disappear onto the back patio. I say, good for them. It's too crowded in here for those cuties, as into each other as they are. I doubt we'll see them the rest of the night." She stopped talking long enough to take another sip from her drink. "Anyway, Robby, did you mean it when you said you would play tennis with me tomorrow? I need to practice if I have any chance of making the team here."

"Uh, yeah, sure," Robby said, aware Jamie's eyes were becoming angry. He knew there had to be an explanation for what Ali had said. She was new, she was probably just confused. Still, he wasn't surprised to see Jamie take off in the direction of the patio.

"I knew that girl was trouble. I said it from the get-go," Walt mumbled, watching as Jamie tore out of the room.

"Shut up, Walt," Robby said. "Sometimes, you irritate the hell out of me."

"Robby, was it something I said?" Ali asked, wide-eyed.

"Don't worry about it, Ali, but yeah, it was. I guess you don't know, but Sarah is Jamie's girlfriend, not Michael's." Robby paused, when he saw Ali's eyes well up with confused tears. "But, seriously, don't sweat it. They'll work it out, I'm sure."

The truth was, he wasn't sure at all. Robby had not liked the look on Jamie's face before he had left the room. He had seen that look a few times before and knew his best friend too well. Things were about to get ugly.

Everyone was too busy watching the patio door to notice Ali glance at Charlotte through her tears—and smile.

❋ ❋ ❋ ❋ ❋ ❋

Jamie's thoughts were racing as he made his way to Michael's patio. How could she do this to him in front of everyone? And with Michael Capitano? The guy was a loser. He had only put up with him to make

Sarah happy. Talk about a joke...Sarah had played him. He had spilled out his heart to her, told her he loved her, and it had meant nothing. She had made a complete ass out of him.

He flung the patio door open and sure enough, there they were, just as Ali had said, wrapped up in each other's arms. For a moment, all Jamie could do was blink, drunk with alcohol, disbelief and rage.

What happened next was a blur. He thought he heard Sarah say something but he didn't stop to listen, knowing that nothing she said mattered. It was Michael he was focused on, only Michael. Lunging towards him, he knocked over a couple of chairs that were in his way, sending them crashing over. Michael put his hands out, as if to ward him off, but Jamie came at him hard, pushing him to the ground and throwing himself on top of him.

His right fist connected with Michael's jaw, causing him to grunt in pain. Furious, Michael brought his knee up, kicking Jamie hard enough to send him flat on his back. Michael tried to hit him again but it was Jamie who swung first. The two began to wrestle, exchanging punches, until Jamie felt strong arms pull him back. He heard Robby's voice, somewhere mixed in the background with the roaring in his head. Despite his best effort to break free, Robby and Walt were able to pull him to his feet, but Michael was still on the ground and Sarah was leaning over him.

Jamie yelled something that made no sense, even to him, as he tried to get loose. Then, somehow, he was back inside, sitting on the couch, trying to catch his breath. Robby was there with him, telling him to take it easy, over and over again. He didn't want to take it easy. He wanted Sarah to explain to him what had just happened and why she had been out on that patio with Michael Capitano all over her. But Robby, Walt and Gaston wouldn't let him up.

When Jamie finally managed to get back outside, both Michael and Sarah were gone. He leaned on a chair, hung his head and closed his eyes. He suddenly felt sick to his stomach. And he knew it wasn't the alcohol causing the feeling.

CHAPTER FIFTY

Amelia collapsed on the bleachers, exhausted. Amazingly, Sarah was still going strong. The girl was determined to keep running, even though practice was over. Amelia reached for her windbreaker, suddenly feeling the cold.

"Hey, you."

Amelia looked up to find Derek standing next to her. She tried to hide her happy surprise. "Oh, hey, I didn't see you walk up."

"I don't doubt it. You look beat."

"I'm totally wiped out. I can't believe Sarah's endurance. Look at her. I can't tell you how many laps that makes but I really think the girl could run a marathon today."

Derek followed her gaze to the track where Sarah was running. He nodded in agreement. "Wow. She doesn't even look winded."

Amelia sighed. "I'm seriously beginning to worry about her. It's been two weeks since Michael's party and her break-up with Jamie. She keeps everything inside, acts like everything's just great. But she's hurting, I know it. I really thought she would be better by now. After all, this is Sarah we're talking about."

"Have they talked about it?"

Amelia squinted up at him, trying to see more clearly through the bright afternoon sun. *What's this all about? Seriously, you're genuinely concerned about Sarah? Dude, it wasn't that long ago she let you have it in front of everyone. What are you doing here? And why are you so hot, Derek?*

"Are you kidding? They're both way too proud," she said aloud.

"Yeah, I saw Jamie at lunch today. He seems to be fine."

And now, hot or not, you're getting on my nerves.

"Great. I'm really happy for him," Amelia replied, sarcastically. The last thing she wanted to hear was that Jamie was fine when she knew Sarah wasn't.

Derek threw his book bag over his shoulder. "Yeah...so, I'd better get going. I've got a chemistry test tomorrow and I want to lift some weights before I go home."

"I'll see ya." Amelia forced a quick smile and turned to look for Sarah. She was still running.

"You know," Derek said carefully, "if you ask me, it's too bad Jamie and Sarah broke up."

Amelia watched Sarah run by them. "They broke up for good reason."

"Maybe, but if they just talked about it, instead of pretending they don't care, there could still be a chance they might work things out."

Amelia could feel her heart begin to race. She wondered if Sarah and Jamie were the only ones he was referring to. She looked up at him. "The trust is gone, Derek. I don't think they can get it back."

"See, I think you're wrong about that," Derek said, his voice so quiet Amelia could barely hear him. "I think if you want something badly enough, there's always a way to get it...if you're willing to change whatever you did wrong. But...I guess what you're saying is, there are no second chances." Derek met her eyes and held them.

Amelia felt her heart pick up even more. It was so loud, she wondered if he could hear it. Here was the conversation she had hoped to have for months now. She thought of Sarah, lifted her chin and shook her head. "It would be hard. Trust isn't easy to get back. And they'd both have to forgive each other."

He surprised her by laughing. "There's nothing for him to forgive, Amelia." Derek paused and looked towards the track at Sarah. "He'd be an idiot to give up on her. He may put on an act and all, but I'll bet he knows..." he paused again and looked back at her, "that a girl like her is one in a million."

Amelia looked down at the dirt. Hope fluttered inside her traitorously loud heart. Derek continued, his voice still quiet, "So, you think, in time, she might forgive him?"

For a moment, Amelia played with a pebble in the dirt with her shoe. Then, she looked up at him and smiled. "I don't know. Anything's possible, I guess."

Derek grinned down at her. " Yeah, it is. See ya tomorrow, Amelia."

"See ya." She watched him walk away, wondering exactly what it was that had just happened between them.

Was that an apology and a promise, all in one? What just happened? Am I reading too much into what he said? And if I'm not, can I really trust him again?

Amelia sighed. She thought of Lexi, smirking at her in the halls when she knew no one was looking. Could she really forget Derek had cheated on her the way he had? They had yet to talk about what happened. They had gone to Michael's together, but the fight between Michael and Jamie that night had pretty much ended any chance of the subject coming up. And that was really the last time she had talked to him until today. She had considered the night at Michael's a clean break, an attempt to be friends. She'd thought it was closure. But now, she wasn't so sure.

She would talk it over with Sarah. As always, Sarah would know what to do. Amelia gathered their things and walked down to the track. First, she had to get her to stop running. Her best friend was doing her best to collapse rather than call it quits.

"Sarah!" she yelled at the top of her lungs. "C'mon! Let's go!"

What was she going to do about Sarah?

CHAPTER FIFTY-ONE

Sarah made her way through the crowded school hallway as nonchalantly as she could. She had spotted Jamie, Walt and Gaston the moment she had walked out of her calculus class, although she had pretended not to. As her bad luck would have it, they were standing just feet away from her locker. She did her best to appear preoccupied as she made her way to it and buried her head inside. She began switching out her books, all the while wishing her heart would stop its frantic beating.

It made her angry that he still affected her so much. It had been over three weeks since they had broken up and he had made no attempt to speak to her. She had felt certain he would have tried by now, that he wouldn't have just let her go without a fight.

You were wrong, genius. It's past time you accept the hard truth: He's glad it's over. And he's definitely over you. Sarah slammed her locker door shut.

"Well, that makes two of us," she mumbled to herself.

"Talk to yourself much?"

Sarah whirled around, alarmed at who may have overheard her. She relaxed when she saw it was Derek. "Among other things," she admitted, determined not to look at Jamie, who was now standing directly behind them.

"Me too. Hey, if you've got a minute, I need to ask you something."

Sarah became aware he was shifting his weight, obviously uncomfortable. She knew whatever it was he was about to ask her had something to do with Amelia. *Forget about your ex-boyfriend and his declarations of love punching him in the gut. Focus, this is about Amelia.* Sarah forced herself to concentrate. "Sure. What's up?"

"Well, it's about Amelia."

"Why am I not surprised?" she asked, with a sympathetic smile.

Derek shrugged and smiled meekly. "I want to ask her to the prom."

"So, ask her." Sarah knew she wasn't being much help but Jamie was still in her peripheral vision. He was laughing and that irritated her. *I'd like to give you a big-style punch in the gut right about now.*

"Do you think she'll go with me?"

"Honestly, I don't know." *If only Michael would walk by right now so I could flirt with him...*

"C'mon, Sarah. Help me out, here. I mean I think I might have a shot at getting her to forgive me. I know I hurt her and I don't know why I did it because...because she's the best thing that's happened to me in a long time."

The sadness in his voice got to her. Sarah forgot about Jamie standing so close. Derek sounded miserable. More than that, he sounded sincere.

"I don't want to go with anyone else but her but I don't know if she is ready and I don't want to screw things up by moving too fast and pushing her further away. I...I just really want to take her to the prom."

"Derek," Sarah chose her words carefully, "I think you should tell her exactly what you just told me. And then, be patient with whatever her answer is."

Derek nodded. His shoulders slumped and Sarah began to really feel sorry for him. "You have to give her time. It's hard to get trust back once you've lost it. Some people can't do it. But Amelia's heart is so big, I think she can."

"You really think so?"

Sarah smiled, encouragingly. "Yeah, I really do."

Derek nodded. "I'm gonna ask her. Thanks, Sarah."

Sarah gave him a quick hug. "Be romantic about it. She loves romantic gestures."

Derek smiled. "I'll do my best." He paused, as if thinking something over. "And how about you, beautiful Greek woman? Are you still going with..."

"No, no..." Sarah interrupted, knowing what he was going to say. "I...I'm not going. Steve's is super busy and..." She stopped in mid-sentence, as Charlotte breezed by them, walked straight to Jamie, and linked her arm through his. Sarah's eyes widened. They were back together!

Wow. He sure didn't waste any time...

Realizing she was allowing her emotions to show, she looked back at Derek and smiled. "I'm sorry, I stayed up late studying for a French test and I'm out of it today." She kept smiling—but her eyes were furious.

"C'mon, Sarah, get over him. He's an idiot and she's...well, she's pretty, but she's completely plastic." Derek's sympathetic tone was more than Sarah could take.

She forced another smile, making every possible effort to hold back threatening tears. "Thanks, Derek, but trust me, I couldn't care less what he does or who he does it with. I've got to get to class. Good luck with...everything."

"Thanks. See ya!" he called after her, as Sarah quickly disappeared down the hallway.

From the corner of his eye, Jamie watched her go.

⁕ ⁕ ⁕ ⁕ ⁕ ⁕

It wasn't until a while later that Amelia found her sitting on the wall behind the gym, the very same spot where she had first met her best friend. Sarah was staring blankly into space, unaware she was even there. Amelia knelt in front of her and gently put her hands on Sarah's knees. "I've been looking everywhere for you. You okay?"

Sarah closed her eyes to keep from crying. She hated to cry. She wasn't going to now, not over this, not over Jamie Nelson.

"He's back with her." Her voice was barely a whisper.

Amelia squeezed her knees, lightly. "I know."

Sarah turned her face away. "I'm okay. It just sucks that I made this mistake again. I knew I shouldn't have trusted him. I knew it and I ignored it. I knew he would use me until he got tired of me, just like Jake did. I knew he would hurt me, I knew it and still I let him do it..."

Amelia stood and sat on the wall beside her. Silently, she put her arm around her. Sarah sighed and laid her head on Amelia's shoulder. For a few moments they just sat there. Amelia rubbed Sarah's arm. Sarah sighed again.

"Tell me about Jake, Sarah," Amelia coaxed, her voice steady and comforting.

Sarah stiffened. "Jake's the previous asshole I fell for in New York." Her voice was angry. "Why, Amelia? Tell me, why do I keep doing this to myself? It's not like I don't know what the Jakes and Jamie Nelsons of this world are all about. Believe me, I do. And yet, I keep falling for them. I mean, what is the matter with me?"

"Aw, sweetie, nothing's the matter with you. You're so strong, Sarah, and you've had to be so in control of things. But you have to realize you can't control your heart, no matter how hard you try. No one can. I know you're hurting right now but I think, maybe..." Amelia paused, when Sarah's shoulders began to shake. She heard muffled sobs and realized Sarah was crying. She had been about to say she thought Jamie was hurting too and that he still loved her, but she didn't. Instead, she held her best friend close, rocking her back and forth gently, much as a mother would have.

She had never seen Sarah cry before. It was all she could think to do.

CHAPTER FIFTY-TWO

Nick was beginning to worry. He searched the gym one more time for his sister but there was still no sign of her. She had told him she would be there. Basketball was Sarah's favorite sport and the varsity girls were in the play-offs. He spotted Amelia and Hudson in the senior section, but Sarah was not with them.

He checked his phone for any messages. Maybe Steve's had gotten busy and she had gone in to help. But he didn't see anything from Sarah or their dad. Nick frowned. He had a feeling her absence had something to do with Jamie. He was there, of course, surrounded by his buddies and the cheerleaders. Nick didn't try to mask the look of distaste that overtook his face as he watched Jamie flirt with Charlotte Sanders. She was hanging all over him. And he was loving it.

Maybe Sarah had been right not to come. She would have only been upset to see the two of them together. Maybe it was too much for her to handle. Nick dismissed the thought even as he thought it. If he was sure of anything, it was that his sister was strong, a true survivor. It was because of her strength that he was even alive...

Nick still had nightmares about the night of the fire. He remembered every detail, especially the intense heat and the horrible smell of the flames, as they had engulfed everything in their path. In his dreams, he saw himself as he had been, paralyzed with fear, helplessly watching the flames viciously lick their way into his room. Sarah had burst in, completely in control and unafraid. She had wrapped him up in his blanket and guided him out into the yard, out of the fire's range. She had ordered him to stay put and he had tried to argue because he had known she was going back in, but no words had come out of his mouth.

Instead, he had watched, terrified, as she ran back into the raging inferno. He'd waited, his teeth chattering with fear. He had locked his eyes on the spot where he had last seen her and prayed she would return to it, his body shaking uncontrollably. It had seemed like an eternity before she had finally emerged, smiling between spasmodic coughs as she ran to him. She had collapsed on the ground next to him, gasping for air and dropping between them what she had risked her life for.

It was two framed pictures. One of the four of them together, taken soon after Nick was born, and one of their mother alone, smiling. He had broken down and cried then, his sobs deep, yet quiet. Sarah had pulled him close and held him tight.

"Hush now. It's okay, Niko," she had soothed him, even between her coughs. "You're safe. We're fine, we're always going to be fine. Μπαμπα will be here soon."

"Why...did...did you go back in? You left me..." he had sobbed against her chest, his hands clutching her sweater and pulling her even closer.

"I couldn't let her die again, Niko," she had answered. "I just couldn't. But it's all over now. We're okay. Shh baby, I'm here and I will never leave you. I'll always be here, I promise. Let's whistle together, like Mom taught us. Pick a song."

"I...I can't."

Sarah had held his face and wiped his tears. "Yes, you can. You're the bravest boy I know. You and me, we're going to whistle for mom right now. 'Hakuna Matata.' Let's go. On three, Niko. Come on, make Mama proud. One, two, three..." She had held his eyes and started whistling the song, coughing after each long breath. She had whistled into his face until finally, he had given up and joined in.

Hakuna Matata, what a wonderful phrase...

Nick snapped out of his thoughts, suddenly angry. Nothing and no one, not since he could remember, had made his sister break. She was tough and she was smart, way beyond her years. She was the brave one. So, why was she letting a spoiled rich kid keep her away from the game tonight? He had to find her and talk to her. She couldn't let them beat her. He wouldn't let her.

He walked outside, immediately calmed somewhat by the silence of the night outside the noisy gym. He took a deep breath, letting the unusually frigid late March air fill his lungs. Lost as he was in his thoughts, he didn't see Walt Patterson approaching until the older boy stood directly in front of him.

"Hey, Giannopoulos, where's big sis tonight?" he asked, sarcastically.

"Don't see how that's any of your business, *Patterson*." Nick said the name as if it were a disease, feeling his anger flare up again. He knew how Walt had treated Sarah, from her very first day at Lakeview. He hated him for it.

"It's just that I've missed her, since Jamie dumped her." Walt shoved Nick as he walked past him to the gym door. He paused before he opened it and looked back. "But, if I had to guess, I'd say she's out giving Capitano what Jamie got tired of." He laughed at Nick's stunned expression before turning away. He opened the door to go inside.

With a loud, angry yell, Nick threw himself on his back, pushing them both through the doorway and down to the gym floor. Surprised, Walt was unable to react in time to avoid the fist of the enraged boy from slamming into the side of his face. His jaw ached from the blow and Walt moaned angrily as he reached up and rolled Nick off him and onto his back. Both got to their feet quickly but Walt was faster. Nick saw his fist coming and tried to back out of the way but didn't make it. Walt hit him hard on the nose. Nick stumbled backwards, unable to keep his balance, his head reeling and his vision blurred. He tried to steady himself but couldn't. The room was suddenly spinning violently and his face felt as if it were on fire. He started to fall.

Strong arms caught him and held him up before he hit the floor. As if it were coming from a faraway place, he heard Jamie's voice telling him to take it easy. He tried to free himself but Jamie's grip was strong. Slowly, his vision cleared and he saw a large group of kids had crowded around them. With a burst of energy, Nick managed to pull free of

Jamie's hold. Angry, yet still unsteady on his feet, he spun around to look at him. "You...you are the last...person in the world I want...help from," he sputtered out in gasps.

"Niko!" Sarah pushed through the crowd just in time to hear her brother's words. Confused, she looked from Nick's bloodied face to Jamie and then to Walt, before making her way to Nick's side. Pulling her scarf from around her neck, she put a supporting arm around his shoulder and forced his head back, pressing the fabric against his bleeding nose. "God, Niko, what happened?" she asked, more like a mother than a sister, still unable to believe the scene she had just walked into. "Who did this to you?" She looked up, searching the faces around them. Her eyes settled on Walt, taking in his heavy breathing and disheveled state. Robby was holding him back. It dawned on her that Walt was the one who had hit her little brother. Indignant rage coursed through her body.

"Walt Patterson, you are nothing but a pathetic excuse of a brainless coward. Not to mention a complete asshole," she said to him with utter contempt.

"Coming from you, sweetheart, that's a compliment," Walt replied, trying to downplay the embarrassing sting of her words. Sarah looked away from him and checked her scarf. It was quickly becoming soaked in blood.

"We need to get you to a doctor," she told Nick, forcing her voice to stay calm.

She was painfully aware of Jamie standing next to her. She could feel his eyes on her. Her insides flinched when she heard him say her name.

Go away, Jamie, leave us alone. I hate this. I hate the hold you have on me.

"Sarah." His voice was strange, almost apologetic. "He's going to be okay. If...if you need a ride..."

She let go of Nick and turned to him, her eyes defiant. "Let me repeat what my brother just told you, Jamie, since it seems you're hard of hearing. I wouldn't take your help if my life depended on it."

Jamie's eyes narrowed. "Good thing you didn't feel that way at Doogie's."

"Yeah, well, now I do. So why don't you and your badass friends find another eighth grader to beat up on?

"What? I had nothing to do with this!" Jamie said, spitting out each word, glaring at her. "Ask Nick. I walked in on it, the same way you did."

"And you did nothing?" Sarah shouted at him.

"Seriously? What the hell, Sarah? I couldn't stop it!" Jamie yelled back, unable to believe she was standing there accusing him of attacking Nick. "But whatever, right? It doesn't matter what I say, you'll believe whatever you want, every time, no matter what." Without thinking, he grabbed her shoulders and pulled her close. "You're just so perfect, aren't you, Sarah? How can you even stand it? It must be exhausting to always be right about everything," he spat out angrily, his nostrils flaring.

Sarah lifted her chin and met his furious blue eyes with steel brown ones of her own. For a few seconds they glared at each other. When she spoke, it was slow and deliberate.

"I sure was right about you."

They stood inches from each other, their eyes locked together in anger. Jamie's mind began to spin. He tried to find a response, a comeback to the blow her words had dealt him.

But Sarah broke the silence first. "Let go of me, Jamie. I need to take care of my brother."

"You got it," he responded, his nostrils still flaring with anger. He let go of her shoulders, dropping his hands to his sides.

"Besides," she added, as she put her arm around Nick, supporting his weight with her own, sparks flying from her ice-cold eyes, "Charlotte looks absolutely frantic you might miss one of her cheers."

"Not a chance in hell." He returned her sarcasm with a cool grin. "She knows me better than that."

Someone in the crowd let out a whistle. Sarah turned away and did her best to ignore them all as she pulled Nick to the open door. Unable to resist, she kicked it hard with her free leg, slamming it shut behind them.

Walt shook out his letter jacket, righting it on his shoulders. "That girl thinks she's so tough. Way to tell her off, Jamie. You know I hated to hit that kid but he came at me first. You guys must have seen him jump me at the door for no reason at all..."

Jamie shook his head, waving Walt off, unwilling to focus on what he was saying. His mind was still reeling from his confrontation with Sarah. He agreed with Walt on one thing: Sarah was tough. She gave as good as she got. She made him crazy mad.

Yet somehow, when she had stood there hurling insults at him, he had felt alive for the first time in weeks.

Jamie walked away from his friends and leaned against the bleachers. His body ached with the need to go after her. But he wouldn't. He couldn't. Sarah had made it clear she hated him.

Just as it was painfully clear to him that he would never stop loving her.

❦CHAPTER FIFTY-THREE

Sarah changed out of her waitress uniform with relief. It had been an unusually busy Saturday lunch at Steve's and her section had not run smoothly. She had made several errors, something she did not normally do.

She pulled on her jeans and a loose sweater, feeling a little better in the comfortable clothes. She looked in the mirror and realized she looked as disheveled as she felt. There was a large black smudge on her forehead.

Ink? Really? I look like I just rummaged through the dumpster.

Sarah rubbed it off and yanked on the elastic band holding her ponytail. It broke. She sighed, resigned. Turning her head upside down, she brushed the strays from her long hair. Returning to an upright position, she was a little more satisfied with her appearance. She skimmed some lip gloss on her lips, stuffed her belongings into her backpack and pushed open the bathroom door with her back.

She ran headfirst into Andreas, who had obviously been waiting for her.

Sarah groaned, bracing herself for the confrontation she knew was coming. A lecture from her father on how to successfully complete a task was the last thing she needed but she knew there was no avoiding it now. She let her backpack drop to the floor, crossed her arms across her chest and met her father's eyes. He glared at her.

"Numbers 32, 37, 39 and 41. Do those numbers mean anything to you, Sarah?"

"If you're referring to the numbers of the tables I screwed up on today, you forgot 34 and 35." She flashed an indifferent smile but seeing his eyes narrow, reconsidered. She wasn't up to a fight with her dad.

Sarah uncrossed her arms. "I'm sorry, Μπαμπα, I'm not myself today. How about you take the money for my mistakes out of my pay."

"How about you just tell me why you're not yourself?"

Sarah sighed. "I was hoping to have heard back from Clemson by now. Amelia and Hudson have. And I have a research paper that I haven't even...well, I need to work on some more, and yeah, that's about it."

"That's about it? All of it?"

She knew he wasn't convinced. Not even a little. Sarah shrugged and looked away. "Yeah, that's it."

Andreas watched his daughter for a minute. Then he took her chin in his large hand, forcing her to look at him. "What about the boy, Sarah?"

His eyebrows came together as he watched her expression change from nonchalant to indignant. He raised his hands in question.

"The boy is history. He was just another spoiled player with an oversized ego. Amazingly, the North Carolina version of Jake. He was..."

"Was? Did he move? Die?"

Sarah opened her mouth to reply but decided not to. She knew her father was provoking her and she just didn't want to get into details of what happened with Jamie. She straightened her shoulders. "He's history. I don't care about him. I don't want to talk about him. I've just got a lot to do and not enough time to do it. It makes me nervous, that's all." She stood on her tiptoes to give Andreas a kiss on the cheek. "I'm fine Μπαμπα, really I am," she said softly, careful not to meet his knowing eyes. "And I'll do better next time, I promise."

With a quick smile, Sarah threw her book bag over her shoulder and walked past him. She felt her father's eyes on her and knew he had not bought a word of it. He would keep digging, she knew. Sarah sighed. What a crappy day.

⁂ ⁂ ⁂ ⁂ ⁂ ⁂

She saw Jamie as soon as she walked outside.

He was sitting alone on one of the park benches that lined the broad sidewalk. Sarah felt her lips part in surprise. Her insides began to churn and for a moment, she could do nothing but stare at him. Recovering somewhat, she walked towards him slowly. Jamie stood, shoving his hands into the pockets of his jeans.

"Hi."

"Hi," she replied, relieved to hear her voice sounded normal.

"How's Nick?"

"His nose is broken."

Jamie nodded, saying nothing. The silence quickly turned awkward. Then, he motioned to the bench. "Would you sit with me for a minute? I want to talk to you."

Sarah adjusted her book bag on her shoulder. "I'm kind of in a hurry."

Jamie sat down, his eyes tired. "Just for a minute, Sarah," he said, his voice quiet and undemanding. "Please."

Sarah dropped her book bag to the ground and sat down next to him. She felt a strange sense of dread as she waited to hear what he had come to say. She had thought he would try to talk to her for so long. Now that he was finally doing it, she wasn't sure she could handle the words. "How long have you been out here?" she asked, in an effort to break the heavy silence and calm her nerves.

"Long enough, I guess. I've been sitting here hoping I could clear the fog in my brain. But I haven't had much luck." Jamie paused, battling between telling her what he had come to say and saving face. He wasn't sure there was a way to fix this. And he could still walk away with his wounded pride. He kicked at a rock in the dirt, took a breath and held it for a second. "I want to talk about what happened at Michael's party."

Sarah didn't reply. Jamie glanced at her and found she was staring straight ahead. He rubbed his palms on his jeans and clasped them together, resting his arms on his legs. "You went with me, but you were with him. All night. And then, I saw you..." He paused, trying to ignore the familiar wrenching feeling in his stomach at the memory of Michael and her on the patio that night. "I can't get that picture out of my mind,

Sarah. I still don't know what happened out there that night. But I know I should have talked to you about it and not reacted the way I did. I… that's what I wanted to tell you."

Sarah sighed. "What, so *now* you *maybe* believe I didn't cheat on you?" Her voice was bitter as she struggled against threatening tears. She kept from looking at him, knowing she would come apart if she did. "It's been over a month, Jamie."

"I know it has. A total shit month. Look at me, Sarah. This is hard enough. The least you can do is look at me."

Sarah shook her head, refusing to do as he asked. Jamie leaned over and gently turned her face towards him. "I'm used to getting my own way. God knows, you've informed me of that more than a few times. And I know it's not cool, Sarah. It's just how it's always been. And you—you sort of took everything about me that I was sure of and turned it all upside down. And the weird thing about it is, I didn't mind. In fact, I was glad you did. I know you don't believe me, but it's the truth." Jamie looked away, rubbing his palms on his jeans again, struggling with himself and his words. He had never laid his feelings out for anyone but her. He was no good at it.

"You know how I felt—damn it, how I feel—about you Sarah. You're the first girl I've ever loved. I don't 'maybe' believe you, I believe you. And I admit I acted like an idiot at that party. But you gave me reason to. You hung out with another guy all night. You didn't care that all our friends were there. You didn't care what it did to me. I know I needed to change some things to be with you and I got that, I tried. I'm still trying like hell. And I'm still willing to do what it takes to be with you, but there's one thing I won't change: It's all or nothing with me, Sarah. The scene on Michael's patio with his hands all over you plays over and over again in my mind and it sucks. And I'm not apologizing for that. If you choose to be with me, it's all or nothing."

Jamie stood, exhaling deeply. He had gotten out what he came to say. The fog finally seemed to lessen in his brain and he felt better than he had in weeks. Shoving his hands in his pockets, he looked down at her, waiting for her reply. He hoped she understood—and that it still mattered.

Sarah looked up at him, her brown eyes glassy. "I gave a friend a hug. You knew Michael and I were just friends. I never gave you any reason to doubt me, Jamie. You were just mad because I wasn't hanging on to your every word."

"That's almost funny. It's not like you ever made a habit of hanging on to my every word, Sarah. Also, I would never want you to."

"Also, your friends were all watching, right, Jamie? Because, let's be honest, that night was about them as much as it was about Michael. From the beginning, everything changed when they were around. Your friends don't like me. They don't think I'm good enough for you. To their credit, they don't even pretend to. And maybe, what happened, happened because deep down, you agree with them a little."

Sarah stood and turned her back to him so he wouldn't see the tear that had rolled down her cheek. Quickly, she wiped it away.

"I cannot believe you just said that," Jamie said, moving to stand behind her. Sarah heard the anger in his voice. It matched her own. She turned and faced him.

"And I can't believe you just lectured me on fidelity and loyalty. You refuse to call that night what it was because it suits your ego not to. You, Jamie, you," she pointed a finger at him, her eyes changing color as they did when she was heated, "decided to ignore me so your friends wouldn't think you were too into me, right? Am I getting warm? I mean how cool would that be? No, instead you stayed true to form and hung out with the *in-crowd*, protecting your status. Only you didn't count on the effects the alcohol would have on you." She let her finger drop. "Or that I wasn't going to fall apart because Jamie Nelson, God's gift to girls everywhere, wasn't paying attention to me."

"What? I told you I loved you in front of this whole damn town! What the hell do you want from me?" Jamie gave up trying to reign in his temper. "Do you ever listen to anything I say?" he growled, so close she felt her breath catch in her throat.

Determined not to let him intimidate her, she nodded. "I listen, Jamie. Now you try it: listen to me. You and I are too different to work. I'm glad you admit you like getting things your way. That's impressively honest. But I'm not like you. Nothing comes easy for me. Nothing. It's why I don't care about fitting in with the cool kids. I just want to be happy. I'm not going to stand here and judge you..."

"Seriously? You're not?"

Sarah ignored him and continued, her voice steady. "I don't want to judge you or even defend myself to you. The truth is you have many special gifts, Jamie. But you refuse to see the big picture. You have to accept that our differences are too big to be ignored. Everyone that matters to you sees it. Your friends see it. And your mother is number one on the list." Sarah sighed, her emotions suddenly sapped. "I can't even say I blame her. She would die if she knew about my dad. That's the real problem, Jamie. Just circumstances, the way we've both grown up."

Another tear ran down her cheek, giving away her feelings. She wiped it firmly away. "It's not like I haven't been here before. I have. It's why I fought this attraction from the beginning. I'm so tired of heading down dead-end streets. I know life is hard. And I know better than to make it harder. But you...you were so convincing, and I let myself believe that it might be different this time...but it's not. It's always the same script —with the same ending."

Her tears were unstoppable now. Sarah sat down on the bench, covered her face with her hands and sobbed. Jamie felt his anger dissolve into something that felt like fear as he watched her cry. He had not wanted to know about the guys in her past. Now, everything was on the line. Now, he wanted to know.

He sat next to her on the bench. "Who was he, Sarah?"

"It doesn't matter," she said between sobs.

"You're wrong. It matters. And you're going to tell me, if it takes all night. I'm not leaving until you do," he warned in a voice that told her there was no changing his mind.

She knew she would be wasting her time to try. She straightened, wiped her tears and breathed deeply. Jamie knew she was making up her mind—and waited. When she finally spoke, her voice was little more than a whisper. "His name was Jake. He was my boyfriend last year in New York. He was our school's best soccer and football player and every girl wanted to be his girlfriend. But Jake chose me." Sarah looked at him, her eyes still wet with tears. She shrugged her shoulders. "Sound familiar?" He started to respond but she held her finger to his lips. "No, don't say anything. Let me get this out. My dad hated him. Jake was a bad player and Dad saw through him from the beginning. But I…I was obsessed with the whole idea of dating a guy like him. I believed everything he told me. I ignored what my friends thought, what my family thought… every single red flag. I was stupid, so stupid. And then…"

Jamie felt as if he were crawling out of his skin. He was painfully afraid of what she was about to say. She paused and he couldn't stand the silence. "And then what?" he asked her, staring ahead, hating that her feelings for this Jake had been so strong.

Sarah shivered. She closed her eyes, as if to block out a horrible memory.

"Sarah? Tell me. And then?"

"And then…one Saturday night, I stormed out of my widowed father's home, refusing to babysit my little brother so he could go to work, all so I could be with Jake. I still remember Niko waving to me from the window. He looked so scared. But I didn't care. I was out of control. That night Jake took me to a really freaky party. He had never done that before but I guess he was pretty sure that I would do anything he wanted at that point. It smelled so bad, I knew there were drugs, and still I stayed and partied with all those awful people. Jake loved it, he had made me a bad girl and it empowered him. We went upstairs and started making out. He started going too far, too fast and I told him to stop." Her voice was monotone, almost trancelike. Jamie watched her, wanting her to finish but at the same time wishing she wouldn't.

Sarah opened her eyes. "He wouldn't stop. He was drunk and I don't know what else. At the time, I didn't think he did drugs, but now I'm sure he did. Anyway, I fought him. He tore my clothes. I kicked and scratched and screamed. But he was so much stronger than me. He laughed, slapped me and told me girls like me liked it…and then…my dad broke through the door. I'll thank God for that always. Dad saved me. From rape, maybe worse. It was the lowest moment of my life, except for the day my mother died."

"Because you loved him and he betrayed you like that," Jamie said, devastated at how that made him feel.

Sarah shook her head and looked at him. "No. Because Nick was there. He just stood at the doorway and cried. My dad couldn't leave him, he was too young; so he had taken him with him to look for me." Her voice dropped to a whisper. "I hit rock bottom at that moment. But, no. I never loved Jake. He played on my loneliness. I had lost my mother and she and I were very close. She was my best friend. She was incredible."

"I don't know what to say. You should have told me."

"I've never told anyone. I don't think about Jake much anymore. But I do think he came into my life for a reason. He taught me a lesson I'll never forget."

The fire was back in her eyes. Jamie tried not to get lost in it. *She didn't love Jake! She had never loved Jake!* He tried to think of what he should say but his mind was spinning from all she had just told him. Sarah had opened up to him. Again. He knew her well enough to know that meant she still trusted him. He ached to hold her.

"I'm not Jake, Sarah."

"Oh God, no, you're not. You're good inside. Jake was a dark soul wasting away. He used me—or at least he tried to. I don't think you're the same at all. At first I did. I couldn't believe there was one of you in every town." She smiled a little at that. To his surprise, so did Jamie.

"But then, I realized it wasn't the same. But the differences between us are. They build walls that limit and shape us. It's why I know we could never work, Jamie. It's about the circles. People who live in one, stay inside it. You need someone like you, someone from your circle who has grown up the way you have."

"You're wrong about that," Jamie said, quietly, covering her hand with his.

Sarah pulled her hand away and stood. Picking up her backpack, she slung it over her shoulder and met his eyes. "Someone your friends and family will happily accept." She straightened her shoulders. "Someone like Charlotte."

She started to walk away before she burst into tears again. She had only taken a couple of steps before she felt his arm on hers, pulling her back. She turned and looked at him, her lower lip trembling.

"I know what I need, Sarah." His voice was steady, his eyes wounded. There's nothing going on with Charlotte and me. She's a friend, like Michael is to you."

Sarah laughed, sarcastically. "That's a good one. I go to the same school as you do, remember?"

Jamie's eyes narrowed. "I was mad at you." He spat out the words.

Sarah could see he was getting angry again but the subject of Charlotte got under her skin and she didn't care. "Oh, please, Jamie, spare me the horseshit. What was it you told me the other night?" She tapped her chin and pretended to think. "Oh, yeah, you said *she knows you better than anyone*."

Jamie surprised her by hauling her up against him, bringing her face just inches from his. "Why do you have to make me so crazy? I listened to you. Now listen to me. I don't care about Charlotte. I sure as hell don't give a damn about Jake. And if Michael Capitano comes near you again, I won't be responsible for what happens." Sarah didn't have a chance to respond before he lowered his mouth to hers. He stopped, just short of kissing her, pulled back and cupped her face with his hands. "I don't want the circle, Sarah. What I want, what I need…is you," he said, against her lips.

Sarah closed her eyes and allowed the kiss. His mouth took hers gently at first, then urgently, like he was starved for her, and she responded without thinking. For all her previous resolve not to, she surrendered, melting into him like she always did, loving the feel of his arms around her.

But only for a moment. She couldn't do this. She knew what she had to do.

Jamie felt Sarah stiffen, knew she had changed her mind and let her go. He took a step back to keep from touching her again.

"I'm sorry, I didn't mean to do that," he said, his breathing uneven.

Sarah laid her hand on his chest and looked into his handsome face, her eyes clouded with sadness. "Jamie…please, if you care for me at all, please don't ever do it again. After everything that's happened, after what I told you today, after what you already know about my family, you've got to understand we can't do this." Her lower lip trembled again. "I'm sorry, but I mean it, my mind's made up. You and I can never work. That's reality." She smiled sadly, a lone tear trickling down her cheek.

"We tried, Jamie. We both tried. It's time to let each other go."

Dropping her hand, she turned and walked away.

Jamie made no effort to stop her. Instead, he watched her walk straight into a perfect sunset. He knew he would see that picture of her in his mind for the rest of his life. He wanted to be walking with her, his arm carelessly flung around her shoulder. But it was not to be.

He sat back down on the park bench and stared blankly at the empty sidewalk. He had seen the resolve burning in Sarah's eyes. He knew, without a doubt there was nothing more he could say or do.

It was over.

CHAPTER FIFTY-FOUR

Andreas Giannopoulos stood behind the bar at Steve's wiping down bar glasses. But his mind was on his daughter. Glancing out the window, he frowned to find Jamie still sitting on the park bench, looking like he had just lost his best friend. Andreas pondered that for a moment. He had observed the confrontation between Sarah and the boy and used all his self-control to keep from going outside and putting an end to it. Her body language had told him she had been upset. And the memory of Jake Holbrook was still fresh in his mind.

He looked over to where Niko was working on the night's schedule. He wasn't surprised to see the concern on his young son's face as he, too, paused to peer outside at the lonely figure.

Andreas let out a sigh of frustration. He still was not sure he cared too much for Jamie Nelson, Doogie's or not. But he knew, without a doubt, his daughter did. This was not like Jake. She had fought him then, but he now realized the issue had been about her right to choose who she spent time with. This was different. These past few weeks, since she had argued with this boy, Sarah had not been herself. His heart ached for her. God knows he had given her a lot to deal with the night of the farmhouse. Even so, she had approached every day since with courage and a light heart, per usual. She had forgiven him his past. Because of Sarah, he had even begun to forgive himself a little.

Andreas felt his heart swell with love for her. Sarah carried a burden of worry now that she knew of his past. She was too smart for her own good. Not to mention strong and fearless. Just like her mother, she was. Andreas sighed again.

Her indomitable spirit was what he admired most about her. Watching her run from a boy after all she had been through? It simply would not do.

Andreas could not afford not to interfere. Not this time. Throwing the dishtowel on the counter, he moved out from behind the bar in long, determined strides, motioning to Niko that he would return.

⁂ ⁂ ⁂ ⁂ ⁂ ⁂

Jamie had not noticed the sky turn dark, nor did he notice the bitter cold that had replaced the brisk afternoon. It was the merry jingling of bells on the door that finally jarred him from his thoughts. He looked up to find Sarah's father walking towards him.

Jamie got to his feet quickly and extended his hand, an automatic gesture inbred by his mother. Andreas shook it firmly, as he studied the tension in Jamie's face. "Where is Sarah? Did I see the two of you talking out here earlier?"

"Yes, sir," Jamie replied awkwardly, intimidated, as he often was by Andreas's gruff, straight to the point manner. "But...she left."

Andreas narrowed his eyes. "I see. So, you've decided to park yourself on this bench instead of making sure she gets home safely. Where you Southerners get your gentlemen reputations is beyond me."

Jamie swallowed. "I don't think she would have let me walk her home, Mr. Giannopoulos." He shook his head, miserably. "In fact, I think she would have hitch-hiked rather than let me take her anywhere."

Andreas smiled at that. Then, he sat down and patted the seat next to him. "I won't argue with you there. Sit down, Jimmy. You don't mind me calling you Jimmy, do you?" Jamie shook his head and sat down next to him. "It's just more Greek sounding and I like a good Greek name like Jimmy, you understand?" He didn't wait for Jamie to respond. "Anyway, Jimmy, it's true, when Sarah makes her mind up about something," he paused long enough to whistle, "good luck trying to change it."

Andreas spread his arms out and then brought them together in a loud clap. Talking and gesturing went hand in hand in Sarah's family. Jamie had found it amusing, especially when they got riled up about something—which was often. He nodded in agreement and wondered where this was going.

"She's so like her mother, my angel is." Andreas's voice took on a gentler tone. He leaned back, looked upward and sighed, as if remembering the past. "I'm going to tell you something, Jimmy. I had a hard time convincing Maria I was worthy of her. She was cautious around men, having been brought up in Greece, by parents who sheltered her." Andreas looked at him sharply. "It used to be the Greek way, Jimmy, not to allow young girls to date. I used to think it was ridiculous, until I had Sarah, you understand?" Jamie nodded. Andreas seemed to be satisfied with that and continued, "Of course, my wife thought all that was overdone, so I've tried to be less strict with Sarah, especially because I see the head she carries on her shoulders is solid—again, like her mother's."

Jamie nodded again, not wanting to interrupt. Andreas stretched out his long legs and stared straight ahead into the night. "Sarah likes to think she's tough, that she can endure anything," he said, his voice suddenly weary. "And I suppose she is. It's not what I wanted for her, but she has been through a lot of pain for a girl her age. Some of it, because of me. Still, she has not let any of it rob her of her zest for life." Andreas paused and looked at Jamie. "So, I'm going to get to the point, Jimmy. I can't change the past, but I can protect her from the future. I don't want to see her hurt anymore."

Jamie looked down at his feet. "Yes, sir."

"And tonight, I don't have to be her father to see her heart is breaking."

Jamie sat completely still. Now that he knew why Andreas had come outside to talk to him, he was at a complete loss for words. What could he say? Andreas was right. Sarah was hurt—but so was he. He had given her his heart, and she had given it right back to him. *Does Andreas know what happened? Did Sarah tell her father everything?*

"So, talk to me, Jimmy. Tell me what's happened. Tell me why my daughter is so out of sorts that she's been walking around snapping at everyone for weeks. She's acting like me, for God's sake! And why did she run away from here tonight, like someone was chasing her? The Sarah I know doesn't run."

"I...I'm not sure, sir," Jamie answered honestly, meeting the older man's eyes. "I never meant to hurt Sarah. She...she means a lot to me."

"But...?" Andreas let the question hang.

"But...she made it pretty clear she wants nothing to do with me."

Andreas nodded and slapped his hands against his knees with finality. "Well, that's that, then." He stood, grimacing as he rubbed his back. Jamie noted he did that every time he stood, and even in his state of total misery, suppressed a smile. He liked Andreas. He liked him a lot. Coming to his feet, he once again extended his hand.

"Thank you, sir," he mumbled, not knowing what else to say.

Andreas shook his hand, still grimacing. For a moment he said nothing. Then he looked up into the star-filled sky and blew out his breath in the cold night air. "It's almost April and it's freezing. I thought spring in the South was supposed to be warm. New York was warmer than this." He looked back to Jamie. "Do you want something to eat?" he offered, back to his usual gruff manner, as if everything was settled.

"No, thank you, sir, my family is expecting me for dinner."

Andreas brushed off his apron and started walking towards the restaurant. "You have a fine family, Jimmy. I especially like your father and brother." He paused to look at Jamie again. "How is your brother? I have not seen him since that night by the river."

"He's doing well, sir."

"I'm glad to hear that. Bring him by when he's in town. You boys did a good thing that night. No one would say it was smart, but it told me a lot about the Nelson family."

"Thank you, sir." Jamie watched him walk away and realized Sarah's father was actually beginning to like him a little. The irony of that was not lost on him.

She dumps me and her dad wants to hang out...

At the door, Andreas turned. "Like I said, Jimmy, I had to fight hard to win my Maria's affections. She had millions of reasons why the two of us didn't belong together. It's the only thing I ever heard her admit she was wrong about." He chuckled at the memory, then quickly grew serious. "But I knew. I knew I couldn't let a beautiful, strong woman like her go, just as I know it's useless to ever again try to find another like her. She was one in a million, my Maria was. But God found reason to take her from us." His voice cracked with emotion. "I can't say I'll ever understand why, but every time I look into Sarah's eyes, I know she's still here. She has Maria's eyes; they change by the minute; they soothe, challenge, explain, comfort and fascinate. Ah, she's just like her, my angel is." Andreas winked at Jamie and smiled, knowing he was soaking up every word.

"I'm pretty sure Sarah's made up her mind. Unless..." Jamie tried not to sound hopeful, unsure if he was reading her dad's words correctly.

Andreas pulled the door open. "Unless you find a way to change it."

"Mr. Giannopoulos?"

Andreas paused, his large frame filling the doorway.

"Sarah told me about Jake. I would never hurt her, sir."

"I see. And has she told you about me?"

Jamie nodded. "Bare bones, sir. She told me what she said I needed to know." His voice got quiet. "No matter what happens, I won't ever hurt her—or your family."

"I know you won't. Believe me, we wouldn't have had this talk if I thought you would." He paused. "Looks to me, you're a fighter, Jimmy. It's a good thing to be."

He went inside, gently closing the door behind him.

⁂ ⁂ ⁂ ⁂ ⁂ ⁂

When Jamie pulled into his driveway, some ten minutes later, he found Robby sitting on the wall waiting for him.

Robby jumped down as Jamie got out of his car. "Ten guesses on where you've been, bro." He threw the basketball he had been holding at him.

Jamie caught it and shot towards the basket. "Ten guesses is like seven too many. Not the odds I want." He missed the shot and bounced it back to Robby. "What are you doing here? I thought you were hanging out with Sherri tonight."

Robby caught the ball and shot it. It swished through the net. "Nah. She's out of town. Guess I'm stuck with you." Robby passed the ball to his friend, sensing his tension. Jamie shot it again. This time he made it.

Robby threw his letter jacket to the ground. "Lucky shot. Let's play."

Jamie grinned, taking his own jacket off. "Lucky, my ass. That's skill, brother. And you're going down. First one to thirteen wins. Where are the guys?"

"Just shut up and play. And not sure. Probably at a party somewhere but I didn't feel like sticking around to find out where."

Jamie took his first shot and made it. Robby rebounded and dribbled past him to score. Jamie got the ball and eyed his friend. "Nice shot. Do that in play-offs next week."

"Thanks. I plan to."

"Since when do you not care where the party is?"

Robby shrugged and smiled. "I don't know, I guess, since she's kind of who I want to hang out with and she's not there."

Jamie spun around him and got ready to shoot.

"You know, like you and Charlotte."

Jamie missed the shot. Rebounding the ball, he slammed it with both hands. "There is no me and Charlotte."

"No shit. So why don't you tell Sarah that?"

Jamie looked at his best friend, not angry, as Robby had expected, but defeated. He shrugged his shoulders. "I did. This afternoon." He looked away and let the ball fly. It swished neatly through the net. "She wants nothing to do with me."

Robby stared at him in surprise. The part where Sarah had blown him off, he could understand, after what had gone down between them. But this was not the Jamie Nelson he had grown up with. Jamie was actually shaken up. His feelings for Sarah were deeper than Robby had realized. Not knowing what to say, he said nothing. He picked up the ball and the two friends played basketball, the way they had in that driveway since they had been kids. The game ended 13-12, with Jamie the winner. Robby picked up his jacket to go.

"Good game, man. See ya tomorrow."

"Since you're not going out, stay and have dinner," Jamie offered. He tried to sound casual. The truth was, he didn't want him to leave. He didn't want to be alone with his thoughts of Sarah and everything that had gone wrong.

Robby smiled in his usual, good-natured way. "Sure, sounds good. I'm starving."

They walked to the back porch and Jamie pulled open the door. The aroma of something delicious filled the air. For no reason at all, it made him think of Sarah. He wondered what she was doing.

"Don't let her go, man," Robby said, as if he had read his thoughts. "Nothing was going on with her and Michael. Sarah's not into him, dude. I've been keeping an eye out and I'm telling you, there's nothing there."

Jamie nodded, dejectedly. "I know. I took too long to figure that out, though. She's done. I blew it."

Robby frowned. "What's up with that attitude? So, the girl's a challenge. When have you ever backed down from a challenge? I should have told you, but I've liked Sarah from the get-go. From the minute she emptied that tea all over Walt, I couldn't help but like her. I mean, who does that?" He laughed and Jamie smiled at the memory. "Even Walt likes her, man. I think he's even got a little crush on her."

"Well, that's one thing I don't have to worry about. Sarah hates his guts."

Both boys laughed at that. Sobering, Jamie shook his head. "Seriously, man, this girl won't let up on me. From the first day I met her, it's been...

I don't know...like something I can't explain. I remember every second with her, every word." His voice trailed and he looked away. "I love her. I really love her. But she wants me to leave her alone. And I know I should respect that."

Robby mulled that over for a minute. "James, I'm not gonna lie to you. For some reason I have never understood, you've always gotten the girls. Looking back, should it have been me? Probably, but whatever. Regardless, this particular girl, you've fought for. The odds you want are there. She knows you're willing to put in the effort. You just gotta stay the course and show her you're not going anywhere. You say you love her. That's the real deal. She'll see that in time and she'll come around. Sure, Sarah can be a pain in the ass, but she's worth it. I think she's good for you. It's gonna work out, man."

Jamie pictured Sarah's reaction to being called a pain in the ass and smiled. "You really think so?"

"Yeah, I do. I really do."

"You didn't see her face when she told me it was over."

"Still not buying it, mopey. She loves you."

Jamie shook his head. "I'm not so sure. But thanks, man. I appreciate it."

Robby pulled him into a quick hug. "Trust me, bro, I'm the smarter one. Stay the course. For now, let's go see what Daisy cooked that smells this freaking good."

The boys made their way to the kitchen and surprisingly, Jamie felt his mood lighten. He nudged Robby's arm. "So, you think in the end even she can't resist the ol' Nelson charm, huh?"

"I said I don't understand it, dude. Shut up and get me some dinner."

Jamie laughed. "Up for a little FIFA afterwards?"

"Yeah, as long as you don't get all pitiful and lovesick on me again. And don't think for a minute I'll let you win like I did outside."

CHAPTER FIFTY-FIVE

The Lakeview High gym roared with applause as Jamie sunk a three-pointer with one minute left on the clock. He could hear Sarah cheer above the crowd and smiled to himself as he ran back down the court. *She's got some lungs on her. Like her dad. Maybe it's all Greeks,* he thought as he wiped his eyes to see more clearly. The score was tied.

Robby brought the ball down the court, faked like he was going to pass to him but drove in for a lay-up instead. He made the shot and got fouled. The crowd roared, on their feet.

"Rebound!" Sarah bellowed. From the free-throw line, Robby smiled at him as he waited for the ref to pass him the ball.

"Sounds like you'd better get the rebound if I miss."

"Can it and make the shot, you pansy."

Robby laughed, squared up and swished it. Jogging backwards down court, he looked over at Jamie running next to him. "Guess I just saved your ass."

"That'll be the day. Just focus and don't screw up now."

"No fouls!" Sarah yelled.

"I won't." Robby laughed. "She scares me."

Jamie laughed, too. "Yeah, me too, a little."

Coach Willis blew the whistle for a time out. He glared at Robby and Jamie, as they ran to the sideline. "Am I missing something funny, gentlemen?"

"No sir, Coach," Jamie replied, any trace of laughter gone.

Coach Willis shook his head. "Huddle up and listen," he ordered, popping his marker to diagram the next play on his clipboard.

The boys huddled in. The play called for Jamie to shoot from the baseline after they wound the clock down.

"Kill the clock!" Sarah called out.

Coach Willis looked up at Jamie. "Is that your girlfriend, Nelson?"

Jamie shook his head. "No, sir."

Coach looked over to where Sarah sat in the stands. Jamie did too. She was waving to Nick, making his way up to her.

"Hm. All the same, son, I would make this next shot if I were you."

"Yes sir," Jamie said, ignoring Robby's grin.

Coach brought their hands in together. "Let's help Nelson score tonight, boys."

The team cheered, Jamie shook his head and the ref blew the whistle.

Seconds later, the game was over. Jamie didn't make his last shot, but Robby had secured the win. Lakeview was going to the play-offs for the first time in eight years.

Chaos ensued in the gym. Coach Willis found Jamie in the crowd, threw him his bag and pulled him into a bear hug. "Good game, Nelson. Now go get the girl."

Jamie laughed. "Thanks, Coach, but to be honest, that's a taller order than getting to the play offs."

"All the more reason, son. All the more reason." He slapped Jamie's shoulder with affection before moving on to shake hands with a parent.

Jamie scanned the crowd for Sarah. There was no sign of her or Nick. Finally, he spotted Amelia and Hudson. Hudson ran over and threw her arms around him excitedly.

"What a game, what a game! Great job, Jamie!"

"Thanks, Hud. Hi, Amelia."

"Hi. Great game." Jamie didn't miss the lack of excitement in her voice.

"Thanks. Were Sarah and Nick here?"

Hudson laughed. "You've gotta be kidding. Did you not hear her? I think I'm now deaf in my left ear."

Jamie grinned. "Yeah, I did, actually." He noticed Amelia looked tense. "Anything wrong?"

"Um…no," Amelia replied, biting her lip.

"You sure?"

"She's worried about Sarah," Hudson interjected. "She worries too much."

Jamie's smile faded. "Why? What's wrong, Amelia?"

Amelia chewed on her lip. Then, she sighed. "Probably nothing. I don't know. But Nick came in and was freaking out about something. Sarah didn't let him explain. They tore out of here before the game was even over."

"I'm sure they need her at Steve's," Hudson said, rolling her eyes at Amelia. "Seriously, girl, you need to chill."

But Jamie's expression turned serious. "Did you hear anything Nick said, Amelia?"

Amelia shook her head. "Nothing except *the lights are back*. It made absolutely no sense so I know I heard him wrong."

For a moment, Jamie stared at her. Amelia stared back. "Doogie's," she said. "Of course, like at Doogie's."

"What about Doogie's?" Hudson asked. "What are ya'll talking about?"

Careful to not let Hudson see, Jamie motioned for Amelia to stay quiet. She nodded, ever so slightly.

"I heard there might be a party there later. Bet she's making sure Nick doesn't try to go," he said. "Anyway, I'd better get back to the locker room. See ya'll later."

"That makes sense," Hudson said, giving Amelia a playful shove. "See? Don't worry, Grandma, she's fine. She's just being a good older sister."

Amelia smiled and nodded. Jamie winked at her.

"Bye, Jamie!" Hudson called after him. She was too excited to notice he headed for the door, not the locker room. But Amelia did. Sighing, she let Hudson drag her through the crowd.

She would try texting Sarah in five minutes. Again.

❋ ❋ ❋ ❋ ❋ ❋

Jamie ran to his car, fishing his keys out of his duffel bag as he ran. He pulled out of the school parking lot and headed for Steve's, scanning the sidewalks for any sign of Sarah and Nick. There was none.

Damn it, Sarah, where are you?

Stopping for a red light, the thought occurred to him she may have texted. He pulled his phone from the console and checked it. Nothing. He swallowed down the bile in his throat, his mind racing. *Where would they come? Sarah, where did you go?*

It wasn't until he was almost at Steve's that he realized he had no plan. He slowed and tried to think. Driving past the restaurant, he scanned the parking lot for Sarah's bike. It wasn't where she always left it; neither was Andreas's car.

Jamie pulled in to the car wash next door. Parking, he turned off his lights. He could not see inside the restaurant. The blinds were drawn.

It only took a few seconds for him to make up his mind. Sarah would not like it, but there was no other choice. Picking up his phone, Jamie punched in his father's cell number.

CHAPTER FIFTY-SIX

"Dad, where are you?"

"Sorry, son, just leaving the hospital. I had a patient with complications. Did we win?"

"Yeah. Listen, Dad, can you come and meet me? I need to talk to you. Alone."

"Are you okay? Where are you?"

"At the car wash, next to Steve's. I'm fine, I'm in my car in the parking lot."

"At this hour? They're closed. What are you doing there?" Then, as if thinking better of it, he added: "Never mind, I'm on my way."

Jamie felt a rush of relief. "Thanks, Dad. Don't tell Mom, just come."

"All right, son. I'm five minutes away."

Jamie hung up, grabbed his jacket and turned off the ignition. Five minutes felt like an hour, but when he saw his father finally pull in to the parking lot, he quickly jogged over and got in his car. "Hi, Dad. Thanks for coming. Can you kill the lights?"

Dr. Nelson looked him over. "Are you hurt, son?"

Jamie shook his head. "I'm fine. It's Sarah. I think her family is in trouble and I don't know what to do to help them."

Dr. Nelson turned off the car. "Tell me what's going on."

"I want to, but you can't tell Mom. It's about Sarah's family. Give me your word."

"Slow down, Jamie. Take a deep breath. Does anything you are about to tell me have to do with you, your brother or your sister?"

"No, sir."

"All right, then, you have my word."

Jamie nodded, relieved. Then, he told his father all of it, leaving nothing out. He explained he didn't know who the men were or where they would be. But he did know they were the men the gang of boys at Doogie's were working for that night with Nick. He told him they were bad news. They had said they wouldn't come back. But they had—and Nick had recognized the flashing lights, same as the night at Doogie's.

Dr. Nelson picked up his phone. "You did the right thing not trying to find them yourself, son. I'm damned proud of you."

Jamie watched him, confused. "You don't sound surprised, Dad."

"That's because I'm not." He punched in a number and held his phone to his ear. "I had a gut feeling there was something more going on with Sarah's dad after the night at Doogie's. So, I called Wyatt. He, Jack, Teddy and I did some digging."

Jamie fell back in his seat and groaned. "Jesus, Dad, all of them? Why didn't you tell me?"

"Because it was supposed to go away."

Jamie heard his uncle Wyatt's deep voice come on the line. "Hey, big brother. Is my favorite nephew in the play-offs?"

"Yeah. Listen, Wyatt, looks like we have some new developments on that out of town real estate deal I had you look into. I need your advice on it. Can you meet me?"

There was a moment's pause on the line. "Sure, Doc. I have some time before dinner. How about we get a drink at Susie's? You drive, I'll head over to your office."

"Sounds great, thanks." He hung up, powered off his phone and turned to Jamie, who watched him, wide-eyed. "Turn your phone off, Jamie and give it to me."

"What is going on, Dad?" Jamie powered off his phone and handed it to him. "Are you in the CIA or something? You really are a doctor, right?"

"Damn it, my cover is blown. Yes, I faked every surgery for twenty-five years."

Dr. Nelson grinned at his son.

Jamie held his hands out in frustration. "What real estate deal, what drink at Susie's dad? Can you please tell me where we're going?"

"Uncle Wyatt told me if anything like this happens, I was to make that call and say just that. He will meet us at my office and Teddy and Jack will probably be with him. Uncle Wyatt will ride with us to The Meadowview, not Susie's—so we can't be traced. I don't know about Jack and Teddy. They are ready for this, son."

"Ready for what, Dad? Maybe you can just tell me what the hell is going on?"

Dr. Nelson nodded and started the car. "First, open the glove box. There are some pliers in there and a blue wire. Cut it. It's the navigation."

Jamie stared at him.

"Do it now, son. C'mon, stay with me here." He leaned over and popped open the glove box. "Cut the wire."

Jamie picked up the pliers and snapped the wire next to them in two. The navigation screen instantly went blank.

Dr. Nelson smiled. "Atta boy, Teddy. The emergency call light's off, too."

"That's great, Dad. No one can find us as we go to what? To fight the freaking mob at The Meadowview, wherever the hell that is? Next you're going to tell me Uncle Wyatt's got guns and grenades stashed under your seats."

"Relax, son. Take a deep breath. Back in the day, The Meadowview was our favorite steak house, a couple of miles out of the city. It's closed now."

"So, what's our plan, we're going to shoot the bad guys at an abandoned steak house?"

Dr. Nelson grinned. "No shoot-out, son. No guns or grenades, either. We're law-abiding citizens. Although, wouldn't that be something?"

Jamie sat back in the seat again. "No, I don't think it would. Dad, you sound like you like this. Whatever *this* is. What the hell is this? What is happening right now?"

"Keep your head, son. It's always your best weapon. We are not in danger. So listen. Here's what I know: Sarah's dad got mixed up with the Romanos, a white collar mob family in New York. He did some jobs for them, changed course and got out. Should have been a clean break. But, apparently, they like him and don't want to let him go."

"How do you know all of this? What's a white collar mob family, Dad?"

"Between your two uncles, there's not much they can't know if they decide they want to look. And the Romanos steal, they don't kill."

Jamie let that sink in. His dad's brother, Wyatt Nelson, was the United States Attorney for North Carolina. His dad's cousin, Jack Nelson, was the Attorney General. He had never thought his parents sought out information from them. *Well, obviously, they do.*

Aloud he said, "And Uncle Teddy?"

His dad shrugged. "Sheriff Ryan knows all that goes on around here, son. Had he made it to that game tonight, I'm betting he would have called me before you did."

They pulled into the parking lot of the medical offices. Jamie squinted to see better in the darkness. His uncle walked out from behind the building, blending with the night shadows. Dr. Nelson pulled up next to him and popped open the door locks.

Wyatt Nelson slid in the back seat behind Jamie and dropped a large, black duffel bag into the empty seat beside him. He smiled at the blank navigation screen. "Good man, Doc. You remembered. Take off, Jack and Teddy will meet us at The Meadowview." He met Jamie's eyes and grinned. "Hey there, Jamie, heard you had a good game."

Jamie stared back at him, unable to find words to reply. Gone was the usual work suit his uncle Wyatt always wore. Instead, he had on a black t-shirt tucked inside black pants.

And an armored vest over it.

CHAPTER FIFTY-SEVEN

"Sarah, what are we going to do? He's not here." Nick's brown eyes were huge with worry as he came flying out of Steve's kitchen.

"Shh, Niko. Keep your voice down and try not to look upset." Sarah motioned towards Sheriff Ryan, sitting in a booth with two other officers.

Nick followed her eyes before looking back at her. He tried to steady his trembling chin. Sarah smiled at him reassuringly, and took his hand in hers.

"Good job, buddy. He's okay, don't worry. Is Lucy in the kitchen?"

Nick nodded, a tear escaping down his cheek. Quickly, he wiped it away.

"Come with me." Loudly, she added, "The dishes aren't going to wash themselves, Niko. Let's get to it." Sarah pulled her brother into the kitchen. Once there, she paused to look out the window towards sheriff Ryan's table. He was reaching for another piece of pizza and laughing at something one of the officers was saying.

Sarah sighed in relief.

"Isn't Ricky dreamy?" Lucy came to stand next to her. "God, policemen are hot."

Sarah didn't respond. Instead, she took Lucy by the shoulders and turned her to her. "Luce, where's my dad?"

Lucy's smiled faded as she took in Sarah's troubled expression. "I don't know, babe, he left about half an hour ago." She looked at Nick, whose chin was trembling again. Putting down her tray, she reached over and pulled him into her arms. "What's going on?" she asked, reaching out one arm to take Sarah's hand in hers.

"I can't tell you. But I need you to watch Nick and act completely normal, especially until the sheriff and those officers leave."

"Why, where are you going?" Lucy's eyes grew large.

Sarah squeezed her hand. "Lucy, I need you to help me right now. Don't ask me any questions because I can't answer them. All I can tell you is I know where my dad is, and I'm going to go get him." She reached over to ruffle Nick's hair. "Don't worry, Niko, I promise everything will be okay."

Nick wrapped his arms around Lucy and began to sob. "No, it's not. Don't let her go, Lucy."

Sarah pulled him out of Lucy's arms and squatted down, gently wiping his tears away. "This isn't about what you did, buddy. It's a long story. And I promise to tell you all of it later. But right now, I need you to be big. I need you to help me help dad out of something *he* did. We can do it, if we work together. Those policemen are trained to sense trouble and I'm not going to lie to you anymore, Dad's in trouble."

Nick stopped crying. "I'm going with you."

Sarah shook her head. "No, Niko, you're not. You're going to stay here with Lucy and you won't leave her side. Both of you are going to act completely normal. You're going to laugh and joke around and you're not going to say anything to anybody."

"Sarah, whatever this is, your dad would want you to stay here. Just wait here with us," Lucy said, her voice laced with worry.

Sarah looked up at her and shook her head. "Lucy, I need your help and I don't have time to argue about it. I need your car. I know I'm asking a lot of you but I need you to watch Nick, I need your car and most of all, I need you to never tell a soul any of this happened." She looked into her brother's tear-streaked face. "Niko, trust me. I can do this, if you help me. Dad needs us tonight and we can save him, if we work together."

Her phone buzzed and she pulled it out of her pocket hastily.

Hope you're okay. Huddy and I are coming to Steve's.

"Lucy, Niko, listen. I'm out of time. Amelia and Hudson are coming over here and I can't stop them. I can't be here when they do. I don't have time to explain. You must absolutely not tell them anything about this. This is a family secret and Luce, like it or not, you've just been initiated. Please, keep Nick in your line of vision and make something up that makes sense to the girls. Keep them here until I get back, I don't want them going to the house."

Lucy nodded, pulling Nick against her. "Go. But tell me where. If you're not back in an hour, all bets are off. I'm calling the police."

Sarah shook her head. "Niko, keep your phone with you. If I think I need to, I will send the address. But don't call the police. Call Jamie. He'll know what to do."

Nick's eyebrows snapped together. "Jamie? Jamie knows about this?"

Sarah exhaled. "Sort of. Enough to help, anyway."

"I hate Jamie Nelson. I will never call him. Just send the address and Lucy and I will handle it."

Sarah and Lucy shared a small smile. "Deal. We'll do it your way," Sarah said, her heart swelling with love for her brother. She leaned down and gave him a quick kiss on the cheek. "I trust you and I know you trust me. Be big. We got this. You and me, like always. I'll see you back here in a little bit," she whispered in his ear.

Nick gave her a hug, wiped his eyes and walked to his locker to get his phone.

"Sarah, listen..." Lucy began.

"Lucy, please just give me the keys. I don't want to scare him anymore than he already is but I have to go *now,*" Sarah interrupted, her voice desperate.

Lucy pulled her car key from her pocket and dropped it into Sarah's hand.

"Thank you so much," Sarah said. She hugged Lucy tightly before turning away.

"Sarah!" Lucy tried to grab her arm but Sarah was already at the door. Pulling it open, she looked back to find Lucy's eyes were full of tears. "I got your back. We'll do our part. Be safe and don't worry, everything will be smooth as pie here. I won't let Nick out of my sight, I promise."

Sarah felt a tug in her chest. "I know. Luce, I..."

"I love you, too, kid. Now stop wasting time and let's get things back to normal around this place." Lucy shooed her away, straightened her apron and picked up her tray. "C'mon Nick, let's get this show on the road. We've got to cook up a story for Amelia and Hudson. Any chance your sister gives us some help with that before she tears out of here?" she called over her shoulder towards Sarah.

The sound of the door slamming was Sarah's only reply.

⁕ ⁕ ⁕ ⁕ ⁕ ⁕

"The Giannopoulos girl drove off about twenty minutes ago. She used the back door and the waitress's car," Sheriff Ted Ryan spoke quietly into his phone. He watched as Amelia, Hudson and Nick laughed together a few booths away. "Her friends are here, with her brother. No sign of the dad. No one out of the ordinary here."

Wyatt paced the desolate Meadowview parking lot. "Jack just left their house. She didn't go home. All's quiet there, too."

"So, it's going down at the farmhouse. The boys and I will head there now."

"Wait ten minutes, Teddy. As soon as Jack gets here, we'll head there, too."

"You got it." Sheriff Ryan hung up and took the last bite of his pizza. "Damn that was good," he said, rubbing his stomach. "Ricky, get the tab, would ya? Time to go."

Exactly ten minutes later, they had settled up and were out the door. Their patrol cars were parked behind the restaurant. Sheriff Ryan tossed Ricky his burner phone as they walked past the dumpster. Ricky stepped on it, crushed it and tossed it in, barely breaking stride.

CHAPTER FIFTY-EIGHT

Sarah parked Lucy's car on a dirt road near the old farm. She had not told her father but she had gone back a few days after the night she had followed him there. She had walked every inch of the land and learned the farmhouse layout from the windows. If the Romanos ever came back, it would be to the farm. She had wanted to get her bearings and have the advantage of knowing the place, in case she ever needed to.

You always said preparation is key, Mama. I think this plan just might work. So far so good, anyway. We need you. Stay with us, okay? She kissed two fingers, held them to the sky and looked up. Then, she crossed herself and said a quick prayer.

Crouching low around the front of the car, in case they had a lookout, Sarah made her way to the bushy over-growth, thick with weeds and kudzu. Pulling her phone from her pocket, she turned on the flashlight and quickly covered it with the bottom of her shirt to keep the light to a minimum. On her knees, the light low to the ground, she moved through it, feeling her way. In seconds, she found the path she had cut out for herself. Killing the light, she started to run for the farm, keeping as low as she possibly could.

When she got there, she saw no one, just as the time before. Still, she kept by the trees and bushes as she ran. The night was dark and cloudy but Sarah was glad for it. She knew the path this time; she didn't need the moonlight.

Pale light glowed from the farmhouse ahead. Sarah slowed to a brisk walk. The sedan was there. And so was Andreas's car.

As quietly as she could she approached the side of the house. She knew there was only one window on that side; she knew the furniture layout and that their backs would be turned to her; and she knew it was too dark for them to see her.

Reaching the window, she smiled. It was barely cracked, just as she'd left it. Sarah crouched by it, took her phone and turned on the video camera. She held it up, just below the window sill. She could hear their voices perfectly—and she would record every word.

"Just one more time, Andreas," one of the Romanos said. "You train Joey on this one delivery and we call it even."

"I said no." Andreas sounded old and weary. Sarah fought to keep the phone steady.

"Andy," another Romano voice said, "for the last time, we're not asking. You gotta do this thing for us."

"Mr. Romano, I told you, I won't do it. We had a deal and I took you at your word. Instead of keeping it, you put my son in danger and I won't forget that. But I will let it go. I'm not as stupid and naive now as I was when I was young. I've grown a little smarter. And I've taken steps to protect myself and my family from you. The wise thing for you to do is get in your car, go back to New York and leave my family alone."

Sarah shut her eyes. *Help him, Mama, I think I'm the only step he's taken.*

A chair scraped and she heard someone's fists hit the table.

"Damn it to hell, Andy, is that a threat?" Whichever Romano it was, he was angry.

"It's a promise, asshole. Get out of my town." Another chair scraped. Andreas didn't sound old anymore. Sarah barely recognized his voice. She shuddered.

Mama, I'm scared. He's too angry. He needs to walk out. But he's not, I know it.

"Both of you, calm down. Andreas, look at me. Listen real good. You're upsetting my big brother right now and that's not going to turn out good for you. In fact," he paused for a moment, "last time you upset him, he set your house on fire."

Sarah brought her free hand to her mouth to keep herself from gasping.

The fire wasn't an accident...

She sagged against the wall in disbelief, her mind racing with awful memories of smoke, fear and loss. And now, rage. They could have died that night, she and Niko. They had lost everything. She clutched the phone with both hands, too angry to cry.

Just then, she heard a click. Quickly, another followed. "May God damn you to hell, Romano," she heard her father say.

Oh God, he's got a gun. And so do the bad guys. A chill ran down her spine.

"Put those down, Andy," the voice of the older Romano brother said calmly.

Those? Two guns? Dad, what are you doing?

"My children almost died in that fire. This ends today, boys. You're both going to hell. And if I have to go with you, I'm ready to take my chances with the devil."

"Stop and think, Andy. What will this solve? Even if you kill us and we kill you, the family will come after your kids. Think, Andy, you're smarter than this. Put down the guns, sit down and shut the hell up so we can figure this out."

"He's outta control, V. Who you tryin' to impress with your two guns? Me?"

"You shut up too, Mike. Put down your gun."

"Not before Rambo does. I told you he's got shit for brains."

He's going to die in there. I have to do something.

Sarah stopped recording, stuffed her phone in her pocket and closed her eyes. She took a deep breath and let it out slowly.

You have to go in there. Now. Run.

Her eyes popped open. She thought she'd see her mother standing in front of her. She had heard her voice, clear as day. Sarah jumped up and ran towards the front door.

When she turned the corner, out of nowhere, strong arms grabbed her. A man's hand clamped firmly over her mouth.

Sarah screamed but no sound came out. She kicked and struggled but the man's arms only tightened around her. He picked her up as if she weighed no more than a feather—and carried her into the darkness.

CHAPTER FIFTY-NINE

"Sarah. I'm here to help. I need for you to be very quiet."

Sarah tried to make sense of the words. Her heart was beating so loudly, she wasn't sure she had heard the deep, unfamiliar voice correctly. She grunted and kicked, trying to twist out of the man's hold. He pulled her more tightly against him.

"Sarah. Your father's life may depend on you right now. Stop making noise."

Sarah stilled. The man loosened his hold around her body. But not her mouth.

"I work for the North Carolina Attorney General, Jack Nelson. Jamie sent for us. We are here to help you and your father but I need your help to do my job. First, I need for you to be very quiet. When I take my hand away, I need your word you won't make a sound. Nod if you understand. Nod if I have your word."

Sarah nodded, her eyes wide with disbelief. The man took his hands off of her and she almost fell forward. He reached out and steadied her.

"Don't speak, just listen," he instructed, his low voice a whisper. Sarah nodded again and slowly turned to face him. He was some kind of police officer, dressed in all black. Her lips were numb as they gaped open. He wore an armored vest. On it was a seal with FBI in large white letters. Her eyes dropped to the gun in his belt.

"My name is officer David Wilson. I'm not going to hurt you, Sarah. I need you to stand behind me because they are about to go in the farmhouse. As soon as they do, we stay as close to the tree line as we can and get you to my car."

Sarah's eyes became panicked. She shook her head.

"Sarah, this is happening. We are going in and we are going to get your dad out alive and well. The only thing that can stop that is you. If he sees you here, he will panic. And he is holding two guns right now. Panic is the last thing he needs." Officer Wilson took out his radio and clicked it on. "Sarah and I are good to go," he whispered into it.

Sarah watched him, her whole body numb, her mind unable to catch up with anything he was saying or doing.

Just then, the yard exploded in light. Sarah saw what looked like an army of dark forms emerge from behind police cars and black SUVs. Guns drawn, they stormed the farmhouse from all directions.

"Now, Sarah. Stay behind me and stay low." Officer Wilson took her hand and pulled her further away from the house, running close to the woods as he had told her they would. Sarah had no choice but to follow him. When they reached a black SUV, he opened the back door and motioned for her to get inside.

"No." Sarah shook her head. "I won't get in. My dad needs me."

"In you go, kid. There's no time for this." Officer Wilson picked her up, threw her in the back seat and closed the door in one fluid motion. Stunned, Sarah watched as he drew his gun. With a quick, reassuring smile, he turned and ran towards the farmhouse.

Furious, Sarah lunged for the door to follow him. It wouldn't budge. She tried again. The lock wouldn't open.

Suddenly, she sensed movement. She wasn't alone in the car. She spun around, expecting to see another officer. Her eyes widened in shock and disbelief.

Jamie sat quietly in the darkness beside her.

CHAPTER SIXTY

"Sarah, don't be afraid. Everything is going to be all right," a familiar voice said from the front passenger seat. Confused, Sarah squinted to see more clearly in the dark.

"Dr. Nelson?"

"Yeah, honey, it's me."

Sarah stared at the shape of him. "What is going on, what is all this?"

"Jamie told me your dad was in trouble tonight. What he didn't know is I had done some digging on my own after Doogie's. My brother, Wyatt, is the US Attorney here. I asked him and my cousin Jack to look into your dad, discreetly, of course. It was between us, I didn't share what I learned with anyone. Bottom line, we know about the Romano family and your dad, Sarah. And we want to help him—and Nick and you."

Sarah felt the blood rush into her face. "Officer Wilson said he works for Jack Nelson. Your cousin is the Attorney General?"

"Yeah, we like to say we keep it in the family: They catch the bad guys and I sew them up when the bad guys leave their mark."

"Dr. Nelson." Sarah sat very still, her voice small. She would not look at Jamie. "You're saying you know my dad worked for the Romano family in New York."

"I know your dad's a good guy who made a bad mistake."

Sarah dropped her head into her hands. "What's going to happen to him? Are they going to arrest him?" she choked out, dreading the answer.

"No, Sarah, they're not. Don't worry, they will explain it all to you as soon as they finish up in there. Trust me, they're ready for this."

Sarah sat back in her seat, her mind spinning. She wasn't sure what was happening was good. Still, she didn't think it was bad, either.

"Look, they're coming out. That means they found a solution. Officer Wilson is coming back. And I see your dad with him."

Sarah watched as her father walked towards their car with officer Wilson.

Thank you, God. Oh, Mama, he's all right. I can't believe it.

"Is...is that the Sheriff with them?" she asked, tears streaming down her face.

Dr. Nelson nodded. "Well, honey, Sheriff Ryan married my first cousin, Emmie."

Sarah kept her eyes on her father. "Of course, he did. Why wouldn't he?"

Dr. Nelson tried to hide his smile.

Officer Wilson pointed to the car and Andreas started to run. Reaching her door he pulled it open. Sarah catapulted herself into his arms and held on tight.

Together, they sobbed. Words they both needed to say would wait for later.

❋ ❋ ❋ ❋ ❋ ❋

"Everything go okay in there, Dave?" Dr. Nelson asked, as officer Wilson secured his seat belt and started up the car. Andreas drove past them down the dirt drive towards the road, his arm thrown protectively around Sarah.

"Smooth as silk." He winked at Jamie through the rear view mirror. "Good thing you spotted your girlfriend by that window, Jamie. She almost blew this whole thing up. She's a fighter, that one." He held up his hand. "Look at those teeth marks. DeeDee's going to freak out when she sees this." He chuckled.

"She's not my girlfriend, sir, I blew that a while back." Jamie shrugged his shoulders at the officer. "And she's going to be seriously pissed at me for this."

"Give her time, kid. Her dad's off the hook and that's no small thing."

Jamie shook his head. "You don't know her like I do. I promised not to say anything. Next thing she knows, the entire justice department shows up."

Officer Wilson laughed and put the car in drive. "I gotta say, from what I saw, tonight, the Romanos might just get off easier than you, Jamie."

"Yes sir, I think they might."

"Well, you're about to find out how mad that little lady is. After we pick up your car from the Meadowview, Jack said to head to Steve's. We're all meeting there. Minus the Romanos, of course."

Jamie groaned. Looking back, he saw his uncle Jack's SUV following them.

"Where's Uncle Wyatt?"

"He said he needed a minute with the Romanos alone. Had Teddy take their phones outside, too. He said they'd be right behind us after Teddy's boys escort the Romanos to the State line. I don't know what that's all about but I wouldn't want to be the Romanos right now, in that cabin with your uncle Wyatt, " Officer Wilson said.

"Do you know what it's about, Dad?"

"I have no idea." Dr. Nelson mulled the information over. "It's safe to say that's how Uncle Wyatt wants it. I'm with you, Dave, I almost feel sorry for them."

"But you think he's okay? I mean, they're mobsters."

Officer Wilson looked back at him through the rear view mirror and winked. "They're no match for your uncle Wyatt, kid. Besides, your uncle Teddy's in there with him. And for whatever reason, he's not too fond of Italians." He chuckled.

Jamie nodded but didn't respond. He couldn't get his thoughts straight. The whole night had been crazy. Even worse, Sarah had not spoken a single word to him.

CHAPTER SIXTY-ONE

"What the hell is this?" Vito Romano sat next to his brother at the table in the cabin. "We agreed to your terms already. This is bullshit." His eyes narrowed as he watched Wyatt quietly say something to the sheriff.

"Shut up, Romano, before I change my mind about letting you go," Sheriff Ryan snapped back. He spoke to two officers standing at the door. "Wait for us outside. And make sure those cell phones are off."

"Sounds like you don't want your government to know how you treat civilians," Vito said, his eyes narrowed. His hands balled into fists.

Wyatt walked to the table, leaned close to him and smiled. "Now, see, Vito, that's funny to me. If I were you, I'd be worried about *your* relationship with the United States government. Seeing as every branch of it has your number, you piece of shit."

Michael Romano looked at his brother. "We need a lawyer, Vito."

From the doorway, Ted Ryan chuckled.

Wyatt straightened, pulled over a chair and sat down. "Okay, let's cut to the chase here. First, we review what happened here tonight: We were alerted of unusual activity by a concerned citizen who saw you pull into what everyone in this town knows is an abandoned farm. Sheriff Ryan and his officers answered the call and came here to find you holding Mr. Andreas Giannopoulos, a Kernersville citizen, at gunpoint. Mr. Giannopoulos is fairly new to our city and was simply here to see if the farm was for sale when you jumped him."

Vito shook his head. "This is unbelievable."

"Yes, that's what Mr. Giannopoulos thought as well. Here he was, innocently looking for land to build his home when he was attacked and dragged into this cabin by drug dealers. Classic bad luck."

Michael glared at him. "The way I see it, you and country-Earl over there know Andreas worked with us. That means there's a trail. Your story don't hold water."

"*Doesn't* hold water, you ignorant piece of shit," Ted said.

"What?" Michael looked over at him.

"Sheriff Ryan is correcting your grammar, Mr. Romano." Wyatt smiled.

"God, you Italians piss me off." Ted took his gun out of its holster and twirled it in his hand before putting it back.

Wyatt kept his eyes on Vito. "Looks like you're the brains of this family. Tell your brother not to interrupt me again." He leaned back in his chair. "Trust me, you don't want to make Sheriff Ryan angry." Ted nodded slowly and crossed his arms across his chest.

Vito shook his head and brought his fisted hands together on the table. His face began to turn red.

"Ah, Vito, I see you're beginning to understand. There is no trail that leads to Andreas Giannopoulos. Only a trail that leads to you."

"So, you just made up false paperwork. And who has it exactly? What is this, blackmail?"

Wyatt leaned in. "We represent the United States of America, Vito. We don't blackmail. As for who has it, I can't say for obvious reasons. I will advise you, however, to get your accounts in better order. Interestingly enough, I had a call from the IRS about you, just the other day."

Vito's face got redder. His fists tightened together on the table.

"Let me guess. The IRS agent is your brother."

"Not an agent, Vito. The head of it. College roommate."

Vito's fists slammed on the table. Furious, he stood up. Michael looked from him to Wyatt, wide-eyed.

Ted's hand went to his pistol. "Sit down, capomandamento."

Vito's eyes narrowed into slits. "Remind me of your name, Sheriff."

"It's public record, donnie-boy. Like your tax returns. Look it up—or don't. I don't give a shit. Now sit your ass back down."

Vito's nostrils flared. Slowly, he sat down. Wyatt tapped two fingers on the table.

"Focus, Vito. You dragged Mr. Giannopoulos into this cabin and probably would have killed him and buried his body out here, if the good sheriff hadn't shown up."

Michael snorted. "We don't kill nobody. Ever."

Wyatt's eyes stayed on Vito. "That's what Mr. Giannopoulos thinks, too. But you and I know differently, don't we, Mr. Romano?"

Michael turned to his brother. "What the hell's he talking about? We never killed nobody. Tell him, Vito."

Wyatt watched the color drain from Vito Romano's face.

"That's it. I want a lawyer."

Wyatt leaned in close to him. "Sounds like you might have gone that one alone, Vito. Maybe Mike doesn't know you hired the furniture delivery man to drive his truck into Andreas Giannopoulos's car."

Michael looked at Wyatt, his eyes wide again. "No, that never happened."

Wyatt nodded. "Yes, it did. We have proof, Vito. Andreas wanted out and you couldn't risk him telling what he knew. Gene Steadman owed the bank—your bank—money. He was desperate to not lose everything so he took the deal: Gene caused the accident to shut Andreas up for you. And you forgave the loan."

Michael's eyes turned to his brother. "What's he talking about, V?"

Wyatt leaned in even closer, his voice little more than a whisper. "Except Gene didn't have the brains to make sure Andreas was driving the car that day. He rammed his truck into Maria Giannopoulos and the two children instead."

Vito cracked his knuckles. "What do you want?"

Michael sat back in his chair, his expression stunned.

"It's more about what you want, Vito. What you need. Because you and I both know, if Andreas Giannopoulos ever finds out you killed his wife, there is nowhere you or your family can hide. He's a killing machine when it comes to the enemy; he's got the medals to prove it. It's why you want him so badly, isn't it?"

"Vito. What the hell did you do?" Michael leaned on the table and dropped his head into his hands.

Vito ignored his brother. "I said I want a lawyer. Now."

Wyatt shook his head. "You don't need a lawyer Vito. We made a deal tonight and unlike you, we keep our word—unless the deal is broken."

Vito snorted. "What you're doing is illegal. Nothing you say will stand up in court."

Wyatt's eyes showed no emotion. "A dead man doesn't need a lawyer, Vito. Andreas will find you no matter where you run. You're smart enough to know that much." He stood up.

"So, the sheriff will escort you out of the state now. As for the rest of us, we were never here. What was said here tonight stays here. It stays here unless you make one wrong move." He looked from Vito to Michael and back again. "Listen closely to this part: If anyone in the Giannopoulos family even sprains an ankle, all eyes will be on you. And I mean every branch of the United States Justice Department. Paperwork and witnesses will materialize." He paused. "And I gotta tell you, asshole, I hope it happens. You murdered an innocent woman and destroyed countless lives with your drug deals and money laundering." Wyatt pushed his chair neatly under the table.

"Lucky for you, we feel the Giannopoulos kids have been through enough. I don't want to have to put their father in jail for ridding the world of you. Otherwise, you'd be in a holding cell right now."

"Damned straight you would." Teddy shook his head in disgust.

Wyatt turned his back to the Romanos and picked up his bag from the floor. "So, go back to New York. Or hop the first plane to back to Italy, it doesn't make a difference." He nodded to Ted as he walked past him but turned back as he opened the door. "I'd hate to be you, Vito Romano, when you meet your maker. Maybe you can do something to help yourself with that, I don't know. It requires a conscience." His eyes were ice cold. "All I know is, one wrong move from any of you, tonight's deal is off. And your day of reckoning comes sooner than later."

Wyatt walked out of the cabin without waiting for a reply.

CHAPTER SIXTY-TWO

Late into the night, with the CLOSED sign on the door, Wyatt shared a pizza with his brother, nephew and cousin Jack at Steve's. Sarah and Nick listened in stunned silence as he told them the Romanos would never be a problem again. Andreas listened too, until Wyatt finished explaining the government was aware of the shady dealings of the Romano family over the years.

"Mr. Giannopoulos, I know you had a friendship with the Romano family in New York. I want you to know our investigation turned up nothing you should be worried about. Consider this case closed, as far as you are concerned." Wyatt paused to smile at Sarah and Nick. "It's important to not talk about what happened tonight. To anyone."

"Yes sir," Nick stammered, his chin trembling.

Sarah took her brother's hand in hers. Timidly, she met Wyatt's eyes.

"We understand. And we can't thank you enough for helping us."

"Gentlemen, I don't have the words to say thank you," Andreas said, his voice shaking with emotion. "I don't think I ever thought I could come back from this." He wrung his hands together on his aproned lap. "I can only apologize to all of you." His voice wavered and his eyes grew misty as he looked at Sarah and Nick. "I was a stupid kid. And then," his voice cracked on a sob, "I lost your mother. After that, I lost my mind. I will be ashamed of it the rest of my life. I never would hurt you, I..." His shoulders began to heave.

Sarah and Nick stood and wrapped their arms around him. Andreas held them tightly, as they consoled each other, grief-stricken, yet relieved and hopeful at the same time. It was a new start. They could leave the past behind them—for good.

Wyatt and Dr. Nelson smiled. Jack wiped a tear. But Jamie kept his eyes only on Sarah.

I love you. Don't quit on us. Look at me, Sarah. Say you forgive me.

As if she heard his thoughts, Sarah turned and met his eyes. Jamie watched as they slowly filled with fire. She was angry. He looked away.

Andreas let his children go and dabbed his misty eyes with his apron. "I owe you more than I can repay. Somehow, my prayers have been answered and I thank you, from the bottom of my heart. I promise you this: I will do for someone else, a great good, as you have done for me." He put an arm around Sarah and Nick. "As you have done for my family." He smiled and ruffled Nick's hair. "Of course, pizza is on the house tonight. A round of beer, everyone?"

The suggestion was met with enthusiastic cheers from the men. Andreas bowed and walked to the bar. Lucy blotted her running mascara, sniffed and pulled beer mugs out. Nick ran over and hugged her tight around the waist as she poured. The restaurant echoed with joy and laughter. Sarah smiled as she watched them before turning to Jamie.

"Jamie, can I talk to you outside for a minute?" she asked, her tone sober enough to put the revelry at the table on pause. She didn't wait for a reply, instead walked briskly towards the front door.

Dr. Nelson laid a supportive hand on Jamie's shoulder. "This one's all you, son. Good luck."

"Yeah, I'm gonna need it," Jamie answered as he stood. Jack tried to hide his smile. Wyatt let out a low whistle.

Sarah unlocked the door just in time to let Sheriff Ryan in. She was unsure how to greet him. But Ted smiled and rubbed his hands together.

"Hi, Sarah. Tell me they saved me some pizza. I'm starving."

Sarah tried to smile back. "Yes sir, of course." She chewed on her lip, shifting her weight nervously.

"You running track this season? My daughter Olivia really hopes so. She says you're the best runner on the team. If you sprint the way you long distance run, I'm looking forward to it. I watched you run with

Jamie last fall and I gotta tell you, I was impressed." He paused and winked at her. "And my nephew was too."

"Thank you, Sheriff Ryan."

"Sure thing."

Sarah's lip quivered. "No, I mean, thank you. For...all this."

Ted put his hands on her shoulders. "Listen to me, young lady. Some people shouldn't walk this earth—but they do anyway. When I can play any part in getting them out of my town, I'm honored to do it. Now, don't you waste another minute worrying about the likes of them. They're gone for good. You understand me?"

Sarah nodded. "Yes, sir. It's why I can't thank you enough."

Sheriff Ryan winked at her again. "You gave Officer Wilson a run for his money tonight. I enjoyed seeing it. Between that and your daddy's pizza, I'd say we're even."

Sarah groaned. "I may have bitten him. I didn't know he was a good guy."

Sheriff Ryan stepped back, laughing heartily. "You just might have a future with the police force, Sarah. Dave tells me you recorded a confession tonight. You keep us in mind when you choose your career. I can make Dave and you partners and you can help us toughen him up." Sarah nodded and burst into laughter, as well.

They were still laughing when Jamie walked up.

Sheriff Ryan held out his hand. "Hi, Jamie. Congrats on the win tonight."

"Thanks, Uncle Teddy."

No one spoke further. Ted looked from Jamie to Sarah noticing neither would look at each other. Tension permeated the air. He knew it was time to take his leave. Good-naturedly, Ted slapped Jamie on the shoulder.

"Okay then, kids, I'm gonna go hit the pizza table. Y'all stay safe." He looked towards the bar. "You got another one of those?" he called to Lucy, who was still pouring beer. Lucy nodded and motioned him over.

"Sure do, Sheriff. Ricky coming, too?" she asked with a coy smile.

"Fool that he is, he went home, darlin'. Dave too. A couple of mama's boys if you ask me, but what can I do? Slim pickings, these days. Just pour one for me."

Nick came out of the kitchen with a tray of clean glasses. He smiled as he handed one to Lucy. "Hi, Sheriff Ryan."

Ted smiled back. "Hello, Nick. I just tried to enlist your sister to the police force but she laughed at me. How about you? What do you say?"

Nick's eyes filled with excitement. "I say, yes sir!"

Ted winked at him, taking the beer mug from Lucy. "Deal. Come see me when you're out of school. I'll save you a spot, son." Nick beamed and Lucy giggled.

Sarah sighed. Without looking at Jamie, she pushed open the door and walked outside. She didn't hold it open and it slammed shut.

Jamie tried to ignore the muffled laughter behind him as he opened the door and followed her.

CHAPTER SIXTY-THREE

Sarah watched as he walked towards her. He stopped when he got close, put his hands in his pockets and waited. She crossed her arms across her chest. Her eyes blazed with anger.

"You told."

Jamie felt his own temper flare. "You gotta be kidding me. That's what you're going to say? Where would you be right now if I hadn't?"

Sarah shook her head. "I don't know. All I know is I trusted you—and you told."

"I had to. It's the only play there was."

"But you promised, Jamie. You gave me your word."

"I promised I would save you. That's what I promised."

"Did it ever cross your mind to tell me you're related to the entire justice department? What if my telling you had caused my dad to go to jail?"

Jamie exhaled. "Lower your voice. I didn't tell any of them. I didn't tell anyone until tonight. My dad did that on his own after Doogie's. I didn't know about any of it."

Sarah snorted. "Right. I totally believe you."

Jamie shook his head. "Whatever, Sarah. You know, until this minute, I thought all I wanted was for you to forgive me. But you know what? I'm over it."

"You're over it? What does that mean?"

Jamie shrugged. "It means I'm glad you don't have to be scared any more. I'm glad it's all taken care of." He paused, leaning closer to her. "Because of me."

"Because of you? Wow. That's good though, because I'm over it, too. I just would like to ask you, not for me, but for Nick, can you please not tell anyone else about my dad and the freaking mob?" She too, leaned in close, her eyes furious. "Can you try, Jamie? It shouldn't be that hard; it's a small town and you've already told half the people in it."

Jamie glared at her, inches from her face. He threw his hands in the air. "I'm not talking to you anymore. You're yelling at me for doing the right thing. I'm done."

He turned and started to walk away.

"Jamie, wait," Sarah called out to him, her voice small.

He paused without turning around. In the stillness of the night, he heard her sigh.

"It is because of you. You saved us tonight. It just scares me they all know."

Jamie turned back. For the first time all night, she looked afraid. He felt his anger melt away. "It's over Sarah. Uncle Wyatt and Uncle Jack have taken care of it." He took a step towards her. His heart leapt in his chest with hope.

A second ago, I'm done. She says one nice thing and I'm putty. Shit.

Sarah looked past him into the restaurant. "Why are they laughing at us?"

Jamie turned to look through the window. Sure enough, his family was watching them, grinning. His eyes narrowed. Instantly, they all looked away. Except for Teddy. He held up his beer mug and smiled cheerfully. Jamie shook his head. "Because they can see I'm getting chewed out."

Sarah looked up at him, confused. "And they're laughing?"

Despite his roller coaster feelings, Jamie smiled at her. "Yeah. They love it. Because that never happens and they think it's funny."

Sarah thought that over. "You mean they've never seen anyone mad at you before?"

"Not really. I mean, at least not a girl screaming at me in a parking lot."

Sarah rolled her eyes. "I'm not screaming."

"Well, it's pretty obvious, you're mad."

"I *am* mad, Jamie. I'm mad because maybe I could have handled this without them all knowing. We'll never know because you just took over."

Jamie shook his head. "You couldn't have handled it alone and you know it."

For a minute, Sarah didn't speak. When she did, her voice was small again. "What if they tell, Jamie? What if they forget, like by accident, I don't know."

"They're professionals. They won't."

Sarah wrung her hands together. "Does your mom know?"

"No."

Sarah's phone lit up and she sighed again. "That's Amelia. She's been waiting for me at my house. I guess I'd better go before she calls whatever form of police is left."

Jamie smiled. "There isn't any."

Sarah tried not to smile back but failed. "God, what a mess. On my way home I'll have to start practicing the whole 'my dad decided to explore buying a farm because he wants us to start farming and walked into the middle of a drug deal by accident' story."

Jamie laughed. "She'll buy it. Just don't say too much. And tell her to keep it on the down-low."

Sarah raised an eyebrow. "Yes, that seems to work every time."

Jamie shrugged, sobering. "I would do what I did again. I'm not sorry."

Tell her you love her. That she's safe now. That you'll give her a ride home.

Instead, he said nothing.

"Well," Sarah said, "I'd better get going."

"Yeah, it's been a long night. I'm glad it's over."

Sarah nodded and looked away. "I know you are, Jamie. Sorry I yelled at you. And thanks for," she motioned towards the window, "all of this."

"Sarah, wait a minute."

That's not what I meant. That's not what I meant at all.

But Sarah had already walked past him into the restaurant. She didn't speak to anyone, instead went straight to the kitchen. Lucy and Nick hurried after her.

Jamie did not go back inside. He waved to his dad and uncles through the window and walked to his car. Neither the Nelsons nor Sheriff Ryan came out to say goodbye.

It was obvious to all, goodbyes had already been said.

CHAPTER SIXTY-FOUR

"I still cannot believe he actually asked me! I mean, he was so adorable, so…oh my gosh, I sound like such a dork!"

Sarah had to laugh, as she hurriedly swapped out her books and slammed her locker door shut. Turning towards Amelia, she couldn't help but laugh again. Her friend's excitement was contagious. "No, you sound love-struck. Slow down and tell me everything. But in two minutes. I can't be late again."

"Wait!" Hudson appeared and threw her arms around both Sarah and Amelia. She looked at Amelia and nodded. "Now, go. I can't wait to hear this. Everyone's talking about it! Best *prom-posal* ever!"

Amelia smiled. "Hudson, you were there!"

Hudson giggled. "I was. But I want to hear it again. It's the most romantic thing I've ever seen…"

"And I missed it? How did I miss it?" Sarah wailed. "Tell me what he said!"

"Oh, sister, it's not what he said. It's how he said it," Hudson explained, with an exaggerated, dreamy sigh.

"How did he say it then?" Sarah grabbed Amelia's arm, her eyes wide.

"Okay, listen," Amelia began. "So, Huddie and I went to Three Spoons last night."

"It was really afternoon. Almost dusk," Hudson interrupted. Sarah glared at her.

Amelia nodded. "Right. Almost dusk. So, anyway, we left and took the steps down to Falls Park to walk home the long way."

"Yeah, we were exercising." Hudson shrugged when Sarah glared at her again. "What? We totally were."

"Hudson. We have two minutes before class. If you speak again before this story is over, I will hurt you," she warned. Hudson's response was to stick out her tongue.

"Okay, okay, three-year-olds, stop, both of you," Amelia said, laughing. "So, anyway, we walked down the stairs and there was Derek, standing in the park in a button down, khakis and tie. He was holding roses."

Sarah's mouth dropped open. "Oh, wow! And he asked you to the prom?"

"Not with words..." Hudson sighed again.

"How, then?" Sarah looked from Hudson to Amelia, excitedly.

Amelia smiled. "Well, he had spelled 'PROM?' out in front of him. With...candles."

Sarah clamped her free hand over her mouth. All three girls squealed, their heads close together like they were in a football huddle. "Amelia! That is the sweetest thing I've ever heard! Sarah hugged her friend hard. "I'm so happy for you!"

Hudson jumped in on the hug and the three friends laughed. When they finally pulled apart, Amelia sighed and looked at Sarah.

"Do you think he's changed? Do you think I can trust him?"

Sarah nodded, still smiling. "I do. I think there's hope for ol' Derek, after all."

Amelia smile was so big it covered her face. "Well, I'm taking things slowly this time. Time will tell. But one thing's for sure: This is going to be a very interesting prom."

"Are y'all talking about the prom?" Ali Brockman walked up to the group, a cheerful smile on her face.

"Oh, hi Ali," Amelia said, still beaming.

Sarah tried to listen as Ali talked about the prom preparations. She had never gotten a good vibe around Ali Brockman, although she had no reason to dislike her. It was just a gut feeling; something about her just wasn't quite right. She was nice as she could be to everyone, popular or not, and everyone seemed to like her.

Including Amelia and Hudson. If my best friends like her, I should like her. I really do have trust issues...an honest reaction after the mob burns down your house, but still, I need to work on that.

Sarah tucked away her negative thoughts and forced herself to pay attention to the conversation. For a minute, she succeeded, but then her mind wandered to Jamie. *I wonder where he is...* She was relieved to hear the bell ring.

"Huddie, we'd better get going. We've got that French quiz..." Sarah smiled at Amelia. "More details later?"

Amelia nodded. "Good luck on your quiz."

"She doesn't need luck. She translates everything into Greek first and figures it out. Weird, yes, but she smokes us every time," Hudson complained, as she hugged Amelia bye.

Sarah laughed. "Whatever works, right? Just so you know, it is not a work out to walk home 'the long way' after you eat ice cream."

Ali laughed. "Y'all crack me up. I jut love y'all! Prom is going to be awesome!" She grabbed Sarah's arm, excitedly. "Sarah, who are you going with?"

Sarah shrugged. "I'm not going."

Ali laughed again. "Of course you are, silly. You're only the prettiest girl in school." She pulled them all close to her. "Okay, I'm not supposed to say because it's a secret but the votes are in and I know who the prom king and queen are!"

"Oh, well, you really shouldn't tell us..." Hudson whispered, giggling. "But really, tell us anyway."

"Yes, our lips are sealed!" Amelia chimed in.

Sarah smiled. *Note to self: Stop judging people. She is sweet and kinda funny.* She leaned in closer to hear.

"Well, it was close. But it's real-life sweethearts! Jamie and Charlotte!"

New note to self: first impressions are golden. What a bitch.

Amelia worriedly watched Sarah's eyes turn to ice as she listened to Ali, who chatted on obliviously for a moment before she noticed the group had gone awkwardly silent. Ali smiled nervously, looking from one to the other. "I'm sorry...did I say something wrong?"

"On, no, Ali, of course you didn't," Sarah replied, with a cool smile. "Jamie and Charlotte are perfect. They were made for cheap crowns on their heads—and each other."

With that, Sarah turned and walked away. Hudson shot Amelia a worried look. "See y'all later," she said and hurried after her.

"Man," Ali said, watching them disappear down the hallway. "I shouldn't have said anything. I thought she was over him. I didn't mean to make Sarah mad."

Amelia shook her head, reassuringly. "No worries. Sarah's not mad at you. Anyway, I've got to get to history class." She paused and gave her friend a quick hug. "Let's study for chemistry during our free period, okay?"

"Sure! See ya then!" Ali called after Amelia, her voice sunny again. Amelia had covered for Sarah, so no one would think she cared about what Jamie did and with whom. But Sarah had been upset, all right. Just as Ali had known she would be.

Hugging her books to her chest, Ali smiled as she made her way to class. Charlotte would be very pleased.

⁂ ⁂ ⁂ ⁂ ⁂ ⁂

She had totally failed the French quiz because of him, but at least it was over. Sarah walked to her locker slowly, absorbed in her misery. *What's it going to take to stop thinking about him? Messing up your grades? Or messing up your life?* She sighed. *He's with Charlotte... He's the freaking prom king. Charlotte's prom king. King and Queen of Shallowness. How many signs do you need? It's time to get over him. Enough.* She reached her locker and hung her head inside, trying to will herself to focus on which books she needed for her next class. But it was no use. She could hear voices buzzing all around her in the crowded hallway. It seemed they were echoing her thoughts of Jamie...All she kept hearing was his name. She closed her eyes and took a deep breath, determined to clear her head. *You're losing it, girl. Get a grip...*

It was a moment before she realized she wasn't hearing his name over and over in her mind. Her head snapped up and she opened her eyes. *Wait...they really are talking about Jamie...*

Curious, she turned and began listening in on the various conversations around her. Everyone was talking in excited spurts. And everyone looked worried.

"They just came in and grabbed him out of class...took him to the hospital...it's his dad...Dr. Fox put his arm around his shoulder and told him...he ran out...it's bad...they drove him because he couldn't drive himself...it was a heart attack..."

Stunned, Sarah stood completely still. Dr. Nelson? A heart attack? No, it couldn't be. He was so fit—and a doctor! Silently, she made her way through the crowd of students and out the door to the front of the school. Once outside, she took deep breaths and tried to take in what she had heard. She tried to calm her racing heart but her mother's death was all she could think about. Unbearably painful memories flooded her mind. Dr. Nelson had saved her family. She had to do something to help Jamie.

"Sarah?"

She jumped, startled. Turning, she saw Michael standing behind her. He was watching her, concerned. "I saw you come out. Here, take my jacket. You're shivering."

"Thanks." Sarah took the jacket, numbly. Michael helped her put it on. She looked up at him, her eyes brimming with tears. "Michael, can I borrow your car?"

"My car? Yeah, sure, of course." He fished his car keys from his pocket and dropped them in her hand. "You're going to him, aren't you," he said, more than asked.

Sarah nodded. "I have to."

Michael studied her for a moment. "Are you sure about that?"

Sarah nodded again. "I won't be gone long."

"Sarah." Michael's voice was gentle. "I'm sorry, but I have to say it: What if you get there and Charlotte is with him?"

She half-smiled, reached up and kissed him on the cheek. "Well, then I'll know he is okay. And I'll get your car back to you sooner."

Michael said nothing more. There was no changing her mind and he knew it. He shoved his hands in his pockets and watched the coolest girl he'd ever met run through the parking lot and the cold, drizzling rain.

Jamie Nelson, you're one hell of a lucky guy, even if you don't have enough sense to know it, Michael thought to himself. *Hope some of that luck rubs off on your dad.*

CHAPTER SIXTY-FIVE

It wasn't hard to find him. Jamie was sitting alone in the corridor outside his father's room. His head was bent, his hands clasped tightly together between his legs. Sarah let out the breath she had been holding. She had found him but suddenly, she was unsure of what she had come to say. Still, she couldn't take the time to find the right words. The pain she knew he was in tore through her. God help her, she loved him still.

She walked over to him, expecting him to look up and see her. He didn't. She sat down in the chair beside him. "Jamie?"

He looked at her then, tears running unchecked down his cheeks. She had never seen him cry and wasn't prepared for what it did to her. It was difficult to hold her own tears back. She was suddenly flooded with emotions of protectiveness at his vulnerability; remorse; concern; and dark, painful memories of her own.

Stay strong. It's his turn to need you.

"I'm so sorry... How is he?" Sarah kept her voice steady.

"Not too good. We don't...the doctors don't know if he's going to make it. They said he experienced 'dramatic cardiac arrest'."

"Well, I know he's going to make it. He's strong, in great shape and he's a Nelson. That means he's completely determined to have his own way."

Missing her meek attempt at humor, Jamie nodded, absently. "He knew it was happening. He was able to call out to mom for help before he passed out. Thank God, he knew the signs. Thank God Mom was home." Jamie got up and walked to the window. Cold rain pounded mercilessly against it. "We argued this morning. I was a complete ass. I said things I shouldn't have. I didn't mean any of them...I..."

Sarah moved to stand beside him. Gently, she laid her hand on his arm. "Your dad knows you didn't. He knows you love him, Jamie, and he is so proud of you." Her voice was soft and comforting. Jamie turned to look at her and Sarah tried to smile. "I know I haven't known him that long but I saw it every time he looked at you. Remember Christmas dinner at your house? I loved the way your parents soaked up every word you said. Even that night at Doogie's, he was so proud. Not to mention when he summoned the cavalry and singlehandedly saved my dad. He did all that to protect you, Jamie." Her voice trailed as his hand covered hers. He picked it up, bringing it to his lips and brushing a soft kiss against it. Tears trickled down his cheek and onto her hand. He made no effort to wipe them away—or mask the fear in his eyes as he looked at her.

It was her undoing. Sarah put her arms around his neck and pulled him close to her. "He can beat this, Jamie. I know he can. Believe it, pray it with all your heart and I promise you, he will," she said softly into his ear.

His arms came around her and he hugged her so hard it took her breath away. He buried his head in her hair.

"Jamie."

Daisy Nelson's voice was firm, almost reprimanding. Sarah immediately pulled away from him, swiping at her eyes, wondering if something had changed in Dr. Nelson's condition. Despite her reassurances, dread flooded inside her.

Jamie's voice reflected the same anxiety. "What's happened, Mom? What did they say?"

"Nothing yet." Hearing the panic in her son's voice, Daisy softened her tone and tried to smile. She stepped closer and rubbed Jamie's arms. "I'm sure we will know something soon." Leaning in, she gave him a kiss on his tear-soaked cheek.

The lack of news was unsettling to Jamie. Without another word, he walked away. Sarah sighed. She wondered if he would try to find the doctor and get an update himself. It would be a Jamie thing to do. Jamie was many things, but patient was not one of them. Sarah knew better than to follow him. He was experiencing a lot of different emotions and she remembered each and every one of them all too well. He needed to be alone to sort them out. She felt her eyes well up with tears again. Her heart ached for him.

Sarah walked to a chair and sat down, aware that Daisy Nelson's eyes were on her. She smiled at Jamie's mother, nervously. And wondered if her decision to come had been a good one. *God, I hope they didn't tell her about the Romanos.*

"Thank you for coming, Sarah," the woman said, her voice steady yet flat.

"I hope I haven't intruded, Mrs. Nelson," Sarah replied, her heart beating a little faster in her chest. "I thought I might be able to give Jamie some support. I just know Dr. Nelson is going to be okay."

"Yes, well, we all hope so. I'm sure Jamie is comforted by your being here."

Sarah blinked, surprised at both her words and kind tone, knowing full well that Daisy Nelson had never liked her dating Jamie. She had made little secret of her continuing disapproval, though Sarah had sensed it from the first time she had met her. She understood it now, even felt she deserved it. Jamie's mother had a soft spot for her youngest son. He was her pride and joy and deserved the very best life had to offer. Not a girl from the wrong side of town who worked at the local pizzaria. Not a girl who had put both Jamie and Ben's life in danger that night at Doogie's. And definitely not a girl whose father used to be "the Delivery Man" for the Italian mob.

"And James, he...he would be happy to know you are here. He likes you very much, Sarah, always asking Jamie about you, telling him what a genuine and pretty girl you are...I'm not always as insightful as he is about...things, but I think now he was right...just...just as he always seems to be...to be right about...everything..." Her voice cracked with emotion and she looked away, bringing her hand to her trembling chin, as if to steady it.

Just as Sarah was trying to decide how to respond, the door of Dr. Nelson's room flew open and his doctor stepped out. Daisy Nelson rushed over to him. Sarah stood, but kept her spot, her eyes riveted on the exchange between them. Jamie and Hillary came running and Sarah realized they must have been somewhere nearby. Her heart began to race again. Holding her hands behind her back, she crossed her fingers and watched their anxious faces for what seemed like an eternity...until Jamie's joyful *whoop* filled the hallway. New tears filled Sarah's eyes as she watched him pick up both his mother and sister and spin them around, all three of them sobbing with relief and happiness.

Sarah laughed through her tears at the sight they made, allowing a wave of relief to wash over her own body. It was then Jamie looked her way. Letting go of his family, he walked over to her, wiping his eyes, and smiling broadly.

"Don't keep me in suspense," Sarah said, still laughing. "Good news?"

Jamie laughed too, joyful tears still in his eyes. "Yeah. The best. He's going to be fine." His voice softened as he took in her tear-streaked face. "You came. Thank you."

Her pulse quickened. Standing in that hospital corridor with him, her heart light and filled with joy, clarity struck fast and sudden.

I don't care what happened before this. Not about Charlotte or Michael or everyone at school. Not about the Romanos. Or Jake or how different we are. None of that matters and I was a fool to ever let it. I still love you, Jamie.

"I'm so glad he's going to be okay," she said, instead.

Jamie watched her and for a brief moment she was afraid he had read her thoughts. When he spoke, his voice was strange. "The doctor said we can go in and see my dad now. We can't stay long, so if you'll wait, I can drive you home."

"No, no, take your time with him. I...I actually need to get back to school. I have...um...Amelia's car."

Jamie nodded, taking in her sudden nervousness. "Okay, well it's started raining and it's freezing out there. Let me give you my jacket at least."

"Oh, no thanks, I already have one." Sarah walked over to the chair where she had dropped her jacket and picked it up, realizing too late that Jamie would recognize it as Michael's. Her heart dropped. Braving a quick look at his face confirmed her fears. She had ruined everything! Again! And there was no turning back.

She had already lied about Michael's car to keep him from misunderstanding her using it. And now, she had flaunted Michael's letter jacket in his face. It was useless…a disaster… Sarah looked away and slowly put the jacket on.

"I'll see you later, Jamie," she managed to say as she turned, desperate now to get out of there, wishing she could run to the elevators.

"Sarah. Wait."

Sarah closed her eyes and took a deep breath. Determined to hold herself together, she forced a smile on her face before turning around. "Yeah?"

Grabbing his letter jacket from a nearby chair, Jamie walked to her. He said nothing at all, just held it out.

Sarah stared at him. "But I already have…"

"Yes, I know you do. I heard you the first time. About the same time I noticed Amelia's keys look different than they used to." Sarah unconsciously closed her hand tighter around Michael's keys. Jamie dropped his eyes and followed the movement before looking up at her again. "It's just that I thought I would ask you to return that one to your...*friend*. And wear mine instead."

A slow smile made its way across Sarah's face. She tilted her head as if she were in deep thought. "I wouldn't want you to be cold without it," she said, widening her eyes to look concerned.

"Worry about your pansy friend getting cold, not me."

Sarah held back a laugh and slid out of Michael's jacket. Putting it down, she took Jamie's from his outstretched hand. She hesitated, her eyes twinkling playfully. "I don't know if you are aware but the ground hog saw his shadow. That means six more weeks of winter. You may be cold for a while, even though it's almost spring."

Jamie kept his eyes on hers. "I'm hoping to find a remedy for that."

Sarah put his jacket on—and smiled. "Feeling pretty confident, aren't we?"

Jamie grinned. "What can I say, it's turned out to be a damn good day."

"And you can't help yourself, it's how you roll, Big Style."

"Since the day I was born, my mama always says."

"Good grief." Sarah burst into laughter, rolled her eyes and shook her head.

Jamie laughed, too. Then, his expression sobered, his eyes softened and he moved closer. Gently, he pulled her long hair free of the jacket so that it fell around her shoulders. "That's my girl," he said, so quietly, she wasn't sure she had heard it.

Sarah felt her heart skip another beat and her pulse quicken. She bent and picked up Michael's jacket, tucking it under her arm. "I guess I'd better go. Your family's waiting for you. Please tell your dad I'm glad he's okay."

Jamie smiled. "I will. Tell your friend I'm glad he's getting his stuff back."

Sarah smiled back, turned and walked to the elevators. The doors opened and she nearly collided with Robby as he frantically ran out. He stopped to stare first at her, then at Jamie, his surprise obvious. Sarah stepped around him, turned and cheerily waved at both of them before the doors shut. Robby waved back, then spun around, his arms spread wide. His mouth gaped open. His eyes went huge with shock.

"Really? Seriously? That was Sarah? Less than two weeks ago, you're moping like a little girl in the driveway and now she's wearing your letter jacket and you're standing there grinning like a fool? How do you do that? Dude, what did you do?"

Jamie shrugged his shoulders. "It's a damn good day, bro."

Robby laughed. "I'd say so. The nurse downstairs says your dad's in the clear."

Jamie nodded with relief. "Yeah. I'm about to go see him. Thanks for coming, man."

"I would have gotten here sooner, but they wouldn't let us leave. Beats me how Sarah got out." Robby peeled off his wet jacket and dropped it in a chair. "The rest of them will be here soon. The whole school is worried about you, man."

"Hang on a few minutes while I go see him. I haven't even been in yet."

Robby grinned. "My guess is that has something to do with who just got on the elevator. I honestly don't understand how you do it." He shook his head at his friend. "Damned Nelson charm is unstoppable."

Jamie laughed and gave Robby a hug, slapping him soundly on the back. "She had a whole lot to do with it, buddy. And thanks. I took your advice and manned up."

Robby hugged him back. "I'm glad for you, man. For your dad, for all of it."

The two pulled apart and Jamie started jogging backwards. "Will you wait for just a few minutes? Tell anyone else who comes?"

"I'll be here."

Jamie paused outside the door to his dad's room and listened to the laughter coming from inside. His family was in there, waiting for him. He was so grateful for it. He felt his heart turn over with joy at the second chance he had been given with his father. Maybe even with Sarah. Lifting his eyes upward, he uttered a few words of thanks. Then he opened the door and joined the celebration.

CHAPTER SIXTY-SIX

Lakeview's prom was a huge success. *There isn't anyone missing,* Sarah thought to herself as she scanned the room once more for Jamie. *Except for him.*

Sarah tried in vain to pay attention to what Hudson and Amelia were saying. They had been so sweet to let her ride with them. Hudson had come with Reed, who Sarah liked a lot. He was shy but very funny. He watched Hudson whenever he knew she wasn't looking and Sarah thought that was adorable. He was one of those guys who was not quite sure how to show a girl he liked her, but Sarah could tell he was a keeper.

Amelia had come with Derek and the two of them were all smiles. Sarah had gotten dressed at Amelia's house and was there when Derek came to pick them up. The way he had looked at Amelia told the story of what was to come for the two of them. She was so happy for her best friend.

They had picked up Hudson and Reed and gone to Hughey's house for pre-prom pictures. Jamie had been markedly absent. Sarah didn't know what to think of that. She knew it had been a tough week for him. Dr. Nelson had suffered complications from an infection but it was all under control and he had gone home yesterday, according to Amelia. But Sarah had not spoken to him since the hospital. In all honesty, she was grateful for the time. She had needed to think. There was a lot she wanted to say to him and she had decided she would say it, whether it still mattered or not. After what happened at the hospital, she had reason to hope he felt the same way she did. But he had not called all week. And he had not tried to take her to the prom. Sarah sighed into her drink. *At least he's not here with Charlotte. Yet.*

As if on cue, Charlotte walked by. She met Sarah's eyes and smiled smugly. Sarah ignored her. But she had to admit, Charlotte looked flawless, as usual. She watched her join Jocelyn, Sidney, Gertie, Ali and Lexi and say something that sent them all in a fit of laughter. Lexi looked over her shoulder at Sarah. Sarah ignored that, too.

Gee, wonder who they're trash talking...it must be exhausting to work that hard at being mean...

She pondered that for a minute. High school had to be the drama headquarters of the world. But one of the many things she had realized over the course of the last few days was that the Lakeview *"it club"* had never truly been her problem, any more than Charlotte or Michael had. She had been her own worst enemy. She had been stubborn and unwilling to bend and meet Jamie halfway. She had let her pride and fear of being hurt again rule her actions. Her reasons for pushing him away had seemed so reasonable at the time. But now she realized they were just what Jamie had once told her they were: her defense mechanism against what scared her.

It's time to make a change, Sarah. You've wasted enough time worrying about yesterday or tomorrow. It's time to trust in the here and now. It's time to trust in him.

"Are you talking to yourself?" Amelia asked her, amused.

Sarah jumped, spilling her drink, but thankfully not on Amelia's beautiful white gown. "I hope not! I thought I was thinking. God..."

"What's with you tonight? Everything good?"

"Not really, but I hope it will be. Amelia, have you seen Jamie?"

"Nelson?"

"No, Jamie Richards," Sarah replied, sarcastically.

Amelia looked confused. "Who's Jamie Richards?"

"Amelia! Yes, Nelson! James H. Nelson, III! Have you seen him?"

Amelia cocked her head. "Why do you care? Girl, why so jumpy? Last time I checked, you didn't want to hear his name; you said..." Amelia paused to look at her pointedly. "Wait. Has something happened you haven't told me about?"

Sarah sighed, her eyes scanning the room again. "Maybe something happened. Maybe not."

Amelia moved, purposefully blocking her view to gain her full attention. "Sarah Giannopoulos. What does that mean? My blood pressure is going up right now."

"I'm sorry. I didn't say anything because you've been so excited about Derek and to be honest, I'm not even sure anything really happened."

Amelia glanced over and saw Hudson was telling Derek and Reed a story. She pulled Sarah away to a nearby table. "Sit down and talk to me," she instructed, her voice firm. "Now."

"Now? Amelia, I..."

"Now."

Sarah didn't argue any further. She had wanted to talk to Amelia about things all week. She sat and faced her, letting out a deep breath as she did so.

"There *is* something. You're never like this. I can't believe you didn't tell me."

"I'm sorry. In my defense, I couldn't get a word in during 'Derek-fest', these past few days."

"Okay, whatever. But look how hot he is and give me a break."

"Noted and done."

Amelia smiled. "Now that we've got that settled, spill. What happened?"

Sarah leaned forward. "I saw Jamie at the hospital on Monday. I mean, I went to see him. I thought his father might die and I just couldn't stay away."

"I am attributing the fact that I thought I just heard you say 'Monday' to the loudness in here. Because you could not have possibly said 'Monday'."

"Derek, Derek, Derek, candles and button downs in the park, blah, blah, blah, Amelia."

"I am going to ignore that. So, what happened? Did you talk to him?"

"Yeah. And we connected, like we used to."

"And?"

Sarah smiled. "And…afterwards, I thought there still might be a chance for us."

Amelia's mouth dropped open. "Whoa! What? *Us*? I thought you said there was no *us*; that you told Jamie that two Saturdays ago; and that there would never be an *us*. I don't understand, I…"

"Amelia," Sarah interrupted. "I want Jamie back."

Amelia threw her hands up, then sat back in her chair and smiled. "She finally admits it. I had begun to give up hope."

"Well, don't start celebrating yet. Just because I want him back doesn't mean it's actually going to happen. He hasn't called me all week. And I'm here alone. Maybe he's done. Maybe he's tired of all the attitude I've given him."

Amelia sat up and shook her head. "I seriously doubt that. I think you are the only one who has never understood how crazy that boy is about you. Maybe that's because you didn't know him before. He was kinda arrogant."

Sarah laughed. "Was?"

Amelia laughed, too. "Well, let's just say he's changed a lot and every bit of it was for you. We all know Jamie Nelson is one hell of a catch." She reached over and squeezed Sarah's hand. "But, honey, so are you. You came here, scarred and knowing no one, and yet you're the girl we all wish we could be. You're beautiful, but more than that you're strong, confident, smart and fun."

"Aw, wow. Thanks, love. So are you."

Amelia shook her head. "No. I'm not. But I'm learning from you and I'm a lot stronger and happier than I've ever been in my life." Her eyes teared up. "You're my best friend, Sarah. I waited for you all these years—and you were totally worth the wait."

Sarah leaned over and hugged her. "You're my best friend, too. I swear I don't know what I would do without you. You know I have a complicated past and you never push to know all about it. You accept me as I am and I can't begin to express what that means to me. You strengthen me, Amelia. Please don't make us cry, your mom paid a lot of money for these make-overs."

Both of them laughed at that. Sarah scanned the room again and sighed. "I guess he's not coming. Maybe it's time for me to read the signs."

"You mean like the signs he held up outside of Three Spoons? Right before he told you he loved you in front of everyone on Main Street?" Amelia held up her fingers. "Yes, Sarah, let's do count the signs. Let's see, he sang to you, risked his life in a fight for you..."

Sarah pushed her hand down. "Okay. I know, you're right. I'm just sorry for a lot of things—and I want to tell him so. I really hope he shows up," she said, her voice quiet but hopeful.

"No worries. He will. He's had a tough week and he was probably sorting things out like you have been. He's proud and his ego is pretty bruised. But he knows better than to let you go. He's too smart for that." She paused, as if something had just occurred to her. "How did you leave it at the hospital?"

"Well, Jamie found out his dad was going to be okay and oh, yeah, his mom was actually nice to me."

"That's key."

"And a first. Anyway, Jamie was so happy and I said I had to go and he said he was really glad I came and..."

"How did he say that?"

Sarah smiled. "He said: You came. Thank you."

Amelia pondered that for a minute. "That's actually perfect."

"Yeah. It was sweet. So then, he offered me his jacket so I wouldn't be cold because it was weirdly cold last Monday, remember?"

"Yeah, yeah, it was cold, end of the world, weird weather, blah, blah, it's all my family talks about at dinner. So, you took the jacket and then what?"

Sarah squirmed in the chair and scrunched her face. "Well, I didn't actually take the jacket because I already had Michael's. Along with his car keys."

"Oh, Sarah," Amelia groaned. "Jamie recognized them?"

"That would be a *yes* on both counts. Hard to miss a letter jacket but he even knew the keys weren't yours, even though I tried to tell them they were."

"Oh, God."

"Exactly. I mean, of all days to be wearing Michael's jacket..."

"And he was furious. Bless."

Sarah shook her head. "Actually, no. Here's the part where I think something happened. I was practically running to the elevators, completely ticked off with myself, when he stopped me and asked if I wanted to give Michael his jacket back and wear his instead."

Amelia's mouth dropped again. "You *think* something happened? What is it going to take with you? I swear, Sarah, if you didn't take it and throw Michael's jacket in the nearest trash can, I am literally going to choke you. And I don't care if that up-do comes undone, either."

Sarah laughed. "Calm down, crazy. I took it. I wore it. But no, I did not throw sweet Michael's jacket away and you are horrible to suggest I would. I left it in his car."

"And that's it?"

"Pretty much. Except he might have said 'that's my girl' when he pulled my hair out of the collar, but I'm not sure I heard that right."

Amelia threw her arms up again in exasperation.

"I am so mad at you! You kept this from me for a week?"

Sarah laughed again. "Amelia, I swear you are turning greek, with all your hand gestures and drama."

Amelia took a deep breath and let it out slowly. "Okay, here's the thing. The boy has laid his feelings out for you again. If you want him, the ball is now in your court. You've got to do something very un-Sarah-like: *show him.*"

Sarah stood and looked around. "Yes, I realize that. Why do you think I'm here, dateless? To watch him get crowned *King of Cool with the Queen of Shallowness and Evil*? If he shows, I'm going to tell him."

Amelia stood, too. "Tell him what, exactly?" she asked, her voice hopeful.

Sarah smiled at her best friend. "That I love him. And that I want to try again."

Amelia clapped her hands and let out a squeal of delight. She hugged Sarah excitedly. She just knew things would work out. Jamie and Sarah belonged together.

"This is so perfect, Sarah," she beamed. "It's the prom. The most romantic night of high school." Amelia was suddenly more glad than ever her mom had insisted Sarah had her hair and make-up done with her earlier that day. Sarah was stunning in her brown silk gown. It was low cut in the back, but clung to her body as if it were made for her, and had a small train that elegantly swirled as she walked. Her hair was up and her make-up was perfect. *Ali was right: she's the prettiest girl in school. Best of all, she doesn't know it,* Amelia thought to herself. "You look incredible tonight," she said out loud.

Sarah smoothed her dress and smiled nervously. "Thanks, best friend. Thanks to you and your mom, I think I look decent."

"More like indecently great. And he's going to show, stop worrying."

"Hope so."

"Sarah, trust me. He's coming. When he does, just this once, no matter what, follow your heart and not your logic. You don't always have to be sure of the right course. Because there's no way to be. Sometimes you have to trust your instinct. This is one of those times. What I'm trying to say is: don't change your mind."

"You mean, lose my nerve."

Amellia put her hands on Sarah's shoulders. "It's go-time. Go find him."

Sarah blinked, suddenly panicked. "Go-time? No…I…let's go talk to Derek, Hudson and Reed first."

Amelia shook her head. Turning her around, she gave her a gentle shove. "Now. I'll be here, if you need me."

Sarah looked over her shoulder, nervously. "Promise?"

"I promise. Go."

CHAPTER SIXTY-SEVEN

A few minutes later, Sarah found him. She came out of the bathroom and there he was, laughing with Robby, Gaston and Walt in the hallway outside the gym. For all her carefully rehearsed plans to boldly walk up to him and start a conversation, she barely managed to smile meekly at the group before hastily retreating back into the gym.

Really, Sarah? Really? What is the matter with you? You've waited all week, and you just walk by him, like a scared little girl? Her mind raced furiously with options, escape from the emergency exit being one of them. She took a calming breath. *Like Amelia said, I can't think about it. It's go-time. I'm just going to do it.*

Turning back, she flung open the door to the hallway.

And hit Jamie square in the face. He jumped back and brought his hands up to his nose.

Oh, God. Did you just break his nose?

"I'm so sorry...are you okay?" she asked him, horrified. He nodded, even as he rubbed his nose. Sarah relaxed enough to notice he looked incredible in his tuxedo. She nodded back, unsure of what to say. Suddenly, her heart was beating as loudly as the drums inside the gym. Jamie dropped his hands to his side. His nose was red.

"I think I'll live, Miss Giannopoulos," he replied with an easy grin. Besides, I've 'run into you' before. Lucky for me, you're not on a speeding vehicle this time."

Sarah smiled at the memory, feeling some of her nervousness melt away.

His eyes grew serious. "You look amazing, Sarah."

And it's back. "Thank you, Jamie, you look very handsome, yourself."

"Are you headed somewhere? I wanted to talk for a minute."

"No...I was just looking for Amelia," she lied.

"I see her in there, dancing with Derek." Jamie moved closer to point out the pair and Sarah felt her body tingle from head to toe.

"Yeah, I see them," she said softly, wondering if he felt it, too. She glanced into his eyes. He met her gaze and neither looked away.

"Can we talk, Sarah?" he asked her, his voice strange, like the day in the hospital.

She smiled. "Let me guess. You want your jacket back."

Jamie laughed, shaking his head. In doing so, he took a step back and created a little more space between them. Suddenly, Sarah felt ready. "I have a confession to make," she said, almost shyly. "I wasn't actually looking for Amelia just now."

Jamie looked surprised. Sarah clasped her hands in front of her, allowing some of her nervousness to show. "I was looking for you. I..."

"Come with me," Jamie interrupted. Taking her hand, he led her down the hallway and into Mrs. Dixon's English classroom. The room was dark, except for a single candle flickering softly, its light dimly lighting the corner of the room. With a backwards glance of surprise at Jamie, Sarah moved towards it and saw it was on the desk where she normally sat. Next to the candle lay a corsage, wrapped around a gold bracelet with a heart charm on it. Sarah gasped in wonder. She sat down in the chair and picked it up.

"It's beautiful," she said, without looking up.

Jamie smiled, pulled out a chair and straddled it, facing her. "I'm glad you like it."

Sarah looked up at him. "I love it, Jamie." Their eyes met and held.

"The first time I really got a good look at you was in this room. You were late and you ran in looking all flustered, your hair all over the place and your clothes a mess. I realized you were the same stranger that had almost run over me on her bike that morning. And hands down the most beautiful girl I had ever seen."

Sarah felt her cheeks redden and was glad for the darkness. She looked down at the lovely corsage, again.

Jamie watched her. "You don't even realize how beautiful you are, do you, Sarah? Just like I didn't realize I got the biggest break I'd ever gotten when you finally agreed to go out with me. I blew it, over and over again. Just when I thought it was hopeless, that the damage I'd done to us couldn't be fixed, you came to the hospital."

Sarah looked up, ready to tell him why. But he didn't let her.

"I couldn't believe my eyes when I looked over and saw you sitting next to me...like...like an angel. I can see why your dad calls you one. You can't know how much I wanted to talk to you, especially after Steve's that Saturday and everything you told me. Especially after what you told me about Jake. I was trying to figure out how to do it, how to get you to believe in me again, when I saw you run out of the gym with Nick after the region game. I swear I was coming after you alone but then I realized I couldn't save you without help. So, I called my dad. I swore him to secrecy before I told him anything. I had no idea, I swear to you, that he had found out about the Romanos and your dad on his own. Or that he had done it through my uncles. I was as shocked as you were with what went down that night."

Sarah nodded. "I know. I'm sorry. I'm so grateful for what you did."

Jamie shook his head. "I'm the one who's sorry, Sarah. I shouldn't have been so proud, and I should have explained everything better at Steve's. I should have been there for you because I can't imagine how scared you must have felt. But I wasn't. I didn't. I just let my stupid pride take over. I was completely miserable after that. I was angry with everyone but most of all, myself. I didn't know how to fix it. Then my dad had the heart attack."

His voice cracked with emotion. Sarah started to speak but he held up his hand.

"Please, let me get this out."

Sarah nodded, unable to take her eyes off his.

"Thank God he was okay. I have never felt such fear, such despair as that day. I looked up and there you were. And I knew what it cost you to come. I knew your pride was hurting, too. Most of all I knew you had already been through the greatest loss there is. And yet, there you were, standing beside me." His voice cracked again and he paused to regain his composure. This time, Sarah didn't move. Only waited.

"So, I planned to bring you here, give you the corsage and ask you to be my prom date. If you came with Michael, I don't care. I'll wait until after he takes you home. I'll wait all night if I have to. All I want is one dance with you tonight. So I can keep it in my memory as the best moment of my life because I know it will be."

Sarah felt her cheeks redden again. Her heart thumped in her chest.

"Sarah, all week, I rehearsed everything I want to say to you in my head, at least a thousand times. And now, here you are, and for all my planning, I still don't have it straight. I guess that's because I can never really think straight when you're this close to me."

"Jamie, I..."

"Wait. Before you say anything, let me finish. Because what I want to say most of all is that I'm sorry. I've been such an ass. But I never meant to hurt you. Or lie to you, or doubt you in any way. There's a lot I need to work on and I know that now."

Sarah sighed. "I did my share of screwing things up, too, Jamie."

He looked into her beautiful face and forced himself not to reach for her. He had come to say more. But for that moment, he just wanted to look at her. She looked so innocent, so pretty, he could hardly keep his mind on what he needed to say. His eyes locked on hers. "I tried to listen to you, Sarah. I tried to get you out of my mind. I tried hard. But I can't do it. You're the first thing I think about when I wake up in the morning and the last one I think about before falling asleep each night. It's been that way since that very first day, right here in this room."

"I used to care so much about what others thought about me. I think now, my ego depended on it. I did what my friends and family expected me to. Always. But you came along and changed all that. You showed me what it's like to be free, to be myself. God, I didn't know what I was missing. It feels so damn good. I just want to be with you, Sarah. I want to sit and talk with you, laugh with you, fight with you, play basketball with you in the driveway, sit next to you in a movie theater, eat pizza with you at Steve's, watch you run, watch you do anything at all. I want to catch your eye from across a crowded room and feel that incredible rush I feel every single time I look at you."

He paused and Sarah watched him, too stunned to say anything, wondering if she were in a dream. The dim candlelight flickered across his face. It was a moment she knew she would always remember.

"You said to me once that I didn't trust you," Jamie continued. "You're wrong about that. I've always believed in you, Sarah. You know who you are. It's me I lacked faith in because I guess I had some soul searching to do. But that's all in the past now. You changed it and there's no changing back. And despite what you say, I think you care about me. I hope that I'm right about that, but even if I'm not, I want you to know I'll accept it. What I need to tell you, what you have to know, is that I love you, Sarah Giannopoulos. I love you and I'm not going to stop, no matter what. And I know I'm totally screwing this up right now. I'm going on and on and I'm not saying anything right." He looked down at his hands and then back at her. "It's because I can't think. Hell, Sarah, if I'm going to be honest, all I keep thinking is that if I don't reach over this desk right now and kiss you, I'll die."

For a moment neither of them said anything. Then, keeping her eyes on his, Sarah pushed the candle and corsage out of the way and leaned forward. Pulling on his hands, she urged him towards her until his face was bare inches from hers. "Please don't die on me, Big Style," she told him softly, her eyes glistening with tears. "We haven't had that dance yet. And I got a new dress."

Jamie smiled against her lips as he brushed them gently with his. Pulling his hands from hers, he cupped her face. "I really love you, Sarah," he whispered, his voice full of emotion, his own eyes glazed over. Sarah closed the distance and kissed him. It was a soft kiss, full of promise.

"Jamie," she whispered, as their lips parted, moments later, "I really love you back. I really, really love you back."

❋ ❋ ❋ ❋ ❋ ❋

Amelia knew the minute Jamie and Sarah walked into the gym that they were back together. She grabbed Derek's hand and squeezed. "She did it! Hudson, let's go talk to her!"

But Hudson was one step ahead of her, already out of her seat and halfway to Sarah. Amelia hurried behind her, smiling excitedly, and even more so when her eyes met Sarah's happy ones. In her haste, she tripped over her dress, landing in Jamie's chest.

"Woah there," he said, laughing, as he steadied her.

Amelia untangled herself and tried to appear casual, failing miserably, of course. "Well, hey, you two! What's up? Having fun?"

Jamie and Sarah laughed; Hudson rolled her eyes. Jamie pulled Sarah to him and winked at Amelia. "Looks like I found myself a prom date."

Amelia laughed. "I see that." She winked back. "Good work."

Jamie smiled down at Sarah. "Yeah, turns out, she can't resist me."

Hudson and Amelia laughed. Sarah arched an eyebrow. "I only said I'd be your date because you got me a corsage. Wipe that smug smile off your face, Big Style."

Jamie grinned from ear to ear. "No way. I'm smiling all night tonight, baby. Get used to it."

Sarah laughed and turned into him, wrapping her arms around his neck. His quickly circled her waist and he pulled her closer. "I am crazy about this dress," he said into her ear, "and about the way your back feels right now. Let's dance and leave."

Sarah smiled and nuzzled his ear. "Wanna know a secret? I like making you crazy. We're staying all night."

"Really, you two?" Amelia said from behind them. Jamie and Sarah turned to look at her. She was trying not to smile but her words came out in bubbly laughter. "Guys, we're actually all still standing here."

"Yeah," Hudson agreed. "We are standing here. We deserve better than this, Sarah. Which is why you will stop practically making out in the middle of the prom and come to the bathroom with us." She looked at Amelia. "And your dress is torn."

Amelia gasped and picked up the hem of her dress. "Bless it, you're right. Come on." She grabbed Sarah's arm, pulling her away from Jamie. "Let's go fix this. You can make out with your date later."

Sarah laughed and shrugged her shoulders helplessly at Jamie, as she let her friends drag her away.

Still grinning, Jamie made his way to the refreshments table. He saw Robby, Gaston and Walt standing a few feet away and walked over to them.

"Where have you been, Nelson? Haven't seen much of you tonight," Walt said, his eyebrows raised in question.

"Here and there, man." Jamie glanced at Robby and grinned again. Robby smiled and held his fist up. Jamie pounded it with his own.

"Well, I don't know what that's all about, but Charlotte is not happy. She's been looking for you, buddy. And I wouldn't want to be you when she finds you," Walt said, letting out a whistle.

"Heads up, Nelson," Gaston warned. "Looks like she's spotted you."

Jamie turned to see Charlotte walking over to him, a big smile on her face. The guys were right. She was smiling, but somehow she looked mad.

"Finally, I've found you, handsome," she cooed, reaching up and straightening his bow tie. "Dr. Fox is about to announce who won *King* and *Queen*." She smiled up at him, knowingly, and linked her arm through his. "Let's go watch."

Jamie pulled his arm back. "I'm good right here." Robby hid his smile behind his drink. Charlotte's eyes turned furious, but only for a moment. She smiled, again.

"Good idea. We'll stand back here," she said, smoothing her hair.

Jamie looked to the stage and sure enough, Dr. Fox was moving to the microphone. The hair stood on the back of his neck. Why did Charlotte want him to watch with her? What had she cooked up now? King and Queen? His jaw tightened.

Oh, God, please, no...not now, not tonight.

"Good evening and welcome everyone to Lakeview's Fiftieth Anniversary Prom," Dr. Fox said into the microphone. "It's a special year and a special night. And now the moment you've all been waiting for: the votes are in for this year's King and Queen of the night. Drumroll, please. I am proud to announce your winners: Miss Charlotte Sanders and Mr. James Nelson!" The gymnasium echoed with applause while Charlotte beamed, took Jamie's hand and pulled him towards the dance floor. Jamie had no choice but to follow, his mind racing.

Shit. Of all the rotten luck. Stay in the bathroom, Sarah, stay in the bathroom.

They reached the dance floor where Dr. Fox and Ms. Dixon were waiting with the crowns. Jamie glanced towards the gym door as Ms. Dixon placed his on his head. The crowd cheered again and the band started playing a slow song. But he just stood there, watching the door, as if in a trance.

"Jamie? We're supposed to dance," Charlotte said sweetly, between her teeth. Her eyes gleamed with excitement. He looked down at her. Suddenly, he was furious.

Pulling her close, Jamie let her see his anger. "How are you doing, Charlotte? Are you feeling tired? All that scheming you do has to be taking a toll." He squeezed her hand and brought it up between them. "You knew about the vote, didn't you? No big surprise there. You'll do anything to get what you want, you always have." He let go of her hand and leaned in closer. "I used to think you were something special. I even took up for you. But guess what? Game over, Charlotte. That joke you lied about? It's on you. I see you for what you are now. One day soon, everyone else will, too. I want you to remember that while we're dancing. And afterwards, I want you to stay the hell away from me."

Charlotte gasped, her cheeks turning as red as her dress. She knew all eyes were on her or she would have clawed at Jamie's face for saying what he just had. She smiled up at him, coldly. She would not give him the satisfaction of knowing how his words had shattered her.

The lights dimmed further and Jamie pulled Charlotte closer, cursing his bad luck. He didn't want to have to look at her. Glancing again at the gym door, he noticed Robby was trying to get his attention. Jamie squinted to get a better look, realized Robby was motioning to him and understood. *Robby's going to keep Sarah out of here until this damn dance is over.* He felt welcome relief wash over him. *Even if he doesn't, even if she sees, she won't be mad. I have no choice but to be up here. She knows now how I feel about her. Damn, she's been right about Charlotte all along.*

The photographer's flash suddenly blinded him. He looked down to find Charlotte flashing her perfected, plastic smile. He cursed his bad luck again.

Then, before he could even register what was happening, Charlotte wrapped her arms around his neck and kissed him.

⁕ ⁕ ⁕ ⁕ ⁕ ⁕

Robby threw open the gym door just in time to watch Sarah run away down the hall. Calling her name for her to stop, he took off after her.

❦CHAPTER SIXTY-EIGHT

The first thing Sarah saw when she walked into the gym with Amelia and Hudson was Jamie dancing with Charlotte Sanders. She blinked, but the vision remained. They were dancing indecently close and Charlotte was smiling contently. Sarah froze, knowing she shouldn't react. She had known Jamie was going to be crowned *prom king* but she had not thought he would dance with her. Especially, not like that...Her eyes misted with tears and her heart started pounding wildly. Why did they look so right? She felt as if she had been drifting in a wonderful dream and just woken up.

Then, as if it were a scene in a movie, playing in slow motion, she watched them kiss. And felt her heart break in two. She felt as is she could no longer breathe.

With a muffled sob, Sarah turned and ran from the gym. She bumped into Robby as she threw open the door, heard him call out to her to stop. She didn't. Sarah ran until she got outside, gulped in air greedily and threw off her heels. She needed to cry, but she couldn't. All she could do was breathe. And run.

She ran until she came to her wall, the wall where she and Amelia had first met, the place they always came to when they needed to talk. But she knew even Amelia couldn't help her this time. She dropped to the ground, her back against the wall, and brought her knees to her chest. She looked up into the star-filled sky.

"I was wrong, Mama. I guess I talked myself into thinking it could work. But I should have remembered what I've already learned, like you always taught me to. This time is so much worse than Jake...because I love him. But you saw them in there. They're perfect for each other,

Mama," she whispered, feeling the pain of saying the words out loud sear through her. "He kissed her...and all I can think about is how much I love him. And that he needs someone like her. Not like me, I've known that from the beginning. God, if his mother knew about me, she'd die. I know I have to let go, Mama. I don't know if it was all a lie. I don't know because I believe there's a part of him that means what he said tonight. Oh, Mama, none of this makes sense...but it doesn't matter anymore. I love him...I love him enough to let him go."

"What if he doesn't want you to?"

Startled, Sarah came to her feet. Robby held her shoes out to her, doubled over as he tried to catch his breath. Sarah took them, angry that he had found her and even more disturbed that he had overheard what she had just said.

"What are you doing here, Robby? Did you follow me?"

Robby nodded, still breathing heavily. "Yeah, Cinderella, I did. Didn't you hear me calling you? Since Jamie's in there dancing his way to *royal doom*, I thought you might need a friend — and your shoes." Straightening, he held his side and grimaced. "Damn girl, you *are* fast."

He smiled. She didn't. Robby shrugged, his expression sobering. "Come on, cut him some slack, Sarah. Don't put him through this again."

Sarah shook her head. She didn't know how much he had heard but she was not changing her mind this time. "Don't put *him* through this? Seriously? He just kissed another girl! No. It's over. It's never going to work, Robby. You saw what I saw in that gym. I'm not that girl, the one who refuses to read the signs."

"You sure did leave in a hurry. Seems to me you should give him a chance to explain. You just said you love him."

Sarah sighed, her anger diffused. "I don't expect you to understand. I do love him. How could I not? Jamie's a golden boy. Everyone loves him. He's destined for great things and I want them for him. But I'm not what he needs. We're just too different."

"That's a load of crap."

"Excuse me?"

"You heard me. My impression of you is that you're not a girl who lies to herself. Are you really reading signs? Then how can you miss the big one, the only one that counts? He loves you. The thing is, you've got to trust someone you love, Sarah. You can't just run every time the going gets rough. And you're right, maybe he is a golden boy. He's got a buffet of choices; always has, always will. But he chose you."

Sarah blinked, confused by the unexpected sense his words were making.

"Everyone expects Jamie to act a certain way, to achieve greatness," Robby continued, moving closer to her. "We always have around here, and probably always will. But of all of us, Sarah, it's Jamie who has been true to his feelings. I haven't. I'm his best friend and I gave him hell about you because I thought being with you meant risking things I now realize he doesn't give a damn about. He's fought hard to be free of all that crap. And you? You're lying to yourself. This isn't about reading the signs. It's about being scared. You lied to Jamie, Sarah. You told him you trusted him. Charlotte's grasping because she knows she's lost and you're selling him out, just like that. That kiss, that whole scene was all a show for you. And you bought it, no questions asked. That doesn't say a whole lot about your faith in Jamie."

Sarah blinked, then swallowed. "Oh, God."

"Yeah." Robby's voice was quiet.

Sarah hugged herself, rubbing her shoulders. "Even if you're right, I'm not going back in there," she said, almost in a whisper.

"Well, you can be damned sure he's not coming out here," Robby replied firmly, ignoring her wounded tone. "I've known Jamie all my life, Sarah. He won't come after you this time. He'll tell himself he's done all he can. He's a proud one and his pride's taken one hit too many. He'll cut his losses and move on—even though he's in love with you."

Sarah's shoulders slumped. She looked towards the twinkling lights outside the school building. "I'm scared, Robby."

Robby nodded, reaching his hand out to her. "I know. But in this moment, you have a choice to make. You of all people know the race isn't over until you cross that finish line, right? Stay the course, Sarah. You love him. He loves you back. Sure, he's a pain in the ass, sometimes, but you make him better. You guys are the real deal."

Sarah put her hand in his and looked up at him. "I would love to see his face if he knew you just called him a pain in the ass with an oversized ego."

Robby smiled. "Our little secret. Let's do this. I'll be right by your side."

You don't always have to be sure of the right course. Sometimes you just have to follow your heart, Amelia's words from earlier that night played back in her mind. Sarah picked up the front of her gown with her free hand and took a deep breath. "All right."

Robby squeezed her hand, supportively. Sarah stepped into her heels and the two of them began walking towards the gym. Robby didn't let go of her hand when they reached the door. He opened it and stepped back, to let her in.

Sarah looked inside. "I...I don't think I can do this, Robby," she said, her voice small. "What if it's too late already? They're all gonna see."

"Sarah, listen to me. I'm your friend and I'm telling you, you have to go back in there. But once you do, once you talk to him, if you still want to leave, I'll take you home. I don't care who sees and I won't leave you, no matter what. Deal?"

Sarah looked up at him, surprised. "You'd do that for me?"

"Sure. But only if you promise to walk. I'm not running after you again. These damn rental shoes are hell."

Sarah smiled. "I promise. But you have to promise to go to law school. I'm pretty sure you'll sway the jury every time."

Robby laughed and held open the door. He wasn't sure how he had managed to get Sarah there. He wasn't about to let her think about it and change her mind.

⁂ ⁂ ⁂ ⁂ ⁂ ⁂

Jamie stepped back, pulling Charlotte's arms off of him. "What the hell is wrong with you?" he growled.

The band stopped playing. Charlotte smoothed the skirt of her gown and looked up at him, coolly. "What's the matter, Jamie? Scared your precious Sarah might get mad at you? That you'll have to run after her again, like the lap dog you are?"

The room fell silent. Jamie glared at her, furious. Charlotte sneered back at him, lifted her arms and adjusted her crown. "Did you really think I would let you get away with talking to me the way you just did, Jamie?" she said, softly so only he could hear. "Oh, yes. Your little girlfriend saw the kiss." She smiled, contently. "And, trust me, she won't forget it anytime soon."

Jamie watched her, his angry expression changing to one of pity. "You don't even know how pathetic you are, do you, Charlotte?" He took his crown off. Charlotte shrugged indifferently.

"None of this is real, you know. None of it will matter after we graduate." Jamie's voice was loud enough for everyone to hear. It was strange to him that after all she had done he would feel sorry for her. But he did.

He stepped closer, put his hand under her chin, and forced her to look at him. "High school's over, Charlotte. And so are you."

Letting his hand drop, Jamie turned and walked away. Shaken, Charlotte watched him go. Her eyes panicked, she looked to where Ali, Lexi and Jocelyn were standing. All three looked away.

The room silently parted as Jamie walked through, searching for Sarah. Amelia stepped out in front of him and laid her hand on his arm. She shook her head, her eyes filled with sympathy. Jamie stared down at her as realization dawned.

She left? Again? She left me. She's gone.

Every thought in his head felt jumbled, as if his brain was in a fog. He tried to make sense of it all. He couldn't. After everything he had said to her, Sarah had left. She had not given him a chance to explain.

He nodded, as much to Amelia as to everyone else watching him in that gym. Slowly, he turned and walked out the door.

Amelia cupped her mouth in her hand. She knew from the look she had just seen on Jamie's face that he wasn't going after Sarah this time.

Oh, Sarah, what have you done? You just threw it all away.

Her heart broke for both of them.

CHAPTER SIXTY-NINE

"Here he comes, Sarah." They saw him as soon as they stepped inside the hallway. Robby gave Sarah's hand a gentle squeeze. "You got this."

Sarah tried to respond but her breath caught in her throat. Jamie walked down the hallway towards them, his tuxedo jacket slung over his shoulder, his eyes locked on hers. She stiffened at the coldness she saw in them. Her heart began to hammer in her chest again. A few steps short of reaching them, Jamie stopped. His eyes narrowed angrily.

Sarah panicked, felt the urge to turn and run. Robby's hand tightened around hers.

"Hey, bud. Sarah's been looking for you," he said evenly.

Jamie looked down at their clasped hands, but not at Robby. He showed no sign of acknowledging the words. Slowly, his eyes came back to hers. They were filled with something more than anger. They were indifferent and hard.

"Jamie! Wait!" Amelia came flying out of the gym, Hudson and Derek following close behind. Seeing Sarah and Robby, they all fell silent. Sarah took one look at Amelia and Hudson's tear-filled eyes and felt her chin quiver. No matter what, she had the best friends in the world. She saw Gaston, Walt and Hughey walk towards them and realized for the first time, that despite their differences, Jamie did, too. She glanced up at Robby, grateful for his support. He smiled down at her and motioned his eyes towards Jamie.

Sarah lifted her chin and met Jamie's stony gaze with what she hoped was a defiant one of her own. She let go of Robby's hand. *Go-time.*

"You promised me a dance," she said, her eyes betraying her and welling up with tears.

He didn't answer her. His jaw muscle contracted as he watched her, his expression giving nothing away. The silence was deafening.

"It's okay if you don't want to anymore." Her voice was barely a whisper.

"You left." His angry eyes bore into her.

"I'm sorry."

"That kiss was bullshit. She kissed me."

Sarah nodded. "I know."

I know. Finally, she did. Watching him stand there, seeing him battle his wounded pride, she knew beyond any doubt: This was the boy she would love forever. His strength and goodness were real. He would never betray her, not with Charlotte or anyone else. She had taken the long way, but she knew that now. She would never doubt him again. And she was ready to fight for him. No matter what the outcome.

"And after the dance, Sarah? What happens then?" Jamie asked quietly, his eyes never leaving hers.

"I was hoping you would maybe take me home. I don't have a ride."

His eyes narrowed into slits. "You don't have a ride? That's it?"

Sarah nodded. "The thing is, there's only one I want. Turns out once you ride Big Style, no other ride will do," she said, with a small shrug of her shoulders.

Jamie said nothing.

"I understand if the answer's no," she continued, "but if you do decide to dance with me, I want the ride afterwards. As well as one tomorrow—and every day after that." Her eyes watered. "Because it also turns out, you're kind of it for me."

He didn't reply. Sarah held her breath and waited for him to make his choice. He stood unmoving, tall, serious, devastatingly hot and completely in control, his eyes still burning into hers. She shrugged again, her own eyes brimming with tears.

Then, his expression softened. Hope sprang inside her.

"Like I stand a chance, when you look at me like that. Like I ever have," he said, his voice hoarse. Dropping his jacket to the floor, he opened his arms to her. "I'll drive you wherever you want, whenever you say, just please come here, Sarah."

Sarah threw herself at him, burying her head against his chest. "I love you, Jamie," she said against his heart.

His arms closed around her and he held her close. "God, baby, I'm glad to hear it. Because I'm crazy in love with you." She looked up at him, her eyes glistening with happy tears.

For a moment, Jamie stared at her, taking in the perfect picture she made, tucking it deeply into his memory. Softly, he kissed her forehead, then her lips. Pulling her close again, he hugged her tightly.

"Not all night, though. One dance and I'm taking you up on that ride," he murmured against her ear. "You don't fight fair, Sarah. You know what your eyes do to me. They make me forget everything. They always have. And you knew I'd be crazy about this dress with brown being my favorite color..."

Sarah laughed through her tears and pulled back enough to look at him. "Bet you wanna kiss me right now, Big Style."

"Hell, yeah I do."

So Jamie did. Then, he picked her up and swirled her around.

"Just for the record, y'all are both gigantic pains in the ass," Robby said, his smile huge. "Can we please get back to the party now? I actually have a date, you know."

Jamie and Sarah both laughed. Derek put his arm around Amelia and pulled her close. Hudson boldly kissed Reed. When she let him go, he looked dazed but happy.

Putting Sarah down, Jamie picked up his jacket from the floor and put it on. Sarah smoothed her dress and straightened her corsage. She smiled at her friends in the crowd and blew a kiss their way. Then, she reached over and kissed Robby's cheek.

Robby flushed. "Don't make him jealous, Sarah. I'd hate to ruin a happy ending by having to beat his ass." The crowd laughed and Sarah hugged him before turning back to Jamie. Lifting her chin, she gave a small curtsy and held out her hand.

Grinning broadly, Jamie bowed, then took her hand in his. He brought it to his lips before tucking it safely in his arm.

Whoops, whistles and cheers filled the hallway, as everyone made way for them. And Jamie led Sarah to the dance floor.

EPILOGUE

The warm May sun was unusually intense, as the graduation ceremony of Lakeview High School took place on the football field. Jamie didn't mind the heat. He was sitting next to Robby, as they had since the day they had started kindergarten together. He made a very real effort to concentrate on the speaker's advice for the future. But his mind kept drifting away.

Scanning the stands, he spotted his mom and sister videotaping and taking pictures. His dad winked at him proudly and Ben gave him a thumbs-up sign. The Nelson Justice Squad members were all in attendance. Jamie grinned. It had all worked out. His dad's health had returned. And his family, even his mom, had fallen in love with Sarah.

It had not taken long for an accounting of Charlotte's actions at the prom to reach Daisy Nelson's ears. Always a lady, no one was surprised she had not reacted to the gossip. But heads turned the following week when Daisy unexpectedly showed up at Sarah's track meet. She had sat next to Andreas Giannopoulos and cheered as if Sarah were one of her own. And from that day on, Daisy treated her like she was.

Leaning forward, he looked down the row for her. Sarah caught his eye, smiled and waved a tiny wave before motioning for him to pay attention. Jamie leaned back in his chair and again tried to listen to what the speaker had to say. He felt as if he were on top of the world. It had turned out to be the best year of his life. Summer was waiting and after that he would be going off to college. He had chosen Clemson University, along with Robby and Derek. Best of all, Sarah would be there, too.

He knew they would have their share of problems during the next four years. Just as he knew they would work them out. And when the time was right, he would ask her to marry him. There would never be anyone else for him but Sarah. She was the one. The answer to a prayer he never knew he'd prayed.

She was his beautiful, fiery-eyed angel. Andreas would have to share the nickname, but Jamie didn't think he'd mind.

He caught the word "destiny" from the celebrated speaker's speech. Leaning forward again, he waited for Sarah to look at him. "*Destiny*," he mouthed silently, pointing his finger her way.

Sarah smiled. Watching him smile back at her in his cap and gown, her insides bubbled with happiness.

She searched the stands for her father and Niko. Finding them, her heart filled with love and pride. *I'll miss you both so much*, she thought to herself. She had decided on Clemson, partly because she wanted to be close enough to come home, in case they ever needed her. But she knew she didn't have to worry about either of them anymore.

Home...this place would forever be home to her now. Still, she couldn't wait for college. Amelia and Hudson would be there, too. And Jamie. She wanted to pinch herself. She felt as if every dream she'd ever hoped for had come true.

Sarah clasped her mother's worn photograph more tightly in her hand. *It's all worked out, Mama, just like I'm sure you knew it would. I know college will be incredible. But I'll still need you to watch out for me—and for them.* She glanced back up at her family and noticed a small cardinal fly by them. Shielding her eyes from the overhead sun with her hand, she followed it until it disappeared into the bright blue sky. Sarah smiled. *But then, you always do, don't you, Mama?*

"Class of 2023, your future is waiting," she heard the speaker say.

Sarah met Jamie's eyes. Together, they threw their hats in the air.

Go-time.

THE END—almost

Fifteen years later

Nick Giannopoulos sat alone at a cliff-side cafe in Positano, Italy. The day was picture perfect on the Amalfi Coast. It was late April and the crowds had yet to take over the serene landscape as they did in the summer season. Nick breathed in the fresh salt air and took another sip of coffee. His beeper lay concealed under his jacket on the table. A Navy Seal was always on call, even here.

His cell phone vibrated and he pulled it out of the pocket of his jeans.

"Niko? Are you there?"

Nick smiled. "Hi, sis. I'm here. Does the baby have you up in the middle of the night again?" He checked his watch. It was two o'clock in the morning in America. "Or have you and Jamie been out painting the town?"

Sarah laughed. "Baby number four is going to do us in. Nicky is determined to stay up all night like her namesake. So, how are you? Livvy and the kids love Italy?"

"Yeah. They really do. I actually left them sleeping at the hotel and am having my coffee at a little cafe, reading the paper. I caught a pretty awesome sunrise."

"Sounds peaceful. Wish we were there."

"Me, too. Did Jamie win his case yesterday? Teddy says it's a big one."

"The jury is still out. But he's hoping so." Sarah laughed. "You talk to your father-in-law every day, even over there?"

"Pretty much. He calls to annoy Livvy, more than talk to me. How's Dad?"

"Good. He brought us dinner earlier. All the family came."

"Well, tell them all hello next time you see them. And get some sleep. I'm going to wrap up reading my newspaper while I still have the chance."

Sarah laughed again. "Enjoy the view, little brother. And kiss Livvy and the kids. I love you."

"I love you too, Sarah."

"Oh and Niko?"

"Yeah?"

"I'm so proud of you. Uncle Wyatt and Uncle Teddy were arguing at dinner over who is more responsible for inspiring your career. The only thing they agreed on is that you'll make Navy Commander in record time. Dad just beamed with pride."

"Thanks, sis. We'll have to wait and see about that. Hope so, though."

"So, between us, which one of them was it?"

"I'm gonna have to go with Teddy, since I married his daughter. But only because you're not an option. For the record, I'm proud of you, too."

"Because I'm saving the world, one diaper at a time?" Sarah giggled.

"You actually are."

"Sure I am. With spit up all over me. Go read your paper and enjoy your vacation, Niko. You've earned it. You're still the bravest boy I know."

"I'll call you soon."

"Sounds good, I'm sure I'll be awake. Bye."

Nick hung up the phone and checked his watch.

Should be anytime now.

He opened his wallet and pulled out the worn photograph of his mother. She smiled up at him, her expressive eyes filled with love. Gently, Nick ran his fingers across her beautiful face. After a minute, he carefully slid the photograph back in place, pulled out a five euro bill, and lay it under his coffee cup. Then he folded up his paper.

The sound of a boat engine pierced through the quiet and Nick looked up.

Hello, boys. Right on schedule.

The sleek fishing boat sliced through the crystal blue water with ease. Nick could see the two men aboard readying their rods for a quiet day of fishing.

He stood, grabbed his newspaper, jacket and the beeper under it. He smiled warmly at the waitress, who wished him a good day in Italian as he walked by. Stepping off the sunny veranda and inside the darkened dining area, Nick pressed on the beeper, the slight movement unnoticeable beneath all he carried.

Down on the water, the boat exploded into a blaze of fire. The thunderous sound of it filled the room but Nick didn't look back. He stepped out of the cafe unto the street.

That's for Maria Giannopoulos. Ciao, you Romano sons of bitches.

Still hidden beneath his jacket, he slid the beeper into the folded newspaper and discarded both in a roadside trashcan. He leaned down and pretended to tie his shoe until he heard the soft pop of the device self-destructing. People began to run past him towards the railing, trying to see what was happening below. From far away, sirens sounded.

Special Agent Nick Giannopoulos slung his jacket over his shoulder and began the short walk back to his hotel. He whistled "Hakuna Matata" all the way there.

THE END

FEMINESSE©

(noun – a female with finesse)

(verb – to finesse being female)

Two blended words: for a motto with moxie

One goal: empowered girls and women

Dear Reader,

I hope you enjoyed Sarah's story.
Feminesse every chance you get, like she does!

xoxo,

Petra

Printed in the USA
CPSIA information can be obtained
at www.ICGtesting.com
CBHW070956260224
4585CB00010B/6